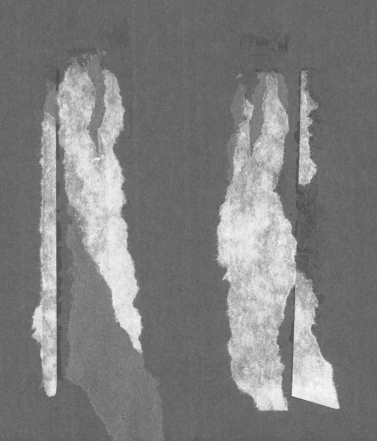

RAIN VILLAGE

✳

RAIN VILLAGE

Carolyn Turgeon

UNBRIDLED BOOKS

This is a work of fiction. The names, characters, places and incidents are either the product of the author's imagination or are used fictitiously, and any resemblance to actual persons living or dead, business establishments, events, or locales is entirely coincidental.

FIC TURGEON (handwritten)

Unbridled Books
Denver, Colorado

11/06 B&T 24.95 (handwritten)

Library of Congress Cataloging-in-Publication Data
Turgeon, Carolyn.
Rain Village / Carolyn Turgeon.
p. cm.
ISBN-13: 978-1-932961-24-9
ISBN-10: 1-932961-24-0
1. Girls—Fiction. 2. Short people—Fiction. 3. Farm life—Fiction.
4. Difference (Psychology)—Fiction. 5. Women librarians—Fiction. 6. Mentoring—Fiction.
7. Fathers and daughters—Fiction. 8. Circus performers—Fiction. I. Title.
PS3620.U75R35 2006
813'.6–dc22   2006016142

1   3   5   7   9   10   8   6   4   2

Book Design by CV • SH

First Printing

for my mother, father, and sister

PART ONE

﹡

✳

CHAPTER ONE

That tramp! Black-haired Jezebel!"

My mother's voice screeched into the house, from the yard. Up in my room, I thought a storm had come until I saw the bare windowpane, the butter-colored sun streaming in.

I ran down the wooden steps and out the front door, peered through the railings on the front porch. My father was out by the hedges again, clipping as if some devil had possessed him, sweat streaming down his face and the shears sprouting from his giant body like antlers. For two days now all we'd heard were the sounds of metal slicing against metal, twigs being snapped through and dropping to the ground. The crops in the field were going to ruin, but my father didn't care. Our front yard was already adorned with an elephant, a lion, and a peacock with a spray of leaves fanning behind it. The hedge he was attacking now was fourth in the line that hemmed in our yard, blocking it from the country road that stretched all the way to town.

"STOP IT!" my mother screamed, beating on his back with an umbrella. My meek, religious mother who spent her days bent over in the fields and her nights bent over a Bible. "Stop that infernal clipping!"

No one could so much as raise a voice to my father without his hand coming down on them. I winced for my mother and braced myself for the beating that would surely come, once my father went back to normal. *If* he ever went back to normal. I had never seen my father get himself into such a frenzy. Two days ago he'd returned from market with a basket half full of eggs, picked up the clippers, and started going at it. Now the slicing sounds had made their way into our dreams, and we didn't know if he'd ever stop.

I heard my sister Geraldine behind me, breathing loudly, hunkering down and pressing her face to the rails. "It's that new librarian," she whispered. "Mary Finn. The one that's making all the men crazy."

"He sold eggs to her in town just before this started," she said.

I leaned back against the steps. *Mary Finn.* I knew exactly who Geraldine was talking about, of course. When Mary Finn had arrived in Oakley earlier that summer, farmers had suddenly started walking miles out of their way to pick up the classics of English literature, and a constant stream of women had started coming by to visit my mother, whispering about the new librarian's wild gypsy past and the secret lovers who visited her after the library closed. Men wouldn't be able to sleep for days after Mary Finn walked by, the old gossips said, and if her blue cat's eyes met theirs, they were liable to start writing feverish poetry late into the night, or painting murals filled with flowers and beautiful women, set in places they'd never seen.

"A woman like that is nothing but trouble," my mother clucked, as if she were commenting on a bad harvest. But I saw her clutching her rosary beads, which she started carrying around everywhere even though we didn't have an ounce of Catholic blood in us. I saw the way she began watching my father out of the corner of her eye.

My mother turned and saw us crouching on the steps. "Get off of there!" she screamed, storming toward us. "Geraldine, get in the fields and help your brothers! Tessa, get back to your stretches!"

Geraldine took off running. I turned to the house, but my mother reached me before I could get away and grabbed me by the collar. "You stay on that bar until supper, Tessa Riley," she hissed, dragging me into the kitchen. "No wonder you're not getting any better. You don't even care that everyone thinks you're a *freak?* You don't want to improve yourself?"

She pushed me to the window, and I scrambled up and grabbed the curtain rod she had rigged for me, back when she still thought my body could pull and stretch out like taffy. Hanging there, I could see Geraldine and my two brothers bent over the corn outside. The sun seared into their skin. As my mother slammed out of the room, I closed my eyes and listened to the sounds of metal against metal, of twigs snapping and falling to the ground. Tears slipped down my face. I was not a normal child: I was twelve years old but just barely cleared four feet; the kids I passed on the way to market called me a munchkin or a freak; my hands were shaped like two starfish and as small as plums.

Mary Finn, I thought. I honed in on the idea of her, grabbed on to it as if she were a talisman. I just couldn't imagine anyone—or any*thing*— that beautiful. My mind set to wondering about it, about what she was like. If she would be as mean to me as all the rest of them, or if maybe there was something different about her, that same thing that set all the old hags on edge. The more I thought, the more I felt something crack open in me. Before then I had always kept to myself. I had gone whole days without touching another human being or making a sound.

One morning a few weeks later, long after the hedge incident we'd vowed never to speak of again, my entire family except me left to look at the pumpkins a farmer had grown two miles down the road— so big, they had heard, that two people could fit into each one. I waited half an hour before dropping down from the curtain rod and heading to the town square. With a pounding heart, I sat on the curb in front of the Oakley courthouse to watch the people pass. I sat stiffly, self-consciously, and tried to ignore the kids who walked by laughing. After an hour, my back and legs were starting to ache, and I wondered if I should go to Mercy Library itself to find her, though I had never been there before and the idea filled me with terror.

It was then that I looked up and saw her, and I knew right then and there what all the fuss was about. There was no mistaking her—nor was there any mistaking the old women who crossed themselves as she passed by, the men who stopped right in their paths and were moved to dance or song or tears. She carried a straw basket filled with red and yellow vegetables, with some papers and books poking over the side, and she walked through the square with her head up, her black hair glittering in the light, so wild it was like a field of weeds. She wore silver earrings that hung to her shoulders and a bright skirt that swished around her feet as she moved. The other townspeople scurried past or loped along, but Mary walked calmly, like a dancer, her back perfectly straight. I gazed up at her and thought she was the most beautiful woman I'd ever seen, with her blue eyes and brown, freckled skin; she was the kind of woman that adults are wary of and children love—you could just imagine that she had cabinets filled with candy when your own parents had only milk and grain.

When Mary turned her cat's eyes on me and then started walking toward me, I gasped out loud. I didn't even know where I was. I felt like I was traveling up and down a muddy river on some long, open boat, or slashing my way through crazy branches and trees in some huge rain forest. The funny thing was, I'd never even known those other kinds of places existed before I saw Mary Finn walk toward me with that hair no earthly comb could ever get through trailing out behind her, smile at me, and sit down by my side.

She smelled of the spices my mother baked oranges in. Her wrists jingled with bracelets. I felt myself enveloped in her scents and by her hair that brushed my bare shoulders and made me shiver as she sat down.

For a few moments she just sat next to me, stretching her tanned legs into the street, smoothing her skirt over her knees. I could only sit and stare. I watched her hands and her calves and thought how her skin seemed warm, like a blanket, or bread just out of the oven. When she turned to me and smiled, I felt like I'd been struck.

"What a perfect little girl you are," she said. "Why are you sitting here alone?"

I stared at her. I could barely believe that she was sitting right there in front of me. Mary Finn, who was the closest thing to a movie star Oakley had ever seen.

But she just rubbed her brown arms and stuck her hand in her hair the way other women stick combs.

"Did you know that stars die?" she said. "They burn themselves out and they fade from the sky, but they are like ghosts."

I looked at her.

"There are no ghosts," I said quickly, then felt my face grow as red as the radishes my parents bent over to pick each day.

"Oh, but there are," she said, smiling at me with her crooked teeth and lifting my right hand into her own. "You see this pinky right here? This little half-moon on the bottom of your pinky nail? It was once a star, you know, a star burning in the sky, but when it came time for the star to disappear, it just fell to the earth instead. Every part of your body—the moon on your pinky nail, the blue rim in the center of your eye—was once part of a star."

Not even my own mother had ever been kind to me like this. I felt all lit up and almost glowing, imagining my body spread across the night sky like an explosion, sparkling down to the half-moons on my fingernails.

"And so the stars come back to haunt us," she said, "the way every-thing else does, sooner or later."

That night I couldn't stop thinking about it—me, Tessa Riley, sit-ting in the town square in front of everyone, talking to *her*. I stared at my flat body in the mirror, wondered what it'd be like to have that sort of presence in the world, to curve and slope and glide. Later I could barely focus on my stretches, and just swung listlessly from the curtain rod. I *had* to visit Mary Finn's library, I decided. I convinced myself that my mother would understand, and as soon as my family came trooping through the house, ducking through the doorway and smelling of sweat and roots, I crossed my fingers and asked her if she would take me to Mercy Library for the first time.

The walls trembled as they slipped the great sacks from their shoul-ders and dumped them onto the long wooden counters. "What?" my mother said, whirling around to look at me. "You are not going any-where near that *witch*. Absolutely not."

My father was silent for a long moment. "You know, girl," he said then, as he reached down to grab a sack of vegetables, bringing it down on the kitchen counter with a thud. Bits of earth fell to the floor. "All that really matters is a handful of dirt and a perfect oval potato. The rest is just pie in the sky."

"But I want to see what it's like," I said. I had never spoken back to my father before, and I saw his eyes slightly widen. "I can't help in the fields anyway, and I can do my stretches at night." It was true. The pota-toes were so big I had to use both my hands just to hold one of them. Each kernel of corn was bigger than one of my front teeth. My broth-ers and sister could hold three ears in one hand, and I felt like I was sur-rounded by giants.

As my father continued to haul up the sacks, my siblings began scrubbing the potatoes and radishes furiously, tossing them into large tin buckets, and my mother boiled a pot of potatoes and carrots for one of her famous stews. I was on the floor with corn strewn around me.

"Listen to me," my father said, with a menace in his voice that hadn't been there a second ago. No one outside my family would have even noticed it, but every single person in that room recognized his tone and what it meant. We caught our breaths and waited. "That place is *unholy*. You will not set foot in there. There's enough for you to do here." He flashed his face back at me, then breathed out heavily, relaxing. "Just *pay attention*, girl, and the husk'll come peeling off like banana skin."

He turned back to the sink and we were all silent then.

Usually my father's disapproval could put a halt to anything brewing inside me. His disapproval could freeze up a river, it seemed, in the middle of June. But something had shifted in me, and that night I lay in my bed, listening to Geraldine snoring from the other side of the room, and I thought and schemed and reflected.

The next morning I dutifully hung from the bar. My muscles were so strong I could hang for hours, and on most days I just lifted myself up and over it or tried hanging from my ankles. That morning I hung still as a board, dreaming of my escape. Waiting. I stared out into the fields, at my parents' and siblings' bodies bent over the crops, the sun burning their backs. The corn jutting up.

When it came, lunch seemed to last for hours. I stood on a stool stirring the stew, as usual, while Geraldine set the table and my father and brothers rested in the den. At the table, I shoveled in my food without tasting it, trying not to stare at the clock or my family's shrinking bowls of stew. I could barely sit still, and more than once my mother had to warn me to stop fidgeting.

"Yes, ma'am," I said, my feet burning, my whole body straining toward that library across town.

As soon as the bowls were washed and the house empty, I hurried outside, crouching down in the dirt road so my family wouldn't catch sight of me. I scrunched myself alongside the corn and moved as quickly as I could toward open space. Once I was out of their line of vision, I ran and ran and nothing else mattered. The whole countryside smelled thickly of manure and growing vegetables and cut grass, but I ran so fast all I smelled was wind. It was exhilarating, breaking their hold like that. I could barely breathe, and my muscles burned from my shoulders down to my calves, but I laughed and whooped when I reached the main road that stretched through the farmland: the fields of crops and the creeks and rivers that crisscrossed our part of the world like veins. I followed the road through the country and into town, sweeping past all the people who stopped in their tracks and just gaped at me. I didn't care. For a minute I thought: the world would be so beautiful, if it were just this, this feeling right now.

Finally the library loomed up in front of me. The air seemed to go cool and misty, all at once, as if a thunderstorm were about to burst on us. From the outside the place looked like a massive barn more than anything else, except for the piece of metal swinging from a stick out front saying "Mercy Library" and the fact that it had been painted stark white. There wasn't much around it, just piles of overgrown grass and clumps of dandelions and some trees hanging down into the road, one with branches so long they scratched across the library's roof. I stared up at the library, my heart pounding so hard it threatened to break through my chest.

It was the farthest I'd ever been from home. Already it felt like hours and hours had passed, though it couldn't have been more than forty-five minutes. For a moment I considered turning back, but something inside me wouldn't allow it. All the bravery buried within me seemed to push up to the surface, forcing me to take another deep breath and walk toward the front door. This is my chance, I thought. My one chance for something new.

Just then an old couple pushed out past me.

"I *saw* the way you were looking at her!" I heard the woman hiss to the man under her breath.

"I was getting book advice, Meg, *book advice. . . .*"

Startled, I slipped out of their path as they barreled by, then stepped into a vast, almost church-like space with old wood floors and a breezy high-beamed ceiling. Light streamed into the space from the huge windows on either end, illuminating the dust in the air. Towering shelves divided the room, all painted different colors. Books poured from every box, every shelf, every basket, and every drawer. To my left was a large desk with books and cards spread over the top, an ashtray filled with half-smoked cigarettes. People milled around with books in their arms, but quietly, as if afraid of making a sound. I could have sworn I heard the sound of rain, but when I glanced out one of the long windows on the far wall, the sun was flaring and the sky bright blue. The whole place smelled like smoke tinged with spices and must.

I realized I was standing there with my mouth open, so I snapped it shut and forced myself toward the shelves. I picked an aisle without even looking and began wandering through it, running my fingers along the spines of the books. I stopped and plucked one off the shelf, stared at the black markings inside until I grew dizzy. I heard a sound then and looked up to see a couple standing at the end of the aisle, kissing. When a man turned in and started toward me, I nearly fell over with fear— until I realized he wasn't paying me any mind at all, but was staring intently at something through a gap on one of the higher shelves.

Suddenly I heard the faint sound of sobbing. I looked around, startled, then tiptoed over, as far away from the man as possible, to peer through one of the openings myself.

I saw a woman with a scarf pulled over her face, sitting at the table and crying. Mary Finn sat across from her. I heard the shush of whispers but could not make out what they were saying. The two women were almost opposites: the one hunched over and covered from head to toe, the other awash in color, her black hair coiling down her bare arms, her tanned, freckled shoulders glimmering as if with oil. Mary's eyes were intent on the woman across from her, and she reached out her hand to the woman, patted her arm. I moved closer, out of one row and into another, and another, where I could hear. It was one advantage of my size: I could move quietly, as if I were not there at all. By the time I was able to see again, Mary had set out a deck of cards—tarot cards, I would learn later—and was explaining them to the woman. Then, for a moment, the woman's scarf slipped and I saw her face in profile, only for a split second before she quickly covered herself again. It was Mrs. Adams from down the road, I realized, shocked. But she was different now, rubbed raw and bare. I could *see* her sadness, slipping off her body like smoke.

"But how can I make him stay faithful?" I heard her whisper, her voice all twisted up from any way I'd ever heard it.

"I have no mind for vision or prophecies," Mary whispered then. "I just know what the cards say. But if I were you I would wear a yellow skirt and toss yarrow root in his tea before bed. It will keep him close to home when he wants to wander." She reached down and held up a handful of something green and glittering, then quickly wrapped it in a kerchief and slid it to Mrs. Adams.

"Thank you," the woman whispered, wiping her face. Mary looked up then, straight at me, through the books. Her eyes like cat's eyes, blue as sapphires. I ducked. A moment later I heard Mrs. Adams shuffling away, and prayed Mary was following her.

My heart pounded.

"What are you doing, little girl?" I heard Mary's smoky, low voice over me and looked up. The scent of gingerbread wafted down the aisle.

"I'm sorry," I whispered, but she just smiled and beckoned for me to come toward her.

"Have you come to visit me?" she asked. "These women, they always want my advice. They think I'm some kind of *witch*." She made a spooky face and I laughed without thinking. "Then they ignore me on the streets, pretend they haven't come by to tell me their heartbreaks and woes. They're embarrassed that they have hearts at all, I think."

I smiled. "I sneaked out of my house. I've never been here before."

"Come," she said. "There's probably a line out the door by now."

I began following her through the stacks to the front of the library, staring at her multicolored swirling skirt.

"Have you come for some books, too?" she asked, looking back.

I blushed. "I can't read," I said.

She looked at me with surprise just as we came to her desk, where three people stood waiting for her return. All old farmers, I realized, with their hands full of books. I expected them to be angry, having been made to wait like that, but they all lit up and practically shone as Mary came near them.

"Well, we'll have to fix that," she said, winking at me, before taking her seat behind the desk. "Why don't you sit next to me while I help these gentlemen?" She smiled up at the first man in line as I sat on a stool nearby.

"Shakespeare, I see," Mary said to the man. "The sonnets. They'll make a romantic of you yet, Joe."

I swear that old farmer blushed all the way down to his collarbone. "I liked *Troilus and Cressida*," he said. "You were right about that'un."

Mary smiled, then picked up another book and put it in with the one he was holding. "You'll like this even better."

I watched Mary check out books for at least half an hour before the library began emptying out. I stared at her mass of hair, so black it seemed to glint blue in parts, and her brown shoulders. My sister had brought home a movie magazine once and I had felt the same way then, looking at the women with pale hair and dark lips, their eyebrows like swooping lines across their foreheads. I touched my hair with my hands, imagined my body stretching up and filling out, covered with swishing fabrics like the ones Mary wore. *This is what it means to be a woman,* I thought. She picked up each book and thumbed to the cards in the back, and I watched her strong, sure hands.

I sat on the stool, praying she wouldn't tell me to leave.

After a while, when the library had cleared out, Mary turned to me. "It's busiest in the mornings and evenings," she said. "Mostly I have the afternoons to myself." She smiled. "So tell me, why don't you know how to read? Aren't you in school?"

"No," I said softly. "My folks don't believe in schooling. I'm supposed to work in the fields with the rest of them, but they don't want me on account of my smallness." I could feel my face growing red and lifted up my hands to cover it.

"Don't believe in schooling?" she said. "What do they have you do all day, then?"

I looked up at her, nervous, but saw she wasn't laughing. "I used to have to do chores but my house is so big, I couldn't do much. I can't do anything right is what my mama says. Sometimes I sneak out and hide in the fields or come to town to watch people. My mama wants me to eat potatoes and stretch my body in the window so I'll get bigger. Then I can make my contributions, she says."

"Well, you should have visited me sooner because *that* doesn't sound like much fun at all." She laughed. "That's the craziest thing I've ever heard, in fact."

I took my hands slowly from my face and rested them in my lap. I looked up at her and smiled.

"You know," she said, leaning in closer, "I didn't get along with my family either."

"Really?"

"Yes," she said. "My father was not a nice man. I left home as soon as I was able."

"Oh, one day I would like to do that." All of a sudden it seemed possible that I could leave Oakley some day, just like that.

"You will," she said. "There's a big place for you in the world, no matter what you think now. You're like I was when I was your age, back when I thought I had no place at all."

I just looked to the floor, my heart beating wildly.

"What do you love to do, Tessa?"

I looked up at her, afraid she was making fun of me. "Me?" I asked.

"Of course."

I scrunched up my mind and thought hard about her question. I could barely think of anything I *liked*, let alone loved. I knew I didn't like farming or shucking corn. I knew I didn't like Oakley, or my giant, ravenous family, or the vegetables that spilled from the counter and sink and onto the floor. I knew I didn't like the way I felt all the time, so freakish and small, so scared of everything.

"I don't know," I said, finally, watching the light streaming in from the windows and slanting through the air. "This is the only thing I've ever loved, being here right now." It came up on me just like that, the realization that there was nowhere I'd rather be, that *this* was as close to happiness as I'd ever been.

She smiled. "It's a good place, this library. Like entering another world. You can open up any of these books and just forget about the fields and rivers outside, the farms and horses. The past."

"It's so different here," I said. "You're so different."

She peered into me and shook out a cigarette from a pouch beside her. The tobacco and paper crackled as she lit up. "Tell me about yourself, Tessa Riley," she said.

I stared at the crazy-quilt skirt my mother had sewn for me, fingering the hem. I felt paralyzed, convinced I could never speak of my own life out loud, but I still felt the stories beating at my throat and lips.

"I have a sister named Geraldine," I began, "and two brothers, Matthew and Connor. Geraldine and I share a room and the ceiling is as high as the stars. My mom's name is Roberta, and my dad's name is Lucas. They don't notice me much, though. They're always busy in the fields."

"Really?" Mary asked.

I nodded solemnly. I'm not sure what possessed me then, but for the first time in my life my mouth just opened and everything came rushing out. I told Mary about the wooden house and the fields, and the rows of gem-hard corn we based our livelihood on. I told her about my favorite log and my father's terrifying hands. I told her about how my mother made all my clothes out of the scraps of my sisters' and brothers' jumpers and dresses and pants. And I told her about how my mother laughed at me as she stitched my skirts and blouses, how she called them "clothes for a baby's doll."

Mary leaned toward me and touched my arm. "They just have their own vision," she said. "For people like you and me, the world is different."

I thought of the world outside my window, and the one I dreamt about when I was out in the fields alone. Not knowing what to say, I just looked up at her and smiled.

She stood and stretched. "I'm making some tea. Want a cup?"

"Yes, please," I said, though I wasn't quite sure. She winked at me and started walking to the open space beyond the stacks, on the left side of the room. Her sandals clacked dully on the floorboards. Alone, I stared at her desk, trying to memorize everything on it before she got back—the glossy cards and scattered notebooks, the rumpled papers for her cigarettes, a discarded silver bracelet, a tiny clown figurine painted red and yellow. I wanted things like that someday, I decided. Things of my very own.

Soon the whole place smelled like herbs. When Mary reemerged with two steaming cups of tea a few minutes later, it seemed like the most exotic thing in the world. I peered into my cup, staring at the greenish water with the herbs floating at the top.

"It's my special recipe," Mary whispered. "It will make you *irresistible*."

When I took a sip it was like drinking grass and sage.

"I have an idea," she said, setting down her cup. "Why don't we write out your name? It's such a good name; it's a shame not to set it down somewhere."

We grabbed our tea and she led me out the door, over to a pile of wood stacked against the building. The sun, low in the sky now, made the landscape blaring and golden. I shielded my face with my hands and stared into it: the mountains hovering in the distance, the sun seeping through them like melting butter.

"Here we go," Mary said, pulling a long twig from the pile. And she did the most amazing thing. She knelt close to the ground and began drawing shapes into the dirt.

"That," she said, pointing, "is a T. For Tessa. Do you hear that? Ta." Her mouth moved slowly over the sound, then spat it from the roof of her mouth.

"*Ta*," I said.

As the sun dipped lower and lower into the horizon, Mary carved into the ground and broke my name into a stream of sounds and shapes: the crossing lines of a T and an E, the two snake shapes spinning out next to them, the shape of a swing set when you see it from the side. The letters seemed to swarm through the dirt, sparkling as if they had a life of their own.

"Your turn," she said. I grabbed the twig and Mary guided me through each letter, slowly, until my name lay across the dirt twice—once in her elegant hand, and once in my own scrawl. When I was done putting my name there, I don't think I had ever seen anything so astonishing.

"I did it! I can do that!" I cried.

"By the end of this month, little girl, you'll be able to read words straight from the page. Why don't you come back tomorrow and I'll show you some new letters? In the afternoon?"

"There are more?" I asked, and then I thought about our name at Riley Farm, set out for the world to see. It was all so overwhelming to me, but Mary just laughed.

"I'm not sure what my parents will say," I said. My heart began to sink then. I had no doubt this would be my first and last visit to Mercy Library, and that I would pay for it as soon as I got home.

"I know they don't believe in schooling, but wouldn't they like you to learn to read and write?"

"My father doesn't believe in it. And my mother wouldn't want me to learn here, from you." I clapped my hand over my mouth. "I'm sorry," I said.

"You know, Tessa," Mary said, bending down to me. Her earrings swung back and forth and made a tinkling sound. "There have been more popular women than me in the world—among the womenfolk, that is. It's all right. But it'd be a real shame for you to go through life without any words. You're a smart girl."

"Thank you," I whispered, wondering why I felt like crying. I was so afraid I would never see her again, that I would wake up and realize I had only dreamt this. Fear clenched my chest as I imagined endless days surrounded by giant corn, the smell of earth on my hands, my family towering over me and stomping through the fields. It was like flying through the clouds one minute and dropping back to earth the next. I looked down at my name carved in the dirt, and I leaned down, snatched it from the earth, and dumped it in my pocket.

"Now give me a hug and get out of here," she said, and leaned in and gathered me up. For a second the strong spice scent was everywhere. "I hope I'll see you again soon, Tessa Riley. Come visit me anytime at all."

Walking back through town, past the fields and farmhouses, I felt like a completely new person. I grasped the dirt in my pocket with my fist, felt it tingle in my palm, and stared up at the black star-speckled sky. The dirt crunched under my feet. I closed my eyes, listening to the rhythm of my walking, the lusty sounds of crickets and frogs in the distance. It was August, and the nighttime just made the heat seem thicker and more wet, like a substance I had to wade through. My heart pounded. The world was bursting with life. I took my time getting home, breathing the night air in and out, stretching out my arms to take it all in. Even if my father beats me black and blue, I thought, this day will have been worth it. No matter how bad things get, I will have *this day*.

When Riley Farm appeared ahead of me, I squashed the dirt in my hands, steeling myself, preparing for anything. I crept across the front lawn, deafened by the sounds of the crickets and cicadas, and pushed through the front door as quietly as possible. The house felt so stark and prim against the lush night. I felt a knot form in my throat and stay there. I stood for a moment in the dark, empty hallway, barely breathing, then heard the clattering of silverware coming from the kitchen. I stood for a few minutes longer, suspended between two worlds, before I tiptoed into the kitchen, to the round oak table we all crowded around.

My father and brothers shoveled bread and stew into their mouths, not even looking up. I took my seat next to my sister, and my mother handed me a bowl without saying a word.

"Where have you been, child?" my father asked.

I froze. "I'm sorry, sir," I said, staring into my stew. "I was doing my stretches outside."

I felt his eyes on me and winced.

Tessa, I thought, squeezing my eyes shut and focusing on the dirt, the shapes, the sounds pulsing from Mary's tongue. *Ta.*

"Eat your stew," he said, in a voice so tight I thought it might whip out and lash me. Later, I knew, he would make up for whatever he was holding back now.

✳

CHAPTER TWO

I came from a long line of farmers whose lives were controlled by seasons and whose skin was hard against the wind. My family had been on that Kansas land longer than anyone could remember, and our name was Riley, a name marked on our front gate and on the windowsills, we were so proud of it. The Rileys were a strong clan, my mother always told us. We came from the earth and our arms hung heavy at our sides.

When I was born the midwife lifted me into the air and screamed; she thought my mother had birthed some kind of rodent, I was so small. Once they'd finally cleaned me off enough to see that I was a normal baby—though I was about a third of the size of the usual kind—my mother decided not to call me Geraldine after her sister, as she'd planned to do. "Geraldine is no name for a munchkin," she said. "Geraldine is a name that'd stretch two city blocks." So my mother plucked a name out of the sky and called me Tessa, and I got a Geraldine for a sister two years later—a baby sister as big as a tree stump.

I don't think it's any stretch to say that my mother hated having such a strange creature emerge from her body, but she tried her hardest to challenge fate and whatever devil had played such a trick on her. She taught me to do backbends and headstands and cartwheels, and made me do stretches every day in the kitchen window, but while Geraldine grew and grew till her head bumped the ceilings of the shops in town, I remained what I was: a terrible mistake. *Please,* I whispered into air every night, holding the word on my tongue like sugar, but when I got to four feet, time stopped for me and the world went on and left me behind.

Probably my mother tried loving me as long as she did out of disappointment, pure and simple. Geraldine, despite her gift for growing, was an ill-tempered, dumb child at best, one who snorted and cried when she didn't get enough to eat, and my brothers were not good for much besides hauling in our crops and trampling down everyone else's. Of course, when it came down to it, my siblings were far better children than I and kept that farm running and food on our plates, but I think my mother could have used someone to talk to sometimes, someone with a bit of soul in them. I guess it's an easy thing for me to say now, when seeing my mother again is about as likely for me as sprouting fins, but I think my mother could have found a friend in me back then if I hadn't shamed her so much. Some things aren't ever meant to be, I guess. All I know is that it's a terrible thing to be born someone's failure in this world.

When all is said and done, though, maybe that was what saved me. I was so light my feet barely made dents in the moist earth outside. Sometimes I passed a mirror and wasn't sure whether I was reflected back in it. And little by little I just slipped away; people have a habit of doing that sometimes—just falling away, out of some lives and into other ones, out of one world and into the next. I ate dinner with my family every night, and I slept in the bed my father had carved for me when I was less than a year old, but little by little they just stopped seeing me is all. By the time I was twelve, plenty of times my parents didn't even notice whether I was in a room or out of it, and more than once my mother ran right into me because she didn't know I was there.

Once I stopped staring out the windows and longing to feel the ceilings of buildings with my head, the world took on a different shape. I stopped even pretending to do chores. The days became silent and mine, and I began to think that maybe there were other things besides rows and rows of corn and radishes, and I began listening to the silence in the house, wondering at what lay beyond the fields and the trees that marked out our land.

And then the world opened itself to me like a mouth.

The next day, as soon as the dishes were washed and dried, I sneaked out into the early afternoon and set off running, as if I couldn't get to the library fast enough. I didn't even look at the landscape around me or slow down for breath when a gaggle of teenaged girls laughed as I ran past.

"Weirdo!" they called. "Freak!"

I didn't pay attention. Everything in the world that mattered to me was reduced down to that library across town.

But the moment I burst in the doors of Mercy Library, I became shy, and nervous. I stood by the door, unsure what to do next.

"Tessa," Mary said, looking up from the front desk. Her eyes immediately dropped to my arms and legs. "Your parents weren't too mad? You're okay?" She walked over and put her hand on my shoulder, looked at my neck and face.

"No, it was fine. I'm fine," I said. I smiled up at her.

She breathed out. "Good," she said, laughing. "You look like you could use some relaxing. Why don't we make some tea? They'll be lining up any second, so we have to hurry."

She rushed through the stacks, pulling me after her, back to an old stove tucked in the corner. I was so excited I was practically skipping.

When we came to the makeshift kitchen, I laughed out loud. Everything with Mary was a great adventure. I loved the little stove, the jars of dried herbs lined above it. I loved the elaborate locked box made of ivory sitting on a table to the side.

"What's in here?" I asked.

"More herbs," Mary said, "for every kind of ailment. Powders and vials." She leaned in to me, put her face next to mine. "You can cure most anything with these herbs, you know. Sprinkle them into tea and soup. Bite down on a clove for a toothache, brew up mixtures of mint and nettle and fireweed to soothe a broken heart." She held up a small bag and let me peer into it: the herbs glimmered and shifted inside, and a faint whiff of smoke drifted into the air.

"You *are* a witch!" I said.

"I'm gonna get you and make you ride my broomstick!" She reached out for me and I screamed and laughed. "Here, we'll need a stool for you, won't we?" she said then, standing up. "So you can make tea, too."

I beamed up at her, unable to imagine anything more exciting.

Mary pulled up a stool from one of the stacks and set it in front of the stove, then pointed out all the various herbs on the shelves above. I could just reach them from the stool, my belly pressed into the front of the stove. We set a pot of water to boiling. As we waited, we wrapped two small piles of herbs in two cheesecloth pouches and dropped them into two mugs. "Now you just pour the water over and let it brew," Mary said, ruffling my hair.

Tea in hand, we made our way back to the front desk. I couldn't take my eyes off my cup and walked slowly, deliberately. With relief, I set it down on the desk and breathed in the hot herb scent.

Suddenly the door slammed open. I turned to see a woman walking hesitantly into the room, someone I didn't recognize from the farm or square.

"Hi," she whispered, approaching Mary and eyeing me nervously. "Can you help me? They say you can see the future." She walked in small steps toward the desk.

Mary set down her tea and laughed, a warm, rich laugh that made me think of honey. "I used to know a woman who could see the future—visions, she called it—but I've never had that gift, my friend."

The woman just stood there. "I don't have anywhere else to go," she said. "I'm being eaten alive, and there's nothing I can do. *Please* help me." Her face was flushed red. Her breath labored and quick. There was a yearning so strong in her I could almost reach out and stroke it there beside her.

"What is it?" I asked, surprising myself. I had never seen anyone so raw before, just laid bare.

Mary turned and looked at the woman then. "She's in love," she whispered. She rose from her chair and walked toward the woman, staring right at her.

The woman shut her eyes. Faint lines stretched out from her eyes and mouth and faded into her hair. You could see all her days in the field, all the harvesting she'd done. Her cow-milking hands were red and chapped.

"She's burning up," Mary said softly, pressing the back of her hand against the woman's forehead. "Tessa, could you make up a batch of tea, black leaves with cranberry bark crushed in, maybe?" She winked at me. "The last jar on the left and second from the right."

I nodded and scurried off my stool as if an army were beating at the door.

My hands shook as I pushed a stool up to the side of the stove and climbed up and stared at the jars. Mary's words jumbled in my head. *Last on the right or left? Second from the left?* I squinted at the black markings scribbled on tape stuck to the jars but couldn't make them out. The herbs inside looked reddish black on either side. I panicked, then reached out and grabbed the last jar on the left and the second from the right. *This is wrong,* I thought, close to tears, as I sprinkled a bit of herb from each jar onto a piece of cheesecloth and folded it into a pouch.

By the time I was done, I could hear sobbing from the front of the room. I raced back, holding up the cup so it wouldn't spill. The tea made me a part of this, and I felt *necessary* in a way I never had before.

The woman was hunched over Mary's desk, weeping.

I set down the tea in front of the woman. "Here you go," I said, my heart pounding.

"She's in love with her neighbor's husband," Mary whispered.

The woman jolted up then. "I can't help it," she said. "I feel so dirty, like a criminal. I feel it in every vein of my body."

"I know," Mary soothed. "I know. My friend Tessa here made you some tea; why don't you try it?"

"Yes," the woman said, picking up the cup. "Oh, yes, I'm sorry, thank you. My name is Beatrice, by the way. I come from outside Springfield. I'm sorry for this, for being this way."

Mary leaned over and put her hand on Beatrice's shoulder. Her hair fell forward as she peered in Beatrice's face. I watched Beatrice take a sip of tea and was relieved when she didn't collapse afterward.

"I've been in love like that, too," Mary said.

I was confused. "But isn't that good?" I asked. Not that I knew anything about it.

"Sometimes," Mary said. "If you're loved back."

At that, the woman began crying again. "I keep looking for him everywhere. I stand at my window so I can see him tending his crops outside. I dream his face when I go to bed and then when I wake up in the morning."

"It's like a sickness," Mary said, nodding. "It is."

"I've gone to meet him in the barn. He doesn't love me, doesn't want me, but I've let him do things to me that I've never even let my husband do. He uses me up and then zips up his pants and leaves me lying there, like some whore. And I go back and back. I whisper *I love you* to him, but he never even looks me in the eye."

"Keep drinking your tea," Mary said. "It'll help. Cranberry root always soothes an unrequited love. I'll give you a handful before you leave, from my garden in back."

Beatrice smiled slightly and downed the rest of her tea. I watched, fascinated, as she wiped bits of root from her lips.

"Thank you," she said, looking at me. I looked down, blushing straight to my toes.

"You need to boil cranberry root every day," Mary said, "and drink it with your meals, and whenever you are feeling like you really need it. Put a black curtain over that window you watch him from, and hang garlic across the top. You can also sip honey water mixed with cinnamon to make your sleep more dreamless. If you want to dream, just not of him, boil cranberry root, too, and use that water with the honey."

"Yes," Beatrice said, sitting up straight. "Yes, I'll do that. I want to be free from this." Already her cheeks were becoming less flushed. Her face seemed to soften, as if we'd sprayed it with mist.

"Wait here," Mary said. "We'll get you some herbs to take home."

We went back to the kitchen. Mary reached for the second jar on the right, lifted out some of the cranberry root, and dropped it in a small paper bag.

I breathed out in relief. "I was so scared," I said. "I thought I'd picked the wrong one. I couldn't remember." I cringed then, wishing I'd kept my mouth shut.

"It doesn't *really* matter," Mary said, lowering her voice. "When you're foolish about love, herbs can only help so much." I looked up at her, shocked. Mary tied up the bag and winked down at me.

When we came back, Beatrice seemed a different woman from the one who'd skulked through the door a half hour before. She clutched her bag of herbs and radiantly offered Mary a small stack of bills.

"Thank you," Mary said, taking the bills and hugging Beatrice as if she'd known her forever. When Beatrice leaned down to hug me as well, I found myself hoping she would always be the way she was right then.

The moment the door closed, Mary turned to me and rolled her eyes, letting out a deep breath. She handed me two of the bills in her hand, then rolled up the rest and thrust them in her skirt pocket.

I looked toward the door, and at Beatrice's empty cup of tea, and at the two bills in my palm. "But is it wrong?" I asked, a pang of guilt sweeping through me. "To take this?" I clutched the bills in my hand. "It feels weird. She was so sad."

"We didn't ask Beatrice to come here," Mary said. "If she wants to give us her money, let her." She shrugged. "And of course she's sad. Who isn't?"

"Oh," I said. I looked at the ground, confused.

"A cup of tea can't change someone's heart, no matter how powerful the herbs in it are. The herbs have a mind of their own, you know." She laughed. "But you make people believe in extraordinary things, and extraordinary things will happen. The rest is up to her. It's the same as in the circus."

"The circus?"

She grinned at me. "Well, you know," she said, raising her eyebrows and leaning toward me, "I was in one before I came here. I performed on the trapeze. I wore glitter all along my cheeks and down my arms, and turned circles in the air." She drew out the words, filling them with flour-ishes. I forgot all about Beatrice.

"Trapeze?" I repeated.

"A long bar and two pieces of rope," she said, "hanging from the sky. Like a swing. You can sit on it or swing from your shoulders or ankles or knees. You can even hang on it from your chin."

My eyes were enormous as I stared at her. "What was it like?" I breathed. "What did you do?" I pictured Mary in the air then, like a bird. Her chin resting on a bar the way she rested it in her hands and peered down at me, sitting behind her desk.

"It was like flying," she said, smiling and widening her cat's eyes. "Like having no weight to you, no bones, no skin. It was like melting right into air. And I did flying-trapeze acts, too, with a catcher."

"What's that?"

"You swing out, holding the bar with your palms, and just let go." She stretched her arms in front of her, pushing away the air. "You just fly, Tessa, and in those moments you can twist or do somersaults or just keep your body pressed into one straight line until the catcher catches you. But in those moments, time stops completely."

I laughed. "Time can't stop!"

"Of course it can," she said, pretending to be offended. Then she leaned down and whispered in my ear: "Because it's magic. Up there, that high, there are no rules!"

I was still giddy that night at the dinner table, bursting with it. I was so desperate to share my news and excitement that I actually looked around the table—at my mother's worn face, my brothers' smirking mouths, Geraldine's hulk on the other side of the table. I imagined telling them all about Mary and the circus, releasing the words and letting them explode over that table like fireworks. For a minute I imagined that we would all laugh together. Then my father glanced up and met my eyes, and the words died in my throat.

Later, in the quiet of the bedroom, I looked over at Geraldine. Her bed was parallel to mine, on the other side of the room. A faint bit of moonlight streamed in the window, illuminating the squares on the quilt that covered her. Her dull brown hair spread over her pillow.

"Guess what?" I whispered.

"What?" I heard, a second later.

"I know a secret."

Geraldine threw off her quilt and sat up. She glared at me. "Tell me."

"You have to promise you won't tell Mom and Dad," I said. I wanted so badly to tell someone. The words were bubbling out of me; I could practically see them floating in the air.

"I don't have to do anything, munchkin. Tell me now!"

I sat back on the bed and crossed my arms. After a moment, she sighed loudly. "Fine," she said.

"Okay," I said, my pulse racing, my heart in my stomach. I lowered my voice. "Did you know that Mary Finn was in the circus?"

"What are you talking about?"

I squinted in the dim light, focusing on her face. "No, really," I said. "She flew on the trapeze. She said she knew people who could eat fire!"

She looked at me suspiciously. "That's the dumbest thing I ever heard."

"No, no," I said. "She knew boys covered in fish scales, girls with wings! She said she knew men with bodies as tall as skyscrapers or as short as daffodils." The words spilled out on top of each other.

"How do you know?"

"I met her!" I said. "I went to her library."

Geraldine sat still for a minute, then said, "What's she like?" She looked at me with wide eyes, waiting. For a second, she seemed almost shy.

"Oh, she's wonderful," I breathed. "She's so beautiful and she smells like cinnamon and she tells the best stories and can tell fortunes, too."

"And she was really in the circus?"

"The Velasquez Circus, the famous one from Mexico."

"I know them!" she said. "They came to Kansas City last year."

I spent the next half hour talking about Mary—the library and jars of herbs, the men who lined up to check out books from her. Geraldine listened, rapt.

"I know Mom and Dad don't like her," she said, hugging her knees, "but I think she looks like a princess."

"Me too," I whispered. "I want to be just like her."

At that, Geraldine let out a huge guffaw. "You? You could never be like her! You're too ugly," she said, the old smile creeping over her face. "And a freak!"

She turned her back to me then and collapsed onto her bed, snorting.

Shame shot through me, into every part of my body. I lay back in my bed and pulled the covers over me.

CHAPTER THREE

The next morning, I woke up dreaming of the circus. Mary and I on the flying trapeze, soaring over everyone, while men breathed out fire on all sides. We took off into the air and just kept on going, past the fire and through the circus tent, up into the sky above. I looked down and saw my family, no longer gigantic but tiny specks, down below. Good-bye, I waved, grasping Mary's hand.

I woke up with a pounding heart, and felt disappointment wash over me as I looked around the dusty, wood-filled room, and at Geraldine's body slumped on the bed across from me. I glared at her, wished I could will her away completely.

I sat up and rubbed my eyes. It was only a matter of time before she told on me, I thought, but there was no use in punishing *myself*. I slipped out of bed and stepped into my clothes.

"Where are you going?" Geraldine asked, sitting up.

I ignored her, couldn't wait to get away from her and from all of them. Today I would not even bother to wait until after lunch. I ran down the stairs and into the front yard as if a ghost were chasing me.

Mary looked up as I burst through the door of Mercy Library. I almost stopped in my tracks, she was so dazzling. "I was about to close up for an hour and head into town for a few things," she said. "You want to come?"

She stood by the front desk, dropping her keys and some letters into her purse and then swooping it up and over her shoulder. I nodded and watched, fascinated, as she slipped a pair of wing-shaped sunglasses over her face and rubbed her forefinger into a small pot that was open on her desk, then spread a dark coral color over her lips, the same color as her toenails in her open sandals.

"Let's go," she said, brushing past me and reaching for my hand behind her. She locked the door and we ran down the steps and into the grass, her skirt swishing around her ankles.

I had to walk fast to keep up. "A beautiful day, isn't it, Tessa?" She grinned down at me and gestured to the trees and sky. It was late summer and the air was filled with the scents of grass and flowers, the faint traces of hay and manure. The sky was bright blue and the leaves dripped and trembled against it. I could hardly believe it was the same world I had lived in before, that I'd just run through to get to the library, to her.

Our feet crunched in the gravel as we passed the lumberyard. I was so proud. I'm *not* a freak, I wanted to say to everyone we passed. *Look.* I wished Geraldine could see me right then, see that I didn't need her, or any of them.

"So what do you want to do when you grow up?" Mary asked, reaching down and flipping up a lock of my hair.

"I don't know," I mumbled, embarrassed.

"Oh, come on. Surely you must love something, right? Maybe dancing? I can see you as a dancer, something like that." She spun around.

"I would like to work in the library someday, too," I said. I looked at her shyly. It seemed like a bold thing to say, but she didn't look surprised.

"You can do that now," she said. "I was thinking maybe I could pay you a bit to stay in the afternoons. You can help me sort the books, keep up with the paperwork. You can look after the desk while I'm talking to the folks who come in wanting fortunes and spells." She opened her eyes wide and made a witchy face as we stepped into the street that led to the square.

I laughed. "Can you really tell fortunes?"

"I can see that you're about to get *chased!*" She shrieked and howled and I ran right into the center of the square. We collapsed on the ground, under one of the huge oaks that shaded the little park. From there, if you craned your head around in a circle, you could see every shop and restaurant and bar in Oakley, lining the square. In the distance you could see the green of the hills, the cut-up lines of the fields and crops.

"Can you see my fortune?"

"You," she said, "will be something special. I can see that much. Does that make me a witch?" She tapped my nose, then pushed herself up into a sitting position.

I just lay there on the grass, staring at the sky, then at the people rushing past on the roads surrounding us.

"Look." I pointed. I saw Mrs. Adams hurrying along with a bag of supplies.

Mary looked over, shielding her face with her hands. She nodded casually, then lay back down on the grass.

I glanced at Mary, surprised. "But don't you want to talk to Mrs. Adams, see how it went? Yesterday she was so sad."

"I never talk to people like her outside the library."

"Why not?"

She smiled and shook her head at me, sitting up again. "Watch," she said. "Meg!" She waved her hands. Mrs. Adams glanced back and then practically ran into the grocer's that bordered the south side of the square.

My mouth dropped open. Mary shrugged, laughed at my surprise. "They're all like that. Ashamed. What are you going to do? Take their money and let them get on with their lives."

"Was it different in the circus?" I asked.

"Different? It was another world! One day you'll see for yourself. You'll go there and everyone will look at you and see the same thing I do, a *gorgeous and amazing* little girl. You'll know that I wasn't just some maniac. Now, are you going to be my *official* librarian's assistant or not?"

"Yes," I said. "Yes, yes!"

"Okay, listen up: I need some paper and some more pens. Why don't you go to the stationer's, then meet me at the post office."

She handed me a couple of bills, winked, and walked off. I stood for a moment looking after her. Mary seemed so bright and out of place in the midst of the Oakley town square. When she reached the street, she turned around and waved.

"Don't just stand there like a bump on a log!" she yelled, laughing at me and all lit up by the sun, and I dashed off, my cheeks burning.

It seems ridiculous now, but I felt, for the first time, *grown up* as I entered the store. The bells rang as the door swung shut behind me, and I was hit with the sharp scents of ink and fresh paper. I walked nervously into the aisle, toward notepads full of creamy, lined sheets. I picked up a couple, then set them down, trying to remember what kind of paper I'd seen at the library. I thought as hard as I could. Finally, I picked the white loose paper, with shaking hands. Another ten minutes or so later and I had selected a set of shiny black pens.

When I paid at the counter, I was shocked that the old man didn't give me a second glance but just handed me my change along with the paper and pens in a bag.

I ran to the post office, thrilled, clutching the bag in my hand.

No one was at the front counter. I stood, waiting, and then heard the sound of Mary laughing, from a back room. Sneaking behind the counter and piles of packages, I tiptoed into the hall stretching off the main office. A second later I came across a half-open door. Peering through the crack, I saw Mary, her mouth open as she kissed a tall, mustached man. His right hand was tangled in her hair, the left one cupping the side of her lower back, pulling her toward him. Her hand snaked between his legs.

My heart raged with jealousy. I ran out and sat on the sidewalk out front. I had thought Mary was my friend, and now I felt betrayed, abandoned. *I should just leave now and go home,* I thought. *Forget about her, and everyone.* Tears dripped down my face. I heard people passing by, whispering to each other, but I didn't care.

"Tessa," I heard then. I looked up and wiped my face. My heart skipped a beat when I saw my mother's friend Ruth standing over me. "What are you doing? Is your mom around?"

"No," I said quickly. "I'm just running an errand."

"Is something wrong?"

I looked up into her pale, pinched face. "Nothing is wrong," I said. Just then, at the worst moment possible, Mary walked out of the post office, her cheeks flushed and hair even more wild than usual.

Mary saw the tears on my face and Ruth standing over me; she took it all in, in an instant. "What the hell are you doing to her?" she said, striding up to Ruth. "What's wrong with you?"

Ruth backed away and looked from Mary to me, and back again. "I just saw her crying," she said. "I wanted to know if she was okay."

"Well, why don't you mind your own business?" Mary asked. She was fierce, like a lioness, and I couldn't help but feel happy that she was so quick to defend me. I didn't correct her.

"I'm sorry," Ruth said, giving me one more look and then practically running away. I watched her, guiltily. I knew I'd have hell to pay later, at home, but when I looked up at Mary that didn't seem to matter.

"Are you okay?" Mary asked, turning to me.

I nodded. "I'm fine."

"I don't know what's wrong with me today," she said. "I just don't care, or something. You know what I mean, Tessa?"

I didn't, not really. But I wanted to.

"Yes," I said.

"Good, now let's head back, *assistant.*" Mary rubbed my shoulder with her palm—a friendly, sisterly gesture that made me feel sparkly and whole. As hurt as I was, I just basked in her, her kindness to me.

That night my mother stood waiting for me at the door. "Where were you today, young lady?" she asked, staring straight down at me.

"I took a walk."

"Oh, is that what you were doing?" she asked. "Strolling about like a little princess while the rest of us work?"

"No, ma'am," I said, bowing my head. "I just . . . I just wanted to go into town."

Behind my mother I could see Geraldine crouched on the top stairs, peering down at us. When she saw me looking, she opened her mouth wide and smiled.

"So I heard," my mother said. "I heard all about you gallivanting around town today, prancing around like some fancy-pants. You think anything in town is more important than your dusting and sewing, miss? You think you can miss even *one day* of your stretches?"

My mother knew I could barely reach anything in that house well enough to dust it, and she never trusted me with the sewing work.

"I won't even wait for an answer to that," she said. "I know exactly where you were and who you were with. I don't know what you and that tramp had to talk about, but so be it. We'll just see what your father has to say about the whole thing." She turned away then, toward the kitchen.

"No!" I screamed, running after her. "No, please don't tell him! I didn't do anything wrong!" My mind scrambled and grasped and then hit on the only thing I could think of. "I went to get a job! I did talk to that librarian, but it was to get a job!"

It was as if I had suddenly become someone new, and she stopped and looked me over, suspicious. "What kind of a job?"

"Helping out in the library. Helping with the books and with buying things. Today I bought paper and pens, for the library. So I can contribute to the good of the family." It was a phrase I'd heard my father use: "Now maybe you'll start contributing to the good of the family," he'd say, usually while working one of us over.

"I see." She kept staring at me. "And what are you getting paid for these valuable services, if I may ask?"

"A dollar a week," I said, pulling a number out of air.

"A dollar? Every week?"

It wasn't a lot of money, but I knew it was enough for my mother to buy cold cream at the corner store, for my father to buy drinks at a tavern in town, for them to splurge once in a while on meals of steak and fish.

Her face changed and she didn't seem as angry anymore. She stared at me so long I started to feel woozy. "Well, then, as long as you do your sewing in the evenings, that might be all right. I don't think your father will have too much of a problem with it, if you're contributing."

She looked at me for one moment longer, her face softened now, before turning back to the kitchen.

I breathed an enormous sigh of relief, but it didn't last long. My father had to agree, and then I'd have to convince Mary to pay me a dollar a week. I steeled myself for whatever was coming. Then another
thought came: How could I help in a library if I couldn't even read? I
thought of all those books and marks and tea labels and felt faint. I ran
outside, in those moments before dinner, and tried to remember the letters Mary had shown me when we had written my name in the dirt. I remembered the T and the beautiful S shapes, and I traced them again and
again, burning them into my memory.

At the dinner table my mother told my father about my new job.

"I know she will be working for that woman, Lucas, but a dollar a
week *would* be a nice contribution."

"Tessa has a job!" My brothers laughed, and I glared at them.

My father leaned back in his chair and looked at me. He had a long,
drooping face with a large cleft in his chin, and he almost never looked
at me directly. His stare seared into me, made me feel exposed and un-
clean. I dropped my eyes immediately. "Well let's just make one thing
clear," my father said, finally. "I never want to hear about that woman or
see a book from that library in this house. You got it?"

"Yes, sir," I said, staring into my stew.

"You see to that, girl." He slammed his fist on the table, and
I jumped in my seat, tried to control the shudder that ran through
my body.

My voice dropped to a whisper. "Yes, sir," I repeated.

His eyes bored into me. "Okay, then," he said, turning from me
and looking around the table, satisfied. "Now we can all make our contributions."

"Is she really a big slut?" Connor asked, after a moment, laughing
with his mouth full.

"I think she's pretty," Geraldine said softly.

At that, my father reached his huge hand over and smacked her right on the face. Geraldine just sat there, her face like a beet. As usual, I dared not say a word.

"Mary?" I asked the next day, as she showed me how to organize the books by number.

She stopped what she was doing, turned to me right away. "What?"

"I did something terrible," I said. I was so ashamed I wanted to disappear into the floorboards. I didn't look at her, knowing that the want was written on my face in glaring letters. "I told my parents that you were going to give me a dollar a week. That woman you saw me with yesterday talked to them, so I told them that, and they said it was okay. I'm sorry."

"Tessa!" she said then, releasing all the tension in her body and letting out a low laugh. "You're going to be working with me. You think I'm not going to pay you?"

"Do you really want me to work for you?" I asked.

"Of course," she said. "Aren't we a team?"

"I wasn't sure," I said, even more embarrassed, cursing myself for getting into this situation in the first place. "Is a dollar okay?"

Mary laughed and bent down till we were face to face.

"And that dollar goes straight to them, right?"

I nodded.

"Shit," she said. For a minute she just stared at me, but like she was looking at something past me. Then she said, "Okay, listen: I'm going to pay you a dollar fifty a week, or six dollars a month. You keep those two dollars. You do not tell your parents about them and you do not even *touch* them, okay?"

I nodded, afraid to speak.

"Your being here will help me a lot," she said. She dropped her voice to a whisper, though there were only a few people in the library. "I was thinking about getting help before this, but these people? I couldn't stand being around any of them that long. With you here, I can do more of my other work, you know?"

I nodded again, though I had no idea what she meant.

"Fortunes," she whispered, laughing. "The library gets money from the county and late fines, but there's real money in fortune-telling, if people believe in you. I learned *that* much before I came here. Maybe I can even give you a raise after a while."

But I couldn't imagine anything better than that two dollars. I had never even had a penny of my very own. "Thank you," I said. And then, blushing, "Why are you so nice to me?"

"Why? We're friends, Tessa. And you're not like the others around here. There's something different waiting for you, out in the world. You remind me of me when I was your age."

"Really?"

"I was so much like you," she said. "So scared, with no idea of what I could do, how big the world was. When I got to the circus, everyone was so different, and it was the first time I felt at home, anywhere. Do you know what I mean?"

I looked at her, and the stacks of books behind her. "Maybe," I said.

"You will know. I guarantee it. This is not all there is, by any stretch."

"Thank you," I whispered. I breathed in her spice scent and looked at the bracelets dangling from her wrist, which made a slight *tink-tink* noise as she moved. "Why did you come here, though," I asked, "when you had the circus?"

"That is a long story, little girl," she said, and I saw a wave of something pass over her. *Something bad,* I thought, but did not know what to say.

"Where did you live before?"

"A place called Rain Village," she said. "A sad place, sadder than a willow weeping over a country pond. It's where I was born and raised."

"Rain Village?"

"It was strange there, Tessa." She seemed far away from me then. "A place where rain shimmered onto the river and water never reflected the sky above it. A place where leaves and pine needles fell into your hair and stuck to the bottom of your feet, and everyone had a secret. It rained all the time, hiding us away from the world."

I stared at her, transfixed. "Why did you leave?"

"I just did," she said. "You can always leave. Always. That's why you should save your pennies, little girl. You know what I used to do to hide money from my parents? And then, later, from everyone else?"

I shook my head.

"I sewed it into my skirts and shirts," she said. "In the hems. But in your case we can just keep a box here, okay? So whenever you're ready to get the hell out of here, you'll have your money with you. In the meantime, why don't we celebrate with a glass of champagne?"

"Okay," I said, though I was sure she was joking. When she disappeared and came back a moment later with a bubbling glass in each hand and a big silver box tucked under one arm, I just drank it all in and laughed.

Rain Village, I thought later, and imagined leaves clinging to my hair, soaked through with rain.

CHAPTER FOUR

I immersed myself in Mary and that library, and the books surrounding me. During the day I learned to shelve and check out and check in, and I soaked in the stories Mary read to me, listened carefully as she recommended books to the farmers who lined up at the library doors each morning. Though I couldn't read very well yet, soon I, too, could recommend books to people based on the way they moved through the room, the way they looked at me as they approached the front desk. I gave my mother a dollar every Friday, and my own two dollars a month piled up, along with the money Mary gave me from what she earned telling fortunes and selling herbs. I was always conscious of the money I had sitting in that silver box: it seemed to chain me to a mysterious but thrilling future, one far away from Oakley, Kansas.

I worked every day from morning till evening, and then at night I sneaked my way into the fields. With a book spread before me I struggled with those marks that covered the pages until early in the morning when my family started to rise. I lay back in the field, the corn swaying all around me, above my head, and the moon shining through and lighting up the pages. The more I studied those pages, the more different everything seemed: the cornhusks pulled back to reveal rows of shiny jewel-like kernels, and the moon marked out the shapes of the corn and the stalks, spooky and wonderful against the sky.

Every day I brought in a list of questions and problems for Mary, and with one glance at the page I was reading she could erase all the roughness and all the awkwardness I'd brought to it when I was struggling in the fields alone. Her voice was rich and low, humming in my ear, and everything she saw she saw differently from any way I had thought to see it before. The stories and words stayed with me, overlaid my mind and heart and protected me from the world outside the library, my world back home. As time passed and the words on the page came into focus for me, I'd sometimes open a book and forget to breathe, I'd slide out of myself so completely. I'd jump up, astonished and gasping for breath, to see Mary looking over at me from her desk, smiling curiously. I would drop a book from my hands sometimes, feeling its beating heart under my fingers.

I loved the cigarette smoke that coiled above the library desk, the shapes carved into the wood, and the way Mary sat bent over some book, her right arm tossed to the side, her fingers playing with the crinkling paper of her cigarette. Though on most days the men were lying in wait for Mary out front and the women practically formed a line behind the library stacks, pretending to look through books while anxiously checking the door Mary was sitting behind with someone else, there were other days when we had that long stretch of afternoon all to ourselves, to read or talk or play cards or just work to get all those books shelved before the next round of scholars and heartbroken women. Those days were heaven for me: I had a million books pulsing around me, and Mary, too, had story after story inside her, so vivid they pressed into the corners of the library, into every nook and cranny, and leaked out the windows that had been cracked open and were jammed crooked into their frames. I would wait for those moments when Mary would look up and tell me a story, or read me some ravishing poem by Christina Rossetti or Robert Browning, or a tract on gardening, or a line about dreams, tulips, or Egyptian kings.

"Listen to this, Tessa," she said once. "One of my favorites." Her face was pink, her hair blacker than I'd ever seen it. Happily, I set down the dictionary I was studying and stretched out on the wooden floor.

Mary held the gold-paged book with trembling hands.

"On either side the river lie
long fields of barley and of rye,
that clothe the wold and meet the sky;
and thro' the field the road runs by,
*   to many-tower'd Camelot."*

I soaked the words in through my skin, breathed them in and out. I had never heard of Camelot, but all at once I pictured it: the river and rye, all tinged with blue, the magical place in the distance that all the workers turned to, dreaming. I imagined castles and towers like in the old stories Mary had read to me.

"And up and down the people go,
gazing where the lilies blow,
round an island there below,
*   the island of Shalott."*

She smiled, making the words lilt and sing.

"Willows whiten, aspens quiver,
little breezes dusk and shiver,
thro' the wave that runs for ever,

by the island in the river,
 flowing down to Camelot.
Four gray walls, and four gray towers,
overlook a space of flowers,
and the silent isle imbowers,
 the Lady of Shalott."

The words ran through my veins, seeped into me and made images appear all around me. I could have reached out and touched the willows and aspens, as light and soft as silk. I didn't even know what the words meant, all of them, but I could *see* them, see the woman trapped in the island by the river, the garden outside. Suddenly I felt heartbroken.

The poem went on, and I watched the boats skimming down the river, the people walking by, the woman in the tower weaving and singing, cursed if she looks down at Camelot.

"Why can't she look?" I asked suddenly, angrily, turning to Mary.

She looked up and shrugged. "She'll be cursed," she said. "Curses are funny things."

I held my breath and listened. *Don't look,* I thought. *Don't look.* When Lancelot entered with his broad, clear brow and helmet, I held my breath.

"She left the web, she left the loom,
she made three paces thro' the room,
she saw the water-lily bloom,
she saw the helmet and the plume,
 she look'd down to Camelot."

"No!" I called out, as, in the poem, the web flew out and mirror cracked. I covered my eyes.

The next thing I knew, Mary was closing the book and kneeling beside me. I peeked out and saw her shaking her head, marveling at me. "It's not real," she whispered. "It's just a poem."

I put down my hands, flushing with embarrassment. "I'm sorry."

"Don't be sorry," she said. "Don't be." And then she smiled down at me. The world went back to normal.

I breathed out in relief. "I hate Lancelot," I said.

"Me too," she said, laughing. "Now how about some tea?"

I remember those days like hot baths after days spent in the snow. Sometimes we'd just sit cross-legged on the floor, a picnic lunch spread around us, as she told me about the strawberry farmer and his mistress from town, or the boy who was engaged to two girls at once, or the post office station manager's wife who was pregnant with a dairy farmer's child. Mary knew every strange, clandestine thing that happened in Oakley. Not too much happened in Oakley outside these sordid affairs of the heart, though: no crimes of passion or big, earth-shattering events. The town was too small to attract the traveling shows that dotted the Midwest through the summers, and you'd have to travel all the way to Kansas City for anything worth seeing. Once, some boys in town got in trouble for defacing the scarecrows that rose out of the cornfields, and that caused more of a ruckus than anything else had in months.

Sometimes we were silent for hours at a time. I would read while Mary just sat there quietly, rolling her cigarettes or trying to organize the papers Mercy Library received each day, the copies of wedding licenses or birth certificates that we'd haul to the vast file cabinets downstairs.

"Why do we bother with this?" I asked once. "What does it matter?"

Mary ran her hands along the cabinets, until she found the right one. She slid it open and began leafing through scattered papers and folders. "Here," she said finally, pulling out a few thick sheets of paper as if she were a magician. "Some librarian before me filed this right after you were born," she said. "Look. Tessa Riley, born to Lucas and Roberta Riley of Riley Farm."

I stared down at the sheet of paper, the harsh, typed words. She flipped through the papers, showing me all of them.

"There are files for Matthew, Connor, and Geraldine, too, and Lucas and Roberta. Your whole family, right?"

I nodded. It was so strange to see our names laid out like that, as if our lives had enough precision to them that someone could type out the details like that—but there they were, their names next to mine.

"You never talk about them," she said. "Why don't you ask your sister and brothers to visit one day?"

I looked up at her, startled. "Oh, no," I said. "No. Please don't do that." The idea of Geraldine or Matthew or Connor in Mercy Library seemed all wrong. I pictured them storming through the aisles, books crashing to the floor as they clomped past. I imagined the looks on their faces when they saw me drinking tea with herbs floating at the top.

Mary slipped the papers back in their folders and shut the drawer. "It was just an idea," she said, flicking her finger against my arm. "So, no more Rileys here if we can help it. I'll put a big sign in front that says they're not allowed."

I smiled, relieved, but sadder, much sadder than I had been before I'd seen my name in black type. Later, without Mary knowing, I went back and back to those papers, which almost tore in my shaking hands. I looked at the names of my parents and felt the most profound sense of longing and loss, though I barely recognized then that that was what it was: loss of the most heart-wrenching kind, despite the books raging with life around me, despite Mary and her kindness, her beautiful words and stories.

By and large, it was the men in Oakley who had begun reading books—bringing candles into their rooms late at night to read the *Canterbury Tales,* perusing Montaigne while sitting in tractors or on bales of hay. They loved coming into the library and showing Mary how they'd read the selections she'd made for them, telling her about their favorite parts and lines.

Women sought Mary out more shamefully, in whispers and with scarves pulled over their heads. Beatrice and Mrs. Adams were only two out of what must have been five hundred women who came to see Mary when I was there. In my first year of working at Mercy Library, I heard women confess to hating their children; to loving women instead of men; to cheating on husbands with all variety of other men, from farmhands to cousins to the traveling salesmen who sometimes appeared at our doors with cases full of perfume or makeup; to hating their lives, our town, and the fields that kept all of us wrapped around their fingers; and to desiring any number of things so strongly that they could barely eat or sleep or get through the house- or farmwork they saw pile in front of them each day.

Several months into my new working life, I was sitting on a small rocking chair near the table, struggling through a book called *Sister Carrie* that Mary had picked out for me, while Mary sat behind the desk with a deck of cards spread out in front of her. She played absentmindedly with her cigarette as I spat out each word, fitting my lips and mouth around them. The cards snapped as Mary shuffled them between each game. The day had been particularly grueling: we had talked to a woman having an affair with a boy half her age, despite her husband's legendary temper. Mary seemed especially quiet, melancholy.

"Love, that's all anyone asks about," she said, sighing. "It's pathetic." We finished closing the library together, then walked out into the balmy spring night, down to the river that ran a mile or so behind the library. We stretched on the grass by the river.

She turned to me. "Have you had any boyfriends yet, Tessa?"

"Me?" I looked at her, truly astonished.

"Of course," she said, winking.

I didn't know what to say. "Have you ever been in love?" I asked, finally.

"Oh," she said, a smile forming. "Yes. Not for a long time, a very long time, but yes."

"What is it like? Who was he? Is he the man from the post office?"

But she hardly heard my questions. Her eyes closed; the sweat glistened on her brown face. The warmth of her skin seemed to radiate all around me. I crept up close to her and put my face next to hers.

She said finally, "No, his name was William. From Rain Village. His body was perfect, like a sculpture you'd see in a museum, and he was just made like that. He would walk around naked, very casually, as if it were the most natural thing and his body were above such things as shame or modesty. Like a child's white hair. As if he didn't even know it."

She seemed far away from me then, and to be talking to herself as much as to me. I squinted up, following her gaze. I felt that if I concentrated hard enough, I too would see him—naked, walking like a cat.

"He was pale, almost completely white. He was only a boy, you know. His hair was like the palest blond dipped in the ashes of a forest fire and his eyes were dark like wet river rocks. Sometimes he couldn't sleep, and then he'd stalk around and curse the rain and the dark, and me. I would huddle in the blankets and block out every single thing but the warm imprint of his body, the faint smell of eucalyptus still in the bed."

She stopped, and the night was quiet. All we could hear was the light lapping of the river, the slight wind stirring the grass and weeping willows and oak.

"His voice," she whispered, "was soft and clipped, as if he'd been born in some other country. But he hadn't been. Sometimes he could sit for hours and never say a word. He would carve designs into wood. If I moved or sighed, he noticed; he was always watching me, like I was made of glass."

Her voice was so low I had to lean forward.

"He died. He drowned in the river. I remember how white and cold he was in the water, the leaves sticking to his skin. It's why I left. Why I left Rain Village the way my older sister had before me. I left my mother, father, sister, and everything I'd known. William died in the river, and the leaves were like leeches on his skin."

The night seemed to have darkened. Mary looked at the sky. I shivered, and she turned to me, reached up and touched my hair.

"You will fall in love, too. You won't be unlucky like me." She pulled herself up and sat cross-legged, facing me. "I left home. I just left, left my family and the rain and the river. And I went all over, and then I came here. Sometimes that is the best we can do in life: seek out new families and homes when the old ones have failed us."

"Is that when you joined the circus?" I asked.

"Yes," she said. She tilted her chin to the sky, her hair sticking every which way. She reached out her hand and slipped it into mine. Her long fingers dwarfed mine, and my pale skin seemed to glow next to hers.

"Do you miss Rain Village?"

She nodded, bending her head to her chest. "We lived in a stone house," she said a moment later, smiling slightly, "in the middle of a forest. A forest as big as the sky. The river where they found William ran almost straight through the forest, about a ten-minute walk from our house. It was a river unlike any you've ever seen, Tessa."

"I've only seen one," I said. "This one right here."

"You haven't ever traveled out of here?"

"My father would never let us. He says the world outside of Oakley is filled with evils."

She smiled. "I don't think Oakley is immune to that, no matter what your father says. And why blame the world when it's right here?" She tapped her chest.

"I think he has evil in him," I whispered. "He makes all of us cry, sometimes. Is that evil?"

She looked at me. "Yes," she said. "I think it is."

"I want to travel," I said. "I want to see Rain Village, and the circus." I tried to call forth a picture in my mind. "What was the river like?"

"Oh," she said, closing her eyes but holding my hand tight, "it was filled with salmon and other pink fish. The fishermen used to set their lines and let themselves drift along the water. They'd fall asleep like that, sprawled out on the fishing boats, the rain plinking down on their bodies."

"That sounds terrible," I said. "All that rain."

"It was weird," she said. "No one there complained about the rain, the dampness. There it was just normal. When I left, I baked myself in the sun, and I've been brown ever since. Before, in Rain Village, I was as pale as a ghost. I didn't even know how curly my hair was until I left home and saw it dry for the first time."

"That's not true!"

"Oh, it is," she said. "There, my face was covered in freckles, from the rain. When I left my skin turned completely clear. See?"

I leaned in and stared at her face, her brown, smooth skin. I gasped. "It's true!" I said.

"Unless I'm lying, of course." She laughed, and I was relieved, seeing her happy. "Everyone there was a storyteller, you know. At night the fishermen docked their boats and everyone gathered to tell stories. The water would have turned black by then, and if it weren't too cloudy all the stars would be out, like they are now, like salt sprinkled over ink. Everyone who looked normal and friendly in the daylight turned spooky at night, with the flickering light and the black water behind them."

"What stories did they tell?" I asked, not even noticing Mary's spice scent anymore, the scent of rain was so forceful in my nostrils.

"Oh, all kinds," she said. "Gossip and legends, kids' stories, stories about our past."

"Tell me one!" I begged, pressing my hands together.

She raised her eyebrows at me. "You really want to hear one?"

"Yes!"

"Well," she said, "one of my favorites was a story about a prince and a peasant girl. My mother used to tell it when I was a kid."

"What was it?"

"Okay," she said, lowering her voice as if she were sharing a great secret. She leaned back on the grass and I lay next to her. Her hair spread out in corkscrews that tumbled down over my shoulder. I picked up strands of her hair and wrapped the curls around my fingers, and we lay there side by side.

"There was once a beautiful peasant girl," she began, "who wore dresses that came up to her chin and ended past her toes. The girl lived in a tiny cottage with her husband, who was a good strong man who worked the fields."

I laughed, imagining him in the fields in Oakley, the ones I ran past every day. I could *see* it.

"One day a prince rode into town on a gleaming black horse. He was so rich that every time he opened his purse men and women gasped as if he held the moon in there. But those women didn't have a chance. When the prince saw the peasant girl, he fell instantly in love and was determined to marry her. He didn't care whether or not the girl loved him back, and didn't let the fact that she already had a husband deter him one bit. The peasant girl was not interested in the prince at all, and when he began hunting her down in the fields, she was sure that the devil himself had found her. 'Help!' she cried, and ran like a ribbon through the crops, so fast the prince thought she'd disappeared. But this only made him more determined; he bought the most luxurious home in town and moved into it that day."

I closed my eyes, picturing it, imagining a red ribbon streaming through the cornfields, whooshing out into the road.

"Soon enormous crates began arriving, one by one, filled with all the prince's earthly belongings. He settled in and began trying to lure the girl in every earthly way—hosting lavish parties, sending jewels to her house, writing her poetry-filled letters—but he did not understand the strength of the girl's love for her husband, or her religious fervor. Finally the prince realized that to possess this girl he'd have to find a way to bind her to him forever, so he sold off every single possession he had ever owned: every last jewel in his gigantic jewel vault, every richly brocaded shirt, every solid-gold candlestick and fork, every exotic bird in his private atrium. When the last item had been sold and he wore nothing but a simple peasant's shirt and overalls, the prince sold his soul to the devil. He took the sum of his earthly life and brought it to a famous jeweler, who spent a month in his laboratory, mixing it all up in a great iron vat until, finally, he produced one perfect, sparkling opal ring, a ring more valuable than any ring made before or since."

Mary sat up and pressed her hands into the grass. I thought of every beautiful thing I'd ever seen, reduced down to one stone. My mind wrapped around that image and held it close.

"The next time the prince saw the beautiful peasant girl, he approached her without a fear in his heart. Not even God could save the peasant girl from the fate that had been given her, the strength of that ring and the devil were so strong. Her heart split into pieces, the girl walked into her husband's barn and came out on her favorite horse. Then she stopped, and the prince leapt upon it, and neither of them was ever heard from again. Until the day he died, the poor, abandoned husband prayed for the soul of his lost wife, who had disappeared into the world and, by all accounts, lived unhappily ever after.

"They used to say that the prince and the peasant girl founded Rain Village. People used to whisper it," Mary said. "They said that that was why we were all so heartbroken there, because it had been passed down by our ancestors."

"Really?" I asked.

"Yes," she said, nodding slowly and whisking an eyelash from my cheek with her thumb. "You cannot escape your fate, Tessa, or where you come from."

I looked at her and was surprised to see how strange she looked, as if something fierce and sad were beating its way out of her.

"What is it, Mary?" I whispered, but she just reached out and entwined her fingers with mine.

CHAPTER FIVE

My thirteenth birthday came and went that second summer. I'd been working in Mercy Library for almost a year. It felt like more time than that had passed; I felt like a whole new person and marveled sometimes as I watched myself with a library patron, recommending *The Canterbury Tales* or *The Divine Comedy*. Mary waited until we closed the library to present me with my very own rhinestone-covered skirt she'd sewn for me herself.

"Someday you can wear this to dinner with your boyfriend," she said, grinning. "You'll be the prettiest girl in the restaurant."

I turned red down to my toes as I slipped into it. Before she let me look in the mirror, Mary took out a shiny plastic purse full of cosmetics and spread glitter and powder over my face. She painted black arching eyebrows over my own, and drew my lips into a bow. She twisted my hair onto the top of my head and stuck long ivory pins through it.

"Look," she said, and I walked straight to the mirror and peered into it, at the strange sparkling girl staring out. Mary came behind me, resting her chin on my shoulder. "Look at our eyes," she said. "You'd think we were related." I looked back and forth and saw it was true: my eyes looked big and blue, almost sloped like hers, though in my case it was the makeup more than anything else.

"I don't look so terrible," I whispered, and was immediately embarrassed to have said it out loud. But it was true: I looked almost pretty, my light hair falling in my face and piled on my head, my face sparkling with glitter.

Mary laughed. "Of course not," she said. "You're beautiful, Tessa. Don't listen to anyone else. People try to shut out beauty wherever they can in this world, but it's a mistake."

I smiled, traced the lines of my face in the mirror. *Beautiful*, she had said. I couldn't see it, but I basked in it anyway, rocking back and forth so that the skirt swished around my knees.

It was around that time that, one day, Mary sent me into the library's depths with a box of old books for storage, and I came across an old dusty box marked "Circus" in faded letters, hidden behind a stack of ancient encyclopedias. Mary's circus stories had taken on the aura of dreams and myth; this box seemed impossible, sitting here before me. I dropped everything. My hands started to shake as I ripped off the tape that ran in lines across the top. I couldn't imagine being more excited if I'd happened upon a treasure chest just lifted out of the sea.

Breathlessly, I peeled back the box cover. Even through the tissue paper they were wrapped in, I could see the sparkles and rhinestones and sequins of the leotards. I reached in and lifted out the one on top, carefully unwrapped it and held it up in the dim light. The red sequins shimmered; the leotard was so heavy and ornate that my arms grew tired holding it up. I stood up, my breath quickening, and held the leotard up to my chest, smoothed it over my belly. It extended halfway down my thighs. I could only imagine how Mary had sent hearts racing in outfits like this.

I laid the leotard neatly over another box nearby and lifted out the rest, one after another, not even caring if I messed them up, what Mary would say. One after another I pulled the costumes out of their wrappings and held them up: vivid reds and yellows, a brilliant electric blue with clouds of sequins swirling down the sides. The colors seemed to take on a life of their own in that room, throwing light against the walls. I had never seen anything like it and was surprised at how quickly I felt transformed. *This* is what the circus is like, I thought. This color, this life.

Why hadn't Mary shown me this stuff before? Everything she'd told me had seemed so fantastic and far away—it didn't seem possible that anything from the circus could exist right there, in Oakley, in Mercy Library. I pressed my hand along the beaded rim of a black leotard, closed my eyes. I could *feel* it: that sensation of flying, of being over everything.

"Tessa!" I heard Mary calling from the main floor.

Hurriedly, I pushed past the wrapped costumes and found slippers and tights and caps and jeweled combs. I ran my fingers along the length of the heels, the feathers on the caps.

I heard the basement door click open and then Mary's voice, louder now: "Tessa, are you down there?"

"Just a minute!" I cried. I grabbed the leotards and quickly folded them, layering them between sheets of tissue paper, in the box. I heard Mary's footsteps on the stairs, slapped the box shut and shoved it in the corner.

I ran up to meet her.

"I've got a line up here," she said. "I need help."

For the rest of the afternoon I felt that box pulling at me. While Mary told fortunes in the back, I sat and checked out books, barely even looking up as I pulled out the cards to stamp and date them. *The circus,* I thought, imagining myself flying through the air, my body draped in red sparkles. The feel of the sequins and beads under my palm.

"Why don't I go organize some of the files downstairs?" I suggested later, during a brief lull.

"Such a good worker you are," Mary said, laughing. "Why don't we take a tea break instead? God, I'm tired. I want to just slap these people sometimes and tell them to take a look around—of *course* they're unhappy!"

I nodded but was awash with disappointment.

"How long were you in the circus?" I asked suddenly, as we made our way back to the little kitchen.

Mary turned to me. "About five seasons, I guess," she said. She set a pot of water to boil and reached up for the herbs.

"Were you famous?" I asked, and then, before she could answer, "Why did you leave?"

The air filled with the smell of herbs and spices. We heard the front door open and voices fill the room. "Can you help those people?" Mary asked, handing me my cup and avoiding my eyes. She seemed relieved, anxious to get rid of me.

I tried not to look too disappointed. The rest of the afternoon went by quickly, and I didn't have a chance to go back downstairs before Mary and I closed the library. She was in a hurry to get cleaned up and go into town, and kissed me on the cheek before disappearing down the stairs to her room.

Damnit, I thought, pausing outside on the front steps, every cell of my body pulling me to that box downstairs. Calling out to me, like a secret. Reluctantly, I started the walk home. I watched the snow gleam in the moonlight and thought of Mary on the trapeze. There was a *whole world* buried in that box, I thought. A world brighter and more wonderful than anything I could find in Oakley.

As I cut through the town square and the giant oak trees that shaded it, I spotted a branch extending straight from one side, about six feet from the ground. No one was around aside from a few men entering the tavern on the square.

I dropped my bag and leapt up, wrapping my palms around the branch. It was easy, just like hanging from the bar on the window back home. But here I was unrestricted: I swung back and forth, then pushed up and hung from my knees. The bark scraped my skin, but I didn't care. I was a thousand miles away from Oakley, anyway.

The next day I scrambled down into the basement before Mary could stop me. She was busy hauling in water from the pump outside, and gathering herbs from her garden to set to drying.

"I need an old newspaper for Mrs. Olsen," I said. I ran down, past the file room and through the hall, past Mary's room with the mattress on the floor and line of skirts hanging from a ceiling pipe. When I came to the box I pushed past the leotards and caps, and dug in to see what other treasures it held.

I pulled up a pile of circus programs. I grabbed the whole stack of them, spread them across the floor. It was crazy, even liberating and wild, to see photographs of things I had only heard about from Mary. I'd never quite believed her stories were real, and yet there they were: beautiful boys crossing the high wire; a woman hanging from a thin rope by her hair; and then Mary herself in midflight, soaring from the catcher's hands back to the bar.

She was so different in the pictures, different than any way I'd ever seen her. Her hair was pulled away from her face and tucked under a red beaded cap, and her skin practically glowed under the light. Even from that far you could see the tilted shape of her eyes, the soft, fluid lines of her arms and legs as they propelled her through the air. She was a bright, magnetic spot suspended amidst the ropes and hooks and metal rings.

It was rapturous: every single picture spoke of some new wonder, some new way of moving through space. I could barely breathe. With my whole being I wanted that, what I saw in the pictures. Flight.

I closed the programs and stacked them beside me, and then, pushing past more tissue paper and wrappings, I came upon a metal bar covered over in parts with tape, a line of rope extending from either end. A thick braided rope curled like a snake at the bottom of the box. Various chains and hooks and smaller ropes were scattered among the coils.

A trapeze, I realized, and rigging, and a web. I wrapped my fingers around the metal, and I swear they *tingled* with the magic of what that bar could do, where it could take me.

And then I no longer cared about getting into trouble, what Mary would say when she saw I'd been snooping. I grabbed that bar and ran up to meet her as quickly as my legs could carry me.

I burst into the room. It was one of those bright mornings when the sun slanted across the floor and all the books turned warm on the shelves. Mary stood at the front desk, next to a pile of books.

"Mary," I began, breathlessly, "I want you to teach me the trapeze."

Her eyes fell on the bar in my hands, and a strange look crossed her face, one I couldn't place. "Where did you find that?"

"Downstairs, among the boxes."

"You've been sneaking around?" she asked, her eyes flashing up at me.

"I'm sorry," I said, pleading. "I just came across it. I had to look. I saw the costumes, the programs, you flying—it was all beautiful, Mary, the most beautiful things I've ever seen."

"Those things are sealed away for a reason," she said.

"I'm sorry," I said. "I couldn't help it. Please teach me. *Please.*" I stopped when I saw how angry she was.

"Tessa," she said slowly, "I haven't flown on the trapeze for years now. It's ancient history. Put that back, and don't let me see it again."

I was close to sobbing. "But Mary, I can feel it in my bones. I *have* to do this."

She looked at me, her face reddening, and then stalked away. I knew better than to follow her.

For the rest of the day we worked in silence. When the evening came, I stormed from the library, slamming the door behind me as hard as I could. *I don't need her,* I thought, kicking the side of the stairwell, slamming the dangling Mercy Library sign as I ran past. I ran until I reached the town square and the cluster of giant oak trees. I threw off my coat, furiously, and leapt up to one of the branches, started to swing.

As I swung, letting the air soothe me, the cold rip past my tears and anger, I heard laughter. I stopped, turned my head to see a group of kids clustered under another tree, smoking cigarettes and passing a bottle between them.

"Tessa!" they taunted. "Tessa the witch!"

I dropped to the ground. My feet crunched into the snow. I was so angry I felt my body dissolve, until I was one voice screaming through the dark. "I hope all of you die!" I cried.

Before I turned and ran home, I swear they all looked genuinely frightened. I flew through the night in a blaze of rage and heartbreak, then collapsed in the cornfield behind my house, hidden away from the world. I huddled against a stalk, grabbed the root, and bent my whole body around it. Tears of frustration ran down my face.

Finally, maybe hours later, I sat up and stretched, blinked at the moonlight. I turned and looked up through the corn at my house, the dark windows. Shivering, I pulled out my book, *Sister Carrie,* and read about Carrie for an hour, getting lost in her world of factories and concrete before dragging myself off to sleep.

Things remained tense between Mary and me throughout the next day. My tenacity surprised me, but I discovered a stubbornness in myself that I'd never known I had.

"Please, Mary," I said again and again, then rushed off in tears or anger when she refused to budge.

"Tessa, I'm telling you," she said, following me back into the stacks, "I barely remember anything at all."

I kept my eyes on the shelf in front of me. "You aren't that old, Mary. You remember. I *know* you do."

"It's too dangerous, anyway," she said.

"Couldn't you show me just one time?" I asked. My eyes filled with tears, and I turned to her. "Just once?"

"You know, Tessa," she said, "it's beautiful to see you so sure of what you want, so passionate about something. But *why* does it have to be the trapeze? I gave all that up. For good."

"Because I'll be good at it," I said, surprising myself.

She stared at me as I purposefully arranged a pile of books. "I don't think I can do it," she said, finally. I looked up at her and was surprised by the expression on her face, a look of something like wistfulness. Her face closed then, like a trap door, and she turned and walked away.

She avoided me for the rest of the day, sending me back into the stacks again and again with books to organize and shelve. I was nearly crazy with frustration, but when the sun went down I walked home slowly, scheming all the while. I walked through the town square and ignored the group of kids sitting under the tree, even when they tried to provoke me. Maybe I could get Mary to hang up the trapeze and learn by myself, I thought. Riley Farm opened up in front of me, but I barely noticed. Maybe there was someone else who could teach me.

Though I knew that such a thing was unheard-of in Oakley, before Mary Finn.

When I stepped into the house, it took me a second to notice my father standing before me, in the dark hallway. I pulled back in surprise. He'd been watching for me, I realized, from the living room window, and all at once I felt like I'd been caught doing something wrong.

His eyes bored into me. I stood immobilized, my heart skipping forward and hammering against my chest. I saw it then, in his hand. A book. *My* book, the one I had carefully hidden under my mattress the night before.

Slowly, I looked back at his face. He was massive in front of me, a mountain. He could have reached out and picked me up between his fingers, I thought, crushed me under his toe. There was nothing more terrifying in all the world than my father standing there with *Sister Carrie* in his hand. He loomed over me, then leaned forward.

I jumped, sure he would hit me. I braced myself for it, my whole body tensing into a wall of muscle and bone. My father lifted his hand, and I shut my eyes. A moment later a loud *thwap!* shook the house. I opened my eyes, saw my book lying on the floor, its pages twisted and crushed.

"Get this trash out of here," he said. "Get it out *now.*"

He turned and left the room, and I crumpled to the floor, snatched the book up into my hands and under my skirt. How had I let this happen? I knew he would punish me. I could already feel his hands coming down.

I ran from the house and out into the road. Just outside our property I knelt down to bury the book, but then thought better of it. My father's eyes seemed to follow me, wherever I went, and I could think of only one place to go where things would be okay.

I ran to the herb garden in back of Mercy Library, dug out the silver key Mary hid there, and let myself in. I must have been a sight to behold: ragged and out of breath, a mashed-up book in my hands. I made my way into the dark space, hoping Mary would still be there.

The whole place was dead quiet. I felt funny and started tiptoeing through. I passed the little kitchen, and the herbs seemed spooky in the dark, roiling around in their glass jars, glittering and smoking as if they were all dreaming in there. I slipped past, through the stacks and into the main part of the library. Mary wasn't anywhere. It was so dark I could barely see.

I tiptoed to the basement door and cracked it open. "Mary," I called. There was no answer. I peered down but couldn't make anything out.

Sighing, I headed to Mary's desk and sat down, cradling the book in my lap. A power seemed to surge from Mary's seat and rush through me, up my back and arms, to my face. *It's okay*, I thought. *Shhh*. But the panic took hold in my gut and wouldn't leave. Never in my life had I so openly disobeyed my father. I felt tears rush to my eyes and wished Mary were there to comfort me. My father was capable of *anything*. This, I knew to my bones. Could I just stay here? I wondered. It was the first time the thought had truly seized me: maybe I could stay here forever, never go home. Maybe I never needed to see my family again.

And then I heard it: Mary laughing. She must not have heard me before. I swung open the basement door and ran down the steps, toward her room. A faint light shone through the crack beneath her door. How hadn't I seen it before? I almost forgot everything, my relief was so strong.

I pushed open the door and gasped. Mary was crouching on top of a naked man, her body bare and slick with sweat. Her breasts were full and round, her hair nearly wet, sticking to her neck. The man's skin was paler than hers. His hands gripped her hips. I didn't recognize him.

I felt completely shattered. Mary looked up at me, and her mouth dropped open, her hands rushed to her breasts. "Tessa!" she said, and quickly rolled off the man, to her side. She grabbed for her clothes on the floor next to the mattress. The man sat up and looked at me, annoyed.

"What is this?" he asked.

In its way, it might have been worse than seeing my father looming before me, holding the book in his hand. This was Mary, acting like a *slut*. My mother's voice echoed in my head: *a tramp*, she'd said, *a black-haired Jezebel*. I had never felt so betrayed, in all my life.

"You're a slut!" I screamed, my teeth mashing together. "How could you?" My insides were teeming, boiling. I had no idea what would come out of me next, what I would do. "A goddamned whore!"

Tears nipped at my eyes, but I fought them back, translated them into rage and heartbreak.

"Tessa!" Mary cried. "Tessa, stop!" Her face looked crushed with worry. "Tessa, come here!"

She reached for me, but I backed away. "Don't come near me!" I turned then and ran: up the stairs, through the basement door, the stacks, the back door. I heard her calling out for me, but I trampled straight through the herb garden, into the grass. Past the lumberyard, through the town square, and onto the road that led to home. The air was like fingers swatting my face. The moon was like an assault. I thought of Sister Carrie in her factory, longed for the world to be as flat and dull as that, a place where I would never have to feel anything at all.

I cut through one of the farms near my house and then slowed, slumped in the grass. I felt completely unmoored. I could not go back to the library, and I could not go back home, where I knew my father was waiting with his leather belt. I could *feel* him peering into the dark night, and, irrationally, crouched down in the grass so he wouldn't see me. I knew that the sooner I got back, the less of a beating I'd get, but the dread seeped into every pore of my body. Where was there to go? Every minute I was gone made his anger worse, and yet I prayed that with each new second a new possibility would emerge. Could I leave? Go somewhere new? Run off to the circus? Sobs wracked my body, and then finally I went numb, resigned myself to my fate. There was no other place for me but home.

I walked back to Riley Farm and pushed through the front door. The house was silent. I tiptoed through the hallway, peered into the living room. My mother sat on the couch, working on the bright orange sweater she was knitting for Geraldine, who sat on the floor playing dominoes. The house was too quiet.

Then I heard my father behind me. "Let's go, girl," he said. I looked back at my mother, but she just stared at the orange yarn, moving the needles up and down.

I woke the next morning aching all over. My arms were tender and bruised. I tried lying on my back and then winced and sat up. The sun glared in. The night before I had thought I would never return to Mercy Library, but now I yearned for it so badly I was almost in tears. I was late for work already. I could not stay in that room, that house, another minute. I didn't even wash, just pulled on a skirt and top. My heart thudded as I descended the stairs, but one glance out the back window proved that my father, mother, sister, and brothers were already in the fields.

The walk was slow going; every step hurt, moved my body in a dozen directions it didn't want to go. A weight was pressing down on me, too, a deep sadness I had never experienced before. As I walked along the main road, past one of the neighboring farms, I looked up and saw Mary, bending back branches, ducking, and walking from behind a line of trees and into the road about a half mile down. She was wearing a bright red-and-white checked dress with a full skirt that fell to her knees. Her black hair tumbled past her shoulders. When she saw me, she waved and started running. I thought I was seeing things. I blinked, shook my head. Mary never came to this part of town, and would be way too busy opening the library by herself.

"Tessa!" I heard. I looked up and there she was, in front of me. "I was worried half to death." She knelt down and threw her arms around me, and her scent of cinnamon and cloves made me start crying. Her arms pressed into my wounds. She leapt back, stared at me, frantic. "I didn't know what to do. I wanted to come after you, but I didn't want to get you into trouble. What happened?" She seemed to see me then, my wounds and bruises. Her face registered everything at once. I felt like she could see right through me.

"My father found a book under my mattress," I said.

"Come," she said gently, taking my hand. "Let's go."

I nodded, numb, wiping my face. "I'm sorry, Mary," I whispered. "I didn't mean those things."

"I know, sweet child," she said, squeezing my hand. "And if you had, that would be okay and we could talk. You know that, right? Nothing you could say could make us stop being friends."

"Okay," I said. "But I didn't mean them." The image of Mary on the bed flashed through my mind, pulling at my heart, but I blinked it away. "Really."

She nodded. "Anything," she said. "Don't forget that. I'm your friend, Tessa. I love you. Okay? Even if I have other friends, it's not the same. You and I are friends for life."

Tears fell down my face, and I just let them. I clutched Mary's hand, didn't even care when we passed through the town square and people saw me crying. When we got to the library I saw that Mary had set a sign out in front, saying the library was closed until the next day. I looked at her, confused. "Come," she said. She led me to the back of the library, to the kitchen. She pointed to the stool. "Sit."

I watched dully as she opened the ivory box that sat on the table and took out two small pouches. Her face was serious, focused. She shook them up and measured about a teaspoon of powder from each one into her palm, then set a pot of water to boiling. She took a small vial from the box and poured oil into the powders in her palm. I smelled lavender, some type of flower scent, as she rubbed the powder through the oil. "Now just sit still," she said. And then carefully, gently, she pulled off my top. I just sat there as she leaned in and rubbed the oil on the tender part of my right arm, which became warm and then burning hot in an instant. "Shhh," she said, when I started to squirm. She walked around and spread the oil into my back, and then down my other arm.

Next, she lifted my skirt and rubbed the oil into my left thigh, where a long bruise trailed to my knee, and into my calves. She pulled my skirt back down, turned to the pot of hot water, and sprinkled in handfuls of herbs from two of the jars on the shelf above, ones I did not recognize. A few minutes later she drained the herbs through a strainer and wrapped them in a cloth that she pressed down over my right arm, where she had rubbed in the oil. The arm went from hot to cool immediately, and suddenly I felt no pain at all. She repeated the process all over, on my back and legs. Finally, she leaned down and patted the cloth over my face, my closed eyelids, my forehead and chin. She sat back, gently pulled my top back over my head. "There," she said, kissing my forehead. "Now I'm going to show you something. Come on."

I slipped off the stool and was astonished at how different I felt. My skin tingled and buzzed; almost all the pain was gone. I pulled up my sleeve and glanced down at the bruise on my right arm, saw that it had already faded from purple to pale pink. "How did you do that?" I asked. Suddenly I felt more alive, back in the world.

"Herbs," she said, smiling. "Magic."

"But I thought you said they didn't work."

"I said that the herbs have a mind of their own," she said. "That's all." She winked mysteriously, then grabbed my hand and pulled me deeper into the library, all the way to the back of the stacks where there was extra space. I saw a long ladder propped against the shelves, a stool, and a small box filled with hardware. It slowly dawned on me what was happening.

"The trapeze," I breathed. A shimmer of happiness rippled through me.

Mary smiled, climbed up the ladder, and fastened the rigging to a ceiling beam. "Watch what I'm doing," she said. "You may have to do it yourself." At her command, I passed the chains up to her and watched her throw them over the beam, fastening the trapeze ropes to the shackles. Two pieces of rope hung down and the bar stretched between them, about eight feet from the floor. The final effect was so clean, perfect: a perfect shape, a perfect confluence of lines cutting through the air.

"Are you sure about this?" I asked, turning to her. "Are you sure you want to show me?" Guilt came over me; I felt so bad for pressuring her, for calling her names. I felt bad about everything.

"Yes," she said. "I'll teach you to swing on the trapeze in a few days, when you're done healing. Okay? But for now I wanted you to see it, feel the bar. Get comfortable with it."

I nodded eagerly, stretched up to touch it.

"Here," Mary said, pulling up the stool. "Stand on this."

I climbed up on the stool and then stood, reaching out my arms. Mary's hand pressed on my back to balance me.

I closed my palms around the bar, felt the cold metal of it against my skin. It was thinner than the bar in the window at home, and smoother, easier to grasp. I looked at Mary and smiled.

"Can I do it now?" I asked.

"You're not ready," she said. "You need to heal."

"I'm okay, though. I don't feel anything. Just once?"

She sighed, pretending to be exasperated. "Well, then, you'll need to chalk up your hands, and you might as well change into a leotard so I can fix it up for you." She made a face as I grabbed her hands and then jumped from the stool to the floor.

"Here," she said, reaching into a small box on the floor, next to the rigging. "Put on this leotard. I'll put one on, too." I took the leotard she handed me and, with my back turned, slipped out of my clothes and into it. It hung from my body like a sheet. Once Mary was changed, she pinned mine up on the sides.

"Now chalk up your hands," she said, gesturing to the canister she'd set out. "Dip your hands in and rub the chalk onto your palms. Like this."

I pressed my hands in and was surprised by the cool powderiness, the clean smell.

"Now climb back up and grab the bar," she said.

I nodded, swallowing, and climbed onto the stool. Then I looked up at the bar and sprang. I wrapped my hands around it, tried to get a firm grip.

"How do you feel?" Mary asked.

"Good."

"Maybe you can swing a little, and then that's enough for today."

"Can I sit on it?" I asked, tilting my face to her. I loved the feel of air on all sides of me; I had never experienced anything quite like it. When I'd hung from the window, I was so close I could kiss the glass. Dangling from a tree, I'd had to curl my wrists around the branches, making it difficult to move as freely as I could now.

But on the trapeze, my body was like water. I could move in any direction, it seemed.

"Swing back and forth," Mary said, "lifting yourself higher each time." Her hands were on my back, guiding me. "Like this. *Roll* your body toward the bar."

I strained my muscles and pulled myself—awkwardly at first, but on my third try I found myself clinging to the ropes on either side of me, looking out at the same shelves and books I had just viewed from the ground. Incredible. Even sitting there, unmoving, I felt almost transformed.

"I'm impressed," she said. "How did you get to be so strong?"

I blushed. "I don't know."

"Well, that will make everything a whole lot easier, little girl. Now what do you say we get ourselves some lunch and pick this up again a few days from now?"

Giddy and happy, we changed out of our leotards, ran into the garden, and selected the plumpest tomatoes and nicest-looking greens. Mary tossed them together inside while I stood on the stool and cut thick slices of pumpernickel bread and cheese she'd bought at market.

When the food was ready we grabbed our plates and went down to the river. We spread our meal out on the grass. Lying there, my body still warm from the exertion, I felt almost beautiful for the first time in my life. I looked down at my arm and couldn't even see the bruises anymore.

"Tessa," Mary said, putting down her plate, suddenly serious, "promise you will never take a book home again."

"I promise," I said, biting into the sumptuous bread, the tangy cheese.

"I mean it," she said. "I can't stand to see you this way, with these bruises, these wounds. It reminds me of what I went through a long time ago, and you, *you* deserve a thousand times better than that. I wish I could protect you from him, but I can't."

Her voice was shaking, and her face flushed red. I looked at her. I wanted to ask questions, but wanted more to forget about every bad thing in the world, and for everything to come down to just this: this bread, this cheese, this river, and this one, perfect day. I felt tears in my eyes and nodded, bringing up my wrist to wipe my face.

"I was thinking, too," she continued, more calmly. "Why don't you tell your parents that I want you to stay past dinner to help organize the old papers and records? And that I'll up your pay a dollar every week? We can read and practice the trapeze."

"Yes," I said, unable to look at her now. "I would like that."

We spent the rest of the day relaxing by the river, weeding the herb garden, and drinking tea over thick books with gold edges. Going home was almost unbearable, but I forced one foot in front of the other, through the square and the fields.

After that everything pretty much went back to normal: the library was open, I worked a little later each day with my parents' approval, and Mary and I stood side by side stamping the cards and handing the books over to Oakley's farmers and lovelorn men and women. My body was clean and unbruised. The books Mary had picked out for me all lay safely in a stack under the library's front desk.

At the same time, everything had changed. Mary treated me differently, less like a child. I became someone she could talk to about adult things—about William, about sex, about the bearded, mustached man who visited her at night, when she couldn't see him, and didn't want to. I learned some of the secrets of her heart then, but I know now that I should have gone deeper, and seen all that had happened before.

✳

I took to the trapeze as if it were a part of my body I hadn't known existed. Swinging in space, the bookshelves on either side of me, my family didn't matter anymore. The kids in the square, the endless fields in Oakley that stretched and stretched past the horizon—none of it mattered. It was like reading *Sister Carrie* but better, because this time it was all me.

"Now swing," Mary said. "Kick out your legs. Get comfortable up there."

With each moment passing, I felt more present in the world, more sure. I reached up my hands on either side, bent my head back and looked at the ceiling beams.

"I *am* comfortable," I said, as the air ruffled against my hair and cheeks.

"The first trick," she said, "is the knee hang. You're going to separate your knees, grab on to the bar, and then drop. You'll end up hanging from your knees, your hands pressed together between them."

I could already see it. In one instant I did the move; before she could even reach me I let my body fall and my legs grasp the bar. I swung back and forth, hanging there, the world turned upside down. I let go with my hands, closed my eyes.

Mary gasped and rushed over. When she heard me laughing, her body relaxed.

"That's too dangerous!" she said. "You could hurt yourself."

Her disapproval couldn't dull the bliss I felt as I swung my arms back to the bar. Mary reached out for me and grabbed my hands, flipping me up so that I was standing on the floor again.

I jumped around, already longing to be back in the air.

"Now hold the bar and fall under it," Mary said. "Like that. Press your legs up to it, straight across, like doing a split."

I did, and looked down at her surprised, open expression. "That's exactly right," she said.

My body moved of its own accord; my ankles slipped into the sides, where the bar met the rope. I started swinging that way, my hands still on the bar.

"The ankle hang," she said quietly. She walked over, reached up, and placed her hands over mine. "Now hold with your ankles," she said. "Hold tight."

I did, and gently, she told me to unclasp my hands. "I've got you," she whispered. I let go then and let my body fall back. She stood next to me and under me, making sure I wouldn't fall. I stretched my body backward and waved my arms out.

"Like this?"

She hunched under me, her hands stretching toward me, hovering just under my skin. "How does that feel?"

"Nice," I said. I couldn't articulate the way my limbs felt loose and soft, my body completely without barriers, fluid as water. I don't know that I'd ever been happier than I was right then.

"You are so lucky you have that body, Tessa," she said, as I rocked back and forth. "It took me weeks to do that. You're a natural."

It was so easy: I learned the gazelle, where the left leg is straight, the right leg bent up to the front of the right rope, the rest of the body hanging underneath. I learned the toe hang and single toe hang, where you drop from the bar from just one foot.

"What about you?" I asked one afternoon. "Don't you want to take up the trapeze again?"

"Oh, I don't know about that, Tessa," she said.

"Just once?" I asked. "I want to see!"

"After watching you, I think I never should have bothered at all!" she said. "I was all wrong for it, you know. All wrong for lots of things."

"What do you mean?"

"Oh, nothing," she said, and for a moment it seemed like her hair had gotten curlier and her eyes more blue. Like something was pressing down on her. Then she looked up at me and smiled. To my surprise, she bent down and dipped her hands in the chalk.

"Okay," she said, her face open and suddenly radiant. "What the hell?" And with one quick movement she hurled herself to the bar and flipped up on it until she was sitting, swinging back and forth, her legs crossed beneath her and hands gripping the ropes. Her face glowed as she began swinging faster, back and forth, and then pulled herself up to her feet in one graceful movement. In the next second she lifted her feet from the bar and threw them over her head, curving her body into a scythe. She held the position for several seconds, grasping the ropes, swinging back and forth, then slipped back down until her feet rested on the bar. She was ecstatic, whooping and laughing.

The next second, without warning, she dropped her whole body down until she was hanging by her ankles and her hands were nearly sweeping across the floor. Before I could even react, she flipped back up and hung from her hands, twisting her body again so that her waist pressed against the bar, her palms leaning down into it. She kept going, in a whirl of movement: jacking her legs up and to the sides, tossing herself over and under the bar, and then, finally, tossing herself off the bar and landing with a tiny flip and flourish.

She collapsed to the ground, out of breath. I clapped my hands, elated, and then collapsed with her. When I looked up at the shelves and the books, it seemed amazing that we were still there, in Mercy Library. For a few minutes I had been utterly transported, outside time and space.

"I'm going to be dying tomorrow," she said, between gulps of air.

She turned her head toward me. I had never seen her more beautiful.

I became obsessed with the trapeze. Over the next year I practiced whenever I could, with Mary and alone, staying past when the library closed, past when Mary slipped out into the night to meet various lovers or just to be alone with her thoughts, and her demons. Mary agreed to keep the bar suspended from the beams and even rigged a tiny hook to keep it pulled back and out of the way of library customers.

I practiced so hard that my muscles ached and I felt myself solidifying into a hard mass. My hands cracked and bled from twisting over the bar; sometimes I hobbled to the library in the morning—through the dead leaves, and snow, and spring foliage—unable to move my arms or bend my knees, my head still clouded from the dreamless sleep of the night before. I was like a raw wound but as solid as granite, the most substantial I had ever been in my life.

As time passed, my body changed in other ways, too, as if my body's changing and Mary's coming into my life were intimately connected. She influenced me in so many ways, anyway: I also began to carry around the scent of cinnamon and cloves, trailing it behind me and letting it wrap around me when I stood still; I began piling books on the library's front desk, running my fingers across their spines as if they were cats; I lined my arms with bracelets, bracelets I was constantly picking off the ground as they slid off; I grew my hair, too, letting it swarm from my head and past my shoulders. Though my hair was straight and thin, I let months pass without brushing it so that, like Mary, I could claim tangles and knots and ruin my hair with combs whenever the occasion arose. Of course I would never really be like Mary. And I was never beautiful like her until I was in the air.

Maybe it was the way I took Mary into me that made my father look at me in a new light. One day when I was about fourteen, I was walking through the house absentmindedly, dreaming of the Velasquez Circus, when I felt the strangest prickling on my skin. It was like the moment when Mary Finn had sought me out in front of the courthouse, except that now I felt no dizzying excitement of love like I'd experienced then, only the uneasy and dismal sense that I'd been found out.

The living room was the same as always. I looked at the thin burlap sofa so uncomfortable that no one was ever found stretched out upon it, at the bowls of plastic oranges and pears decorating the windowsills, at the splintering, sagging floor, and, finally, at the rocking chair that moved back and forth like a little minnow. That was when I realized the chair was filled with two eyes as big as suns, crackling into my skin and down my flat body. That was when I saw my father, whose gaze pinned me to the spot, trapping me in that little burlapped room my mother had designed to the discomfort of us all. There was nothing natural about it: nothing natural about that house and my being there, and nothing natural about the way my father looked at me from that rocking chair not meant for his body or anyone else's.

I might have thought I'd dreamt it or been carried away by all the crazy novels Mary had me read. I might have forgotten that sensation of shame rushing through me like blood. But that night my father appeared in my bedroom doorway, blocking out the light behind him. I stared at him, tried to figure out what he was doing, but I couldn't make out his eyes in the mass of his body. The whole room was cast into shadows, and my father's silhouette showed up jagged on my wall, like teeth.

"Father?" I whispered. For a moment I wondered if it was someone else, a stranger who'd broken into our house and come for me. I felt fear slide through my body in a cold rush. He was so large, looming there, much larger than he had appeared in the confines of the rocking chair.

"Who is it?" I breathed, my heart pounding. I looked to the bed across the room, but I could tell from the sounds of Geraldine's snoring that she was fast asleep.

"Shhhh," he said. Even with that hushed tone, I knew who it was, yet I had never heard such a soft, gentle sound come from his mouth. A sound that seared over my skin.

"Here, Tessa," he whispered, reaching out his hand. "Mind your sister. See you don't wake her." I could have sworn he was smiling, but even as my eyes adjusted to the light I could not make out his features.

I dared not say no to him. I shook as I pushed back the covers and threw my legs over the bed, toward the floor. The wood was cold under my bare feet as I stepped down, and I stopped and pulled my arms around my shoulders. I could not stop shaking.

"Do as I say, girl," he said, still reaching his hand toward me.

I walked in slow steps across the floor, my arms wrapped around me. He snatched my wrist in his palm as I approached. I glanced back—the room seemed strange, covered in shadow and dark. Geraldine was spread out on her mattress. Breathing slowly in and out.

I followed him down the creaking stairway, through the front hall, back through the kitchen. He held the screen door open for me and then I was outside, stumbling over grass and crops, dirt crunching under my feet. We did not speak. I barely even breathed as I walked on tiptoes behind him, and my mind raced with all the things I must have done wrong to make him come for me at night like this, without even waking Geraldine.

He grabbed my wrist and pulled me into the cornfield. The corn swished on both sides of us. He pushed me down onto the dirt with the corn swaying, hovering over me. The moon was out that night, I remember. The corn stretched in front of it like claws.

I closed my eyes and braced myself for his hands against my skin. When they came they were gentle, slow. I popped open my eyes, astonished. Wasn't he going to hit me? Hadn't I done something wrong?

"Quiet, girl," he said, and I shuddered at the sound of his voice—so soothing, like he was talking to a cat. He crouched over me then and pulled up my cotton nightgown, yanked it over my head and pressed me down again until the dirt cut into my back, into bare skin. He spread me out under him, and his eyes moved over me, mocking.

"You're a strange one all right," he said, laughing, and then slid his hand across my breast. "Barely even a girl."

I stared at the moon over his shoulder. The corn silhouetted against it.

Tears rushed down my face and I whispered "I'm sorry" again and again. I shivered in the dirt, expecting his hands to beat down any second. I tried to cover my bare skin.

He came down on me then, so heavy I could barely breathe. My skin scraped over dirt. Pain ripped and seared through the center of my body, through places I didn't even know could feel. I kept my eyes squeezed shut. The smell of earth and growing things was as strong as if I'd been buried in it. I closed down, didn't even flinch after a while, but my mind raced and flickered and the whole world seemed to be contained inside it. After a moment I imagined I could even see the girl being worked over out there in the dirt, under the corn, but I was so far away I didn't even care. I kept my eyes shut and my mind zeroed in, focused on the trapeze, the feel of the bar in my palm. Air swept under me, split open on all sides. I felt myself soaring over everything then. The pain that ripped up through me, opening inside me like an obscene flower, was happening to some other girl's body, somewhere else.

Afterward he picked me up like I was some sort of wounded bird and carried me inside. I kept my eyes shut as he washed the blood from my legs with a cloth from the kitchen sink. After carrying me back up the stairs, he laid me on my bed as smoothly as a dress you planned on wearing to church the next day. Geraldine stirred slightly but did not wake. When I finally heard the door shut behind him, I turned on my side and wept.

The next day I woke up feeling as if my insides had been scooped out and replaced with fire. Every part of my body hurt as I moved from side to side. I stayed in bed. I wrapped my hips in towels and paper to soak up the blood, and hid the soiled sheets underneath the mattress.

I thought of the library: Mary unlocking the thick wood doors, the line of people that would surely be waiting by now. It felt like a parallel life I had been dreaming about but had never actually led.

"What the hell are you still doing in bed?" Geraldine asked, glaring at me.

I closed my eyes and ignored her, and soon my mother was in the room, already covered in dirt and exasperated to have been called away from it.

"What is going on here, Tessa Riley?" my mother asked. "I will not have you jeopardizing that job."

"I'm sick," I said, looking at her dully.

"Goddamnit." She shifted angrily, then caught sight of something, a dash of blood on the sheet. Her face became softer, almost the way it had been once, back when she loved me and thought I'd keep growing, back when she still tucked me in at night. Something inside me almost caved in right then.

"Well, well, you've become a woman," she said. "A miracle."

I looked at her then, and the feeling I'd had a moment before, that pinprick of longing, disappeared. Suddenly I ached for Mary so much it was a physical pain inside me. I wished I could will her to my side, wished I could ask her to explain the world to me. I winced, and shame seeped into every cell of my body at the thought of her knowing what had happened to me.

I stared at the ceiling. Later, when Geraldine perched herself on the side of my bed and made snorting noises to annoy me, I closed my eyes and imagined myself a million miles away, in Rain Village, with the rain pounding down over me and leaves sticking to my skin.

The next day I felt better but couldn't bring myself to get out of bed and go back to work. I didn't know how I would face anyone, let alone Mary. I was cheap, disgusting, like some old discarded thing. The power I had felt in my body up on the trapeze, practicing twirls and layouts, felt like some lie I had been told. My father had burrowed into me and brought out the truth: that I, Tessa Riley, was a freak, something monstrous. The kids in the square had known. *He* had known.

At my mother's insistence, I went down for dinner that second night. My father behaved as if everything were normal. If it weren't for the sharp ache in the center of my body, the image of the corn bent in front of the moon, haunting me, I might have thought that I'd imagined everything.

The phone rang, and I almost jumped out of my chair. We all looked to my father. The phone never rang in our house and was only there for the direst emergencies.

"Lucas?" my mother asked, her voice tentative, almost meek.

He continued eating, wordlessly. We sat there, and the air in the room grew heavy with his silence. The phone continued to ring.

"Leave it," he said, after nearly a full minute had passed.

The next morning I pretended to leave for work and instead wandered through the countryside, climbing trees and spreading myself out in the fields. Alone, I could just go blank and dull, stare at the clouds until I felt like I was one, too, but even the sight of another human being—a farmer, from a distance—made me want to sob. I could not face anyone. All I could do was stare at the clouds and the sun and dream of flying.

Later, when the sun pounded the earth from the center of the sky, I found a tree with a branch flung straight out to its side, and I leapt up and grabbed it, then dropped until I was hanging down the way I had hung in the kitchen window, from my palms. As I pulled myself up into a knee-hang position, I didn't even care that the bark scraped my skin and tore it off. I pulled myself up and over that branch until my muscles shook and burned.

I wished, suddenly, that I had a rig of my own to set up somewhere. The idea seized me: that the trapeze was the only thing that could save me. That it could burn through my body and make me pure again. Those three clean lines cutting through space, the cold metal of the bar. I longed to go back to it, but every time I turned my head toward town my feet started walking in the other direction, carrying me so far away I would start to get lost.

The next day I had an idea. I had dreamt the night before of my body hurtling through space, and then I'd seen an image from one of Mary's brochures: a woman hanging from a long, braided rope. Twisting her body up to the side. Just one long body and a rope, moving into each other, creating a line from earth to sky.

As soon as the dawn came, I snuck into the barn and grabbed some of the rope my mother hung clothes on. I ran out into the fields, past the corn and carrots and radishes and into the wild land that bordered one side of Riley Farm, where the river ran through. Right there, surrounded by crazy weeds and flowers, a tall cragged tree rose from the ground and draped its branches everywhere. I had often visited that spot when I was younger; even on the hottest days there was so much shade and wetness there that you could burrow into the cool dirt and rest. Acorns and leaves littered the ground, and the smell was deep, like musk.

I inhaled the rich scent and stretched out my arms. Scrambling up the tree, I leaned out from the trunk and looped the rope around the strongest branch, three times to be sure the knot would hold. This was a huge task for me; I had to lean out so far to reach the right spot that I nearly fell twice. When I was finally done, I threw the rope down and watched it tap the earth. I dropped to the ground after it.

Slipping off my shoes, I dug my bare feet into the earth. I placed my palms on the rope and fingered it for a minute, getting used to its feel. I flung myself up then, and out, so that my hands were the only point of contact and the rest of my body darted out to the side. Every muscle in my body strained and pulled, but I felt clean in a way I couldn't on the ground.

I closed my eyes and let myself go: I swung from side to side, wrapped the rope around my waist and fell into it, twisting it further around. The rope cut right into the wounds the bark had made, but I kept going, wrapping my knees over the rope, pressing so tight I could release my arms and stretch them into the air behind me. The world was reduced to the feel of that rope underneath my palm, the sound of its creaking and my own breath. The sense of my body carving lines and shapes into pure space. I hung from one arm and tried to swing myself up, but that was when my body gave out, and—trembling, exhausted—I dropped to the ground and collapsed.

I lay there catching my breath and letting my muscles ease back down. Then I dragged myself to my feet and stumbled down to the river, which stretched behind our farm the way it did behind Mercy Library. I dunked myself in the cool water, let it rush into my cuts and bruises. Every part of me hurt. I closed my eyes and ran my fingers along the scabs that were beginning to form. Everything else wound down and stopped until it was just me, the water, the burning everywhere, and the dark, dank smell of the wet woods.

My body had no end or beginning, I thought then.

Then a strange thing happened: in the middle of all that silence I had a vision, one perfect image of a body whirling like a pinwheel or windmill about the rope, drawing a circle in the air. Up and down—a clean, straight body whipping through the air like a knife. Slicing right through it. I wondered if it could be done, if a body could even move that way. The arm would have to throw itself up and twist, even dislocate a shoulder to come back down. The body would have to be straight and lean and pure.

I pulled myself from the water and ran back to the tree, and didn't even feel it when I wrapped my wretched, split-open palm around the rope and hoisted myself back up. Grunting with effort, I hauled myself upside down with one arm, which shook so badly I was sure I'd drop on my head at any second. And then I squeezed my eyes shut, steeled myself, and pushed my body back down again in the other direction. My shoulder felt like it was splitting in two, then popped out of the socket for the second that it took for me to rush down.

I dropped to the ground, exhausted. Crying from pain. Crying, for the first time, about everything.

When I stumbled home at dinnertime, my parents and brothers and sister stared right at me and gaped. I could feel my father's eyes on me.

"What the hell happened to you?" Geraldine asked. "You look like you got runned over."

My brothers snorted. My father reached over and smacked Geraldine on the face. She didn't even flinch as her right cheek turned red and tears trickled down her face.

"I'll be okay," I said quickly. "I was just working at the library and fell."

"You shouldn't be climbing those ladders, girl," my mother said. "You could slip right through one of those rungs."

I looked to the ground, but all I saw was the image of a lone girl, inscribing circles in the air.

Over the next few days I went back and back. I destroyed my body against that tree, dreamt about it when I was in bed or at the dinner table. My father's eyes followed me through every room in our house, under every stalk in the fields, but I blocked them out with the sheer force of my body slamming against oak and rope. By the third day I could do two twists in a row—with excruciating pain all through my shoulder and upper arm. *The more the better*, I thought, and swung myself back up again.

I knew Mary would be wondering what had happened to me, and I was nagged by the thought of her sitting in the library. But *she* hadn't come looking for *me*, either. As I shimmied up the rope and wrapped my legs around it, letting it sink into my skin, I tried to convince myself that she would know I was all right. Part of me felt that I was in the library anyway, that my real self was shelving books and stamping the book cards, sitting down with Mary to a lunch of vegetables and dark bread, while here, by the river, my shadow self twirled from the tree and back out again, clinging to a length of rope.

✳

CHAPTER SEVEN

W hen I hadn't shown up at Mercy Library for well over a week, Mary came looking for me. I had spent the day by the river practicing, honing my new trick, ripping my shoulder again and again. When I entered the kitchen and saw Mary sitting right there waiting for me, at my parents' dinner table, my mouth literally fell open with shock.

"What are you doing here?" I asked, suddenly furious. She looked so radiant and out of place in the dark wood room, surrounded by my bulky siblings and my enormous, glowering parents. Their skin was pale and blotchy, while hers was golden and smooth. It felt like she was playing a joke on me, purposefully making my world seem even uglier than it had before.

Her eyes widened. "I haven't seen you in over a week, Tessa. I didn't know what to do. I kept calling."

Her words barely registered. I wanted to scream at her, to pull her beautiful hair and slap her. Irrational, I felt that she had come there just to humiliate me, the way she was sitting right next to *him*, my father, as if it were the most normal thing in the world. *She doesn't know,* a part of me whispered, and yet in my pain and frenzy I was sure that she had come just to rub my face in it, my father and I eating at the table together, the unspeakable hanging in the air between us.

I had thought that the rope had burned the anger out of me, but in that moment, as exhausted as I was, as bloody and bruised and beaten, I felt like I could have ripped everyone in that room apart. It was unbearable, her being in that room. I couldn't stand it. *You bitch*, I thought, trembling with rage.

"I was going to come back," I spat. "I got sick. You didn't have to come here. It's no big deal."

"I just didn't know, Tessa." I could see how much I was hurting her, but I didn't care. Her being in that room made everything ugly and sordid about it stand out as if a spotlight had suddenly shone in. I was sure she could see what had happened just by looking at me. That she could take one look at my father and one look at me and know everything.

Geraldine gazed up at Mary in the most pathetic way, and I wanted to smack them both. My sister looked so stupid next to Mary, with her dull brown hair and huge white arms smeared with dirt. They were all dirty from a day in the fields, their faces smudged and worn, their work clothes stained, ripped.

And Mary like some kind of queen at the table, my father sitting just left of her, barely able to look her in the face. My mother standing by the stove, ladling out the stew. I could see how upset she was, the way the spoon shook in her hand. Next to Mary, she looked a hundred years old, a mass of wrinkles and sighs. They had set a place for Mary, I realized, and the idea of Mary at *my* kitchen table eating a bowl of brown stew while my sister and brothers just stared at her with bug eyes was too much for me to bear.

"Why don't you just leave?" I said, and I could hear Geraldine gasp. My brothers stared at me, dumbfounded. At some level I knew my father would not scold me for my rudeness, not now, but, more than that, I didn't care what happened. I just wanted Mary out of there as quickly as possible.

"Not so fast, young lady," my mother said, throwing down the spoon and walking toward me. "You've been lying to us, too, and we want an explanation *now.* You contribute to this family and we rely on that contribution. If you've decided you no longer need to make a contribution, then that is something we'll have to discuss further. Right, Lucas?"

My father stared into his stew, not making a sound.

"You'll get the dollar from this week," I said, before my father could answer. You could feel the shock in the room, and still my father just sat there, not uttering a word.

Mary stood up then. I saw her eyes taking everything in: the bruises on my arm, the scrapes on my hands, my split palms. I could see her struggling, trying to decide whether it was better to stay and try to help or whether that would make everything worse for me.

"Yes," she said quickly. "Tessa will still get paid; there's no issue with that. Whenever she is feeling better, she's welcome back." She looked at me, pleadingly. "I'll see you soon, and we'll talk more then," she said, reaching out her hand to touch my arm. I pulled away. She was shaking, about to cry, but I stood motionless and watched her go.

"Lucas?" my mother repeated.

"Let's leave it alone right now, Roberta," he said slowly, almost under his breath.

The front door clicked shut. My mother pursed her lips and stormed out of the room, while my father just ate his stew as if nothing had happened. When I looked at Geraldine and Matthew and Connor, they just stared back at me. I almost laughed. For the first time I, little Tessa Riley, had rendered my loudmouthed siblings speechless.

I returned to the library the next day. I had no choice. I walked down the main road, through town, and then out past the lumberyard. I had no idea how Mary would react when she saw me, whether she would even talk to me or want me back. Rage and humiliation burned in my heart, and even though I knew she hadn't done anything wrong, I could not make them go away. Part of me wanted so badly to see Mary and have her explain everything to me, yet I could not imagine telling her, or even releasing the words into air.

My heart pounded as I entered the building.

She looked up from behind the desk, stared at me with her blue cat's eyes. I stared back.

"I'm sorry I went to your house, Tessa," she said. "I'm sorry for everything that's happening to you."

"You should be," I said, then picked up a pile of books from the bin to return to the shelves.

I could feel Mary's eyes on me as I made my way into the stacks, my back straight. I could feel her grasping for something to say.

"Your hands," she said, as I reached up to one of the shelves. "I saw yesterday. What happened?" She reached over and took my hand in hers. I snatched it away, but not before she saw the thick scabs and calluses.

"I was practicing," I said.

"Practicing what?"

"By the river," I said. "With a rope."

"What is happening, Tessa?" she asked, leaning down and looking straight at me. "I tried telephoning you. Why were you gone for so long? Are you being hurt? Are they hurting you?"

I looked at her. I wanted so much to tell her what had happened out there in the corn, how sick I was now, and sad. For a moment I considered telling her about the river and the rope, my one-armed swing-overs, as I had begun to think of them. But I couldn't. Something had slipped in between her and me in that cornfield, something I could not control.

"Is it him?" she asked, dropping her voice to a whisper.

Her eyes were dark, and it scared me, the way she looked at me then, as if she knew everything. I dropped my eyes, looked to the floor.

"No," I said.

"You can always come to me, you know."

I heard a tremble in her voice. I met her eyes and had never seen her look so broken, her face soft and slack, as if she'd been hit.

"You can leave home, Tessa. They can't keep you away from the world."

"Everything is fine," I said. I felt dizzy, as if my head were about to explode. "I don't know what you keep talking about."

"Okay," she said softly. "It's okay." She leaned down and kissed my forehead. The spice scent overcame me so forcefully I could barely breathe.

Without thinking, I pushed out my hand and shoved her away. And then everything welled up in me, all at once. I ran to the back of the library and out the door that led to the garden and water pump. I fell into the grass, let everything break free. I was barely even conscious of Mary right there next to me, gathering me up in her arms.

"It's okay," she said. "Shhhhh."

It was as if the broken part of me had spilled out, and I wailed and twisted around, in the grass. Mary kept me bound up in her arms. The pain gnawed at my gut, strangled my throat. I thought of my mother and father and sister and brothers, of how much I used to love them, how hurt I used to be when they laughed at me, when they joked that I was a punishment from God. I thought of the other kids under the oak tree always looking and laughing, and the cornstalks bent in front of the moon, the feel of dirt against my back, the feel of my body and my heart and my entire self being broken down, erased and wiped out. How much I wanted, sometimes, to be wiped out, how Mary was the only person in the world who could fill me again, remake me into something new.

Slowly I became aware of a vague herb smell, a handful of herbs in my face and on my skin. The pain lessened. The broken-glass feeling in my gut numbed, then disappeared. I lay back and felt the words and images leave my mind, until there was nothing left except *that* moment, right then.

I opened my eyes and came back to earth, to the library, to her.

"I'm sorry," I said. "I'm sorry."

"It's okay," she said. "Everything is okay."

I sat up, and my head pounded with grief. "Please," I said. It was a terrible feeling, looking at her right in front of me, feeling her hands on mine, knowing how far I was from her now. *I can never tell her,* I thought. But as she watched me, it was as if she knew what I was think-ing already, as if I had unleashed my whole heart there, in the garden, and she was holding it in her hands.

We looked at each other, and her cat's eyes seemed to grow bigger and deeper, more dark, the way they had before. I felt a whooshing feel-ing through my gut, a tickling, and then a laugh whispered through me.

"You can't let it take you over," she said. "You are stronger than any-thing else, any of these people." Her voice wrapped around me like arms.

I couldn't speak, just stared at her and then at the ground.

"How about I tell you a story?" she said. "Would you like that? Something that happened a million miles from here, many years ago?"

I looked back up at her and felt relief wash through my body, tears start at my eyes. "Okay," I said. I sat back and closed my eyes, let the last vestiges of pain slip away. The spice scent swirled around me. Mary leaned back and draped her arm around my shoulders.

"Once," she said, "in a small Turkish village, there lived a man named Mihalis, who had a son named Costas. Mihalis had eyes the color of kiwis and bright black hair, just like his son."

I pictured it: a man with hair like Mary's, sticking out in every direction and as black as ink. My whole body released and let go, sinking into the grass.

"When the child was a year old, the father decided to leave the village because he wanted to teach his son to be good, and to teach him to live without love, as he had done. Mihalis set out into the world with his baby strapped to his chest. He walked and walked and never stopped to sleep. He wanted so much to be someplace new that his feet wouldn't stop walking when he was tired but began to run, and he ran for six days from the love he'd never found, until he ended up in a barn.

"There the father and his son survived by eating sunflowers, cooking them over a fire. They spent every day lying in the sun reading the clouds and the books they'd brought. The child Costas learned about mathematics, jewelry-making, agronomy, homemaking, horseflies, and seeds. He learned to read as many languages as there are in the world, though he had no one to speak them to."

I laughed at the idea, letting the story overtake me. Mary paused and laughed with me, touching my hair.

"One day," she continued, "when Costas turned eighteen, Mihalis decided to return home to the village he'd left so long ago. He felt safe, convinced that he'd raised a child without love. But Costas was terrified of walking over the edge of the earth, and begged his father to stay. Mihalis tried to describe the wonders of people and other places, but his son could not understand. And when they left their home and Costas began to see other creatures like them, the boy was afraid and filled with delight when he saw that the world did not stop, but kept stretching before them.

"They had only been walking for two days when a group of young girls passed by them. Their bodies looked like fruit trees to the young Costas, who turned to his father and asked what these creatures were that made his stomach drop and his breath grow short. Mihalis turned to his son, who had stopped in the road, and saw his stricken face. He looked back at the young women and saw that one of them had stopped also, and was turned to his son."

I was breathless, imagining it: the group of them paused in the rough, rock-ridden road, the girl's deep black hair strewn with jewels and hanging to her knees, her sad eyes and the sand streaking her legs. *Talk to her,* I thought. I imagined her curving, parted lips. *Go on.* I imagined myself like a fruit tree, wearing sandals that revealed my toes.

"Mihalis remembered then the girl he'd run from. Her image appeared like a storm cloud over him. Mihalis had dreamt of Katerina every night for seventeen years, but the herbs that grew by the pond had made him forget every morning the dreams of the night before.

"*What is it,* whispered his son again as the girl walked toward them. Mihalis knew, at that moment, the waste of seventeen dreamless years; he thought quickly and replied, *It is a kind of duck, and it will eat you.* The son thought for a moment before he spoke again. *I want one,* he said."

I looked up at Mary. "A girl can't be a duck," I said.

"It is all true, Tessa," Mary said, "every last bit of it. Costas never returned to the barn after that. The world was too big.

"You can always leave," Mary said then, looking right at me. "There is always more to discover, more selves inside you that just need to come out."

"Thank you," I whispered.

She paused, then leaned down and kissed my forehead. "Now, why don't you show me what you've been doing on this rope of yours?"

We went inside, and I hauled myself up to the bar, the shelves of books towering on either side of me. Mary went to help the few readers who had gathered while we were outside, then came back to me.

"You're improving, Tessa," she said, as I held my body straight in the air, with only my palms on the bar.

For a moment, I was tempted. I felt my muscles pulling, my hand reaching for the cable on the side of the trapeze. I could show her my new trick, release it into air.

"Why don't I show you how to flip down?" she said, in the moment I spent hesitating. "I think you're ready. And I can show you my own *special* trick, one of the things that made Marionetta so loved and desired."

"Marionetta?"

"That was my name, up there, Tessa. *Marionetta,*" she said, stretching the name out until I could feel it wrap around me.

I forgot about the rope, my new trick, my hours by the river, completely.

She slipped off her skirt to the leotard underneath, then reached up for the bar. She smiled at me and started to swing. For a moment, as I watched her fly through the air, I imagined that there was only this, this moment, right here.

✴

CHAPTER EIGHT

I remained closed in, as if I occupied two separate worlds: the world that my father stood over, a dark, secret place where the moon and the corn masked unspeakable things, and then my world, which was always Mary's. I walked into Mercy Library each day, and the earth-pounding sun turned to mist. The smoke and the smell of cloves and cinnamon wove around me, and I began hearing the patter of rain, seeing the flash of fish out of the corner of my eye, feeling the *swoosh* of the trapeze under my hand. The force of Mary's world was so strong that it even changed the air around her. What would it be like to swim in a river, I wondered, with rain sprinkling all around and fish sliding against your skin? How would it feel to spin five times in the air before dropping into a silver net?

And then I shrugged out of myself and those nights in the field and threw glitter across my skin and tumbled across the floor, as Mary danced and clapped. You could see a wildness in her still, left over from her days on the trapeze: her skin made for circus lights to bounce off it, legs that could curl past her neck and over her shoulders.

More and more I asked Mary about the places she'd lived before coming to Oakley, before she'd taken over the abandoned library on the outskirts of town and begun cataloguing the minutiae of all of our lives.

I stayed at the library so late that my parents would be in bed by the time I got home. In the night I would sneak down to the river and practice, beating my body against the rope. I wound my body down to a spark of energy, so tight that I could fly out of the room, twist and disappear when my father came near me.

I began to imagine that other places and lives existed for me, too, places where I could become what Mary saw in me. "Rain Village," I repeated to myself in the dark, and dreamt of floating boys with white skin. It seemed so far from the stark, bright fields of Oakley, the heavy manure scent that was everywhere, the swooping wooden house inhabited by a father who never seemed to sleep.

Most of all I dreamt of the circus: the sequined women with red lips who'd hang from ropes by their ankles, the men who could order a row of lions to walk on their hind legs, the flames streaming from men's mouths, and the sticks a girl could juggle while hanging by her hair. Mary described these things for me again and again.

What Mary described was like nothing I had ever seen or heard of, and the one thing I needed was something to imagine, something far from home. She told me that after William's death she cried for one year straight. Tears flowed from her eyes and down her face so constantly that tiny rivers of tears followed her wherever she went, and anyone who wanted her had only to look to the ground to trace out her path. She left Rain Village on a boat, she said, and then walked and walked through the country and into the little towns where she eventually became the stuff of legend: at night the townspeople would whisper to each other about the crying lady, and mothers warned their children to keep their windows shut at night, lest the crying lady climb inside and steal them away.

She lived off the vegetables she stole from farmers, she said. Once in a while she would think of settling in a town or village, but who would hire a woman with a steady stream of tears falling down her face?

One time a shopkeeper actually did let her spend a day folding boxes in the back room, but when he saw the pile of boxes that night, perfectly folded but soaked through with tears and falling apart, she was fired on the spot.

And so she kept wandering until, soon enough, the winter came. She had nowhere to go and began shivering at night, when all she could do was try her best to warm herself in piles of hay and straw. Soon even the straw was specked with crystals of ice and snow. The teardrops froze right on her face; icicles hung from her hair.

But unbeknownst to her, not everyone who heard the story of the crying lady turned away in fear. Some lit candles for her, some prayed to her, and some trekked through the snow trying to find her. Some tried to interview her for their magazines, while others proclaimed that she was a hoax, or the devil. But one man, Juan Galindo of the Flying Ramirez Brothers and star of the Velasquez Circus, thought only that she would make a fine addition to the circus sideshow, and Mary, for her part, couldn't have agreed more.

Juan found Mary curled up in a haystack, outside a town famous for its strawberries and loose morals. As he came upon her he gasped: the tears had all turned to ice that streaked her face and her clothing and hair, and her dark eyebrows were sprinkled with frost. She was as pale as the snow that coated the fields. The ice shone and gleamed on her skin and caught the light until rays of colors came off it. When she shifted in her sleep, the ice clanked and tinkled against itself. Juan knew that the woman in the hay would draw crowds in the hundreds. The tears were like diamonds on her cheeks. He gazed at her, and later he would tell anyone who'd listen that he'd never seen anything or anyone so beautiful as Mary right then.

But the moment Mary woke up and saw Juan standing over her, with his dark skin, burning eyes, and the black mustache twisted into a slight curl on either side, she stopped crying once and for all. Her body became so warm that the ice melted instantaneously, and her pale cheeks became rosy and bright. Her heart beat like drums in her chest.

"At that moment," she told me on the library floor, "I knew William was dead and gone forever."

Juan Galindo watched in horror as Mary's entire body flushed with an unbearable desire. The dollar signs that had been floating in his head vanished along with the tears and the ice, until all that remained was one ordinary girl, lying in wet hay. Juan's plans for Mary were over before he'd even had a chance to hear her speak, and in sorrow and disgust he turned back toward the night.

"Wait!" Mary cried, and pulled herself out of the hay. "I'm coming with you."

And there was nothing Juan could do to stop her.

I often thought about Mary walking away from Rain Village to find a new life, and it was around the time I turned fifteen that I really started thinking about leaving my hometown, too. I became convinced that I could persuade Mary to go with me, that she felt as trapped as I did. I began to have long, elaborate daydreams about us traveling the world together in the circus, flying through the air, hearing the crowds roar, and meeting wild, fascinating men like Juan Galindo who would make the sky turn pink, they were so dazzling. Sometimes I laughed out loud, imagining such a glamorous life, and I'd emerge from my daydreams feeling groggy and dazed, heartbroken to be back in the world once more.

The more I fantasized about the circus, the crazier it seemed to me that someone could ever leave such a life, especially to come to a place like Oakley. There are better worlds than this one, I thought. How could Mary not agree, when she was the one who'd shown them to me? By then

I could do one hundred one-armed swing-overs. In the silver box I had hidden downstairs, buried in one of Mary's boxes of leotards, I had three years' worth of savings—well over two hundred dollars.

It took me several weeks to get up the courage to talk to Mary about my plans, but on one particularly hot day, when we closed the library at lunchtime to gather strawberries and then wash them in the river, I took a deep breath and released all my hopes into the air.

The river was lined with weeping willows that hung and dipped into the water, and we dunked the strawberries in before biting off the stems and popping the fruit into our mouths.

"Mary," I said, looking at the juice-splattered grass I'd gathered up in my hands, "I want to join the circus someday, maybe. Do you think I could?"

I was afraid she would laugh at me, though I should have known better. I always should have known Mary better than I did. She threw a strawberry stem into the river and looked over at me.

"Yes," she said. "Of course I do."

"You think I can do it?" I asked. "Could I be a flyer?"

"You are a flyer already, Tessa," she said.

"Come with me," I said, my heart pounding. "We could go together, to Kansas City."

I could not even look at her. The seconds passed so slowly I was sure that time had stopped. I pressed my fingertips into the earth.

"No," she said, finally. "You have to go alone. I cannot leave here, Tessa."

"But why?" I asked. "Why not?"

She would not answer. After a long pause, she said, "I know what it's like to feel trapped, like you do. You should leave before something happens. Something bad happened in Rain Village, Tessa, because I stayed too long."

"Come with me, then," I said.

She reached out her hand and placed it on mine. "I'm sorry," she said, quietly. It felt like I was pressing against glass.

"Why can't you leave?" I asked again. "I don't understand."

"I don't think I can explain it to you," she said. "Sometimes it's just not enough. The world is larger than you can even imagine, but sometimes it just closes in on you until there's no room left."

"But why did you come here in the first place? Why here, out of everywhere? Why can't you leave?"

She hesitated for several long moments. When she finally spoke, the words seemed heavy and ill formed in her mouth. "I heard about Oakley once," she said, "after a show we did in Kansas City. Someone talked of a town out west that was cradled by hills and ripped up by farmland. I kept asking questions, and the more I heard, the more I was sure it was the place for me to rest in. I was so tired then, Tessa. I could not stop thinking, and remembering, and I was just beaten down. I had visions of people following me, hunting me down. When I found out about the library and how it was just sitting here, I knew I had to come."

"But why here? I don't understand."

"I hope you don't ever understand, Tessa, what it is like to be so tired of life."

I didn't understand anything at all. "But why are you tired? Why can't you leave now?" I let the grass drop out of my hands.

"I just can't do it, Tessa. It's in the cards, and in the tea leaves." She laughed at herself, but it wasn't really a laugh at all. Something was happening in her that I couldn't see or touch. "Back in the circus, the fortune-tellers always avoided me; they could see what was coming. I can't help it, not now: I am marked by fate for what I've done."

My heart welled up inside me as I felt the world slamming shut. We stayed there, quiet. I stared out at the water, and at the weeping-willow branches hanging down and grazing the water, and thought that there was nothing else for me in the world—just this, forever, until I grew old and gray. And then I felt tears rising within me like a flood. Suddenly my body was wracked with them, and I opened my mouth wide and cried out every bit of grief in me, every shard of hope that I had taken out during the long nights in my parents' house to comfort me while Geraldine snored in the next bed, while my father stalked through the fields. It was then that I came the closest I ever came to telling Mary about my father. I felt the words bubble on my lips but I did not say them, just let the tears stream down my face. A moan rose up from deep within me, and I howled and cried and whimpered, let Mary cradle my head in her lap and stroke my hair.

"Tessa," Mary soothed, "it is a burden, being young. I know it. Young, with the weight of family pressing down on you. But you will find your way in this one, Tessa. I just can't do it with you. But *you*, you need to do it. To go. You need to make a life for yourself, my child, far away from here."

I looked up at her and realized her eyes were wet, that tears were running down her face. It was the first and only time I saw Mary cry, but I hardly paid attention. I was so furious, and afraid, that I could barely see straight.

"You aren't even my friend!" I shouted suddenly. I pulled away from her and leapt to my feet. "I hate you!"

I did not even think to ask what it was she had done, what the tea leaves had told her, what it was the fortune-tellers had seen.

L ater, when I thought back to those moments, I would always wonder if Mary knew, even back then, how things would turn out.

The past remakes itself in hindsight. By now I can barely trust myself in my own life—I am so haunted, each moment, by the idea of what I will remember, what I will see when I look back, all the things I am failing to see now.

I should have known there was something wrong when Mary began closing the library in order to walk down to the river with me and spend long afternoons telling me her stories. People left angry messages on the door, having walked miles out of their way to catch a glimpse of her, smell her spice scent, or find out what herb to sprinkle in the dinner to make their husbands more kind, or passionate, or dull. But suddenly she didn't seem to care. It seemed strange, too, I guess, that she told me so many new things that last summer, down by the river. That she talked so much, all of a sudden, of Rain Village and its pink fish, which writhed through the river and brought tourists from all over to sample their meat, and that her heart turned so often to William and her terrible, pounding sense of loss over his death. "He should not have died," she would say, her voice so tight and full I thought she should have been screaming. One week Mary and I went to the river every single day, and, when we returned to Mercy Library, she didn't seem to care about the notes on the door, the stack of books, magazines, and papers the mailman had left on the step. She just left them sitting there.

I barely took note of any of those signs, though. I was lost in my own fantasies. The yearning in my gut was so strong—the crazy excitement when I imagined leaving, the terrible fear when I thought of being alone, somewhere new, without her.

That summer seemed to last longer than usual. It was nearly October before the air began to crisp, the leaves started dropping onto the ground and into the water, and the air filled with the smoky, nostalgic scent of autumn. The sky grew gray and heavy and seemed to tap my head as I rushed down the road to Mercy Library, to help Mary rake the furious leaves that blanketed the library yard. The little chimneys of the houses I passed began sputtering wisps of smoke into the air, and Mary made crackling fires to heat bowls of apple cider with cinnamon sticks floating on top.

It had always been the perfect season for her. As soon as the leaves turned we pushed cloves into the skins of oranges and lined the windowsill with them. She put out bowls of nuts that we cracked into piles of shells and dumped into the yard out back. Mary sat at the desk and told me stories about her mentor, the trapeze star Lollie Ramirez, who could see into the future and had tried to warn her brother Luis before he fell from the wire and onto his neck in front of two thousand people.

"She could see it. She could hear him falling before it even happened," she said.

The days grew shorter and I left Mary's earlier, trying to get home before the night was completely black, spooky that time of the year on the empty roads stretching between farms. "I can't bear to watch you go back to that house," Mary would say, holding me close. "I'm so sorry, Tessa."

"It's okay," I said, to reassure her, but she would watch me as if I were about to disappear.

As the days got colder, I'd return in the mornings and Mary wouldn't be in the main room or out back. People would be lined up at the door, and I'd let them in, check out their books, and try to keep everything running smoothly. But more and more they had to fend for themselves, and every evening there'd be piles of books all around, scattered on the floor and in front of the books lined up on the shelves.

I'd run down the stairs to the cold basement to wake Mary, shivering with only a thin sheet wrapped around her, and see that she'd been going through her circus box—the paraphernalia, old costumes, jewelry, and love letters, which she wouldn't let me read. I'd put the things back, fold the box flaps over each other, and set it to the side. I'd start a fire in the little stove and wake Mary with a cup of cider.

"Thanks," she'd say, sitting up and raking her hands through her mass of curls.

"Come," I'd say, "let's go outside."

Autumns in Oakley were magical. From some parts of town all you could see, for miles around you, were leaves on fire—red and yellow and orange, flaring from the trees and coating the ground. Mary was tormented by something—I did not know what—from her past or present, but that autumn all I wanted was to lose myself outside among the colors, to not think of anything else. I sought anything that would pull me outside myself. I could not stand my father, just walking past him in the mornings in his rocking chair. I dreaded the nighttime and hated my body with more passion than I ever had, unless I was on the trapeze. One afternoon Mary dragged herself from her bed and came out with me, wrapping herself in a sweater.

"What's wrong?" I asked, and she turned to me and smiled the crooked smile that lit up her tanned face, bending her blue cat's eyes into arcs.

"Don't mind me," she said, "I'm just tired. It is you I'm worried about, Tessa."

"But nothing's wrong," I kept insisting, my mind full of the circus, the trapeze, the feel of my body rushing through air. And I did not even pay attention as she slipped away.

It was cold and gloomy as I walked to the library one day in late November, tromping through piles of wet, dead leaves. The trees were all skeletons. I couldn't find Mary anywhere. I let in a few farmers who were standing impatiently at the door and left them standing, confused, in the main room. A cold kettle of tea sat on the stove, Mary's mattress downstairs was empty, and she had boxes of memories, more than I'd ever seen before, spread out along the floor of her makeshift room, mixed in with the papers and books. I searched every room. I knelt down and began straightening up her things, waiting for her to return. I picked up her shimmering costumes. I arranged her high-heeled shoes in the box, running my fingers along the length of them, and started gathering up a pile of circus programs to stack on top.

When I finally looked up, I realized it was way past lunchtime. My stomach was grumbling. Where was she? I stepped over the mess Mary had left—I had barely managed to clear a foot of empty space on the floor—and looked once more around the other rooms downstairs and the front and back yards. Shouldn't she have left a note or something? I walked back into the library, stumbling over the boxes and shoes, ignoring all the farmers wandering around aimlessly, books in hand. It struck me then how strange it was that she had taken all these things out after years of never touching them—all the clothes and papers and bracelets and shoes.

I don't know what it was that led me to the river. Maybe I had some kind of premonition, the way Lollie Ramirez had had before her brother fell from the wire, or maybe it started to hit me that something wasn't right in the way Mary had been acting, or in the way Mary had ever acted, burying herself in Mercy Library in the middle of a farm town like Oakley, leaving the circus and her home and her sisters, everything that had ever meant anything to her. Maybe I was a bit haunted, too, by the image of William in the river, pale and floating, and the girl who cried so many tears that they turned her skin to ice. A horrible thought came to me, that I had lost her, right then. It was the oddest thing; I just put the thought out of my head and kept on running.

I ran until I could see through the trees, and then suddenly, from the hill where I stood, the whole thin river lay before me.

What I saw first was the bright color on the river. I thought it was some sort of fish floating on the surface until I recognized Mary's long and brightly patterned dress. It was the dress and colors I had watched deepen in the sink out in back of the library a dozen times, watching Mary knead it in the water and lay it out to dry. I knew how the red and the orange and the silver smeared together under the water, that it was like staring into a dark, blurred sun. I knew how the colors were muted in the daylight, dry, and how the fabric rubbed against the paleness of her ankles.

I saw the white of Mary's face—then her chin turned up to the sky, her dark hair spreading around her. Everything passed so quietly. It was only after a few moments that it struck me that something had happened, though, in a way, I think I had always known it, just as I had always known I would never see her again once I left Oakley. *It is why I haven't left already,* I realized. I moved down past the trees and toward her as two shouting men, who seemed to have just come upon her, pulled her from the river. Careful with her as they pulled her to the riverbank, they lifted her from the water as if she were a child. It was all wrong— them moving and breathing and going red from the effort, and her lying there, blank and dull.

I don't remember how I came to be right there, next to her, reaching for her as if I were the one who was drowning.

Once she was on the ground, I could see plainly how her body was filled with water. I watched the men pump down on her breast and breathe into her mouth. I knelt by her. I stroked her forehead and pushed back her hair. Leaves twisted through it, and I thought back to her stories, the ones she had told me over the years. I had the strangest sense that I was hearing the tale from Mary's lips. If I closed my eyes, I could almost feel the vibration of her voice humming in my ear.

"And then she drowned in the river."

With Mary's head in my hands, her black coiled hair wrapped around my wrists like seaweed, I couldn't see straight. My heart was a blinding light in my chest, blank and searing. I couldn't believe what was happening, yet it was true down to my core; the world had already shifted for me completely. Sometimes, when tragedy enters a life, it can feel like something that has always been there. For me it was as if everything in my life had moved, and had always been moving, toward that moment.

As I held her there, I suddenly noticed a bright spot on her breast. I looked to see if the two men had noticed, but they'd turned away to give me a moment with Mary alone. I leaned into her face until her cold forehead touched my skin. I trailed my fingers down her neck until I felt the thin chain that circled it. On the end of the chain I felt a ring, which I pulled from the dress surrounding it and brought into the light. The light hit it, illuminating the tremendous colors that can only be hidden in an opal stone.

CHAPTER NINE

✳

The world became completely silent. Even the water Mary floated in seemed to have turned to ice. The last leaves on the trees, so bright and furious the moment before, seemed as dull as paper. I felt the most crushing sense of emptiness I had ever felt, and when the others came to stand over Mary's body and carry it away, I could not even see them lifting her from the slick, leaf-covered ground. I stumbled along as they carried her to the doctor's house, and let the townspeople pull me away when the doctor put a blanket over Mary and passed the palm of his hand over her face. I vaguely remember hands on my shoulders and head, murmurs of compassion, but I was blind and dumb that day and for many days after. It was as if every breath of air, every drop of light, had been sucked out of the world at once.

Eventually I ended up at home, very late that night, I think, and my grief was so heavy that the house immediately filled with it, causing my parents and sister and brothers to take to their beds with fevers and sadness. I lay and stared at the wooden slats darting across the ceiling, unable to move. Geraldine snored next to me, her throat catching in her sleep, and the sound was like a hacksaw in my ears. I stared at the ceiling for what seemed like days, closing my eyes and just feeling the whoosh of air, calling back a sliver of the fantasies I'd had about Mary and me in the circus. My illness and grief were so severe that even my mother started coming into the room, yelling at me to get up or lying down next to me to comfort me. It was as if the grief had awakened something primal in her, and she began tending to me the way she would have once, back when she had convinced herself that I was almost normal. She mashed up potatoes into a paste, brought in fresh milk straight from the barn and forced it down my throat. She kissed my forehead, and I thought about how happy that would have made me once, before Mary had given me the world, before it had fallen apart again. Even Geraldine tiptoed in and out of the room, in keeping with the strange hush that had fallen over everything.

But it was harvest time, and the crops had no patience for such grief. Mary's death was the biggest thing that had happened in years, I think, but there was no time for it, as much as everyone spoke and dreamt of Mary, imagining the water filling their own lungs and skin. While my family returned to the fields, one by one, to work from morning till night, I stayed in bed. It took many days for my own fog to begin to lift, and that was when Geraldine told me that Mary had been buried behind the library.

"They said she couldn't be buried in the local cemetery," she said, "because she died in sin."

"Sin?" I repeated, dumbly, though I knew well enough what she meant, had heard my mother whisper the word outside my door. "Suicide," she kept saying, in the same hushed tone she and her lady friends had always used to talk about Mary Finn.

"Matt Tompkins's kid watched her," Geraldine said, looking down, running her palm back and forth along the doorframe. "He watched her wade into the river by herself, and just stop and sink down into it. He had no idea what was happening." She looked up at me and then down again.

I imagined it then, Mary sinking into the river, and it felt like a scene I remembered from somewhere. The memory beat against my head and skin, struggling to come into relief.

"Matt Tompkins found his son crouched down, holding on to a tree, crying. By then you were there, he said, and some others, pulling her out of the water. He said you didn't make a sound."

"The poem," I whispered.

"What?"

"A gleaming shape she floated by / dead-pale between the houses high."

"Tessa, are you okay?" Geraldine asked. I looked up at her and was surprised by the worry that crossed her face, how soft she seemed then.

"She read me so many stories," I said, choking on the words.

"I know," she said. "I saw you sneaking off to read the books she gave you. I saw you hiding them under your mattress."

"You did?"

"Sometimes I would look at them."

"She didn't belong here," I said.

I had the sudden, crazy idea then that I could still steal her away, take her body and bring it back to Rain Village, bury her in the forest, by the river. She had never belonged in Oakley, I thought. I was so strong by then, my whole body powerful and muscled; I could carry Mary across states, I thought, through Colorado, Idaho, up to the Pacific Northwest, where she had told me Rain Village was located. Just the two of us moving through the world, like I'd always imagined.

I clenched my eyes shut, pulled my knees into my chest, and felt like I, too, was being put into the ground behind the library, the chain tangled around my neck, dirt piling up on top of me. Guilt seized me like two massive arms and kept me pinned to the bed, gasping for breath. I just could not think of it: her body in the river, the way we'd pulled her onto the bank. The air itself turned golden with it, heavy like syrup. I saw Mary, again and again, sitting next to me that day on the riverbank, talking about the fate her tea leaves had spelled out for her. Warning me.

"Tessa," Geraldine said, and I could hear my mother then, appearing at the door, feel them leaning into me, but it was as if I had vanished, as if I had never been there at all.

I woke a few days later and found I couldn't bear to stay in my bed a moment longer. Outside, the sky was a pale, smoky gray, and a wind seemed to push through the trees, through the cornstalks, making them sway and shimmer. The world seemed to have been emptied out. The branches pressed into the sky, cutting through it with thick black lines, and there was no sound except for the faint whistling of wind. I lifted the window a crack and pushed my fingers through. The air felt like ice. It was December already, I realized, nearing up on Christmas. At Mercy Library Mary would be brewing cider with cinnamon sticks, baking gingerbread in the tiny stove. On any December day you would find an array of farm folk, their cupboards filled with canned vegetables and jams, their cellars stocked with dried meat and mounds of potatoes, spread through the stacks and at the tables with collections of Boccaccio or Baudelaire or the Brontë sisters open before them, breathing in Mary's spice scents. I thought of all those mornings when I had looked out onto a world just like this, barren and raw and ghostly, and felt filled with life, because of her.

The house seemed unusually empty, quiet. Geraldine's bed was unmade. I had that strange feeling again, like I had vanished completely. Like I didn't even exist. I touched the windowsill, the fine layer of dust that had collected on it. I touched the pane of glass and watched the imprints of my fingertips slowly fade out. Outside, the corn swayed back and forth, dried out and ragged in the winter air.

I realized then that I needed to go back. I needed to go back to the library and take what I could of her, to prove that she had existed, that we had existed together. I pulled on a sweater and pants and boots, I couldn't get them on fast enough, and then I took off, slamming down the stairs and through the front door, past the hedges my father had attacked that strange, ancient morning, onto the road that ran into town.

Mary, I breathed, into air, and she seemed to flare up before me, with her straw basket full of vegetables and books, her dangling silver earrings, and her long skirt that trailed behind her as she walked. "Mary!" I called, and I could just see her there, in the distance, her head flung back, laughing, calling to me. Smoking a cigarette with a book open on her lap. Swinging on the trapeze, whooping with laughter. Floating on the river, her wet hair sticking to her skin.

I flew through the town square and past the lumberyard. I didn't care that I was making people stop in their tracks and stare, or that the cold seemed to slip under my skin, turning my body inside out. I just needed to get back to her. I lived so much in books, I thought, it was hard, sometimes, to tell what was real. I remembered all the times Mary had read me stories and poems and the entire world had seemed to drop away. How many times I had watched the moon, the dirt scraping into my legs and back, and imagined I was in medieval France, or Victorian England, or, most often, in Rain Village, which had sometimes seemed more real to me than anywhere else. How afterward it would take me several seconds to calm down, to come back to the world again. Maybe none of this is real, I thought. Maybe it is all just stories.

My feet thudded against the earth; my breath was so loud it blocked out every other sound. I stopped only when I saw Mercy Library looming before me, and then I stood before it and took it in. The sign creaked back and forth the way it always had, and the old wooden building rose up like an old ship. Nothing seemed different from the way it had before, not really, though there was no one around. No couples crouching around the corner or groping each other under the front stairs, as the town folk were all too likely to do when Mary was there, weaving her spells over everyone. I don't know what I'd expected to change, if I thought the whole place would have burnt to the ground the moment Mary lost her breath. That was exactly what I had thought, I realized. It didn't make any sense for the library to continue standing, or for me to be there before it, staring up at it with my hands buried in my pockets. Nothing made sense anymore.

Slowly I walked toward the front steps, listened to the familiar creak as I walked up them. "I'm here!" I said then, into air, and I almost expected the main door to open and a whoosh of heat and gingerbread to come wafting out to me. For her to be standing in front of me in her long skirt and heels, her hair blackly wild around her face. "Did you like this story?" she would ask. "How real it felt? The best stories always feel more real than your own life."

"I'm here," I whispered, again, pressing my hand against the door, willing her to come to it. Surely she was there, in some form. "Mary?" The wind blew across my face then, shuffling through my hair, and I closed my eyes. "Is that you?" The air calmed, and all I could hear was a deep rustling sound, the shaking of tree branches above me. A weird feeling passed over me, and I started to realize how absolutely alone I was out there. The library in front of me like a corpse.

I shook the feeling off and tried the door. I had come to this library hundreds of times, I told myself; it was just a place like any other place, a place I had known and loved and spent the best hours of my life in, my only happy times. I straightened my back. The front door was locked, so I made my way around the library, past Mary's herb garden, to the back door. I dug at the base of the strongest rosemary bush, and the silver key was there, where it had always been, covered in earth. I heard a tapping sound then, and I found myself looking up, looking for her at the door, my heart lifting, and I realized that I expected her to be there, asking me to hurry inside because there were customers waiting, or because she'd made us some pumpkin soup and rye bread, or because the library was empty and we could practice a bit during the lull. I could almost see her in front of me. If I squinted, she would be there.

I sank down to the ground, into the herbs. The pain seared through my body, like nothing I had ever felt or have ever felt, before or since. Mary Finn had left me. I would never see her again. And I was not prepared to live a life without her. I knew then that I never would have left Oakley while she was still there. Not even to forge a life of my own, not even for the circus, as much as my love for the trapeze and the rope burned inside my body and made me long for something new.

Suicide, they'd said.

I picked myself up from the ground and unlocked the door, pushing my way into the library. Past the stove and the jars of dried herbs, through the stacks, past the tables where she had done her readings, up to the front desk with its trinkets, the silver bracelet and the scattered notebooks, the cigarette papers and the clown figurine. I stood still and closed my eyes. The library was completely silent. Empty. The feeling came back: that the whole world had stopped existing and that I, too, had vanished. It was a feeling I was getting accustomed to, a far more comfortable feeling than the pain that beat up against me and threatened to break through at any moment, dropping me to my knees, taking away all my breath.

I thought of the millions of stories pressing against each other in the library stacks. So many lives and feelings and tragedies. *This doesn't matter,* I thought. *None of this matters.* There were countless other stories to wrap my head around, weren't there? Like Sister Carrie's? The girl who had gone to make a life for herself, who had started in the factories and ended up rich and feted. Just focus on that, I told myself.

I squeezed my eyes shut as tightly as I could but found myself thinking, for the first time, of the river.

Not how she picked herself up from her mattress, tied on her shoes, and walked those few minutes down to the bank. Not what she must have thought as she stood there, staring into the water. Whether she saw her own face staring back at her, or William's face floating on the water, or if she saw another river, teeming with pink fish and rain. Whether she thought of the ice that had covered her skin, Juan Galindo coming upon her as she lay in ice-streaked hay. Whether she thought of leaving the circus, coming to Oakley and to Mercy Library, coming to me.

What I thought about was the feeling she must have had when she felt herself slipping, when the water moved into her mouth and lungs and the water plants twisted around her legs. The way she must have given herself over to the water and felt herself sink into it, become part of it, felt her mind go blank and soft. I stood there by Mary's desk, imagining it. How the water would feel against my own skin, curling into my mouth. How if I allowed it, if I chose it, I would never have to be without her. Never have to go back to Riley Farm. Never have to lie back in the cornfield staring at the moon, or run past the kids in the town square and hear them laughing. Never have to be the freakish, strange girl with hands shaped like starfish and as small as plums. Never have to face my own life. The river was only steps away. I wondered if Mary's feet had left indents in the earth, for me to follow.

I let my mind wind down and stop. Concentrated on the feeling of the water, what I imagined it would be like. Let my mind let go of everything in the world but that feeling, the emptiness of being so far below the earth and air.

I focused so hard on the blackness, the silence, that I stopped smelling, hearing, feeling the faint chill against my skin. I stopped feeling myself at all, and it was then that I saw it. A twirling, tiny shape, a speck really, in the center of all the darkness. Flicking back and forth. Getting closer and closer. Filling up my mind until all I could see was a perfect image of a body whirling around a white rope, cutting cleanly through the air. It took me a minute to realize that it was my own body I was seeing. My own body covered in sequins, stretched out in a smooth, gleaming line, moving around and around, unaffected by gravity, unaffected by anything of this earth.

I opened my eyes and realized there were tears running down my face.

I felt it, deep in my body.

"You need to make a life for yourself," she had said.

"Far away from here," I said out loud, finally realizing what she had meant. "In the circus." The room seemed to spin around me. I could walk into the river, I thought, or I could live in the air. Spin in the air until I became pure light, until I transcended everything. Suddenly the desire moved through me so strongly I almost cried out, and all the muscles in my body seemed to break open, all at once. It was a strange feeling. I thought of wings lifting up and spreading in the air, expanding and unfolding and opening out, and I thought of Mary in the brochure from the Velasquez Circus, a spinning blur of light as she flew through space.

I ran through the stacks to the back of the library, my heart in my mouth, my feet storming across the wooden slats, and I pushed the stool out and leapt up on it, then reached for the trapeze. I curled my fingers around the cold metal. The moment my hands touched the bar, everything felt different. I had a place, I thought, beyond Mercy Library and Riley Farm. As I pulled myself to my feet, gripping the ropes with my hands, I knew I had made a decision.

It's what she had wanted, I thought. What she had seen in me. What she had given to me.

PART TWO

*

It is strange, how people drop out of your life, like tears. The way the whole world can shift and change, the way you can choose to remake it. Choose to become someone new. When I left Oakley, Kansas, I was only sixteen years old, but it seemed so long in coming that I might as well have been fifty. I had never stopped longing to be a part of my family and my town, no matter what, but it was too late for that now; it was too late for a lot of things, and my heart was so chock-full of grief and love and hope and wildness that I thought I would burst with it. As I walked into the ice-cold night, under the black sky sprinkled with stars like sharp diamonds, I thought of Mary, all those years before, heading out into the world, leaving everything she'd known behind. I remembered that first time I'd left my house and taken off running for the town square, determined to find something more in the world.

I left Riley Farm with a bag flung over my shoulder filled with clothes and books, my money and Mary's ring sewn into the hem of my skirt. I wanted to have a life separate from everything that had come before, and back then I imagined it was possible to have a life apart from Oakley and my family, as if I could slip out of my own skin like a snake. I imagined it was possible to have a life apart from Mary and what she had been to me, though I was heading toward a city she herself had created in my mind, and I was going there to find the Velasquez Circus, which I knew came through the city every spring. I was stepping into my future, though everything I knew of the circus was wrapped in Mary's memory and stories, the smell of spices. Before I had simply dreamt that one day I too could work under those lights, unbound by normal laws of gravity and flight. Now I knew there was nowhere else for me, in all the world.

I was not prepared for the grief that moved through me as I passed the neighboring farms, as I cut through the town square for the last time, grief that went beyond Mary Finn. I knew my sister would wake up to find my bed and closet empty, that she would feel under my mattress and find it smooth and bookless, that she would find the small postcard I'd left on her dresser, a picture of a clown I'd found with Mary's things. I knew my father would rage through the house, that the walls would sag and strain with his anger, that Geraldine and my brothers and my mother would have to tiptoe around him for days, eat with their heads bent over their bowls, not making a sound. When I got to the edge of town and the wide, main road that led to Kansas City, I started to run, tears streaming down my face, imagining him coming after me with legs that could run whole miles for every tiny step I took in the snow.

The faster I ran, the safer I thought I'd be, as if sheer distance could separate me from him, my grief, everything of the past. I walked for days and days, from morning till night, without stopping. It was as if stopping would whirl me back to Oakley and to the cornfields and to Mary, floating in the river, her body wrapped in leaves. And so I walked and walked, letting my feet crease and freeze and blister, until one day the city appeared before me, its spiked skyline outlined above the horizon. Mary had told me all about the clanging of streetcars and the grates that cut up the roads, about the laundry hanging from lines that stretched from rooftop to rooftop, and about the smog that curled around chimneys and the office buildings that stacked floor upon floor upon floor until you got dizzy counting them. Years before, she had followed Juan Galindo on the same roads until the icicles disappeared from the tree branches, the snow melted from the ground, and they reached the city that now glimmered with lights before me.

My heart danced in my chest as I gazed at the city; the skyline seemed like a cluster of gifts under a Christmas tree. As I walked closer, with each step the dry grass became sparser and the houses turned to buildings and then to enormous silver fingers that pointed to the sky. Men and women rushed by me dressed in formal clothes, and they would have trampled me had I not taken to moving from doorway to doorway, out of their path. The farther I went, the more the world closed down until I no longer had spaces to run and hide in. I walked until the city pressed into me so tight I couldn't breathe.

The delicate streams that ran through Oakley, the swaying vegetables and buried potatoes, the weeping willows that fell over the river, the endless grassy fields—everything was blotted out by the city, by stark concrete and stone.

My head whirling, I stopped and sat on a set of stairs that led into a small building. I dropped my sack to my side and only then realized how tired I was, how hot and damp my face was despite the cold. A woman stepped out of the building and brushed past me, followed by a dog on a leash. I turned around and looked: it seemed unimaginable that life could exist inside buildings like this. A train whistled nearby. Cars clattered down the street. The air seemed to get chillier by the moment, as the sun fell in the sky. I couldn't believe how a place so full could feel so empty. I pressed my palms flat against the stone of the steps I was sitting on, breathed in the gritty, smoke-filled air. I felt exactly as if I were a character in a book I'd read, and the idea was as weird as it was thrilling. In some ways it seemed unreal, all of it, like I was lying on my back in Mercy Library the whole time, listening to some story; in other ways it seemed like all I'd had to do, all these years, was walk right out of one life and into another. Like Oakley, my family, my past were all things I could have just blinked away.

I stood up. I pushed past people and ducked under railings, looking all around for some way in, some crack in the city's ferocious, dirty facade. A few blocks later I saw a sign, and my heart leapt: *Apartment for Rent.* I had plenty of money. I took a deep breath, walked up the stairs, and pressed the doorbell. I'll be okay, I thought. I patted my pink lace skirt, reaching unconsciously for the weighted-down hem. After several long minutes, an old lady opened the door and peered down at me.

"I'm here about the apartment," I said quickly, before she could shut the door again.

She laughed. "Girl, where are your parents? Is this a prank?"

The woman slammed the door shut and did not open it again, though I stood on her porch for ten minutes more, ringing her doorbell and trying to hold back tears. For a moment I thought longingly of my bed in Oakley, my warm covers and Geraldine snoring across from me.

I turned back to the street. By now it was practically dark. All the streetlamps had snapped on, and the car lights bounced off the pavement, confusing me as I walked along, dragging my sack. Brightly lit stores lined the main streets, which swarmed with men and women who fell against me as they pushed past, on their way to the next place and the next. I glanced into windows to check that I was still there, that I was there at all. I cursed myself for having timed my arrival so badly and being so lacking when it came to understanding the world and its ways.

I walked on, past sleek silver buildings and squat brick ones, open-faced mansions and run-down tenements. Every single thing was like a new description from a book I'd read, come to life.

I turned off the main avenue and onto a narrow side street. After what seemed like hours, the city seemed to quiet down. The streets widened and turned desolate. The buildings expanded and blew smoke across the sky. I stopped suddenly. Factories. Sister Carrie. I smiled, despite myself, at the strangeness of it.

I walked past the first factory and then the second. My eye caught a flash of white to my right. I looked up, realized there was a line of row houses there, huddled together. In front of one was a small white sign. I crept up closer and saw that it said, "Rooms Available. Women only." *Please*, I breathed. *Please.* My heart skittered in my chest as I climbed up to the door. "St. Mary's House for Women," I read, on a golden plaque outside the door.

I rang the doorbell and stood perfectly still, afraid to even breathe. It was pitch black outside by now, and the factories were spooky in the dim light of the streetlamps, the smoke ghostly as it rose to the sky.

A sturdy, middle-aged woman opened the door and squinted out at me. She looked me over and nodded at my sack. "I presume you are looking for a room?" she asked. Her voice was surprisingly delicate for her harsh, thick looks, her sloppy hair stuffed into a bun.

I nodded. My mouth was bone dry.

"Well, let's not catch ourselves a chill. Come in, and I'll show you around."

I stepped forward, let her lead me up a flight of stairs. "Two dollars a week for a room," she said, turning back to me. "Three for room and board. The bathroom's down the hall and the kitchen downstairs."

"That sounds fine," I said, trying to fill each word with a sense of how dependable I was, how responsible. I could hear my voice trembling and was surprised when she just nodded and led me into the dour upstairs hallway, with its gray carpet and walls. She withdrew a ring full of keys and picked through it daintily with her small hands.

"We abide by Christian rules here, though some abide better than others," she said, turning to me.

"Yes, ma'am," I said, and she smiled for the first time, wrinkles shooting out along her cheeks. A minute later I was stepping into a tiny, musty, flaking room with a small dresser and bed, a closet and window.

My heart filled. A room of my own, I thought. No Geraldine. No father's shadow in the doorway. No cornfields outside the window, trees like brushes against the white sky. I thought of the trinkets scattered across Mary's desk in Mercy Library, how I had vowed to have my own things someday.

"It's perfect," I said, nodding, tears pricking at my eyes.

She smiled and raised her eyebrows, then made some quick movements with her hands and passed the key to me, hanging from a wire circle.

"Well, good-night, then," she said, as I handed her three of the dollars I had stashed in my skirt pocket. "My name is Esther, by the way."

"Tessa Riley," I said, and the words felt strange and strong on my tongue, as if I were marking the letters into dirt.

She left, and I walked into the center of the room and just stood with my eyes closed, breathing it in. Letting my relief and sorrow and excitement slide into each corner, over each inch of carpeting and flaking gray-white paint. I looked out the window, at the smoke that seemed to hover above the buildings. I spread myself out on the lumpy mattress and stared at the shadows against the wall. I felt the exhaustion relax from my muscles and spread throughout my body, weighing down every inch of skin, every vein.

And then, without even meaning to, I thought again of my quilt-covered bed in Oakley, and I imagined my mother and father and Geraldine and my brothers, wondered if they missed me at all. If they were worried or sad. I pictured the fields and the wooden floor and the giant countertop covered in dirt and vegetables. A longing moved through me that I couldn't understand. How could I feel homesick? What was wrong with me? They never wanted you, I told myself. I closed my eyes and thought of my mother with her face turned to the wall. I thought of Geraldine alone in our big room, the silence of it engulfing her. I thought of my father bending over me, and the ache went straight to my gut, as if I'd been stabbed.

The light from the streetlamp slanted in and illuminated my closet door. I tossed and turned. I longed for sleep, for peace, to just disappear. *Stop*, I kept thinking. The thoughts came, one after another. The images: Mary floating in the river, the corn and the moon and the dirt pressing into my back. Sitting cross-legged on the library floor as Mary rubbed glitter across my eyelids and cheeks.

None of it is real, I kept telling myself, staring at the outline of a smokestack outside my window. Only this is real, here and now. I clutched my body, imagined that spinning, gleaming girl above everyone, slicing the air right open.

The next morning I rose, showered quickly in the small bathroom, and walked across the street. I was determined not to think about anything but the task in front of me.

"Where can I apply for a job?" I asked a tired-looking woman carrying a smock. She pointed. A sign led to "Applications." The place was desperate for bodies, it seemed, and within an hour a foreman was handing me a smock and a time sheet and putting me to work sewing school uniforms.

I was given my own little station, a chair with a spindly black sewing machine in front of it. I looked around at the other girls, but they all kept on working, their faces bent to the fabric. At first I had difficulty placing the fabric in the right spot, getting the machine to move the way it was supposed to, but by the end of the day I'd gotten it down well enough to keep my job, even if my hands were stuck through with pin-pricks and bleeding. That night I went back to the boardinghouse, ate a bowl of soup and a hunk of cheese with Esther in silence, and fell into bed, dreamlessly.

After several more days I got used to the way the sewing machines clattered like teeth, the feel of the needles jabbing me when I made a mistake. I settled into a routine so dull it seemed to wipe out everything, both my past and my future. Every day I picked up the gray wool vests that prickled under my hands while one hundred girls did the same thing on either side of me, lined up in rows. Time stretched out in a way it never had before, until a minute seemed like an hour and an hour a whole day. My head pounded with the whirring of the machines, which strung vest after vest and skirt after skirt with the same dull thread. I returned to my room so wiped out that I did not even think about the circus or the trapeze, just the bliss of darkness and sleep.

But it was at night that everything returned to me, and I dreamt of Mary floating on the river, her hair coiled blackly and wetly against her forehead and throat, wrapping itself around her neck like ropes; of the opal that was all light, a million points of light contained in one small, swirling face glowing from her breast; of the letters and photographs she had left strewn across the library's wooden floor, the papers she had let pile by the front door; of the leaves that had clutched her skin, the thin, narrow leaves of the tree weeping over her; and of her cat's eyes opening under the water.

Sometimes I dreamt that the river was pressing down on me, too, pushing me to the bottom, where plants and reeds encircled me and my lungs slowly filled with water. I gulped the air, tried to remember how to breathe when I woke up. I cried so many tears into my pillow that I could not believe that my tiny body hadn't shriveled into a dry husk. And for those moments the world was dark and hollow, inside out, until I rose from the bed, covered myself with a smock, and stuck my head under the rusted bathroom faucet. The dreams vanished like mist then. Outside my window, there was only concrete and steel.

On Sundays, my day off, I took to wandering the streets, hoping to spot some sign of the circus—some dash of color in the gray winter landscape—but there was nothing. The smoke covered my clothes with its scent and its weight. The feel of piles of buttons under my fingertips stayed with me even as I wandered the streets or lay on my bed in my room, staring at the ceiling. For weeks I couldn't bring myself to think about the trapeze, and a heavy guilt settled over me, burying me in my new life. My only pleasure was walking to the five-and-dime on Sunday mornings and poring over the shelves for that one tiny, perfect thing, something new to set on the dresser in my room. I bought soaps shaped like seashells, mirrors with pictures of the Eiffel Tower on the backs, tiny figurines, boxes carved with dragons and fish. I could spend whole evenings just lying back on my bed, staring at my growing collection, rearranging the things I had bought.

I didn't realize that I was grieving still, that the grief had exhausted me and wiped out all desire for the future. Often I thought of Riley Farm and the hedges that lined the front yard. What my father had been doing the day he'd carved that giant peacock with the leaves spraying out behind him. How it had taken weeks for the branches and leaves to grow back again, though they'd never taken on the same shape they'd had before. I thought of that feeling I'd had, crawling into bed each night and lifting the quilt to my shoulders, that feeling of being home, as terrifying and sad as it was. You can't just shuck it off, I thought, just as Mary had said. I spent hours imagining my life, rewriting it, as I bent over the sewing machine, as I sat alone in the lunchroom while the other girls chattered, as I wandered the city streets and stared at the lit-up windows, wondering if I would always be alone, if there would ever be another person for me to love.

Slowly the winter gave way to spring, and then flowers burst out of the flower boxes hanging from every window. The trees that dotted the streets turned a bursting green. And after many weeks and months of the grief that clung to me like ice, I, too, felt ready to come back to life, and was able to part that dullness, pull it back ever so slightly and reveal something new, a longing that came from deep within my muscles and blood. One day in April, alone in my room after work, I placed my hands on my flat torso and realized it was mine, my own body, a body that could twist in the air and crumple into a box two feet wide. And then I missed the rope and the trapeze so feverishly that I almost cried out. I left my room and walked the streets until I found a hardware store, where I bought a length of heavy rope. Later that same night I tiptoed down to the basement with a candle and hung the rope from one of the pipes crossing the ceiling, using a ladder I borrowed from Esther. For a dollar more each week, she said, she didn't mind.

The first time I swung up into the air, my muscles ached and burned and my balance was so off that I kept slamming into the wall. But it didn't matter. I worked hard, pushing myself. I returned to the basement after work each night, anxious to climb up to that rope and practice. With one turn after another, I forced my creaky muscles into submission. Seeing me huddled over those uniforms in the daytime, nobody would have guessed that I spent my nights flinging myself into one rotation after another, in the air.

The Velasquez Circus would come any day now, and I was ready.

But the circus did not come that spring, or that summer, and I began to get nervous. I worked and saved every penny I could, eating the beans and bread and soup Esther provided in the evenings and buying small containers of tuna in the factory cafeteria every day for lunch. I stopped visiting the five-and-dime, as if denying myself small pleasures would make the circus come faster. I began to wonder if I'd missed it—if the circus had come and gone without my noticing, if I'd been too lost in all that reflecting and wandering. I was sick of myself and my thoughts, and I couldn't stand another year in the factory. If the circus didn't come to me by winter, I decided, I would just have to set out once again and find it myself.

I continued to practice in the basement until I collapsed into bed each night, exhausted. Days and weeks and months passed. I worried and waited, wondering if my life would ever truly begin. And then finally, after a long, blistering summer that baked the sidewalks, well into an autumn that sprinkled leaves over the city sidewalks and streets, news of the circus finally came to Kansas City. From a fourth-floor window of the factory, I saw posters splashed across buildings and lampposts, even in that lonely part of town. The name *Velasquez Circus* burst above tigers, trapeze stars, and elephants with sequined harnesses on top of their heads. At first I thought I might just be imagining it, I'd been waiting to see that name for so long: *Velasquez Circus*, which seemed to contain everything within it. I was dizzy with excitement.

"Look!" I shouted, pointing. "I'm going to leave with them."

All the girls left their machines and ran to where I stood, pressing in toward the dusty windowpanes, craning their necks to see. I turned to a girl next to me, who looked down at me with wide, surprised eyes. "I know the trapeze. I learned from a famous aerialist. I'm going to do it!" She backed away from me, and I could hear the others whispering, laughing, but I didn't care. Flying Lollie appeared again and again in the posters, her hair glaring red and flowing out behind her, her skin coffee-colored and outlined in dark blue. "Flying Lollie, Dream of the Circus!" the posters screamed. The leotard she wore was made up of thousands of tiny yellow points, and she always lay flat across the bar, her arms spread out on either side like wings.

I didn't even hesitate. That day I told the foreman I was leaving and collected my pay. I gave Esther a week's notice and spent every waking moment stretching in that basement, jumping up and down in place, practicing my one-armed swing-overs and forcing my body to fling out from the rope in a clean straight line, with nothing to hold me up underneath but air.

✳

CHAPTER ELEVEN

I remember my last night in Kansas City as if it were yesterday. I packed my bag, left the boardinghouse, and camped out beside the railroad line on the outskirts of the city. I was suspended between lives, between my grief and the freedom of being out on my own, about to have my greatest adventure. I pressed my starfish hands on the cold railroad tracks, feeling for rumbling. I lay on my back staring at the moon, remembering those nights when I first learned to read among the cornstalks and those nights, a little later, when my father changed the meaning of those fields so completely. Now I was seventeen years old, free of the burden of family and of love, lying next to a line of tracks and staring at that same yellow moon. Everything was open to me.

The night seemed so full and strange, and to stretch out forever. Dirt and gravel pressed into my back. I stayed awake for hours, despite my exhaustion, imagining what I would say and do, how I would find Flying Lollie and tell her about Mary, about everything I'd learned and done. I closed my eyes and imagined Mary was there lying next to me, that I could reach up and wrap my fingers in the coils of her hair. "I am finally here," I whispered. "Can you see me?" I felt a breeze pass over my face and sat up, sure I could smell the faint scent of cloves. "Is this how you felt, too?" In the distance I could see the outline of buildings stamped against the sky. I was afraid to breathe. I closed my eyes again and felt the edge of her skirt brush my leg, her hair curl around my finger. Eventually I fell into a deep, dream-filled sleep, my body curled into a ball next to the tracks.

I woke to the sound of voices and rumbling. I jumped to my feet, confused and disoriented, and saw that people had begun gathering behind me and were rapidly lining up on both sides of the train tracks, for miles in each direction. That was how it seemed—like we stretched out for miles. I gathered up my bag and looked around, as if I would see Mary there, waving to me from the other side of the tracks, the sun lighting up her face, her eyes glowing bright blue. Instead I saw crowds of people, more people than I'd ever seen in one place. My heart fell a bit to be back in the world, but the world seemed to have changed completely. The air was heavy with waiting, longing. Children ran through the crowds, and the people surrounding me took out binoculars to see into the distance. I looked in the direction they were facing, listened as the rumbling on the tracks grew louder. For a moment I felt raw fear press into my gut. This is it, I thought. If not this, then I have nothing. I closed my eyes and imagined my body cutting through the air like a steel blade, slicing through skin and bone and this mass of people until it was just me, swinging up to the canvas and back down again.

When I opened my eyes, the first thing I saw was the color. A mass of sequined colors coming toward me, sparkling under the sun. I saw the trunk of an elephant, the flash of a trombone, and the whirl of the feathers that drifted from hats, capes, and boas. Children cried out with delight all around me, and I found myself crying with them, rushing forward to meet the parade. Confetti whirled in the air. It did not feel real, any of it. I was caught up in something nearly holy, no longer myself. As the parade and train moved forward, I moved back, as we all did, to clear the tracks and make space. I felt the crowd of people behind me as I moved, the whir of noisemakers spinning through the air. Everything blurred together, and I opened my mouth and shouted, amazed that I could be invisible in the midst of all those people. My head reeled with it. What I saw next were the colors draped across the performers' bodies, the shocking pinks and oranges and blues. I remember the green and silver of the gilded wagons rolling past, tigers roaring behind the glittering bars.

I followed the procession, once it had passed, as if I were a child in Hamelin. The earth thumped and shook, the sky hung behind clouds of confetti, and people rushed past me while I struggled to keep up. We traveled like this for a half hour—moving until we arrived in a pristine green field with only the occasional dandelion interrupting, where we watched as spikes were laid into the ground and the canvas tents raised up on them. We watched the train unload, the wagons and cages being rolled off one by one. Tears ran down my cheeks, but I didn't care. I had been waiting my whole life for this, I felt then, even if I hadn't realized it until I'd met Mary Finn. I thought of all those mornings I had spent hanging from the bar in the window, staring out into the fields as the sun burned into my parents' backs, imagining that there was something wonderful in the world, beyond what I could see.

Unloading the train took all morning and most of the afternoon, but it felt like the tents appeared magically, within seconds, all on their own; the pounding of the metal spikes and hammers stopped, the tents rose up in the air, and the landscape was transformed completely. This is what the beginning of the world must have been like, I thought, as one by one the banners went up, the tents flapped open, and the talkers took their places outside, shouting out to the crowds to lure them into each show. The midway curled around the big top in a long circle. Behind the field the train stretched out like a shiny snake. The brochures and fliers I had seen in Mercy Library couldn't begin to capture the excitement of all that hope and desire gathered up in one spot. Like an opal, I thought, everything wonderful ground down and contained within it.

I pressed into the midway with the rest of the crowd, then wandered through the tents and the sawdust. People jostled about everywhere, and the midway was one wonder after another: the sideshows with their flaring banners, the fortune-tellers, the Ferris wheel, the peanut and candy sellers, the booths where you could spin wheels or shoot at lines of bottles to win a plastic trinket. The world flooded my vision and I wanted to stop time, to be able to take it all into me. I couldn't believe that the line of buildings stretching into the sky, just visible from the treetops, was still Kansas City. Everything about the city seemed dull and washed out, a shadow world next to this one that burst with color and life. Smells came from every direction, making my mouth water. I had never smelled things like roasted peanuts, hot dogs and burgers, funnel cakes, after all my years of potatoes and corn, and everything assaulted my senses at once. I walked down the line of tents, where talkers shouted out, selling peeks at the moon for a nickel, or scales from a mermaid's tail for less than that. A man who claimed he had the moon in a jar stopped me as I rushed past.

"Have you ever touched the moon, girl?" he called out. "I have a sliver of it right here."

I stopped, terrified.

"There is a lady in the moon, as you well know, and you can talk to her if you'd like. You can ask her anything you want. Of course she is on the moon, but in here," he smiled, tapping the glass, "I got a piece of her heart."

I approached the man carefully, my whole body shaking, drawn by the glimmering jar in his hand.

As I pressed my coin into the man's palm, he cracked the jar open, just the smallest fraction.

A crowd gathered around us. I watched the jar, the way the light sprinkled out of it like salt. I was mesmerized. Everything spun down to that jar resting in the talker's meaty hands. At first I could hear nothing at all, and I could see nothing at all resembling a woman.

I tilted my head toward the jar so that my ear was almost covering the crack, my hair brushing against the talker's hands. And then, all of a sudden, I heard it: the softest voice in the world, the faintest little cry, whispering to me, "Let me out."

"What?" I whispered, scared to breathe. I heard the crowd around me, pressing in.

"Break the glass," the voice whispered, so low that no one but me could have heard it, and even I, just barely. "Let me out."

Before I could even register what I'd heard or make a move, a thin trail of smoke rushed out of the jar and toward the sky, and I was sure I saw a woman floating inside it. I blinked and looked again; all I saw was a whiff of smoke, then nothing.

I looked up and into the man's face just as he broke into a smile that showed all his teeth. "It's amazing!" he yelled, turning from me. "Now step inside and see the other wonders I've brought back from the sky!"

I was so shaken I had to sit down to recover.

Everything I had ever dreamt of was at the Velasquez Circus and the midway that wrapped around it. The show in the big top was set for that evening, the signs announced, but there was more than enough in the midway to keep the crowds busy until then. My eyes couldn't take in everything at once, but I tried to remember that I had all the time in the world now: I had nothing else in the world besides that. As I wandered through the crowds, people pointed at me as if I were one of the wonders surrounding them. I didn't mind. Everything was fantastic there, and surely I was not as strange as the boy with scales covering his body from his neck to his toes, beautiful iridescent scales that seemed to ring with light. His eyes sought me as I wandered into the tent. I smiled up at him from the crowd, my heart in my mouth.

In the next tent was a man who could swallow ten swords at once and then blow streams of fire from his mouth. My skin prickled from the heat, but I couldn't stop watching him, just as I couldn't stop watching the girl with the wings sprouting from her back, who walked out onto the small wooden stage next door. I huddled near the stage, lit by lanterns that threw shadows onto the canvas walls. The girl walked out in red sparkling heels. I heard them clack across the floor. She had wonderful curving legs and a torso shaped like a violin. Her blond hair unspooled down her back and hung around her face—bright blond hair, like starlight. I thought she might be twenty years old. She turned around and shook off her sequined top, revealing curled-up white feathered wings. She smiled at me with her painted lips as she unfolded her wings slowly, inch by inch, like in the vision I'd had in Mercy Library, until the tips touched the sides of the tent with a *thwack*. Once again I found myself amazed by the sheer beauty of what I was witnessing, of how the world unfolded and revealed itself.

I stepped into the midway as if coming out of a spell, the hush of the girl's wings rustling in my ears. A buzzing sound pulled me into the next tent, where the hugest bumblebee in the world pressed its face against a jar, next to a tarantula so big I could have swung from its legs. The coins slipped out of my hand as I went from tent to tent in a daze. The mermaid girl swam through a glass aquarium, flicking her tail near the surface so that water splashed onto the crowd. The tallest man in the world could have balanced me on one set of fingers. The snakes hissed at me as they slid across the snake girl's body, wrapping themselves around her neck and waist and thighs.

Suddenly music filled the air, from the big top, and everyone started moving toward it. For all the wonders of the midway, it was clear that the real magic took place within the tent that rose up in the middle of everything. Every person I passed seemed alive with the same excitement I felt; I could close my eyes and hear the whoosh of the trapeze, see the darkness shrouding the audience, their eyes glowing out of it, and I could hear the beating of rain. It all ran together—the sounds and smells and images that made up my memory and my past, which was always Mary's past and would always be Mary's past before mine. What had she felt, I wondered, as she stood outside the big top for the first time, surrounded by the talkers, the banners announcing the most astonishing, impossible feats and creatures? I imagined her next to me then: not the Mary I had known but the young Mary, the one who'd followed Juan Galindo and arrived at the same place I was standing now.

The talkers continued to yell into the crowds, luring us into each tent, seducing us.

"Girl!" a voice called. It seemed far away and right in my ear, all at once. I looked up. A fortune-teller sat inside a partially opened tent, beckoning me in. I stared at her, then slowly pushed through the curtain and sat across from her, leaning forward until my chin touched the tabletop. She smiled and her face was like a planet, covered in pockmarks and dropping from her bones. A sign saying "Fortunes, 20 cents" hung above her.

"Here," I said, pulling out two dimes from my skirt pocket.

"Let me see your palm."

I hesitated, then pushed my fist across the table and unclenched it. She put her fingertips on my palm, and I flinched, then looked up at her.

"Such extraordinary hands," she said, studying them. "Hands like this are special. Your love line runs right to your wrist, do you see? You will have a great love in the future, not too long from now. More than one."

"Yes," I said, excitedly. "The trapeze, the circus."

"No," she said. "A man, and not only one." She winked at me. "You'll be a heartbreaker, you know. You wait and see."

I stared at her dumbly, then laughed out loud. "You're making fun of me."

"I never tease about love," she said solemnly, watching me with her large, soft eyes.

I shook my head and stepped back into the crowd, let the fortune-teller's words sink into me as I gave myself over to the spangles and the talkers' ballies, luring us inside the tents.

The sun started to drop in the sky, behind the line of train cars, and everything became more frenzied and wild. The Ferris wheel exploded with light. The crowds had grown even larger, though I had hardly thought it possible. I seemed to be the only one alone. The air smelled like powdered sugar and fresh dough. I bought myself a stick of spun sugar, which tingled and melted on my tongue, then a candy apple I spent an hour licking the coating from. I held the sugar into the light to watch it sparkle and melt. The grass and dust crunched under my feet. Lights started to shoot on everywhere, popping like little explosions from the strings that looped from one tent to another.

The crowds pushed toward the big top, the midway tents started blacking out their lights, and the circus music grew louder and more frantic, pulling us to the main show. I stepped into the big top, past a starry black curtain and into the main space. Grass blades jutted through the sawdust. The smell was sharp and strong. Lights splashed everywhere through the tents, feeling out the corners and the spaces underneath the bleachers. I ducked my way through everyone to find a space up front, squeezing myself onto the end of a bench in the first row.

Within minutes the place seemed crammed with all of Kansas City. I stared, trying to memorize everything: the way the paint swirled through the sawdust, spelling out VELASQUEZ, the way the top of the tent sloped down, jangling with ropes and wires and hooks that seemed to crisscross the whole ceiling. If I squinted, I thought, I could see Marionetta spinning in the air, a blur of light darting from one side of the center ring to the other.

Suddenly the whole place went black. A hush fell over the crowd, as if we were leaning in, waiting to hear a secret. I held my breath and waited.

When the lights snapped back on, everything seemed to break open. Pure white horses, sparkling with rhinestones, ran out like streaks of light from the back of the tent, with beautiful women perched on top of them. A voice boomed out from the center of the ring, and a tall, black-clad man stepped out to introduce the famous Vadala horses. The world turned inside out, and the glare of the lights, the rhinestones, the wonderful pure white horses' manes, the snap and crack of the whips and the bars and the wires, the boom of the ringmaster's voice—all of it just whirled around me like another body, ready to pull me into itself. Under the lights everything would be different, I thought, with a purity and a certainty I hadn't felt before. Once I was under those circus lights, dressed in rhinestones and glitter, flying through the air—then everything, all the pain and hurt and longing within me, would disappear. I was seventeen, ready to slip out of my past and create a new one—a brand-new one, shiny as glass. *Here* was my life, I thought. The one I had always hoped for.

They brought out the cats that jumped through hoops of fire and stood on their hind legs; the clowns who stumbled and leapt across the floor; the girl who hung from her hair and did flips in the air, like a strange insect or bird. I saw the contortionists who could rest their toes on the tops of their heads, their stomachs against the ground. We, the audience, were bathed in blackness, and the performers passed in front of us like a dream. I longed for Mary as I had imagined her, for a friend I could turn to and say, "Look! Look what they can do!" For a brief moment I imagined Geraldine next to me, her face radiant and open the way she had been the night I'd first told her about Mary and the trapeze. "You would love this," I whispered, and then winced as I imagined my father slapping her face at the dinner table, the way she would always just sit there dumbly and grow dark red.

I blinked the thought away.

Next came an act Mary had told me all about, the Flying Ramirez Brothers, Lollie's four luminous brothers who could do flips across the wire, ride bicycles over it, and walk across stacked on top of each other, seemingly unaffected by the laws of gravity. I hadn't realized that men could be as beautiful as Mary had been. I was used to old farmers and foremen; I had never seen a man who could look your direction and make you gasp. The girls in the audience went wild; one woman fainted on the other side of the tent. The brothers did not seem to notice any of the commotion they caused. The wire was just a gleaming silver strand stretching across the tent, but the brothers played with it, teased it, made us believe that at any second they might go crashing to the floor. They never even came close. It was as if they were linked to the wire by their breath, heartbeats, and skin.

Then Lollie herself appeared with Flying Geraldo, soaring across the room. She was dressed like a yellow butterfly, wings hanging off her back, and somersaulted three times before reaching out and grasping Geraldo's hands. She balanced on her head as the bar spun and swung underneath her, and she hung from her feet, hooked into the sides of the trapeze. She was as beautiful as Mary had told me she would be, her hair and lips a flaming red.

I was mesmerized. I think I stopped breathing.

Everything slowed down as the two of them sped through the air so smoothly they appeared to be gliding, as if they had all the time in the world to throw themselves from the bar and into each other's arms, their hands locking in midair, he pulling her up and the two of them swinging back and forth, flipping over each other and the bar as if they were of the same body. *This is what it means to be in love,* I thought, and a longing clutched my chest. I thought of the fortune-teller's words: *You will have a great love.* I had never felt it before, that kind of longing, and it opened in me like a wound. Lollie and Geraldo glided back and forth. All the music stopped, and the only sound was air, the hush of their bodies splicing through it. *Swoosh, swoosh,* as if time had stopped.

When the show ended I felt drained. It had taken all my longing and hope and balled them up until I couldn't see straight anymore, and now everyone was headed back into the midway, or back home to their families, leaving me alone on the bleachers among piles of paper cups and popcorn bags.

For a few moments the tent was almost empty. There was barely a sound, just the roar of the rides and the ballies outside. Inside, everything was as still as a landscape after a storm. I was so nervous I could barely breathe. This was my chance, I thought, for a new life.

I pushed my way past the flap in the tent, the curtain that separated the performers from the audience, and headed to the train cars curled up out back.

A miniature city had cropped up behind the big top, I saw. Aside from the train cars, where the stars of the circus and the menagerie traveled, there were tents and trucks and vans, an army of cooks and vendors and talkers and workmen spread out among the performers. Ignoring the terror that yawned open inside me, I took a deep breath and walked past the small tents that had cropped up across the field, back to the shiny monster draped across the landscape. I hurried past fire pits lined with rocks, little portable stoves heating pots of coffee, camps of families sewing nets and costumes, and blankets spread out over the grass, despite the chilly autumn weather. I saw the bird girl in a tank top, her wings folded up beneath it, carrying a jug of water to a fire. She nodded to me as I walked by, and I looked down, trying to seem like I knew what I was doing, and scurried ahead.

The moon shone down on the metal of the train. Most of the windows were illuminated by light. The performers rushed in and out of the train cars, preparing for night, some in costume and some not, most somewhere in between, with glitter-covered skin and T-shirts. When no one was looking, I hopped onto one of the cars and pushed my way inside. The first thing I saw was the pointed top of the main tent through the dim windows, which stretched out on both sides of the car. The lights sparkling through them seemed different from the way they did outside—almost sad, and nostalgic, flickering through the dim train windows. The car was empty, and a hush hung over everything, the kind that makes you tiptoe and whisper.

Before I had time to look around, a girl entered the corridor from one of the other compartments.

"Who are you?" she said, walking straight up to me.

I jumped with surprise.

"You are so small!" she exclaimed.

I looked up at her, but she had not meant the words unkindly, I saw; she was only about ten years old, and her pale face was smeared with sloppy freckles. Her teeth were giant squares behind her lips.

"Are you looking for the sideshow tents? They're back there," she said, pointing in the direction I'd come. "They sleep in their tents, most of 'em."

"No," I whispered. "I'm looking for Lollie."

"Who?" she asked. As I looked closer, I could tell the girl was a circus child. I would come to recognize them in an instant, with their muscled legs and arms, the sheen of the lights playing across their skin, their callused hands.

"Lollie," I said louder. "Flying Lollie."

"Oh!" she exclaimed, covering her mouth. "You can't see her! She doesn't really see people, you know. None of them do, the flyers, they're snobs. Aren't you in the ten-in-one? I heard they were getting new folk."

She laughed and tilted up on her toes. The smile across her face was like a door being thrown open.

"No, no," I said. "My friend sent me to her. My friend Mary knew her; she used to be a flyer too. A long time ago, though."

My heart was racing, talking to this child. I felt silly, but she was part of something I longed for, fiercely. I felt it then, something I would feel again and again over the years: that the only world I was made for, this world of light and glitter, would never be part of my blood and skin the way it was part of this girl's and Lollie's. I envied her with all of my being, and it was as if she alone could grant me a pass into this life.

The girl looked stunned, I realized, and I felt the old shame come upon me. The words from my mouth just hung there.

But she surprised me again.

"Marionetta?" she asked. "Marionetta the flyer?"

I looked at her.

"Yes," I said.

Her whole face shifted, as much as if the sun had flicked on in front of her, pouring lemon-colored rays through her hair and skin. Her mouth opened slightly. She almost looked as if I'd struck her.

"Do you know her?" I asked. "She had black curly hair that swarmed around her face, and eyes like cat's eyes."

The expression on her face was not disdain, as I had imagined before, but something as soft as wonder.

"We all know her," the girl said. "They tell stories about her over the fire. People say she used to be covered in ice but that she glittered like a diamond. Some even say she murdered someone!"

She laughed. "We all tell stories about her," she said.

It was the beginning of my past remaking itself.

"I'll take you," she said, grabbing my hand. "My name is Ana. My mom and dad do the horses. The Vadala horses, you know. My sisters and brothers and parents are in the show, and I will be soon, too. Now I just feed and brush the horses, bring them out to my dad when he practices."

"I saw the Vadala horses," I said, smiling. "They're wonderful."

We wound our way to the back of the train. All around us performers stood in groups. Everyone stared as we went past, down to the train cars at the end of the line.

She snorted. "Of course they are," she said, and giggled. "They're the most beautiful horses in the world! Later I'll show you. How long will you be staying? I can't believe you knew Marionetta—I can't wait to tell everyone!"

"I don't know how long," I whispered, but she was already talking again.

"Lollie has one of the nicest cars in the train," she said. "My dad says she's a diva. He said Mary was one, too, that she slapped one of the roustabouts when he rigged her up wrong." She squeezed my hand and laughed. "I was just a baby when she left."

We stopped in front of a car that had a flying pink woman emblazoned on the side.

"Oh!" I breathed, surprised.

"See what I mean?" Ana laughed, rolling her eyes. "D-i-v-a." Then she reached over and hugged me, kissed my cheek. I stood unmoving, abashed.

"Bye!" she singsonged, then slipped away. I watched her skip up to a group of young boys and then turn toward me, pointing. I turned to the car quickly and hurried up the steps, into my future, before someone came to throw me off the lot.

CHAPTER TWELVE

It never occurred to me that it was an audacious, crazy thing to do: walking right up to the car of one of the most famous circus stars in history, the famous *Flying Lollie*, expecting to be greeted with open arms. I would later think that it came out of that same need that had first driven me to Mary Finn, that had made me plot and scheme as I hung in the kitchen window. A blind faith and hope and longing that made me demand more of the world than it wanted to give me. I was four feet tall with hands like starfish and as small as plums. The kids in the town square, the girls in the factory, my sister and brothers might have all called me a munchkin and a freak, and I might have been my mother's failure in this world, but I was still able to manage up a feeling that there was something beautiful in me, something they just couldn't see. I'd known it down by the river, when I taught my body how to spin circles in the air, clean and sharp as a knife cut. I'd known it when Mary Finn told me she recognized herself in me, and I knew it as I stood in front of Flying Lollie's train car, clutching my bag, ready for my new life to begin.

I pushed the door to the train open and walked into the narrow hallway. Another door to my right was ajar, I saw, and it swung forward at that moment, just as I was noticing the name FLYING LOLLIE scrolled along the top in large gold letters and before I had a chance to even think about knocking. I had thought I'd have a moment to prepare myself, but then there she was: dressed in spangles and high heels, her hair pulled back and strewn with silver sparkles, her skin like soft sand under the sun. Her hair was even brighter up close, a shock of red against the pale, thinly lined mocha of her skin, and her eyes were large and hazel-colored, rimmed with lashes so long they made her eyes look like stars. She was much more dramatic-looking than Mary. I couldn't imagine her bent over an herb garden or a pot of tea or a crumbling book of poems. She seemed like she would always be wearing stockings and glitter, surrounded by velvet and fur and glass. She was breathtaking. I scrambled to gather my senses and remember why it was I was here, why it was I had sought her.

"Who are you?" she asked, looking surprised and disappointed to see me quivering in front of her. Her eyes searched behind me, as if she were looking for someone else, and then focused in on my face. "What are you doing here?" Her voice was haughty and flecked with Spanish.

"My name is Tessa Riley," I said, rushing through the words. "I'm a friend of Mary Finn."

She just stood and stared, raising a painted eyebrow. It was like a bird's wing over her eye. "How did you get back here?"

"Through the back door, the flaps in the tent. I'm sorry, I had to find you."

She looked me over. "You say you know who?"

"Mary Finn," I said, and then, "Marionetta." My heart pounded. "She told me all about this place. And you, and your brother Luis, your villa in Mexico."

She looked at me a moment longer, then shrugged. "Many people knew Marionetta," she said. "Why are you bothering me about it?" And with one more look at the air behind me, she closed the door in my face.

As disoriented as I was by her beauty, as long as I had anticipated this moment, I had not been prepared for her to reject me. I stood staring at the gold letters that spelled her name, the door that shut me off from everything, all the possibility in the world.

I knocked again.

The door flung open and there seemed to be a different person standing there—her face soft and hopeful, her body pressing forward. When she looked down and saw me, she seemed crushed, and then I almost saw the fury descend on her.

"What are you still doing here?" she said, her eyes watering. "I said go! *Véte!*"

"But I came here for you!" I screamed, suddenly hysterical. "I've practiced for years, for this, to find you!"

I kept screaming after she slammed the door again. "Please!" I said. "Please just talk to me!" I pounded on the door.

I felt a hand on my shoulder and looked behind me. I immediately recognized Flying Geraldo from the ring, though up close he was not the same man at all. There he had seemed romantic and darkly handsome, but here, in the train car, there was something in his eyes I didn't like, something that reminded me of my father. I backed away.

He looked me over once, quickly. "*Véte, niña!*" he said, and made a shooing motion with his hands.

I walked slowly out onto the lot again, then turned and stared at Lollie's door, at the painted lady swooping on the side of her train car. I felt unbound, completely without anchor. The life I had created in Kansas City was gone, dismantled in an instant and forgotten. Oakley was a million miles away. *This* was my life now, behind that shut door. I could almost *feel* myself unraveling, drifting away.

They don't want me, I thought. Of course they don't. I repeated it to myself, then forced myself to turn away, toward the tent and the midway. The lot was darker now, and trash littered the ground. The circus folk were packing up, tearing down the makeshift kitchens, putting away their tin plates and silverware, and disappearing into the train cars and tents. The Ferris wheel hung over the lot like a giant moon.

I looked around. Ana stood a few train cars down, staring at me, and for a moment relief swept through me. I hesitated, then ran toward her.

"Are you okay?" she asked, as I approached. Her freckle-covered face was friendly, but less so than before. "Why didn't they let you in?"

"Lollie doesn't believe me, I guess, about Mary," I said. "Marionetta. That I knew her. She didn't give me a chance to tell her everything. I mean, I could tell you anything about Marionetta."

"Really?" She looked dazzled. I wished Lollie could be a tenth as easy to win over.

"Sure," I said. "She was my friend."

"Did you hear the story of how she came here?" she asked, smiling. "How Juan Galindo tracked her down and found her covered in ice?"

It was as if she'd called forth Mary, right in front of me. I hadn't heard anyone tell that story besides Mary, and I could practically *hear* Mary's rasping voice. My bravado disappeared instantly. All of a sudden tears welled up in me; I hadn't been prepared for them, and for a second I believed I would faint. I could not understand the sweep of emotion coming over me. I was on edge, anyway.

"Yes," I managed to get out. I could feel my face swelling up with grief and longing.

"Are you okay?" she asked. "Where are you going, anyway?"

"I don't know," I said, and then the tears came, splattering down my face, into my hair, down my shirt, over and under the fabric.

"Don't cry," she said, tentatively putting out her hand to touch me. "I'm sure Lollie will talk to you tomorrow. It's Geraldo, you know. He makes her crazy. That's what my parents say, that he makes her crazy from love. Why don't you just go back in the morning?"

"Yes," I said. I gulped in a breath of air. "I'll do that."

"You could probably go sleep in one of the midway tents," she said. "They'll let anyone stay there, my mom says."

"Thank you," I whispered. And I stumbled away, letting the tears come, not caring that the circus folk continued with their business and didn't pay me any mind at all.

I was as invisible there as I was in Oakley, I thought. I realized, with the certainty of stone against skin, that Mary had been the one person who could see me, the one person who would *ever* see me, or care. All my dreams about the circus had been a lie, I thought; and without them, I was empty.

I wandered off the lot, through the now-deserted big top, past the midway tents and the small crowds still hovering around them.

"Hey, girl!" I heard, and looked up to see the fortune-teller smiling at me.

I waved to her, turning my face quickly so she wouldn't see my red, puffed-up face, my swollen eyes and soaked shirt.

"Wait!" she called.

I ran then, covered in tears, my mouth tasting of salt and wet and heartbreak. The night seemed to pull me into itself, and I just ran and ran, off the lot, out of the field, and toward the railway line I had slept next to the night before.

"Mary!" I screamed, stopping and staring at the night sky, the thousands of stars. "I hate you!"

I let my heart open up to the night and thought of her lying next to me, wrapping my hand inside hers, her corkscrew curls streaming over my shoulder and her voice rasping into the cold air. I thought of her talking of Lollie and the circus, making me feel there would be a place for me there. I thought of her walking straight into the river, all the while knowing that I would be the one left behind.

"I hate you, I hate you, I hate you!" The words wouldn't stop coming. "You left me all alone!"

I was shocked at the strength of my feeling, the anger that raged out of me after all those months of moping and mooning, letting the world go dull and blank. I had never been more alone in my whole life. I could die right then, I realized, and no one would know or care. I thought of Mary healing my wounds and putting me on the trapeze, offering me this world that was just as closed to me as everything else, and I sobbed and thrashed over the ground, wearing myself out. I was a freak. Every single person had been right, except Mary, and she had locked herself up in a library, then drowned herself in a river. She didn't know anything, I thought. I kept remembering my last visit to Mercy Library and the choice I'd made, foolishly, not knowing anything of the world. I imagined the river, the blackness surrounding me, entering my body until the whole world just disappeared, and me with it.

The next thing I knew, I found myself blinking my eyes open and staring up at the sun. I didn't even remember going to sleep. My eyes ached and watered, and my skin was caked with dried tears. Grassy dirt stuck to my legs and arms. Scenes from the night before flooded through me, filling me with grief and anger. For a few minutes I lay there with the sun pounding over me, keeping my eyes closed. My head throbbed. I imagined myself staying there forever, in that same spot, pressing my cheek against the grass. My heart was just an ache in my chest. There was no point in moving, I thought. No point to anything at all.

Finally, after an hour or so had passed, I sighed and started rubbing the grass from my legs. I reached into my bag, pulling out the first bit of material my hands landed upon, and did my best to clean myself up with the lacy skirt, wiping it over my face and rubbing myself pink. I winced at how sore I was, how much it hurt to move. Suddenly I felt something scrape against my cheek, heard a rip, and I stretched out my arm and stared at the ripped-open hem, the thing inside it. I shifted my skirt and the sun caught hold of it, making it burn so brightly I had to shut my eyes.

The ring, I thought. *Mary's ring.*

I pulled the skirt into my lap and crept into the shade, under a tree. My breath was short. I could feel my heart fluttering as I pulled the hem back again and let the colors—every color in the world, it seemed, all packed furiously together—shine out. It was everything beautiful, honed down to the size of a penny.

It hit me then: *this* was what I needed. To show the ring to Lollie. I couldn't believe I hadn't thought of it sooner.

I tucked the ring into the pocket of my skirt, and clasped my palm around it. I stood up and gathered my things.

I walked back to the train, rubbing my eyes and blinking against the light. My grief and anger had exhausted me, hollowed me out, and each step felt like twenty. I could already hear the circus music starting up. In the daylight the Ferris wheel seemed a shadow of its nighttime self, but it still glowed with color. I walked straight through the midway, through the tent, and into the backyard of the lot. I knew people were watching me, that I might get kicked out at any moment, but I was too tired to care. I needed to try again, just to know I'd really done it. There was always the factory, I thought. Always other circuses. Always the river.

I moved past the gathered families, the performers all relaxing, sipping coffee, laughing and talking in the grass with bare faces and ordinary, everyday clothes.

I saw Ana sitting on the steps of one of the many Vadala train cars—white horses galloping across them, one after another, so that ten cars strung together seemed like a whole herd—and waved. She sat with another young girl, larger than she was and maybe slightly older, who otherwise could have been her twin.

"Hello!" she screamed, waving at me. Right away I saw her turn to the larger girl and start talking, pointing.

I saw the flying woman on the side of Lollie's train car and was lit with a new sense of purpose. I walked even more quickly. More and more people turned to watch as I walked by; there must have been something in my face, I thought, something making them sit up and take notice.

Suddenly I wanted to show all of them. If there had been rope strung up across the backyard I would have leapt up right then. *Look*, I would say. *Look what I can do.*

I scurried up the steps and into the car. I knocked on the door and then stood, waiting, for a long, breathless moment. There was no response. Raising my fist, I slammed against the door again and again until I felt my fist fall into air and saw her standing over me.

In the daylight she was just as magnificent as she had been before. Glitter still clung to her cheeks, and her hair was like flames around her face. Her clothes were stark and black, her collar stiff. She looked calmer than she had before, but sad, too, as if she'd been crying.

"You?" she asked. "What are you doing here?"

"I've come because Marionetta sent me," I said. "She told me about you, everything, and I've been waiting so long to find you."

She sighed, before I could say another word. "But I told you . . ."

I drew my hand out of my skirt pocket, unclasped my fingers.

Lollie gasped. I looked at her face, reflected in the lights of the ring, watched as the rays of color hit her with the forces of memory, desire, and regret.

"You know this ring," I said. "You know I knew her."

"Marionetta," she whispered, then looked back up at me with her intense, hazel eyes. "Who are you?"

"Tessa," I said, staring back at her. "Tessa Riley."

"I didn't recognize you," she said, nodding.

"Recognize me?"

"I've seen you before," she whispered, and then she stepped aside and motioned for me to come in. She sat, offering me a seat, and I lowered myself onto a velvet chair lined in gold wood. Leaning toward me then, she placed her hand on my wrist. A speck of glitter fell into my palm. She looked straight into my eyes so long that I had to look down. I had a thousand questions beating at me, but something told me to stay quiet, let her speak first.

Gently, she turned my wrist over and traced my palm with her fingertip. At first her touch felt calming, soothing, and then I felt a tingling on my skin, a strange sense that she could see right into me. I resisted the urge to snatch my hand away.

"You were close to her," she said.

I looked into her face. Wrinkles bled from her red lips, and her eyes were soft with age. She wore layers of makeup, I saw, but it looked like it belonged on her face. Like the movie stars in the magazines Geraldine used to bring home, with their white faces and bloody lips. Lollie's shoulders dropped slightly as she looked down at me.

"She's dead," I said.

"Yes."

The ring still beat in my hand, and I clamped my fingers over it, shoved it into my pocket again. "I should have known," I said, without realizing it. "I should have seen it." The words seemed to come out of me on their own. A strange urge moved through me, to tell her things, and I was furious at myself for talking about Mary that way. I didn't want this to be about Mary, I thought. I didn't want to be thinking of her all the time.

"You couldn't have," Lollie said. "When I was a child I *saw* my brother fall from the wire before it happened, and even then I couldn't stop it. The future is full and alive, like a beating heart, but that doesn't mean you can change it."

I nodded, looked out the window of her car and toward the Ferris wheel. I watched it spin around and around, imagined sitting at the top of it and staring down at everything.

"It wasn't an accident with Mary," I said. "It's different."

"It's our fate," Lollie said, folding my hand and setting it on my lap. "It doesn't matter how it comes to us, how it shows itself."

I looked around then, at the little crucifix hanging on her wall, the Virgin statues lined up on her dresser, the rosary beads hanging from her doorknob. An image of my mother came to my mind, her fingers moving down the length of beads, her lips whispering feverishly. The big top swayed in the wind. I felt a tear slip down my cheek and realized I was too sad, too beaten up, to care.

I could have stopped her, a voice said inside me. *You have to pay attention in this world, or things will slip away.*

"She taught me the trapeze," I said suddenly, turning back to Lollie. "That's why I've come here."

"You look so tired, *niña,*" Lollie said, placing her hand on mine and sending that same strange tingling feeling over my skin. "Why don't you take a nap and I'll wake you for lunch? I have an extra compartment."

I realized suddenly how exhausted I was from all the waiting and longing and sleeping on the ground, all the days pricking my fingers with needles in the factory, all the sadness that had sunk into my bones.

"Thank you," I said, nodding. When I stood up my head spun, and I was woozy with relief.

Lollie made us a pot of rose-petal tea and prepared a bed for me then. I fell back onto the mattress and felt I could never leave it.

Still, I did not fall asleep right away. I lay in the bed watching Lollie's costumes shimmer in the dim sunlight creeping through the curtains—from the bed I could see some of the bright banners that decorated and lined the midway. I could hear voices and all kinds of activity just outside the metal of the train car: people dumping pails of water, dragging equipment over the ground, roasting meat over crackling fires, walking in groups under my window.

I lay with my face toward the ceiling, and I stretched my body out in the soft bed. Sleep descended on me in black clouds, but my eyes stayed open. It was too much for me. I was at the circus. It was like falling in love for the first time with something you believe is in your grasp and can change everything.

I woke to the sound of a man yelling. For a moment I thought I was in my parents' house again, in the bed my father had carved for me. I thought I'd dreamt everything until a man stormed through the small door and into my room.

I jumped up.

The noon sun streamed in through the train-car windows. Before I could even register where I was, Geraldo pressed into the room.

"What is this girl?" he yelled, in a thick Spanish accent, turning to look behind him. Lollie appeared in the doorway then. She looked different than she had the night before—less haughty, less dreamy, more afraid.

I sat up in bed and looked up into his flashing black eyes.

"What are you? Why did you come here?" he said.

Lollie raced in behind him and pulled him from the doorway. She slammed the door between our compartments shut, and I could hear the two of them shouting.

"She knew Marionetta," I heard her say. "Leave her alone."

"When were you going to tell me about this? What, she just suddenly appears one night and is in your car the next morning?"

"Just for a day or two."

His voice spilled over the doorway and invaded every corner of my little room. It traveled along the back of my neck, making the hairs stand on end, making me want to bury myself in the earth.

"Get out of here!" I heard her scream. "Back to your *putanas!*"

His voice was like a tree falling. And then I heard tears, and more tears.

"I'm sorry, Tessa," Lollie said later. "Don't mind Geraldo. He is a great, passionate man, an artist. You'll see."

I just looked at her, with a clenched heart. Geraldo could do anything, I thought then, as long as he didn't make me leave the circus. I *had* to stay. I had to find a way to show them what I could do.

"Come," she said. "I'll show you around the lot."

We left the train car and headed toward the big top. Lollie waved at the performers spread out on the grass but kept walking. "Many of us practice there during the day," she said, tilting her head at the canvas. A man walked by us with a sack full of garbage and a stick. We neared the smaller menagerie tent, and Lollie led me inside. I gasped at the tigers in their gilded wagon cages, the elephants tied to poles, the horses in their pens.

"That's Julia," Lollie said, pointing toward a sleek tiger that was sprawled across the floor of her cage. She reached in her hand and petted the tiger, as if it were a kitten. When I did the same, I was surprised at the warmth seeping into my skin, the softness of it.

We stayed for a few minutes with the animals, looking at the snow-white coats of the Vadala horses, so creamy-looking you wanted to run your tongue against them. Then Lollie led me to the midway, over the perimeter of the lot.

"We don't spend too much time around here," she said, "but you might as well see it. There's a tattooed man who hates the sight of his skin so much he covered himself with images of ships and sailors. He has whole cityscapes spreading across his broad back and sweeping down his arms. See?" She pointed to a hulk of a man emerging from a tent right then. From where I was, he seemed to be covered in bruises.

"And that's Clementine." She pointed to the left, and I turned. It was the bird girl, shaking her wings out, airing them in the sunlight. She was so beautiful with her starlight hair and red lips, the wings hanging off her shimmering pale skin and folding along her waist and thighs.

"She can't be anywhere near a pool without her wings sticking together so badly she can't move," Lollie whispered. "Her wings are like a giant ache on her back. She has to spend all day lying on her stomach before heaving herself up and wiggling into her sequined top and skirt. She dreams about water.

"Usually I don't know so much about the sideshow performers," Lollie added. "They keep to themselves. But Clementine and my youngest brother Mauro used to be in love. Quite a scandal." She winked at me.

As we turned toward the cookhouse, a makeshift kitchen and group of tables covered by a tarp, I saw four beautiful men standing in front of it. I recognized them instantly.

"My brothers," Lollie said.

Carlos, Paulo, José, and Mauro were perfect gentlemen as they introduced themselves to me, each more handsome than the last. They all had the same black hair that Lollie did, and curving, lush bodies. "Bodies like fruit trees," I thought, before recognizing the words from one of Mary's

stories. I could barely look at them. I felt like the child Costas, the kiwi-
eyed boy who'd come upon all the wonders of the world at once.

"The Flying Ramirez Brothers," they were called, on the wire or the
ground and in their stretched-out white sequined costumes, cut low in
the front to expose their glistening brown chests. I would learn later that
in the part of Mexico they came from, the Ramirez Brothers were the
stuff of legend, and girls still described beautiful boys as "almost a
Ramirez," or "able to walk on steel wires."

"They'll take good care of you," Lollie said. "Maybe you'll meet my
other brother someday, too. Luis."

My head spun as we went into the cookhouse and sat down. The
brothers' white teeth, pale-coffee skin, and ink-black hair dazzled me. I
could not tell them apart as I looked up at them. Lollie stayed by my
side, her hand resting lightly on my shoulder as we sat down on the
wooden picnic bench.

"It is wonderful that you're here," said the oldest one, Carlos, reaching forward and placing his hand on mine. I tried to snatch my hand
back, but he clasped it with his own. "Lollie says she knew about you,
but she never told any of us about it."

I looked at her, surprised.

"Yes," José jumped in—José, whose hair in later years would turn
white as flame. "Tell us how you got here."

Lollie laughed. "We're thirsty for stories! Whenever news comes
from the outside, we all gather around, and you can hear everyone chattering like birds for days after."

Mauro ran up to the cook and brought back plates of grilled meat
and rice. The talk was easy; before I knew it the whole cookhouse had
filled with circus people, many of whom I'd met on the way over or seen
in the show the night before. I settled a bit into my skin and let myself
enjoy the warmth of all of them around me at once. I told them about

my nights by the railroad, waiting for them, my months working in the factory, where the machines hummed like insects. I surprised myself with how sure my voice sounded. I watched Lollie's face, then looked to Carlos, with his great big hands; Mauro, the youngest, whose sweet eyelashes curled from his almond-shaped eyes; Paulo, my future teacher, with hair flopping in his face and down his neck; and the bad one, José, with his murderer's hand and quick, passionate heart. Soon the brothers would come into focus for me, and I would never mistake one for the other the way I did those first days.

"Did you know, Tessa," Paulo leaned in, "that Lollie saved my life with her vision? Once I was going to ride a black Arabian called Diablo, who would have shaken me off his back like water if Lollie hadn't stopped me from going to the stables herself. After Luis I wouldn't risk it. She could tell me to stay off the wire forever, and I would."

"I can still feel it," Lollie said, "You know, visions don't fade the way memories do. They become part of what you are."

"Mary told me you could see things," I said. "She said it gave her goose bumps to listen to you."

At the sound of her name, everyone turned to me. I remembered what Ana had said in the train car: that all the circus people told stories about Mary.

"She is dead," I wanted to say. "When she died there were leaves tangled in her hair, and I had to pick them out one by one."

But I did not speak.

"Did you know Mary well, Tessa?" Mauro asked quietly.

I had no voice to answer him with. A black hole gaped in me where Mary had been, one that swallowed all my speech. I could feel the blood rushing to my face, my hands fluttering against my plate.

Mauro placed his hand over mine the way Carlos had earlier. But Mauro's touch steadied my hand in an instant.

I looked up at him.

"Yes," I said finally, after a long pause. "I did. I thought I knew everything about her."

I could barely breathe. Mauro stared at me intently, as they all did.

"You know," Lollie said slowly, brushing her hand over mine, "I remember the day she showed up here as if it were just a moment ago, just this morning."

"Really?" I asked. I hadn't realized how much I, too, craved to hear about her, who she was and had been.

By now it seemed that everyone in the cookhouse was gathered around our table or sitting quietly at their own, listening. I was surprised to see Ana at the next table, next to the ringmaster, who was barely recognizable in his sweatshirt and jeans. She waved at me and smiled.

"Oh, yes," Lollie said, laughing. Her laugh cracked her face open until she was more like a girl swinging from a tree over a creek than a regal circus star. "Marionetta. Men used to drop wedding rings outside her door. Movie stars sent her garlands of roses, which she'd dump in the trash bins outside. She was never interested in men like that. Mary had only two loves in her life, William and Juan Galindo. That was how she first came to the circus. She followed Juan here. 'Who is she?' we asked. 'She is a like a dog,' he said."

"'Like a dog.'" I laughed.

"That's what love makes of us," said José.

"Well, I took her in," Lollie continued. "I never liked Juan. For ten years straight he was the star of the Flying Ramirez Brothers. Though his family's name was Galindo, Juan used the name of my grandfathers to spread his own fame until he became the most sought-after, popular star here, even more so than Geraldo is now."

"And women sell clay sculptures of Geraldo in the villages we pass through," Carlos added.

I marveled at the idea of Mary going crazy for such a man, then re-membered Lollie with Geraldo just that morning. If that was love, then I didn't want any part of it.

"So I despised Juan, of course, and was ecstatic at the opportunity Mary presented to me. I could see past what Juan saw—and all he could see was the ice that had melted from Mary's body as soon as he came near it. I saw it all pass before me: Mary, her waist pressed to the bar, her hands gripped around it, whirling and whirling until she was free and flying toward the ground."

"You wouldn't have known it to see her," Carlos interrupted, look-ing across the table at me. "She seemed too wild, way too wild for the trapeze."

"Even my own brothers didn't believe it when I said she would be a great flyer," Lollie continued, laughing. "But I took her in and tried everything to rid her of the smell of spices. I burned her clothes, and I ruined her hair with combs until it swept down her back like feathers. I scrubbed her face and rubbed it with lemon juice, but even the bath-water she soaked in became infused with the scents of clove and cin-namon, and we'd have to drain the water and spend hours rinsing and scrubbing the wooden tub."

When I looked up, I saw the memories coloring all of their faces. Ana sat with her head craned toward Lollie, her face so rapt that she did not notice my gaze. Lollie was like Mary, I realized then: a storyteller. I would come to realize that all of them were.

"But the crowds of people who came to the circus did not seem to mind her scent at all. We heard stories of women who'd return home and brew up vats of hot cider steeped in cinnamon sticks, or put out bowls filled with oranges stuck through with cloves. Men stood outside our trailer for whole days, waiting to catch a glimpse of her. I became used to Mary's scents more quickly than the others, probably because I loved her the most. We were able to laugh with each other and talk late into the night, and we would cook long dinners, wrapping every kind of vegetable in foil and roasting them in a bonfire out back. I listened to her stories on those nights, nights when we sat under the sky watching the moon and counting our wishes on the stars."

"She told the most wonderful stories," I said, quietly.

"Yes," Lollie said, smiling over at me, "she did. Mary and I became as close as sisters during those long talks by the bonfire, until the rest of the circus came to accept her, eventually, the way I had. Her scent came to seem warm and rich, like a jar of honey standing in sunlight, so much so that my trailer became a gathering place where we all met for cups of tea or games of cards spread out over blankets and across mattresses—everyone, that is, except for Juan Galindo, who would call her a devil woman and murderer to his dying day. I never did learn what happened between Juan and Mary in that long walk back to the Velasquez Circus, through the snow and ice, but Juan would have allowed himself to grow old and loveless before he'd take a step in Mary's direction of his own free will, and that was what he did. He faded so quickly that within five years of Mary coming he had left both the Flying Ramirez Brothers and the center ring, and he took to wandering the towns we passed through, staring into shop windows at young girls with yellow hair."

Mauro laughed. "Sometimes a local would lead him back to us," he interrupted, "dropping him off in their cars or trucks or leading him by the hand. Sometimes one of the yellow-haired girls would pull up near the tent, and we'd learn that Juan had been following her through town all afternoon, or that he'd been singing outside her window until she could no longer bear the sound of it."

"It was pathetic," José said to me over the table, in low tones, "for a man who had once been great."

"He was always pathetic," Carlos added. "Then he just shriveled up and went away. It was like all the life had gone straight out of him."

"Oh, but in his day, Tessa," Lollie said, smiling at me, "just watching Juan for a moment was enough to break the world apart. When he burst upon that haystack Mary was sleeping in, Juan Galindo must have seemed like a flame."

Lollie stopped then, her eyes glowing and wet.

"It is strange how one moment can change a life," she said softly, after a long pause, "one moment that rears up on its hind legs to knock you to your feet."

Mauro reached over and clasped her hand. "We never understood when she left," he whispered to me. "She just seemed to fall apart, and then she was gone."

He looked up at me through his curving eyelashes, and I realized he was waiting for me to speak.

Her words echoed in my mind: *I had visions of people following me, hunting me down.* But I could not speak of her.

"We are sorry, Tessa," he said, finally.

"Yes," I said, and wondered if I had ever really known Mary at all.

Soon we could hear the talkers calling out that night's ballies over the din of the clanging pots and pans, using every trick of voice and turn of phrase to lure the townies into the tents where the moss-haired girl flipped her head back for the thousandth time, the fat lady tilted back and forth, letting the ripples of her body spill out behind her, and the reptile boy removed his shirt and let the people sigh or swoon or spit in disgust. You could feel the difference in the air, the way the excitement rode through it like a giant wave, and soon everyone began scattering to prepare for that night's show.

The same electricity crackled through the air as the night before: the groan of the Ferris wheel gearing up, townspeople meeting up with their friends and heading toward the field in groups, coins jangling in their pockets. But I was not part of it that night. I was silent as Lollie and I walked back to the train, and I do not think she minded, herself lost in memory and regret.

"I'm going to lie down and rest," I said, when we reached the car.

"Yes," she said. Then, after a pause, "I know you miss her, Tessa," she said. "I can see her in you."

"Thank you," I said, feeling the tears beating against my heart.

Inside, I spread myself over the mattress. I tried to focus on Lollie's creams and perfumes that lined the little dresser, but her voice curled around me, filling my vision with images of Mary roasting vegetables with Lollie or following Juan Galindo in the snow. She too must have felt comforted once, a long time before, knowing Lollie was close by. I shook the image off me. I saw the opal ring shimmering against Mary's breast, with its thousands of colors. No! I thought quickly of Mauro's curving eyelashes, his black eyes looking out at me through them, but then blinked the image away, furious.

It had been one year since I'd found Mary in the river, I realized then, and I had never, in all the time I'd been away, shared her with anyone else, never heard anyone else even speak her name.

Now stories of her colored the air, drifted across the camps that spread over the field, behind the midway and big top. She was part of the air we breathed. They had all held her name on their lips, had all whispered it in their sleep, just as I had.

Tears slipped over my face. I gulped for air.

I had not spoken of Mary either, not to anyone. I had not spoken of her in the factory, or as I'd passed through the city streets, clamping my hands over my ears to muffle the clanging of the trucks and streetcars, or as I'd waited by the train tracks, dreaming of a new life. The times I'd tried with Geraldine had been miserable failures. To speak of her now, with people who had known her and people she herself had described for me, was too confusing, too strange, and I did not think I could do it, though I knew that the Ramirezes longed to hear of her, what her life had been like. They all did, all the people in the circus, and for the ones who hadn't known her, like Ana, Mary was a legend that swirled through their lives and made them yearn for spice scents and coils of black hair and rivers filled with pink fish.

Even Lollie longed to hear about Mary, though she herself had felt Mary's life throughout the years. I came to understand that Lollie had felt Mary's life in bits, in slivers of images or scents or dreams, not in whole slices as if she'd been there. For Lollie, the world was not open and transparent, like a sheet of glass. Every seer has lapses and gaps, I would learn, moments when the world does not offer itself but lies as flat as a sketch before her. Lollie could feel Mary's heart in moments, feel her leafing through books and shuffling through documents that she would drop into thick files, feel her staring out the library windows during all those long hours she was alone, remembering the feel of rain streaming down her skin, the tang of the river, the mud that sucked at her feet, the pattering and plinking that never stopped. Lollie had felt the pain that had pulsed through Mary's veins, but I, who had been right there with her, hadn't understood or seen it at all.

How could I put her into words? How could I describe the way she walked into a room, the way she boiled cabbage and ham for our lunches, the way she picked me out in front of the courthouse and told me about the star particles in my fingernails? Or the way the stale smell of books and papers and ink was part of what she had been for me, along with the thousands of words and phrases and stories we had shared, the spooky old ballads, the stories of unhappy peasant girls and of boys coming into the world for the first time, the long, meandering scenes set in meadows spotted with wildflowers. She had given me language that could describe feeling and beauty and love, but I could not use it to bring her back to me. And it would not make up for the fact that she was, like everything else, fading away—and no huddle of words could take her place.

When I closed my eyes and tried to imagine her, I saw a woman with ice-ravaged skin, soaking in a bath of cinnamon-scented water.

I could not remember her as I'd known her.

I stayed in bed as Lollie spread glitter through her hair and across her skin, and during her performance that night. I watched the lights bobbing up and down through my window.

Later, Lollie brought sandwiches to me that I let dry up on their plates. When she came in and out of my compartment, she did not make a sound.

"I think I am dying," I whispered to Lollie as she moved through the room.

"Yes, I know," she said. "But you aren't. You are a strong girl, Tessa. You are stronger than she was, even."

CHAPTER THIRTEEN

The circus played in Kansas City for only three nights before moving on. On the third night, after the last show, the roustabouts swarmed around the tent and tore it down. From the train car, I watched the big top fall like a cake just out of the oven. I had my small sack of things with me in Lollie's compartment, but everyone else seemed to become part of a military operation—tearing apart makeshift camps, pulling in lines of laundry stretching from the train windows to the trees outside, dismantling the tents and booths in the midway, compressing everything into the trucks the sideshow traveled in or onto the circus wagons that would be hoisted from the ground to the flatcars using ramps and rigging. They had it down to a science: when those trucks and wagons were packed tight, I'm not sure a penny could have traveled from one end of the car to another without getting stuck somewhere.

It would be the last time I would sit around on a night like that, not knowing what to do with myself. Everyone pitched in, even Lollie and her brothers and Flying Geraldo. I heard voices everywhere and watched, fascinated, as the whole miniature city outside my window folded itself up under the moonlight and disappeared. The Ferris wheel collapsed and the lights popped off and the train shifted and expanded like a living thing.

Less elaborate, the midway took half the time to tear down, and, one by one, the sideshow trucks—some of them plain, others draped in banners and painted with lurid advertisements for the performers inside—roared off into the darkness.

I was lured out of the train car into the night, despite myself, just as they were loading the menagerie back onto the flatbeds. The whole night was filled with voices and the scratching and squealing of wagons being pulled across metal planks. By then most of the cars had been loaded back onto the train—filled with the equipment, the tents and big top, the cookhouse, the seat wagons and stock cars, all stacked before the performers' cars, which varied wildly in size and quality—and the only thing left was to drop the menagerie tent and roll the animal's cages back onto the flatbeds, too. No one even seemed to see me as I slipped from the steps to the ground.

The roustabouts shouted and pulled while others scoured the lot for anything left behind or started piling into the cars. The menagerie was the most difficult part to load, out of everything, and other men stepped forward to help push and pull up the wagons with the big cats and then lead in the two elephants, who strained the ropes so badly I thought the cords would break. It was spooky, looking out over the empty, dark field, the autumn leaves scattered in patches over the grass. It gave me the feeling I was completely alone in the world. The roars and bellows of the animals seemed surreal, like something out of a dream.

"Tessa!" a voice called, and I looked over to see Lollie approaching the car. I was suddenly terrified: She's going to ask me to leave now, I thought. I remembered what she'd said to Geraldo, and my heart stopped. *Just for a day or two.*

She wore working clothes that were smeared with dirt. "You're up! We were loading the rigging; you can never trust these guys to do it right. Are you feeling better?"

I nodded and stared at her, afraid to speak.

"Well, we can settle in, then. You're coming with us to the next place, no?"

"Yes," I said, relieved. Yes.

I went back into the little room. Soon I could feel the train wheeze to a start, then lurch into a steady, chugging rhythm. I sat on my little bed and stared out the window at the fading lot and the branches that seemed to reach out toward the train and try to grab us. It was mesmerizing: the forests and fields, the little towns and cities, all of them blurring past on the outside, lit by the moon or streetlamps, while I sat snug on the bed, alone in the dark.

I heard a tapping on the door, and Lollie walked in. "Why don't you turn a light on in here?" She laughed.

"I like it this way," I said. "Looking out the window. It feels safe."

She smiled, then came over and sat on the bed next to me. For a few minutes we sat in silence, staring out the window at the rushing branches, the looming trees. The train chugged and rumbled under us.

I knew I had to say something, stake my claim. "Lollie," I said finally, "how can I be part of the circus? I want to stay here, to perform."

"Perform?"

"Mary taught me a lot. I can do the trapeze and some rope stuff. I can twirl and do tricks, hang from my knees and ankles."

She didn't seem convinced. "Well, you know," she said, after a long pause, "that may take time. Normally people don't just start performing unless they were born to it. But there are plenty of ways to join the circus: cleaning the horses, selling candy, helping the roustabouts . . . though you might be a bit young for that, a bit small."

The town outside seemed to whoosh by. The streetlamps blurred together and made me blink.

"But Mary did," I said. "She joined the circus. From outside."

"That's true," she said. "But not at first. She had to practice and learn, and she did menial work before she got up there in the ring." She paused and pulled her knees up to her chest, wrapping her arms around them. "So you learned the trapeze, did you? From her?"

I nodded. I was dying to tell her about the space we'd made between the shelves, the magic of that trapeze gliding back and forth under the wooden ceiling beams, but I kept silent.

"Well, why don't you show us what you can do, then? After we set up tomorrow, before the show? In the meantime, we can maybe talk to Mr. Velasquez about keeping you on for a bit, helping out. It's a lot of hard work, though, Tessa, and we're constantly moving."

"Yes," I said. "But I don't mind, I wouldn't mind at all. I have nowhere else to go."

She laughed and leaned into me. "Maybe you're more of a circus girl than I thought."

That night I barely slept, between the clanging and bumping and the nervousness that took hold in my gut. I knew that Lollie was humoring me, but I was determined to show her that I was good enough to perform—and determined to make myself as indispensable as possible. I stared out the window at the fleeting towns and countryside. As soon as the train screeched to a halt early the next morning, somewhere in the middle of Oklahoma, I leapt out of bed, ready to work.

Oklahoma seemed like another world. Oakley and Kansas City were the only places I knew, and on the new lot the landscape seemed scrubbed dry, reddish in spots. The world seemed wider, sadder, but within minutes we put our stamp upon it, and then it was transformed.

We worked all morning. The wagons were rolled off the flatcars and the menagerie was reassembled outside the tent for townfolk to exclaim over for the price of a quarter. I heard the lions and elephants and shivered with excitement—nothing could make me feel farther away from Oakley than that sound.

We ate lunch in the cookhouse, tired and sweaty, having helped to remake the lot until it seemed like that land had always had a huge blue tent rising out of it, a Ferris wheel whirring next to the sky.

"So," Lollie said, setting down her fork, "Tessa is going to show us her trapeze skills a little later. In an hour, maybe?" She looked at me. "That should give us time before the show."

I could feel my face turn red, feel all their eyes on me.

There was silence, and then Mauro was the one who spoke. "Great," he said, winking at me. The rest of them kept eating. I glanced up and saw both José and Ana look quickly away.

I would later learn how opposed they all were to letting in someone new, how they saw themselves as inhabitants of the air and everyone outside the circus as rooted in the earth, like vines.

That hour crawled by. I locked myself in my compartment and stretched my legs and torso, moved my arms around to get them loose and burning. For the first time, I wondered what I would do— what I could possibly do—if I failed. I thought of all the months I'd wasted in Kansas City, and cursed myself.

When the time came, I changed into the leotard Mary had given me and entered the big top.

The trapeze swooped up above me, right in the center of empty space. I would have to climb a long ladder to a platform to reach it. I was used to Mary's trapeze, hanging from a beam in a jam-packed library, and the length of rope hanging from a tree by the river—not this elaborate contraption made of metal and pulleys, stretching down from the top of the tent, swinging in empty space. A gleaming silver net stretched out underneath like something hauled up from the sea.

My whole body was shaking. I looked up at Lollie and all her brothers, and noticed then how many more people were gathering close to the tent.

I had to do it, to go up there. If I could just catch the bar, I'd be fine. Lollie looked at me. "Go on. You can't be shy here," she said.

"Privacy is something you have to give up," Carlos said, winking at me. "Especially if you come as a friend of Marionetta's."

Outside, I could hear the midway starting up, the people beginning to come in. The air had that electric quality, and I could hear the buzzing of the lights, the Ferris wheel spinning round.

This was my one chance.

The bird girl Clementine was in the tent now, I saw, talking to Mauro. Ana and her family stood huddled on the other side. I caught Ana's eye and she waved, just as the Kriminov Twins, a brother-and-sister team from Romania, slipped in and sat on the bleachers.

"Don't worry," Paulo whispered, leaning down. "They're all curious because of Marionetta. Just show us what you can do."

I breathed in. I went to the ladder and climbed up, feeling as if someone else were navigating that thin, narrow contraption instead of me. Slowly, rung by rung, I watched the ground pull away, woozily.

As I stepped onto the platform, I swooned for a second, with nausea.

Paulo climbed onto the platform opposite. He reached out and grabbed the trapeze. "Hep!" he called, throwing it out to me.

His voice was the first thing that threw me off. I reached for the bar, leaping out a second too late. For a moment there was nothing in the world but that bar looming in front of me—until I looked down at the net. I hesitated again, froze, and when I lunged for the bar, I was several seconds too late. My hands stretching out, I fell down to the net, which reached up and smacked my neck and face and legs.

"Are you okay?" Lollie rushed over. "Are you hurt?"

The ropes burned and slashed my skin. I couldn't think.

Mauro pulled the net back and leapt into it, then swept me up and into him.

"Can you move your neck, Tessa?" he whispered, looking right down at me. Even in a state like that—burning with shame, bruised and cut—I was taken aback by him, his beauty. When I didn't answer, he cupped his hand under my neck and pressed his fingertips into my skin, cradling my head with his other hand. He gently moved my head back and forth, then reached over and patted down my legs. The only man I had ever been that close to was my father. I stared up at him, confused.

"She's fine," he pronounced, looking down at everyone to the sides. I didn't realize then how badly the net could hurt you, if you took a bad fall into it. Coming at you in the wrong way, the rope could feel like tiny knives. If you fell at the wrong angle, it could break your neck.

At that moment I could barely feel anything but his palm under my skin.

"You're okay, Tessita," he said. "You want to get out of this thing?"

I nodded, and with one long shift of his body he moved both of us to the side, then held me to his chest with one arm as we jumped down to the ground.

"Don't worry about it," Lollie said, comforting me. "You're not used to the big top. You can try again in a few days."

But I saw that their anticipation had waned. The twins had already left, along with Carlos and about half of the Vadalas. They had expected a pupil of Marionetta and had seen a girl who couldn't even catch the bar. "I want to try again now," I said, staring straight at Lollie.

She looked surprised but nodded.

They have no idea, I thought, what this body can endure.

Paulo ascended again and threw out the bar to me. This time I leapt out and grabbed it, even managed to pull myself up into it before being hit with the empty space around me. From the air, it was even worse than from the ground. Nothing could have prepared me for the way it felt being suspended over nothing, for that one bar to be the only thing in the world keeping you up there. The bar scraped under my legs where the net had cut into me.

Stop being a coward, I said to myself. *Stop being such a freak.* But my hands would not let go of the ropes on either side of me. I could feel every pair of eyes on me, pinning me to the spot. I looked down at the net and felt my eyes fill with tears.

"Let's get her down from there," I heard Mauro say.

Without even hesitating, Paulo leapt out onto a second trapeze and swung out to me. I winced as he approached, but then I felt his arm wrap smoothly around me, whisking me off the bar and into the air. As I heard Lollie yelling for him to be careful, I squeezed my eyes shut and tried not to cry.

When I opened them, I was on the ground, shaking with shame and confusion. I looked up at the bar swinging over us, and then, just behind it, I saw a rope hung up in the top rigging.

My heart leapt desperately. "That!" I said, pointing, hearing the crowds outside, seeing almost everyone else leave. "Let me try that, just for a minute."

Paulo rolled his eyes. "We're out of time," he said. "Just try again another time. Get used to the feel of it."

"We have to get ready now, really," Lollie said.

"Just for one second," I said. "Please. You'll see." Tears ran down my face.

It was Mauro who shrugged his shoulders and asked, "Why not? Let's go."

He unpinned the rope that was hooked into the ground, then maneuvered it down, the way the roustabouts did during the shows. It unfurled, then dropped to the ground like a woman's braid.

I walked purposefully to the rope. I looked up into Mauro's black eyes, then over at Lollie's hazel ones. I blocked out everyone, everything else but Mauro, Lollie, and the rope in front of me.

I grabbed it and shimmied my way up. I could feel the air in the room change as I stopped with my feet about five feet off the floor, as I released my body until I was dangling from the rope by one hand. I twisted the cord around my wrist once, then flung my body up into one of the windmills I had perfected by the river alone. The swing-over.

I was reduced to one motion, over and over. I poured all my rage and sorrow and hope into that one motion: the swing up and back down again, the rotation of the shoulder as it moved out of its socket and back in again. Excruciating, but not the worst kind of pain, not by far.

I did twenty swing-overs in a row. When I dropped to the ground and looked up into Lollie's face, and then Mauro's, I was stunned to see that they were in tears.

"My God, Tessa," Lollie said, after a few minutes. "Where did you learn to do that? Did Mary teach you that?"

I shook my head.

Mauro just stared at me. I could still feel his palm on my neck, and I looked down, embarrassed.

My shoulders felt like they'd been hacked through. The cuts and scrapes pulsed all over my body, from the net.

Mauro looked down at me. His face lit. "You know how beautiful that was, don't you? You are weightless, a blur of light. And the strength you have in that tiny body of yours. Unbelievable."

I blushed down to my toes, beamed in spite of myself.

We could hear the crowds outside, pressing up on us, anxious for the show to begin. The roustabouts started coming into the tent then, cleaning and prepping it, while the concession-stand vendors started setting up the carts that sold popcorn balls and cotton candy and sweet fizzling sodas. I felt like everything about the circus that night reflected the excitement shooting through me. I was an electrical current, one of the lights popping on and off along the midway.

Lollie whispered something to Mauro, then smiled and hugged me. "Wait here," she said a moment later, running off and leaving me alone with him.

"What's she doing?" I asked.

"I think she wants to get the others," Mauro said. He looked in the direction she'd gone. "But we're incredibly late already. So impatient. She doesn't want to wait till later. We've been working on the aerial acts for a while, Tessita."

A moment later Lollie rushed back into the tent—still in her pants, without makeup—with her brother Carlos and a tall, thin man I hadn't seen before.

She was almost breathless as she introduced the man. "Jorge Velasquez," she said. I knew who he was instantly; once a world-famous acrobat, he was now the manager and owner of the Velasquez Circus, founded by his grandfather. He looked delicate and shy to those who didn't know better, but, I would learn, he was as tough as they come.

Mr. Velasquez looked me over suspiciously as he took my hand. He had to dip down so low he was almost squatting.

"This can't wait?" Mr. Velasquez asked, annoyed, standing up and glancing at Lollie. "I've got a sick clown and a goddamned lazy fucking ringmaster I'm red-lighting after this show, I swear to Christ. And now my knees are going to fucking give out."

Carlos was half in his makeup and half out of it. He had on his sparkling performance tights with a T-shirt over them.

Lollie gestured to me, exasperated. "You have to see this, Jorge," she said. "Now."

Turning to me, she softened. "Can you do that—just the exact same thing—one more time?"

I looked up and saw the concession girl staring at me. I turned to Mr. Velasquez and, for a moment, thought of my father.

"Yes," I said, feeling rage bubble up in me.

I shimmied up and did it again—only fifteen this time, but enough. I'm not sure I could have pulled off any other trick at that moment, but the swing-over was *mine*, the trick that cleansed and renewed me, that pushed me past the filth of the world and into a place where I could forget. After each turn I clenched my teeth and thought, "One more. Just one more." I pushed and fell and turned, not caring if my arm ripped from my shoulder at the socket. I just went and went. By the time I dropped to the floor, I was exhausted.

Mr. Velasquez simply looked at me and nodded. "Can you do that again in one hour?"

Before I could answer, Lollie stepped forward and said, "No."

Mauro nodded his head in a agreement. "Look at her," he said. "She's exhausted."

"She's not ready," Lollie said. "Look at her wrists." She took my arm gently and lifted my burned, bloody wrist into the light. "I thought she might be, but she's not. Not yet. We're going to have to fix this, fix up the rope with some padding and loops so she doesn't knock herself up so much." She turned to me. "How long have you been doing this?"

"A while," I said. "I just started again last spring."

"With just a rope?"

I nodded.

"Crazy *chica*," she said, shaking her head.

Mr. Velasquez sighed. "Can you do the trapeze, ladder, rings, silks?" he asked.

"Everything," I lied.

"Next season, then," he said, turning to Carlos before abruptly leaving the room. "Make sure she's ready."

Lollie laughed out loud and hugged me then.

Carlos reached out and took my hand.

Mauro leaned in and whispered in my ear. "That trick will make you famous," he said.

After that it was a mad dash back to the train cars, for them to get ready before the show. Lollie grabbed my hand and I sat with her as she slipped on a soft purple costume that caught the dim trailer light and cast it about the walls.

"You'll need to dream up some costumes now, too," she laughed, as she streaked her eyes with pencil and glitter.

I caught a glimpse of myself in her mirror. With the Ferris wheel lit up behind me and Lollie in front of me, as glamorous as a movie star, I looked radiant. My eyes were bright blue and my face flushed and pretty.

"Thank you, Lollie," I said.

"No," she said. "Thank *you*. I had no idea."

When I ran out with her toward the tent, the show was already about a third over. We ducked through the opening in back and stayed behind the main curtain, along with the other performers who had yet to go on. I noticed then how everyone was looking at me and whispering. The brothers all walked over together and shook my hand, and even Geraldo gave me a short nod. Ana ran up and wrapped her arms around my waist.

"I'm so happy you're staying!" she said.

It was an unreal feeling, and I just let it wash over me.

CHAPTER FOURTEEN

Everything seemed to change after that. Every morning I sat up in the train car and looked around, astonished that it hadn't all vanished as I slept, the lot swarming with life outside my window, the Ferris wheel and the banners. All of it. I could step from the trailer and be in this world that was so ragtag and so glamorous, everyone spread over the lot, talking and laughing and working and cooking and sewing, and then, beyond it, the sideshow, which was its own separate world, equally wonderful. All these things that seemed so unreal were just how I lived now, I realized. I was constantly feeling like I was in a dream, like I was a character in a book I'd read. I thought of the poem Mary had read me once, "The Lady of Shallot," and how I had *felt* that river, that look of Lancelot, while the rest of the world had slipped away. I walked slowly, feeling the sequins on the costumes hanging in Lollie's closet, leaning down to touch the grass on the lot, the sawdust in the tent. I'd walk into the menagerie, smell the thick scent of animals, feel the fur through the steel cages.

No one would ever have believed it, that little Tessa Riley could be part of such a world, or that I would heading to Mexico for the winter to train with the rest of the circus folk. There were only two weeks left until the end of the season, and the new one wouldn't begin until spring.

Some of the performers left for other shows and returned the following spring, Lollie explained to me, while others stuck around, performing in the scaled-down winter shows throughout that part of the world. From December to March of each year the circus worked that way, with most of the performers using the time to settle down into normal lives and prepare themselves for the next season. Many of them met each day at the tents to prepare new acts or perfect old ones before the next season began. The Velasquez Circus holed up in Mexico City, while the Ramirezes retreated to their family villa just outside it and rode in each day to practice. Mary had never explained the intricacies of circus life, and I listened carefully.

There was much work for me to do, Lollie said. The trapeze was the main act of any aerial troupe, so it was important that I become as comfortable flying as I was on the ropes. There were several other aerial acts I could probably master in time for the next season, she said, if I were willing to train with them through the winter. I tried to wrap my mind around it, the idea of living in Mexico, another country, with these people who glittered and shimmered as they moved and spoke with strange lilting accents that seemed to dance on my skin. For my first sixteen years I hadn't left Oakley even once, and now here I was traveling every day, about to go make a home, however temporary, in an exotic, faraway place. I felt astonished all the time at the idea, and couldn't ask Lollie enough about it.

"How long has your family lived there?" I asked one night before a performance, as I watched her line her eyes with thick black pencil. I thought of Riley Farms, the name marked out on our gate and windowsills. My father was so proud of that land and would tell anyone within hearing distance about how his great-great-grandfather had bought it in exchange for a blind cow and a bucketful of seed.

"Our villa has been in the family for hundreds of years," Lollie said, never taking her eyes off the mirror yet making me feel like she was whispering in my ear, "ever since our ancestors set down roots and planted a thousand fruit trees, selling the fruit throughout Mexico. They grew rich and fat until a terrible case of wanderlust afflicted the sons and daughters and almost wiped out the whole line. That's how we became a circus family. Our ancestors took to the roads and learned the gypsy arts. They beat on pots for money, hammered out necklaces from bits of silver, and learned to bend and tumble. When one of the sons married a girl from a Russian circus, they finally organized enough to form their own show, the Fantastic Ramirez Circus."

"That sounds wonderful," I said. I mouthed the word: *wanderlust*.

"They wandered and performed and made men, women, and children fall in love with them, setting up the circus in the centers of big cities and tiny villages or performing in countries so vast and spread out that people would travel on donkeys or by foot for miles to see them. Oh, they were something, Tessita. Devoted fans wrote so many long letters to them that the poor local postman had to carry two sacks on his route each day—one for my family, and one for everyone else. And though my ancestors went as far as Russia and China, they always found themselves returning to just outside Mexico City. It became habit for them to return to the villa every winter and take off with the circus again in the spring. They sold off all of their land except for the villa we have now. You can still see the last of the lemon and orange trees there. Every day we drink the fruit for breakfast, and I used to pour lemon juice through my hair to make it lighter."

Lollie smiled at me, and in that moment she reminded me so much of Mary that I wondered for a second if it was from Lollie that Mary had learned to tell stories. From this great bright family of circus gypsies, so different from the pale, rain-soaked folk she'd left behind. At those moments I felt so close to Mary that I could almost touch her, and yet, at the same time, I felt the most piercing sense of loss, knowing I was just imagining her and how she would have been. I could never truly know what her experience had been, how she had felt when she'd sat right in the place I was now.

"I wish I had come from a family like yours," I breathed, as Lollie twisted her hair into a knot at the base of her neck.

"It is nice," she said, turning to me, "to know where you belong. But you have your gifts too, *niña.*"

I was regaled with stories during those first days as we traveled down through Oklahoma, all the way through Texas, watching the landscape become more and more sparse, and made our way into Mexico. In the daytime I worked on the ropes in the big top, beating myself into shape. At night, after watching the performances from behind the back curtain, I stumbled through the cars into the cookhouse or the common areas where performers met to eat and talk, or wandered outside the cars by the train tracks, where everyone gathered around bonfires to exchange all kinds of stories about the tiny circuses they'd started out in, circuses run by gypsies who'd scatter through the crowd to steal money out of children's hands or who made their money by peddling the flesh of women and young boys. Some told of their most exciting moments in the tent, others about the most horrifying deaths: tigers who'd turned on their trainers, men who'd been trampled by elephants, and flyers who'd crashed to the ground or into the crowds below them. One of the clowns had even seen the most famous circus wreck in history, when a train carrying seventy people and sixty-two animals had run off the track and into the river below, killing everyone and everything on board. I listened to their stories as every fiber in my body burned with pain, then dropped off to sleep before the sun even set.

It seemed like we arrived in Mexico within minutes. The green-and-yellow scrub turned to clay, and the sun seemed to burn right into the ground, set the entire world to flame. I sat with my face pressed to the window, on the bed in Lollie's compartment, and watched the landscape go by in a dull red haze.

We arrived in Mexico City in the late afternoon. Mrs. Ramirez met us at the train station. Lollie and her brothers filled her car to bursting before hiring several more to transport the rest of their trunks and suitcases home. I liked Mrs. Ramirez right away. She was petite and elegant, yet formidable as she stepped out of the car and came marching toward us. I could almost look her eye to eye, and she didn't flinch. She just leaned in, grabbed my hand firmly, and said, "Welcome to the family, *niña.*" The brothers all seemed to compete for her attention, and she directed the procession as if she'd been running a circus for years herself. She was quite a businesswoman, Mauro explained to me, as the two of us bumped through the countryside to the villa in one of the rented cars. "She inherited the savvy of our ancestors. Everyone here loves the circus. Our children don't have swings but long pieces of wire their parents stretch from tree to tree in the backyard. *Mi madre* bakes cookies in the shapes of lions and giraffes, paints huge canvases of circus scenes, and makes shirts with the Vadala horses silkscreened on the back. She is a very rich woman, Tessa."

I listened to him raptly, though he was so handsome I could barely look him in the eye. Instead I stared out at the hills and countryside as we passed out of the city, at the sun as it set over the hilltops, sinking into them until it disappeared. The lush, heavy scent of jasmine filled the air, which was warm and thick despite the fact that it was December. It seemed crazy to me that the world was not coated in snow.

"You will like it here, Tessita," Mauro said, smiling at me, and I smiled back at him, blushing. His eyelashes curled over his eyes and gave his whole face a sweetness that I was sure had broken many a girl's heart. He seemed exactly like the kind of man I'd read about, the kind a woman would light a candle for and not move until it had burned all the way down. I thought of Mary in Mercy Library, all the women who'd come to see her, suffering from love, and vowed to stock up on cranberry bark. I could brew some up for Lollie, too, I thought.

When we pulled up to the villa, sprawling down the side of a hill, I was bouncing with excitement. Inside, it was exactly what I'd pictured: all fresh flowers, white stucco walls and black iron railings, chattering parrots, and embroidered pillows. It was tiled and open, the kind of place you could walk around barefoot and wrapped in a towel, and the scent of jacaranda and jasmine wafted from room to room through the open arched doorways. The others had already arrived, and the house was full of voices and the smell of dinner on the stove. Lollie led me to my own room with a window that took up most of one wall and looked out over the pool, and a bed with crisp white sun-drenched sheets. I couldn't believe it. I loved everything about it: the walls indented in places and filled with figures of saints and crosses, the lemons I could pluck from the tree just outside my window. I did not have many possessions, but I hung every skirt and shirt in the closet and placed a few of the trinkets I had collected in Kansas City on the oak dresser.

For dinner that first night we all sat around a long table by the pool, and that was when I met Lollie's wheelchair-bound older brother Luis, the most astonishingly handsome man I'd ever seen, who lived in the villa year-round, along with Mrs. Ramirez and the maid, Victoria, who had cared for Luis for twenty years and would care for him until the day he died, bathing him each day with a wet cloth, clipping his beard, and smoothing pomade through his shiny black hair. Everyone knew the two of them were in love, Mauro had told me in the car, but if it weren't for Paulo's whispered words at the table, I never would have noticed the way

Victoria smoothed down Luis's hair as if it would break, the way she served up his plates of rice as if sculpting them out of clay. I knew so little of those things back then, and did not expect to.

When Luis bowed his head before me and kissed the top of my hand, I felt like my life could not be more glamorous than it was at the moment, with the moon shining down on the pool and the night obscene with the scent of flowers and *mole*. "Welcome to our family, Tessa," he said, raising his wine to me, and then we all clinked glasses. It was my first real glass of wine.

I glanced at Mauro over my glass and caught him watching me. I drank the wine down in one long gulp, my heart racing.

The next day the circus hunkered down in the lot, which was vacant throughout the spring and summer, and the tents were raised like huge animal carcasses in the faded landscape. Here Lollie and Paulo spent most of their days with me, patiently guiding me through each spin and turn, each toss into the air that brought me to the net, to the bar, or to Paulo's outstretched hands.

I worked eight hours each day in training with Lollie and Paulo. "Paulo is the best catcher," Lollie explained. "I worked with him before Geraldo came." Lollie and Paulo led me up to the platform, forced me to listen to the sound of the bar as it moved through air, to listen for the precise moments as it moved through its arc—rising up to the platform, down toward the net, and back up again at the other side, where Paulo waited for me. They had me memorize the sound of the bar whooshing up to the platform, then going still for a second before moving back down.

"Listen for the silence," Lollie said.

"Now," Paulo said as I stood crouched and tense. "Go!"

I fell again and again and tried to ignore the fear, that hollow feeling as I looked down at that net and, past it, the sawdust. I tried to listen to the bar, but my heart pounded in my ears, deafening me to anything else. I thought of the corn bent in front of the moon and how, in a way, it had saved me, giving me something to focus on when the rest of the world had hollowed out and gone blank. *Block out everything,* I thought, *but the bar rushing toward you.*

The first time I reached out and clumsily grabbed the bar, it was as if I were flying. I twisted myself up to a sitting position and laughed as Paulo and Lollie clapped and whooped.

I was nothing if not determined. My hands cracked and bled from twisting over the bar, my body was covered with bruises. I fell a thousand times into the net. I learned all the infinite adjustments I had to make with my body, the precise alignments and poses that took me from one spin into the next. From the ground you wouldn't have known the searing that ripped through my muscles or the stinging of my hands as I grabbed the bar. You wouldn't have known the deep sleep I fell into each night for ten hours straight as my body desperately tried to heal itself for the next day of abuse, or the way the physical strain wiped out everything else for those first weeks, blissfully. My mind was blank, registering only when a turn cut the air as perfectly as a scalpel or when a bad landing shot pain up my legs and left me without breath or speech.

"Good, Tessa," Lollie said as I spun through the air. "That's exactly right."

I remember floating in the pool after long days of flying, letting the water run over my bruised skin and cracked hands, barely able to move without feeling I was ripping a limb from my body. In the evenings, wonderful smells from the kitchen filled the air as Victoria cooked up vats of beans and rice and pork and pans of fried plantains and *sopapillas* for us to eat at the long table stretched out near the pool.

Outside of practice and eating and the luxury of the pool, my days were filled with stories. The Ramirezes were all storytellers, and I wondered if it was part of the circus life, this constant weaving of words into air. Sometimes I felt I had never left Mercy Library at all, but was still lying on the wooden planks of the floor with my eyes closed, listening to Mary as she described her life with the Ramirezes, all their crazy stories, their larger-than-life personalities, their great passions and lusts.

Carlos, the tallest and oldest Ramirez sibling, was driven by his passions more than any member of the Ramirez family, but he also had the most control over them, enough that he was able to manage his twenty mistresses deftly, without a dissatisfied one among them. Mauro told me about his brother by the pool one day after dinner, when Carlos was nowhere to be found. No one knew where Carlos got the boundless energy, Mauro said, that allowed him to leap from bed to bed and then back to the family breakfast table each morning, where Carlos could always be found setting the schedule for each day's practice. But he somehow managed not only to fulfill his impressive love and professional obligations, but to indulge his great fondness for books. Carlos owned thousands of books, Mauro told me, though I myself never saw them; Mauro claimed that Carlos's collection spanned ten floor-to-ceiling shelves that pressed together and took up three walls of his room. He had tales of explorers, gypsies, and medical doctors, volumes of folktales and physics theorems, and stories of love and sadness propped up against delicate volumes of poetry whose amber-colored pages were so thin you could see right through them. Some of his books were imposing and bound in leather, others were ragged from all the reading he'd subjected them to. I heard each of the Ramirezes on separate occasions muse about Carlos's unbearable schedule, and not one of them could come up with an adequate explanation for his prowess.

At first I couldn't help but feel nervous around Carlos and the brothers, being so exposed, the way everyone was with them. These were men used to feeling out a crowd, the wind and rain and landscape, the audiences waiting for them in each new town and in the bleachers each night. This was necessary with the high wire, Lollie told me. The brothers could gauge the colors of the dreams that influenced each person in the audience's sleep, sensing all the desires and longings the audience would bring to the ring. The feel of the people crowding the bleachers could alter a performance as much as the weight of the air and the speed of the wind, she said. All the longings and sorrows and betrayals traveled through the big top like wisps of smoke, and the Ramirez brothers always felt them. It was this, José explained later, that kept them safe on the wire, allowing them to flirt with it and tease it.

Slowly, over the next few weeks, I started to get used to the way the brothers looked right into you, as if they could see your past and your future. Though Lollie was the only true seer in the bunch, they all had a bit of vision in them, born from years of dancing across wires so thin you could floss your teeth with them.

Lollie's vision might have been the strongest, but it could not protect her from her own fate. As innocent as I was of the world, as amazed and overwhelmed as I was being with the Ramirez family in Mexico, I had spent enough time in that library with Mary listening to heartbroken, desperate women to recognize Lollie's sickness for what it was, and to see that she had no power over it. Lollie was always waiting for Geraldo, who was always doing anything other than coming to find her. Whenever he wasn't at the villa, Lollie stalked through the house like she was in some kind of fever. She would pinch her dark cheeks in the mirror and coat her lips with red gloss. She would brush her hair in long, slow sweeps. She would cover her face with her hands, and I knew: no seer can see her own future, even if it clacks across the floor in five-inch heels.

During the day she was mine completely, guiding my body through spin after spin, laughing with me when I fell or executed a turn so perfectly that she almost forgot that I wasn't born into the circus the way she had been. There was always a difference between those who felt the circus in their blood and those who had actually been born into it, just like there was a difference, in the sideshow tent, between those who had been born freakish, like the woman with hair made of moss, and those who had mutilated or marked themselves. I was a strange one, not fitting in anywhere exactly. But I was burning a place for myself every time I forced my body through the air, slicing it right open.

I pretended Lollie was two separate women: the woman who had known Mary and whom I spent my days with, the seer and trapeze star who had given me a room in her compartment and who made up a bed for me in her own family's house, and the woman who would have stayed on the ground for Geraldo, baking cakes and pastries for him, making his bed for him, wiping the floors he walked on. There was a time when she would have done that, though the circus ran through her blood like a river and forced her face to the sky. I'm quite sure that, back then, Lollie would have said her love for Geraldo was what made her who she was. She could spend whole nights weeping for him, and I watched her helplessly, feeling like I was back in Mercy Library, wishing I could remember what teas to brew, what herbs to give her to chew on.

I learned to ignore Geraldo, and tried to let Lollie's tears meld into all the other noises of the Ramirez house: the chattering parrots, the lapping water, the brothers' smooth voices, the whoosh and whisper of the breezes that passed through the open hallways like spirits. When Lollie shut herself in her room and filled the house with her sobbing, I would sit out by the pool with the rest of the Ramirezes or any number of the guests who dropped by each evening with their hands full of flowers or pitchers of sangria, which Victoria would fill with ice and bits of freshly cut peaches and apple. "There is nothing you can do," José would say when he saw me covering my ears, trying to block Lollie out. "Love is an illusion, and there is a bitter nut at its core." I learned later about how José had shot his one true love Clara through the heart, years before I left Oakley.

According to Mauro, who whispered the story to me by the pool, José had loved Clara since before the two of them could speak, back when they had played together in the park near the town plaza. Clara was the most beautiful child in all of Mexico, and as she grew older it only got worse, making all who saw her feel like they'd been momentarily blinded. The two were to be married, but then José returned one December to find Clara holed up with the town lawyer, whom she had married a few months before. José didn't even stop to think; he took one look at Clara in another man's arms, then turned around and left the new couple's home, picked up Mr. Ramirez's shotgun from the villa's cellar, walked straight back to his one and only love, and shot her through the heart. José didn't even put up a fight after firing the gun but dropped it as if it were burning, folded his body down to its knees, and waited for the town sheriff to come take him away. José spent five years in prison and left a changed man, having sworn off love completely.

I loved hearing these stories, just as I loved watching Mrs. Ramirez sit with her embroidery, her hands transforming bits of white cloth into works of art with her children's names, elephants, and entire miniature circuses blazing up out of them. Just as I loved watching Mauro, whose heavily lashed gaze left a fluttering sensation in my gut.

I often watched Luis, too, imagining how things must have been for him before, when he could throw his arms out to the sides and race

across the wire, or shimmy up a tree the way his brothers still did. While
Lollie paced feverishly in the house and one or another of the brothers
headed out into the night to meet lovers or friends, Luis always sat with
his back perfectly straight, letting the breezes brush against his skin,
laughing quietly, telling soft stories, and gazing every so often at Victoria as she set the table or poured a drink.

Victoria was never far from Luis's side, even as she moved from
room to room in the house, plumping up the pillows and sweeping the
tile floors. No matter how busy she was, she was constantly dashing
onto the terrace or one of the balconies overlooking the pool, whisking
up to Luis's side. "Are you all right, *señor?*" she would ask. "Would you
like some more *café?*" He always smiled up to her graciously, and lowered
his eyes when he answered.

It was impossible not to be affected by Luis's gentlemanly manner,
and it was no wonder that he received fan letters from all over the globe
from women who'd heard legends of his gallantry and gentleness.
Despite his injury, he seemed completely at ease in his body, though
I wondered if he could feel anything below his skin—the racing of
veins, the ripple of muscles, the bursts of joy or sorrow that come from
deep in the body. I was fascinated by his unmoving arms and legs, his
hands propped on the arms of his wheelchair like ornaments dangling
from a tree.

"Do you miss it?" I asked him once, only realizing the moment I
said it how rude it must have sounded.

He was unfazed. "Of course I do," he said, looking at me, "but I can
still feel the cut of the wire under my feet. That is how I tell my students
what to do—I can feel their movements just by watching them, imagining myself in their place. When the world closes down on you, you must
imagine it opening back up again, like a flower."

He winked at me then, and made me blush.

"Sometimes I have felt that way," I said shyly, "in my own body. Like it makes everything close down."

"Before," he said.

"Yes," I said, "before the trapeze."

"Your body was born to fly," he said softly. "It is something that comes from deep in your bones, Tessa. Some people have hollowed-out bones, the kind you can play music on, and those are the people who can fly."

"What happened to him?" I asked Lollie, on one of those rare evenings when she was in a good mood. She had flung her arms around me and announced that we'd spend the evening together, that we'd carry our meat and beans to her room, lock the door, and talk the evening through.

"To Luis?" she asked, spreading out food on the tile floor and handing me my fork.

"Yes," I said. "How did you see it? What happened?"

Her room was large and sweeping, her bed gray and discolored from all the tears that had fallen on it. A smiling picture of her and Geraldo hung over the bed. She saw me looking at it and said, "I know you must think I am crazy, Tessa, but I am sick with love. Around here all the girls dreamt of him, even the ones with diamonds hanging from their ears. You will have much better luck than I've had."

I laughed, embarrassed. "I don't think I'll have to worry about it too much."

"Oh, I don't know," she answered, and leaned in toward me, smiling. "It may happen sooner than you think. Much sooner. Isn't there some-one you think about?"

My mind rushed to Mauro's black eyes on mine, peering at me through their thick, curving lashes, and I felt my face go instantly hot with shame. "Of course not," I said, convinced she was making fun of me.

"I know more than you know, more than you even imagine," she said, tapping my arm playfully. "You underestimate me, but you'll see."

"Please tell me about Luis," I pleaded, and felt my face burn.

"Okay," she said. "Then maybe you'll understand how much I know. You see, I saw Luis the day before he fell from the wire. It was the first time I understood that I had been born with the gift of sight, though I did not quite see it as a gift back then. I was in the backyard of my grandfather's house, nine years old, sunbathing on my back in the hammock he had strung between two oak trees, swinging back and forth.

"Suddenly Luis's face appeared before me as clearly as if he were standing right there, though I could see the shapes of trees behind him and knew that his body was somewhere else. His face was contorted with pain. Tears rolled down his cheeks, and I realized that he was in a bed with a white-dressed woman leaning over him, wiping the tears away and keeping the plaster cast just under them dry. And then from a distance I saw him crossing the wire with dancer's steps, crossing them in front and in back and like a pair of scissors. He smiled to the audience as if the wire underneath him did not matter one bit, as if he could dance on air if he wanted to. His arms stretched out on either side, he was never more beautiful than he was right then, flirting with that wire in the brief moment when he had her all to himself, while my other brothers waited on either side. Then in one swift second Luis slipped— he missed the wire with his hands, and he fell to the ground and broke half the bones in his body. When I saw that my brother would break, I howled and howled and I yanked at my hair and I beat at the ground and I screamed into the sunlit yard: 'Luis! Luis! Luis!' I was on my knees in the yard with my heart breaking, and I said, 'Luis, stay off of the wire!' I said, 'Luis, you will fall from the wire! I saw you fall from the wire!'

"Luis came out into the yard. He smiled, held my face between his hands, and said, '*¿Qué pasa, mi niñita?* What have you done to yourself?'

"He wrapped his arms around my quaking body, and I told him what I had seen. His heart pounded so strong against my ear, and his arms seemed like iron around me. I begged him to stay on the ground for three days, and he said, 'I promise, *niñita*, do not worry about anything at all.' He kissed my cheeks. 'I am strong like an ox, *niñita*, but I will stay on the ground for you.'

"The very next night Luis stepped up to the wire. At that moment I sat innocently in a trailer behind the tent, my mother stroking rouge over my cheeks and twisting a ribbon down the length of my hair. My act came quickly after my brothers', so I rarely watched them myself. Only at the moment it happened did the vision come back. Again I saw him float down, but now I could hear the screaming crowds and running steps and the ringmaster trying to calm the crowds. I heard banging on the trailer door and felt my mother slump to the floor behind me.

"After that I did not speak for weeks, not even to Luis, who worshipped me now as if I were a little Maria. Even so, people came from miles away to hear what I saw, what they couldn't see.

"Later Luis told us how he'd heard my voice in his ear as he fell down from the wire, how it comforted him and told him he would not die as the ground pushed up under him. He said that as he fell he could smell my hair, which my mother always sprinkled with rose petals, and that he felt my hand on his just before he hit the ground.

"'I knew it was your hand, *niñita*, because I could feel your little gold rings,' he said.

"After that Luis liked to call me a saint and a healer, and he kept a candle burning for me all the time, and still does, though I've always told him he's crazy. Victoria used to store crates of candles in the pantry but has complained for years that Luis makes her light a fresh one every day, and makes her sprinkle the dresser top around it with newly cut roses each morning and night.

"'Dolores is no *santa*,' she used to say about me. '*Santas* do not fly on the trapeze or roll across lawns or crawl into boxes meant for heads of lettuce or cabbage. I don't know what that crazy man is thinking.'"

Lollie laughed. "People react in all kinds of way to vision, and I never know what way is right. But I am no *santa*; I cannot stop tragedies from happening, and though I have the gift of sight, sometimes I wonder what it has done for me aside from ruining the world a bit."

Lollie stopped speaking, and I could see the flush on her skin.

"You know I told you, Tessa, about the moments that change our life, how when Mary saw Juan Galindo in that barn the world changed for her completely?" she asked. "My moment was not filled with a passion that licks through the skin and into the blood. The moment that changed my life, you see, was when I saw my brother Luis fall to the ground and break, the moment I understood how death and accidents wait for us, how the world moves without us."

The house was silent except for the breeze whispering through the curtains and the sound of Lollie's breathing, as heavy as if she were asleep. When Lollie spoke of the past she seemed to inhabit it, until I could almost see her transform into the young girl with black gleaming hair and smooth sun-soaked skin. It was hard to distinguish between the weight and shape of her words and the power of the world she was calling back to me.

"Could you feel it in Mary?" I asked. Death seemed like water in the room then, like something you could dip your hands in and touch. "Did you see her in the river? Could you see the way her hair tangled around her neck, in the water?"

I felt strange speaking so casually of Mary's death. I thought back to those days, to the way Mary had let the mail pile at the door, to me running home to shuck corn and help set the giant dinner table. It was a world that stood in my memory like a perfect photograph, something timeless and complete. I could not imagine that my father had continued to exist past the last moment I had seen him, or that Geraldine was somewhere, too, with vegetables springing up under her fingertips. I thought back to those moments inside the memory I had built, the little moments that would seem so significant later. It made me afraid to walk through my life, never able to see the death that must have cloaked Mary back then, that must have been written on her skin and in her tears like an announcement.

"Yes," Lollie said. "I could always see the water dripping on her skin. I could smell the salmon and pine of where she'd come from, see the leaves that clung to her body."

I did not speak.

"That day," Lollie continued, closing her eyes, "I could feel the water swooping in between her dress and her skin, filling her body with its weight. I was in the cookhouse with the others. At first I thought it was just rain, but when I looked around nothing had changed—the day was still as clear as it had started. I felt the breath go out of her body while everyone around me ate their meat and rice. No one knew a thing. I did not say anything. What could I have said?"

"Why couldn't I feel it?" I asked her. "How could I not have known that something was going to happen? I was in her library drinking tea out of one of her cracked cups, straightening the things she'd left strewn over the floor. How could she have been drowning at the same time?"

"I don't know, Tessa," Lollie said.

"Why did she do it?" I whispered.

Lollie reached out and drew me to her.

"I don't know why she did what she did," she said. "Only that it was written on her from the first day I saw her, when she showed up at the Velasquez Circus."

That night I could not sleep. I tossed in my bed, imagining the water on Mary's skin, the crack of Luis's bones as he hit the ground. The world moves without us, I thought. I imagined my father in the cornfield, Geraldine working in her garden, Lollie sobbing in her room from love. I saw myself, younger, back in Oakley, crumpled up on the dirt, clutching my skirt in my hands.

There was no way I was going to sleep that night. I tossed and turned. Each movement revealed a new ache that had burrowed into my body, and nothing brought relief. I lifted my starfish hands and traced the cracks raging through them. "Nothing before this matters," I thought over and over. "I am in the circus now. Nothing before now matters." But nothing could erase the fear wrenching my gut. Is this all there is? I thought. Does everything come back to this exact feeling?

Restless, I slipped on a robe and tiptoed through the hallways, feeling the cool tile under my bare feet. The crosses scattered throughout the house, the twisting wrought-iron railings and candle holders, the earthenware vases filled with roses and other flowers, the sparkling costumes that hung in closets and across doorways and on the line that stretched over the back porch—all of it looked different in the sleeping house, lit only by a faint moon through the open windows.

I let my hands glide over the railings and the walls as I walked from room to room, then past the pool. I plucked a lemon from one of the shimmery trees and turned it over in my hand. I thought of Luis as a young man, falling falling to the ground. I thought of Lollie listening to the screams from the trailer, and I imagined how her heart must have exploded in her chest.

"Nothing before this matters," I whispered, into air.

With every corner I turned, I was convinced I heard the whisper of spirits. Moonlight dappled the walls, a breeze moved through the room, the crosses throughout the house seemed heavy with meaning. Back in Oakley the world had been flat and stark; here it was filled with memory, story, spirit, and all the colors of the circus and the lemons and roses. I could not stop thinking of Luis falling to the ground, the way he sat by the pool each evening as splendid as a sun.

I walked from room to room, breathing in the scent of the jasmine, imagining the feel of the bar under my hands, myself flying over everything. The memory of it pressed against my palms. It was strange to reconcile the quiet lushness of the house with the clean, precise feeling of flight, my limbs cutting through air and forcing it to sweep from my body in waves. A different feeling took hold of me. The house, the moon, the quiet—it all seeped into me until I had so much energy I could hardly stand it, despite the soreness of my limbs, my ravaged muscles and cracked skin. I thought how I had no body, no father, nothing before what I was right then, and I began running through the hallways, racing right through them as if I could not be contained by anything. I felt absolutely weightless then in a way I had never felt on earth, on the ground—as light as pure air, pure feeling and desire. The breath in my lungs felt like glass. This is all that matters, I thought: the clean feeling of air slicing open.

CHAPTER FIFTEEN

The days and weeks passed, and the new season loomed before me. I wore my body down to the bone and quickly mastered the new movements Lollie showed me. At practice I had a much easier time with the rope than the flying trapeze. Lollie and Paulo were both appalled to learn that I'd used only the thick rope from a barn and a hardware store before, and that my wrists were scarred from the countless sores that had opened because of it. Paulo threw away my own rope and insisted I work with the *corde lisse*, the long braided rope all aerialists used. With a swivel and a ring, he attached a padded rope loop to the *corde lisse* for me to slip my hand through to do the swing-overs. The difference was amazing: the trick was still difficult, still required a complete shoulder rotation, but the padded loop made my grasp on the rope more sure and protected my palm and wrist. Suddenly I was able to do fifty swing-overs at one time, sometimes sixty or more.

"Beautiful!" Lollie would call out. "Just keep the leg straight as you turn, lean your body in."

I learned to keep my shoulder close to the rope to control the movement, to polish the violent, angry thrusting of the river and the boardinghouse in Kansas City.

"Here it is about creating poetry in the air, not throwing yourself around without even thinking. The more you harness that energy, *chica*, the more disciplined you make each movement, the more magical you will be. An *artista*."

Every day Lollie, Paulo, and I drove to the big top at dawn. I worked on the ropes each morning before the long afternoons on the trapeze. I came to understand that the Ramirezes had wanted a solo aerialist in their act for a long time but that it was a touchy thing, bringing a new aerialist into an established act, especially when egos like Lollie's and Geraldo's were concerned, not to mention the brothers'. But I was much less of a threat than the sinewy aerialists from the Russian and European circuses the Ramirezes had spoken with. I was so different from Lollie in the air, my quick, strong movements a striking contrast to her more silken, flowing ones. Lollie evoked romance and languor and lushness while I was all raw power and blurring, spinning movement.

"Eventually we can integrate so that you, I, Geraldo, and Paulo can do one long flying act together," Lollie said.

"You are a gift to us from Marionetta," I heard Carlos comment more than once.

Once Paulo and Lollie felt I had the swing-over under control—the centerpiece of my act, they both agreed—they began to teach me other solo acts. The hoop, a bar with semicircles rising from the top and bottom, that spun around, making it seem like you were enclosed in a beautiful bubble. The Roman rings, the two small rings hanging from two cords that I could work like a gymnast, performing numerous tests of strength. The long rope ladder that let you do all kinds of tricks while ascending and descending through the air.

I took to all of these acts much more easily and readily than to the flying trapeze. Despite all the hours and days and weeks we spent on the trapeze, I hadn't been able to master it. I could not catch Paulo's hands and pull my body to the opposite platform. I'd panic, looking down to see that his hands were there, and ruin the trick. I'd either miss it completely or grab his hands clumsily, breaking a clean line or luxurious spin.

What I could do was leap to the Roman rings, pull myself up until my arms shot straight across on either side, and then hang for many minutes, steady and sure, as if I were just relaxing on one of the lounge chairs by the pool. My muscles were unbelievably strong from Mary's library, the river, and the bar in the kitchen window. Of course it helped that I was so small, that my muscles probably outweighed all my skin and bones and blood put together. Lollie could not stay up in the iron cross for more than thirty seconds, her body shaking the whole time.

"I have never seen anyone take to the air so quickly," she said to me one evening as we drove back to the villa. "I almost think Mary passed something on to you in that crazy library. Some people can pass memories or dreams from one body to the next, you know. Maybe that was Mary's power, the reason everyone who saw her fell in love with her."

Paulo glanced over at me from the driver's seat. "I believe it," he said. "But it also comes from your bones, like Luis always says."

I laughed as the heavy night air blew against my skin from the open window.

I felt, for the first time, that I belonged somewhere. Carlos, Mauro, Luis, José, and Paulo were like brothers to me, kissing my cheeks in the morning and at night, making sure I had enough to eat and was never by myself in the city or on the roads surrounding the villa. Victoria taught me to make *flan* and her special *mole*, laughing with me in the kitchen over the huge industrial stove.

But despite everything, Mary was often there, around the edges—not the woman I had known and loved but a reminder, a sense that I had left something undone. Like everyone else in my life, she was split off, between the woman I had known and the woman who stayed with me. And she was separate from everything. As close as I became to Lollie or Luis, I could not tell them about the way Mary haunted me or what it had felt like to spend those long days with her in the library, listening to her voice or watching her brew tea on the stove. I could not tell them about the opal ring that I kept hidden in my room, sewn back up in a skirt, or what it had felt like to come upon her in the river.

And no matter how happy I was, how in love I was with Mexico and the circus, I still dreamt of rain. Some nights I woke with my heart pounding in my chest, longing to leave Mexico and to find Rain Village, which must have been a million miles from the house and the pool and the trees that dropped lemons to the ground. I heard Mary's voice in my ear, thought of the riverboat that snaked up the thin river, how the sky must turn black as the riverboat neared. I saw the thousand colors of the opal ring sparkling up from her neck. I felt a darkness swooping over me, threatening to pull me to the river's bottom, threatening to fill my lungs and drown me.

I would hear her voice in my ear, wrapping around me the way her scent had once.

"There's a secret there," she would say. "I want you to find it."

It was late February when Lollie announced that we had to begin preparing my costume for the new season. We were sipping coffee at the big table in the early morning, getting ready for another long day of rehearsal. All of us were there. It was a normal morning: the sky was hung over a bit with rain, we were quiet and tired, and Victoria had set out a large bowl of mangoes and oranges with a pot of steaming coffee.

I was slathering my toast with butter when Lollie said, "I think we should make you a costume covered with rhinestones, Tessa, so that you'll look like a diamond in the air."

I looked up at her. I had almost forgotten that our time in Mexico was a rest stop for the winter and that the day was approaching for us to gather up the circus and head north, where we would pick up the rest of the acts and start the new season.

"You're ready," Lollie said, smiling over the table at me. "Maybe not for the flying trapeze, but your solo act is more than ready."

I looked to Paulo, who agreed.

"We want your solo act to be part of our main act," Lollie said. "We can work it out with Jorge, your pay and your sleeping arrangements."

I nodded, speechless.

"We can negotiate more then," Carlos said. He turned to me. "We can probably get you twenty dollars a week for now. Jorge, Mr. Velasquez, pays me one lump sum for all of us in the Ramirez acts, and I divvy it up. That should be fair for you and increase profit for all of us. We're a strong act already—the two star acts of the show—but you'll make us even stronger."

"Does that sound fair to you, Tessa?" Lollie asked.

"Yes," I said, overcome. This was more money than I'd ever thought I'd make, anywhere. I would have traveled with the Ramirezes for free.

"We need a name for you, then," Carlos said, clapping his hands and looking around the table.

"What's wrong with Tessa?" I asked.

Mauro shook his head. "Something more."

"Tiny Tessa!" Luis said suddenly. He sat at the head of the table, his wheelchair pulled up to it. "How about that?"

I giggled, clapping my hand over my mouth.

"Bueno!" Lollie laughed, nodding vigorously and spreading her hands out dramatically in the air. "You will be the tiny trapeze girl who glitters like a perfect diamond in the air, a gem in the center of our act."

I looked at all of them. "Thank you," was all I could manage, and I looked down at my coffee.

Luis leaned toward me. "You are going to be magnificent," he said. "Don't worry."

I looked up at Luis, and at Mauro's sweet face and Lollie's open one, the pride beaming through it, and was almost heartbroken. It was too much, all of this—how could I trust any of it? I had thought that Mary had loved me once, too.

Mrs. Ramirez and Victoria worked on my costume for a week straight. They sat in the main den downstairs with a bowl of rhinestones set on the table between them. They sewed each one onto the soft white fabric by hand, then stuck me through with pins in the evenings as they molded the fabric to my skin.

"More rhinestones!" Mrs. Ramirez cried, then plucked the fabric off my body and got back to work.

At night I would go look at my costume, pure white and sparkling in the moonlight, like snow and ice and frost, and I'd close my eyes and think of the spinning girl in my vision. Gleaming, rotating around and around until you could no longer see the lines of her body, just pure light moving through space.

Two nights before we left Mexico for the new season, Mauro knocked on my door. He was dressed in a black suit and hat and held a bouquet of geraniums he'd plucked from the walls surrounding the villa.

"Tessa," he said, before I could speak, "would you go to dinner with me tonight?"

I looked at him, confused. "But I always have dinner with you, Mauro," I said.

"No, no," he said, pushing the geraniums into my hand, "Not here. Outside. In the city."

"Oh," I said, blushing. "You mean . . . ?" I didn't know what to say.

"I want to take you to dinner, Tessa," he said.

"Okay," I said.

"I'll be back in an hour," he said, looking at me from under his thick lashes. He was so handsome in his white shirt and dark suit, his hair slicked back with grease. In one quick movement he kissed my cheek, then left me there in the doorway.

I stood there for a full minute before it hit me that Mauro Ramirez had just asked me, Tessa Riley, out on a date. I touched my cheek where he had kissed me, my face burning, my hands trembling. This was not supposed to happen, I thought. This was not ever supposed to happen for a girl like me.

I dropped the flowers on my bed and raced to the shower. My heart pounded as I slicked shampoo through my hair and slapped scented soap over my skin, and I shook when I stepped in front of the mirror, glaring at my flat body. I rubbed my hair with a towel, leaned into the glass and stared right into my own eyes, blue and wild with fear and excitement.

What to wear seemed like the biggest decision of my life. I yanked out shirt after shirt from my closet—old ragged ones I'd worn in the factory, sweet embroidered ones sewn by Mrs. Ramirez—but everything seemed wrong, dull. Finally I pulled out the rhinestone-lined skirt Mary had made for me for my thirteenth birthday, and slipped it on with a tight white top. The effect was not too bad, I thought, staring into the mirror. My skin looked tan against the white, and I looked summery, like I should be sipping lemonade. Still, I cursed my ridiculous body, my pinched face. I wanted to weep and cry out with excitement, all at once.

I looked at the clock. I had fifteen more minutes—just enough time to get Lollie's opinion. I ran through the bathroom to the other side and knocked on her door, which swung open almost immediately.

"Tessa!" she said, pulling me inside.

"Can you lend me some makeup?" I asked. "Mauro is taking me out tonight, and I want to look nice."

"That's wonderful!" she exclaimed, a little too happy. I realized I hadn't seen Geraldo around for several days, though Lollie had seemed fine at practice that morning.

"That skirt is *muy bonita*," she said. "Why don't you see how this necklace looks with it?" She led me over to the sweeping bureau covered in jars and bottles. Her eyes were red and slightly swollen.

"Are you okay, Lollie?"

"Of course," she said, smiling as she clasped a thick silver band around my neck and let it nestle into my collarbone.

In the mirror, I was surprised at how it glinted. I never wore jewelry. Behind me Lollie looked transformed, glowing. For a moment my mind went to the ring wrapped in a sack at the bottom of my suitcase, and I imagined placing it on my finger, dazzling everyone we passed. I pushed the thought away immediately.

"Thank you," I said, turning to her. "Are you sure you're okay?"

"*Sí, sí*," she said. "Now let's get a little makeup on you, *princesa*."

She reached for a tube of lip gloss, then coated my lips with a series of small dabs. Next she poured powder over my skin, rubbing it in with a large puff.

"*Cierra tus ojos.*" I closed my eyes, and she pulled a pencil across the lids. I pointed to the pot of glitter, laughing, and she sprinkled a few specks on my lids.

"I used to spend hours getting ready for my big dates," Lollie said. "The boys used to beat down our door to get to me, once upon a time, in the last century."

I squeezed her hand and kissed her. When I looked in the mirror I was still myself, but shimmery, better.

Mauro drove and I sat beside him. He told me stories about his family and the villa, but I was so nervous that I only heard every few words.

We drove out of the valley and into the city. I had only seen Mexico City in the daytime; at night it was another world completely, with lights draped everywhere and music filling the streets. I loved the little bands of *mariachis*, squat and bird-like, with their silver-spangled pants and sombreros. They seemed to be everywhere as we pulled the car into the center of the city, near one of the huge plazas lined with restaurants and bars and elaborate buildings.

Mauro looked at me. His eyes glimmered in the dark car.

"Ready?" he asked.

"Yes," I said, smiling up at him, thankful that the nighttime masked the redness of my face, the sweat gathering at my neck. I forced myself to swallow.

He stepped out of the car, then moved around to pull open my door and extend his hand, shutting the door behind me after guiding me to his side. We strolled through the plaza. My skirt swished around my legs. The *mariachis* gathered around us as we walked.

"Care for a song?" they asked. *"Una serenata?"*

"Señor Ramirez!" one cried, and began tiptoeing along the ground in a straight line, mimicking Mauro walking over the wire. "A song for your *novia?"*

Mauro laughed as a small crowd gathered around us. The plaza was full of people: young and old, children and drunks and young lovers and old people singing along to the music. Lights splashed on the stone, and the Mexican flag waved above us. The cathedral bordering the plaza on one side was as elaborate as a wedding cake.

"Por favor," Mauro said, bowing and laughing to the old *mariachi* in front of us. The *mariachis* were all over the place, playing song after song to small groups of listeners. There must have been fifty songs playing at the same time, and the effect was blissful, like a dozen fireworks going off at once.

The old *mariachi* bowed and stepped back, lifting up his violin. A group huddled around him with their own instruments and suddenly the sweetest, saddest song in the world burst out of them. Mauro pulled me in to him, wrapped his arm around my waist, bending down.

"Dance with me," he smiled, and I let my body press into his as he guided me in a slow circle.

"Mauro!" some of them shouted. Or, like the *mariachi:* "Señor Ramirez! I want to join the ceer-kus, too!"

We laughed and laughed and I was dizzy with it.

Later, at the restaurant, everyone knew who we were. The Ramirez family was legendary in Mexico City, and the other patrons kept walking by to look at us, see what we were eating, how we were dressed.

We ordered heaping plates of *carne asada* and turkey *mole*, and the waiters kept bringing out beans and rice and guacamole. Mauro ordered us each a tequila cocktail, and I laughed and protested as I drank it down.

"Are you trying to get me drunk?" I asked, flirting, surprising myself. I took a sip of tequila, and the salt stuck to my lips. Mauro reached over and wiped it off, then licked his fingertips, gentle as a cat. He stared right into me. The blush that came up on me must have started at my toes.

The horns and violins and *guitarrones* and *vihuelas* enveloped us.

"So, Tessa," Mauro said, "what do you think of Mexico now?"

"Oh," I said, "it's perfect. I love everything about it."

He smiled. "*Dime*. Make me see it the way you do."

I mashed down the beans on my plate. The waiter brought over two new drinks for us in icy cocktail glasses.

"It's always sunny," I said. "And the air has perfume in it, with all the flowers. They drape over everything like necklaces, and it makes me think of a fancy woman at a big dance. I love all the buildings and crosses. The music."

"*Sí*," he said. "It suits you here. You look healthy and dark, almost like a *mexicana*."

I giggled. "Oh, and everyone is so peaceful and relaxed, not like at home. There it was always worry and looking to the sky for rain. You know, the farm and everyone not getting along. Telling secrets. Hating things. The world."

"What about your family?" He reached for a piece of meat on my plate, popped it into his mouth.

"They weren't at all like your family. Not one bit. You are so lucky, having the brothers and sisters you do. Such a beautiful mother."

"*Dime*," he said.

"We were nothing alike," I told him, beginning to smile. Something I had never done while talking of my family before. "My sister and I shared a room but barely even spoke. I mean, we practically looked right through each other whenever we were unlucky enough to be awake at the same time, in the bedroom."

He laughed. "When we were kids we just worked and worked, all the time."

"Us too," I said. "Well, not me, really—I was too small to help much in the fields—but my brothers and sister were always out there, breaking their backs."

"You saved your body for other things."

I looked up sharply, afraid he was mocking me.

His eyes were warm and liquidy. "I would hate for you to be any different than you are now," he said.

I let out my breath, unsure of where to look, what to think.

"I think it sounds wonderful," I said, finally, "to spend all day working in the circus."

He laughed. "People think we are free in the circus," he said, "but all of us, we were born into it. It is as natural for me to be on the wire as it is for me to breathe. But you can be anything you want to be, the way Mary could. You are a streak of light."

"I don't know what you mean," I said. "It must be wonderful, knowing exactly who you are and what you are, the way you do."

I felt like I could say anything to him. He was, I realized, just like Mary and like Lollie: someone who'd slipped through the cracks, a friend. I do not think I had ever been more myself than I became at that moment, with him.

"Maybe," he said. "But you can cut a space for yourself in the world. Sometimes, when it's all you know, it's different. You want to have more than one life. You envy the people for whom everything is possible."

His voice was as deep and warm as baking bread. His lips were full, and as I watched him talk, I could feel them on me, grazing my cheek and the sides of my mouth. His hair fell into his face. He smiled as he spoke, and I watched his lips, fascinated.

"I liked you from the first day you came to the circus," he continued, smiling shyly. "I thought I had never seen anyone like you. You just showed up, slipping from one life into another."

"Thank you," I said, not knowing what else to say. I was afraid that if I said anything more, the moment would disappear. I didn't trust anything, yet my life was so different now. It almost made sense for me to be here, for me to be staring at Mauro Ramirez and he back at me.

"Are you excited for the season?" he asked softly.

"Yes," I whispered. "Excited, and scared. Scared to perform in front of everyone."

"You will be amazing," he said. "Enjoy these last two days, Tessita, because everything will change afterward. Everything." He stretched his hand across the table and took mine in his palm.

"I will," I tried to say, but the words seemed to get caught on my tongue.

We drove back to the villa in silence. When Mauro looked over at me I could feel his eyes on me as if they had weight to them, as if he were pressing on me with his fingertips. I lost every breath in my body. It was as if we weren't even part of the world, with the way the moonlight cast shadows through the windows.

When we got back to the villa I felt like everything had changed. At the front door, Mauro looked down at me. I couldn't even see straight. I wanted to stop time, wrap myself around this moment and keep it close. But before I could think or feel, he reached his hand out, cradled my cheek with his palm. I was shocked at the warm softness of it, so different from the skin on my own palms, ravaged by the bar. I stared up at him, unable to move.

As his face neared I saw the flash of his eyes on mine as they moved into the light. I saw the lines of his jaw and then suddenly it was as if I were underwater. His lips pressed on mine, as soft as pillows.

Afterward I stood there in shock, staring up at him. Without even thinking I turned around and ran so fast that everything around me blurred into lines of light and dark.

I rushed into my room, unsure if my legs would still carry me. When I stood in front of the mirror I barely recognized myself with my flushed cheeks and dark, shaded eyes, my body so strangely muscular and bruised from the constant training.

I fell onto the bed. My heart pounded, my whole body trembled. His kiss had crept its way under my skin, past where my father had burned his handprint, past my revulsion at what love could make of a woman like Lollie, or Mary, who had followed Juan Galindo like a dog through the ice and snow. I wrapped my head around it, what would make him do something like that, anyone do something like that, with someone like me. I moved from excitement to fear and back again, watching the stars outside my window.

I did not know what to expect from Mauro the next day. I watched the sky turn pale pink and then slip into yellow, and still my heart would not calm. Again and again I saw Mauro's eyes as his face leaned into mine. What if I had imagined that moment? One minute I was convinced the world had changed, the next I was sure I had imagined the texture of his hair and lips, the scent of his skin. Everything seemed so fragile then, in my life. But most of all I was afraid to look in the mirror and see the same Tessa Riley, the one who used to lie in the cornfields, staring past her father's shoulder at the moon.

Finally the sun reached the top of my window, and I knew I had to leave my room, return to the world to see what was different in it. I got up and bathed, imagining his lips, his gaze over my body as I sponged myself down. I poured water over my torso and watched it drip down my legs to my feet, wondering if I could ever be beautiful to someone like Mauro, or anyone at all. I still was myself, tiny and flat and disappointing: I felt so utterly transformed by Mauro's kiss that I thought I might look down and see rounded, sculpted legs like Mary's, breasts that were full like fruit.

I dressed slowly, in my plain white training leotard and shorts, and pulled my hair back with trembling hands. I slapped cold water on my face. I took so long that when I stepped out of the house to where the pool and fruit trees were, they were all already there: Lollie, Mrs. Ramirez, Luis, Victoria, Carlos, Paulo, José, and Mauro, who looked up at me and smiled as if someone had knocked his face clean open.

"Tessa," Carlos called out, laughing, "we thought you had gone off and run away! Mauro here was about to hop on a horse and run after you."

I glanced at Lollie, who smiled and winked, then looked at Mauro, whose face, I noticed with surprise, was every bit as red as mine.

I wanted to sink into the floor and, at the same time, run leaping toward them all. Nothing made sense to me that day; it seemed like the whole world had gone mad.

CHAPTER SIXTEEN

On our last night in Mexico we all gathered around the long table and ate tortillas, sliced avocados, and fried meat. I knew I was crazy, but I felt the way I used to feel when the sun dropped, when it was time for me to leave Mary's library and head home. My excitement fell into sadness and back out of it again. I wanted to perform, but I almost couldn't bear the thought of leaving the hushed, tile-floored house, the burst-open flowers like explosions along the dusty streets.

Luis sat at the head of the table. My costume hung like a secret in my closet, wrapped in tissue. I sensed a bittersweet sadness in Mrs. Ramirez and Luis, something all circus people feel: that longing to watch the landscape blur by as you go from town to town, to smell the sawdust and feel the lights beaming on your skin. I looked around the table, at Carlos's shining face, José's quiet inward gaze, Paulo's dreamy secretiveness. I watched Lollie with Geraldo next to her, beaming with a desperate sort of happiness, one I recognized instantly after so many days and nights with her. And I turned to Mauro, who looked at me with his inky eyes that made me feel I was being touched.

I decided not to even question it. I would just take it in the way I took in big mouthfuls of the *flan* Victoria made us for dessert.

As we neared the train station the next morning, it was as if someone had opened a jewel box and scattered its contents over the dusty ground. I spotted Lollie's car right away, with the flying woman on the side, then saw the five Flying Ramirez Brothers' cars strung in a row just past it. People were milling around everywhere, loaded down with suitcases and boxes, boarding the train and coming down off it. I caught a glimpse of the Vadala horses being led past. Roustabouts lugged carts and carts of water and vats of vegetables and meat into the cookhouse, which was just in front of the line of gilded wagons that gleamed from the flatcars. You could feel the excitement of a new season like a tangible thing hovering over us.

Carlos rolled down the window and started yelling to friends on the lot. We parked the cars and moved into the horde. I saw Ana, playing with a group of children on the steps leading to the platform. Geraldo and Lollie had left earlier than the rest of us, and Geraldo held court outside the manager's car with Lollie next to him, gesturing to one of the Kriminov Twins and an elephant girl I recognized, who had flame-red hair falling in one thick wave after another.

It was hard to believe we were still in Mexico City.

"Relax," Mauro whispered, leaning toward me. Paulo looked back at us and winked, then ran into the crowd.

We walked into the mass of people, dragging two huge suitcases, my small knapsack, and my finished costume, which Mrs. Ramirez had carefully wrapped in paper. Right away I noticed all the stares in my direction, the way people greeted Mauro *and* me as we walked past. I craned my head looking for Clementine, Mauro's former love. I didn't realize the sideshow wouldn't join us until later.

Ana leapt up when she saw us. "Tessa!" she screamed. "You are so different!" She ran around and around me like a puppy dog, yelping her delight. "You're beautiful! I heard you will be in the show." She leaned into me and grabbed my hand. "Everyone is talking about it! Have you seen the posters yet?" She pointed to a poster draped on the side of one of the walls of the train station.

I looked, focused in, and could not believe my eyes: there I was, right in front and center. "Tiny Tessa!" the poster proclaimed, and showed me zooming toward a bar, my starfish hands reaching forward as my body swept behind. My face was shown relaxed, with thick starry lashes and bright red lips spread into a smile. In the background tigers leapt forward, mimicking the movement of my body, while four tiny figures stalked over the wire in silhouette. "The Velasquez Circus!" screamed over the top, in glittering block letters arching above everything. It did not look like me. The girl in the poster seemed different, beautiful.

Mauro smiled, set down the bags, and pulled me to him. "So what do you think?" he asked.

"How . . . ?"

"Paulo took a photograph of you when you weren't paying attention. The artist painted you from it."

I was completely speechless. My face would be splashed across the world for everyone to see, my image stamped on the paper, my face painted in vivid hues. I imagined my father coming upon it, or my mother, or Geraldine.

Everyone rushed around to congratulate me. "I can't wait to see your act," I heard again and again. Mr. Velasquez stepped from the manager's car and walked over at one point, glaring at me.

"You've got a lot to live up to, girl," he said. "Now that your face is going to be splashed from here to fucking Canada."

We had to wait three days before the first show. We settled into our cars as the train clattered through northern Mexico, where we would meet up with the rest of the performers and workers, then cross the border into Texas. I loved having my own car on the train, loved falling asleep with the wheels rumbling under me, seeing my clothes hanging in my own tiny closet. I hung my costume from a hook on the wall and spent part of one night just watching the moon bounce off the rhinestones. Lollie often came by to visit, lying back on the bed with me and telling all kinds of stories. Sometimes we just sat cross-legged on the bed and played gin rummy for hours at a time. Every night Mauro walked me back to my car after we all had dinner in the cookhouse and kissed me at the door.

The cookhouse was the real gathering place in the train; other than that, people met in each other's rooms or just slept until we reached the next town, where groups of us descended upon the local pubs or just sat around outside by a bonfire, talking about everything: the shows, the crowds, the other circuses hitting the same towns on the same routes. It was a small world, I would discover, with many performers moving between the circuses and sideshows of the various companies. Staying with the Velasquez Circus year after year, the Vadalas and Ramirezes were more the exception than the rule.

Once we settled into the first lot, I tried to keep myself busy every second. I pitched in with everyone else to raise the big top, toss sawdust over the ground, and assemble the tangle of wires and ropes and hooks and poles that would fuel the show. I wandered through the lot as the sideshow hucksters set up their own tents and the cookhouse workers set pots of soups and stew to boiling. All the while I just heard the beating of my heart, the pounding that counted down the seconds and minutes and hours before I would perform for the first time.

The day before the show Lollie insisted on running me through my routine for hours to make sure I hadn't lost momentum with the traveling and setup, all the new people milling around, curious to catch sight of me in the big top.

"I'm okay," I kept telling her. "I know the routine. I want to do the flying trapeze."

"You're not ready," she said.

"Next season maybe," Paulo said, and my heart swelled with disappointment.

I ran through my Roman rings act and practiced the swing-overs. To my surprise, more and more of a crowd gathered in the bleachers just to watch me. It hadn't really hit me yet, I suppose, that anyone outside my small circle would even care, despite the posters, despite the twenty-dollar-a-week salary Mr. Velasquez had agreed to after some hard negotiations with Carlos.

That first morning on the lot, I ran through my swing-over act, then sidled down to the floor, only to see the entire Vadala family staring at me and clapping from the bleachers.

"*Brava!*" Gregorio, the family patriarch, called out. "*Bellissima!*"

"She's something else, *no?*" Lollie called out, laughing.

I was delighted and overwhelmed by the attention. As Mauro continually told me, I would get used to it over time.

Later that afternoon I was flipping around on the rings and then steadied myself into an iron cross. Suddenly I caught sight of something glinting from the bleachers, and looked down to see Clementine, the bird girl, staring up at me. I faltered for a second, then dropped to a hanging position.

"What's wrong?" Lollie asked immediately, rushing up to me.

"Nothing," I said, trying to lift myself back up but unable to. My heart pounded and I could feel my whole body flushing. It took so little to bring the old shame back.

Lollie glanced over and saw immediately what had affected me.

"Come on, sweetheart," she laughed, under her breath. "Don't let *that* get to you. It was so long ago."

But Clementine sat there like a beautiful movie goddess, like one of those stars with pale skin and pale hair, bright red lips, and a full, languorous body. I dropped to the ground, out of breath.

"Tessa," Lollie said, putting her arm around me, placing a hand on my horrified, cringing face. "Tessa!"

"Don't let them see me," I whispered, burying my face in her. "Please take me out of here."

I don't know how long Clementine ended up sitting there, or if she even had any idea what had happened. Lollie sighed and walked out of the big top with me, into the afternoon.

"What the hell is going on?" Paulo demanded, striding out after us. "What the hell just happened?"

"Let it rest," Lollie said.

"What if this happens during the show, what then?"

"Don't worry," Lollie said, more firmly. "It's all under control."

I kept my face covered until I heard him leave, cursing under his breath.

"Love is very hard," she said, touching my hair. "Believe me, I know. You always feel like someone's going to snatch it away."

I spent the rest of the afternoon stretching in the train. I didn't see Mauro until dinner that night, when we all gathered in the cookhouse.

"What's the matter?" he asked.

"Nothing," I said, smiling quickly at him. He slipped his arm around my waist, and I shrugged out of it.

"Don't."

He looked confused but let me go.

Sometimes it felt like I had become a different person in the Velasquez Circus, in the ring and under Mauro's touch. I could look back at my old self and laugh at the girl who had hung in the kitchen window. Other times it felt like I would never be anything but Tessa Riley from Oakley, Kansas. A freak. The girl everyone laughed at except one woman, who had drowned herself in the river and left me all alone.

It was like a sickness. Something I had to let wash over me, then slip away. Eventually I would learn to accept it, like a headache that just had to pass.

The day of the show, I was worried about whether I'd be able to function under the lights and over the crowds, whether people would boo and laugh me out of the ring. I was afraid I'd turn to ice when the moment came.

We practiced for a few hours in the morning, and after lunch I stretched in my compartment, played solitaire with the cards spread over the bedspread. I lay back in the bed and visualized myself in the air. As the sky began to dim, Mauro and I ate hamburgers in the grass near the train, watching the crowds gather in the midway as all the lights flashed on, one by one. I could eat only a few bites, I was so nervous. The Ferris wheel shone with pink lights, and the scents of hot dogs and popcorn mixed with the smells of animals and dust, as the talkers began to lure the crowds in.

Time seemed to speed up, and the whole world felt bigger and more electric, and then, before I knew it, it was time to prepare for the show.

I started shaking, I was so nervous. I could barely see straight as I kissed Mauro good-bye and walked into Lollie's car.

In her dressing room, surrounded by vials of creams and powders, she caked makeup over my face and spread glitter all along my cheekbones and eyelids, then down my neck and arms. She lined my eyes with kohl, brushed powder across my skin, and painted my lips dark red. Then she twisted my hair into a small cap and held it in place with crystal-studded pins.

"*Hermosa*," she said, when my makeup was done, smiling down at me and clasping my trembling hands in her own. "Beautiful. Don't worry. No matter how nervous you are, your body knows exactly what to do."

Her face was next to mine. I could see the line of red tracing her bow-shaped lips. I could only nod, gulping for air.

"The people will see you tonight, and they'll dream about you after they go home," she said. "They'll look at you up there and feel trapped by their own bodies pushing them into the seats."

She pointed to the mirror and said, "Look."

I turned and did not recognize myself. I looked just like the girl in the posters, with my face sparkling with light and my lips drawn in ruby red and shining. My eyes were luminous in my pale face, like jewels. Behind me I saw Lollie smiling, then turning around to smooth the leotard that dipped over her breasts and flattened her stomach. "It's time to get dressed," she whispered, reaching for my leotard with the thousands of rhinestones glinting off it. When I slipped into it, the fabric rubbed against my skin like silk.

I turned back to the mirror and thought, *I will never take this off.*

I wanted time to sit and think, to let my body adapt itself to the makeup and the glitter, but then we were walking through the dark lot, crunching over gravel and discarded candy wrappers, the night air cool on our skin. We could hear the muffled sounds of the crowd, the pounding of horses' hooves.

We entered through the back flap of the big top and stood behind the starry curtain, where Mauro was waiting.

"Tessita," he breathed, when he saw me, "you look so beautiful."

If I hadn't been so terrified already, I might have been nervous next to him. It was the first time I'd seen him in his full costume since the night he'd taken me into Mexico City. His pale costume curved smoothly against his skin, showing every rounded muscle. The kohl under his eyes made them smolder like two small piles of ash.

I clutched his hand and stood stock-still, waiting.

Lollie left us to head into the ring with Geraldo. We watched them perform through a slit in the curtain. Then I noticed the audience for the first time, and it was like looking from the sky to the earth. The sawdust-coated ground seemed to drop out from under me.

It was right then, at that moment, that Mauro leaned down and said, "Tessita, it is time."

The feel of the crowd, the din of moving feet, of breath being pulled in and boxes of caramel corn being rattled and dropping to the ground—none of that had been present when I'd rehearsed with Lollie and Paulo in the ring, not in the final days of the last season or in the winter space down in Mexico. While Lollie and Geraldo took their bows, I hurried into the ring, in the shadows, and sidled up the rope ladder to the platform.

I looked down to see my two glittering slippered feet resting on the platform and, far below them, the sawdust-covered ground.

I stood and waited.

When the ringmaster announced my name, my heart thumped in my chest so loudly it drowned out everything else. I was shrouded in darkness, clutching the bar in my hand, waiting for the lights to flare on and send me hurling into space. "Tiny Tessa," he blared out, to cheers and applause, "now in the center ring."

I could not even breathe.

When the lights came on I just closed my eyes and leapt.

M y act opened with me tearing out in a hoop and then flipping over and over it, catching it with my feet and my palms as it twirled and twisted over the audience. I became a swirling sparkling circle of white before stopping suddenly, splayed out, my arms and feet spread, in the center of the circle. The lights caught on my costume and reflected out into the audience, sitting under me in the dark.

My body moved of its own accord. I cut through the air as if it were a part of me.

One moment I was leaping into the air; the next I was landing on the platform, feeling the sting of the bar in my palms, the platform swaying slightly under me as I adjusted to its surface. The roar of the audience seemed far away. My breath came shallow and quick.

The Roman rings dropped down next as the hoop disappeared into the folds of the tent. I reached for them and went straight into my routine. The iron cross and then a series of positions I had done before on the rope and trapeze. From the rings the movements looked more weightless, fluid.

Finally, the *corde lisse* dropped from the top of the tent and I caught hold of it. Hanging from the padded loop Paulo had designed for me, I blocked everything out and just started to go.

One swing-over, two swing-overs. By the fifth one, the audience had begun calling them out. It buoyed me, gave me a rhythm where I hadn't had one before. I closed my eyes, leaned into the rope, and turned in time to the audience's chant. *Twenty-two, twenty-three . . .*

"Go," I said to myself. "Don't stop." *Twenty-nine, thirty.* I turned and turned, moved my body like a stutter as the crowds counted out each spin.

Up in the lights like that, punishing my body with twist after twist, I didn't actually think; my body took over until I was nothing but breath and movement, the twisting of skin and muscles into one perfect motion after another. *Sixty-nine, seventy.*

On the ninetieth spin, I felt something in my arm give out, and I stopped. I switched arms and hung there by the rope for a second. I could have been back in Oakley, hanging from the barn rope and the oak tree, until I heard the burst of applause hit that tent like a wave. The audience was cloaked in darkness; the light was bright on me and dim everywhere else. The applause seemed to have a will of its own, and it spread through the tent, sweeping right up into me. Without even thinking, I threw out my free arm and did a tiny bow, still hanging from the rope. The crowd screamed and hollered and just kept on clapping.

Then, in one swooping motion, I slid down the rope and to the floor. Standing in the sawdust, I smiled and bowed a final time before running behind the curtain. "And that was the magnificent Tiny Tessa in her Velasquez Circus debut!" I heard the ringmaster call.

"Tessa!" They all swarmed me at once, hugging me and knocking rhinestones from my leotard to the ground. Paulo and Lollie whooped around me, while Mauro slipped his hand through mine and beamed. Carlos bolted toward me and threw me up into the air. I felt myself laughing and laughing, but it seemed like it was all happening to someone else.

"Do you hear them?" Lollie asked. "Do you hear the crowd?"

"They love you," Paulo breathed. "It's amazing, like you have no weight up there."

The crowd did not stop. "Go back and bow, Tessa," Lollie said.

I took a deep breath and ran to the center of the ring. The light hit my skin and reflected off it. I felt like a sliver of glass held up to the sun.

That was when it broke open for me, and the dreamy world I had inhabited until then became shocking, loud. I stared out at the faces in the audience, and I could see them—men and women and children with faces lit up by joy, clapping and whistling and calling my name.

That night we celebrated for hours. Everyone whirled around me with congratulations and kisses. Everyone wanted to shake my hand or lift me up and twirl me in the air. I could barely keep any of it straight. At one point Mr. Velasquez came over and said simply, "Good job." When he left, Carlos leaned over to me, grinning so wide I thought his face might break. "That's as good as it gets, *chica*," he said. "Enjoy it. Drink it all in."

Paulo lit a huge bonfire out by the train cars. One of the concession girls mixed a vat of pink lemonade with rum and started serving it in ice-filled plastic glasses. There was music all around us. The band moved outside the moment that the crowds left the big top and started spilling out of the lot and back to their cars and tents. Mauro never left my side; I looked up at him, woozy, and his face was lit up as if an explosion had been set off.

"This is just like the night Mary performed with us for the first time," Lollie said at one point. "When everything was about to change." She looked at me, drunk and happy. "I knew you were something special, *chica*, the first time I saw you."

I burrowed my face into Mauro's neck and sighed. My muscles were heavy, and my head spun with rum. When the fire finally went down and, one by one, we all drifted off to our cars or tents, Mauro actually had to carry me off to bed.

Later, as I fell into an exhausted sleep, I dreamt of Mary, and my mother and father and brothers and Geraldine sitting in the shadows below me. The lights flashed from my body over theirs, and I swooped and arced and flew. I dreamt that they all watched me the way the audience had, with faces caught up in the fantasy and glamour, the new worlds I spun in the air.

I woke to the sound of someone banging on the compartment door. I turned over and pulled a pillow over my face. The early-morning sun streamed in through the open curtains.

"Tessa!" I heard, and more banging.

A minute later Lollie pounced on the bed next to me. Before I could even protest, she snatched the covers away and thrust a paper in my face.

I blinked my eyes open and saw it: a photo of me from the night before, in mid-swing-over, right on the front page of the town newspaper.

"What?" I sat up straight, grabbed the paper and read about my "glowing face and tiny body," my "endless rotations that left the crowd speechless and stunned."

"Geraldo picked it up in town," Lollie said. "I don't know what he was doing there, but he said everyone's talking about it."

I stared down at the photo. My smiling face, my graceful, arching body.

"Come on," she said, grinning and tapping my back. "Let's get some *café*."

Wide awake, I rushed to throw on some clothes, and the two of us burst into the bright morning, where Mauro and Paulo were waiting. Most of the performers were still sleeping, but there was plenty of activity on the lot: roustabouts at work cleaning the grounds, random circus people milling around, a smattering of fans.

We made our way to the cookhouse. The Ferris wheel hung over us

like a sleeping beast, and the tent just sat there. An open mouth, waiting
for us.

We were passing the big top when a young woman approached us.

"Tessa?" she asked, walking straight up to me.

"Yes?" I looked at her suspiciously. I was completely unused to
friendly attention from strangers, let alone anyone actually knowing my
name like that. She was young and eager-looking, with short brown hair.

"I'm from the local newspaper and would like to interview you for
tomorrow's paper."

"Interview me?"

"Yes, ma'am."

"Go ahead," Lollie said, smiling at me.

I looked up at Mauro, who nodded. "Be careful," he whispered, as I
pulled away.

The woman, Rachel, and I talked while walking through the
menagerie tent. I pointed out the animals to her, the way Lollie had
done for me, as she asked about my background, my life.

"I came from Kansas," I said. "I knew a woman who had been in the
circus, Mary Finn, or Marionetta, and she showed me how to fly. Then
I made my way here."

"You knew Marionetta?" the woman asked, turning to me. "Marionetta the flyer?"

"Yes," I whispered, suddenly uncomfortable.

"I was a huge fan," she said, visibly becoming excited. "We always
wondered what happened to her, why she stopped performing, where
she went. You say you met her in Kansas?"

"Yes," I said. Suddenly adrift, suddenly floating in that water, her
hair wrapped around my neck.

"What was her story? What happened to her?"

I looked up at her. My voice strangled in my throat. *Why did I mention her?* I thought. *How could I be so stupid?* Somehow I still thought of her as all mine, despite everything.

"I can't talk about that," I said finally.

"Well, then, can you tell me the nature of your relationship?"

I looked at the Vadala horses, zoomed my gaze in on their white manes.

"She was my friend," I said. And suddenly my eyes filled with tears. *My friend,* I thought. *My best friend.*

"Where exactly in Kansas did you say you were from? Is that where I can find Marionetta now?"

I shook my head.

"This is unbelievable," she said then, smiling at me, not even noticing my wet eyes and pinched face. "God, we've been wondering about Marionetta for so long, and then you pop out of the woodwork."

The pit in my stomach grew, my heart started to beat faster, and suddenly I realized: *I don't have to do this. I don't have to say another word.*

"I'm sorry," I said, before walking out of the menagerie, then breaking into a run, heading straight to the cookhouse.

Lollie, Paulo, and Mauro looked up in surprise. José and Carlos had joined them.

"That was quick," Lollie said with a laugh, setting down her coffee. "How does it feel to be so famous?"

I sat down and looked at the ground. Before I could even register what was happening, I began to weep.

"What's wrong, Tessita?" Mauro and Carlos asked again and again while Lollie shushed them, stroked my hair.

I looked up at her. When I was finally able to speak, I said, "She wanted to know about Mary. That's all. I couldn't do it." I choked out the words.

"Oh," Lollie said, shaking her head angrily. "Of course. I should have thought of it, warned you."

"Bastards," José said.

"Don't worry about it," Mauro said to me. "Let's have our breakfast and forget about it." He leaned in and kissed me, then went to the line and brought back coffee and pastries. We ate, and I tried to shake it off. More and more circus folk wandered into the cookhouse and congratulated me on my performance.

"Look," Lollie said to each one, displaying the cover article proudly. "Look, they love her. Doesn't she look gorgeous?"

Everyone seemed to be happy for me, kissing my cheeks or shaking my hand, patting my back.

As the day wore on, there were more reporters, each of them wanting to talk to me. Most weren't able to find me; either the roustabouts got to them before they sneaked into the backyard, or back of the lot, or the other performers claimed I'd gone into the city to get my hair permed, or to buy leather gloves, or any number of other things I had never done in my life. I just stayed in the car and stretched and played cards.

Lollie had spread the word fast: no interviews, no reporters. Refusing press also made the sting less biting for the other performers, Carlos said.

"Everyone wants to be where you are now," he said, over a lunch of black beans and *platanos*. "Our livelihoods depend on it, on the people loving us. You've got to be humble to keep friends, *chica*."

I nodded, almost laughing out loud at the absurdity of it.

But that second night, the lot literally overflowed with fans. Backstage, the atmosphere was electric. Even Mr. Velasquez stood back there that night.

"Go get 'em, kid," he said, making me laugh.

Several people came up to wish me luck, but I began to notice, that night, the many performers who looked away when I caught their eye, or seemed to look me up and down disapprovingly when I walked by. Geraldo, especially.

"It is the flying trapeze they all come to see, the act that grabs their hearts and imagination," I heard him say loudly to one of the menagerie girls, who didn't even blink. "Not all this *spin spin spin.*"

I ignored it the way I used to when I walked through Oakley and it was just me and Mary, no one else. I stood behind the curtain in my leotard clutching Mauro's hand. When the time came I scuttled up the rope ladder and stood staring down at the sawdust, past my glittering slippers. This time the applause came before I even began.

A fterward there was no celebration like the night before. Just quick congratulations before we packed up and dismantled the lot, leaving the grass so bare and blank that you'd never know we'd been there. The train whooshed out of town deep in the night, speeding to the next lot, the way it would over and over again. I loved feeling the ground rumble under us. I opened the curtains and watched the dark earth passing by, all the homes with glimmering windows and families sleeping inside, the endless stretches of crops and fields, the jagged cities and quaint towns, the fences strung along the tracks. That night, very late, there was a heavy rain that came slashing across the windows. The air roiled outside. I just lay back and listened to the pattering, the rumbling wheels.

I imagined what life was like in each town, each house, what selves I might have been had I lived there instead of where I did. It was safe, thinking like that, and there was nothing more safe than being in that train car, deep in the night, traveling between lots. I lay back and thought about all the lives unfolding around me, and imagined my family exactly as I'd last seen them: my father in his rocking chair, Geraldine tending her garden, my mother chopping and roasting in the kitchen while my brothers harvested the crops in the fields. What would they say if they could see me now? I wondered. If they could see my rhinestone-drenched costume, hear the applause? Flying across the countryside, it didn't bother me to think like that. With each Spanish word I learned, each kiss Mauro gave me, each footprint I left in the sawdust of the big top, the farther away I got from Oakley, the more separate I was from my own past.

W hen the news about me and Mary broke, none of us could have predicted the way the crowds would react. The morning we arrived at the second lot, for the third show of that first season, Rachel's article came out in the *Tribune*: "Mystery Girl Tessa Trained by Marionetta." The story was picked up by the other papers even as the *Tribune* itself made its way to the next town, and the next.

The crowds went crazy. Mary had been a popular performer, and now there was a mystery behind her leaving the circus, which somehow made its way to me and heightened my "mystique," as Paulo said. Even before the midway opened, people were lining up on the streets, all around the lot, waiting for the show.

"Everyone thinks you have a wonderful, secret past now," Paulo said. "And then they come and you're all light, a spinning blurring thing. It's incredible."

He passed me a copy of the paper as we rested on the grass. There, right on the front, were two photos, side by side: me darting out in the hoop, all lights and sparkle, and Mary, hanging by her hands from the bar, her hair in a long ponytail down her back, as beautiful as I'd ever seen her. I couldn't even trace the mixture of feelings it brought out in me: anger, rage, love, pride, a sadness that blotted out everything.

Mary would always be attached to me, I thought. I would never leave her to forge my own way.

✳

CHAPTER SEVENTEEN

Those first weeks with the Velasquez Circus passed by in a whirl-wind. The pace was frantic and crazed, something I wasn't used to after the unhurried luxury of Mexico, the dull throb of the factory, the long days at Mercy Library. In the circus it was working and crowds and shows and moving to the next lot, always. Building and dismantling, building and dismantling again. Asserting ourselves in the world with the brightest lights, loudest colors, and visions out of a dream.

I practiced every day, learning new tricks and perfecting old ones, adding little flourishes to my standard routines. No matter how crazy everything got, or how many whispers I heard or thought I heard as I walked by, no matter how many fans ran up to me begging for my auto-graph or just wanting to touch me, I could hang from the rope or the bar and feel like everything was normal. Exactly right. I dreamt of the tricks at night, woke up with adrenaline rushing through my body. I learned to wrap my shoulders in a sheet that hung from a steel hook overhead, and to glide through the room, wrapping and unwrapping myself as the sheet shimmered and flapped around me. In time I could wrap the sheet under each shoulder so that it hung out like wings, wrap it around my torso and throw my arms above it so that it seemed I was not held up by anything at all.

And still I tried to master the flying trapeze. I climbed to the platform and stared at Paulo hanging from the cradle, his feet wrapped around it, his body hanging down and his arms stretched out. As he swung, he kept his eyes on me the whole time. He called for me to jump to the bar, and then, once I was there, swinging upward into empty space, he called for me to release my hands and fly into the air, spinning and turning and then reaching out at the exact right moment to place my hands in his.

I swung. I released. I soared in the air, and time slowed down. I could have been up there for hours. Turning, precisely moving my body from one position to the next. And then I froze up at the moment when I should have given myself over completely to the world, to the air, to Paulo's sure hands reaching out for mine.

Again and again the fear spread like ice through my body. I missed his hands and dropped into the net. I became an expert at falling, falling smoothly on my back and bouncing up to land on my feet. Landing on the back was important. Landing on the belly, as I had more than once, could tear your muscles and burn your skin. Landing on the head or feet could result in a broken neck, broken ankles. Luis was like a ghost haunting the ring, and I think we all woke up at least once, our bodies drenched in sweat, thanking God that we could still move our fingers and toes, that we were still whole.

"Tessita, just let go," Mauro told me. "When you're up there, just give yourself up to it. Trust that Paulo is there."

After all my failures, I was surprised sometimes that Paulo still showed up in the tent each morning, dressed in his catcher's outfit. More and more it was just him and me. Now that we were back on the road, Lollie was thoroughly caught up in Geraldo—kissing him passionately one minute, right there in the cookhouse or the tent, and the next minute screaming at him or shutting herself in her train car to weep.

I had more than a sneaking suspicion that Lollie was not altogether happy about my success. She remained my friend and had a vested interest in me, having trained me and made me part of the Ramirez act, but I saw her face when children called out my name and not hers when we went past in the parade. Everyone loved Lollie, but she had been a flyer for twenty years. I was new, brand-new to the world. I did tricks no one had ever seen before.

I saw her looking in the mirror, tracing her fingers along the lines that outlined her mouth and eyes. I sat next to her sometimes and just gazed at her, at how wonderful she was. So glamorous and rounded, so sexy and soft. Her light-brown wavy hair and hazel eyes.

"I'm old," she said once. "Too old for this, for babies, for love. You are lucky, Tessa, to be young."

"Lollie," I said, "you are so beautiful. How can you say that?"

She turned to me. "Men used to line up to meet me after the shows. They used to send enough flowers to fill the villa with roses and tulips. Now look at me. All used up."

"But you're only forty," I said.

"In the circus," she said, "I am ancient. And it is too late for me. I never had a normal life. No family, no babies, no husband."

"You can still be married," I said. "Why don't you and Geraldo marry?"

"He will never marry, and I will never leave him."

"But why?"

"Let it rest," she said, turning from me. She stood up and angrily reached for her bag. "Do not judge me, *chica*."

She left me sitting there. I looked at my own face in the mirror. My blue eyes and pale skin, my small features. I held my hands up under the light and thought of what Mauro had said just a few days before.

"Your hands are beautiful."

"They are starfish hands," I had said.

"Tessita, what you see is all wrong," he had laughed, picking up my hand and holding it out in front of both of us. "These hands are not fish shaped like stars. Why do you say these things?"

I was surprised to learn, slowly, that Lollie was like me. That she hated herself sometimes, felt ashamed the way I did.

To me, she was perfect. I never understood her self-loathing, or what it was about love that could reduce a woman like her and keep her tied to a man like Geraldo, who was nowhere near her equal. Lollie's love for Geraldo pressed down on her like a sieve, but it was only later that I understood how painful it was for her to bear. I did not know back then about how much she had longed for children with Geraldo and how she had been betrayed by her own barren body, while he had fathered at least a dozen bastard children over the years.

Still, I don't think Lollie minded so much that I could not do the flying trapeze. As attractive as it would have been, from a business standpoint, to include me and Paulo in her act, it was only on the flying trapeze that Lollie had Geraldo all to herself. There, under the lights, drenched in glitter and feathers, she could live out the love story she could not seem to have in real life. All his flaws fell away and it was just him, flying to her, cradling her as if she were the most precious woman in the world. Before every performance Lollie had a glow about her, an anticipation, and afterward it was always as if she had fallen to earth. It was a strange thing, how the air and the lights could seduce you like that, making you believe that what happened up there was more real than anything else.

Paulo was the one who wanted me to fly. "It'll come," he said. "In time. And when it does, there will be nothing like it in the world." He was endlessly patient with me as I fell and fell and fell.

I knew his fiancée back home, Serena, had recently sent word that she was pregnant, that it was important for Paulo to make my act first-rate—for the Ramirez act in general, for me, and for the baby growing in Serena's belly. I wanted to master the trick so badly I could taste it, but the fear was bigger than my want. When it came on, it just swept me down to the net like I'd been caught in a waterfall. I looked down at the ground and saw only empty space.

"Concentrate," Paulo would say, but in truth I was concentrating so hard I'm surprised I didn't start levitating.

Despite my frustration, the air gave me a confidence I'd never had before. The deeper we went into the heart of the country and the more times I went into the ring and performed, the more a confidence grew in me, straight out of bone and muscle and blood. It was larger than anything I'd experienced before, even the shame that came over me sometimes, the jealousy I felt when I glimpsed Clementine from the big top, when I sat in the train car and tortured myself with images of her and Mauro in the same bed. It was larger than the corn-clawed moon that never quite left the periphery of my dreams. This was something from deep within my body. A surety, a calmness.

I walked arm in arm with Mauro and felt proud. I found myself in restaurants reaching for salt or butter and realized I wasn't curling my palm over to conceal the shape of my hand. I found myself looking strangers straight in the eye, hugging the fans who pushed through the starry curtain to say hello.

I found myself feeling that I had a presence and a shape that were only mine.

It was only my jealous heart that threatened to unmoor me, for a time. In Mexico I had imagined that Clementine would be there every day, taunting me, but in reality the sideshow could have been a hundred miles away from the big top. As it was, I only caught glimpses of

Clementine. I'd see the white flash of her hair and wince. I'd see her hauling pails of water or wandering through one of the towns we stayed in,
and every vein in my body would grow cold. If I was with Mauro I'd
squeeze his hand and look at the ground, without saying a word.

"What is wrong, Tessita?" he asked. *"Qué pasa?"*

And the words burned on my tongue: *What happened with her? Did you
love her? How can you even look at me?*

They crowded my brain, stuck through me like pinpricks. And yet I
didn't say anything. Even over the countless hours in the ring, on the
train, and wandering over the lot, even as Mauro told me stories about
his life and I told him about Oakley and Riley Farm and the factory.
Even when I sucked in my breath and told him about the day in front of
the courthouse, the endless afternoons in the library, Mary's rich, raspy
voice and card games and her penchant for cataloging and reading out
loud and cooking pots of soup and tea. Even when I told him about the
hair that curled wetly around her neck and the opal that glittered spook-
ily from her breast. The story had been beating within me like a heart. If
I had tried to tell it before, it would have stayed buried in my throat,
bound up in grief.

But I could not ask him about Clementine, and I could not tell him
that when I saw Clementine's perfect starlight hair, I heard my father's
voice again in my ear: *Barely even a girl*, he had said, as the dirt and rocks
pressed into my skin. I felt ugly and ridiculous, the way I had then.

I waited for Mauro to bring up Clementine himself. I walked hand
in hand with him to the cookhouse or to watch the Kriminov Twins
practice in the late afternoons, after I finished with Paulo and showered
in preparation for the show, waiting. Mauro loved watching the twins.
People said the earth had disappointed them so much that they chose to
walk in the clouds, on stilts. One afternoon that first summer, I sat with
Mauro and watched Sergei balance Masha on his shoulders so that her

head nearly grazed the canvas top. The words and questions beat in my head, but I wouldn't ask him. Instead I asked him about the sideshow, about performers like the fat lady, Josephine, whose skin fell from her bones and just kept right on falling, like huge sails.

"Jo is a great lady," Mauro said. "The daintiest woman you'll ever meet. You could scoop up her hands and eat them for dessert." He laughed and pulled me close to him.

I leaned in. "Mauro," I said, "how can you be so close to the people in the ten-in-one? Lollie and your brothers never go near it. The twins and Ana don't."

"Oh," he said, laughing, "they've always been that way—circus folk, that is. It doesn't mean anything. They just have to believe the people come here for them and them only."

"Don't you think they're horrible, though?" I asked, holding my breath. "With their tattoos and scales and wings?"

He looked at me, surprised. "Why, do you?" he asked.

"No." I whispered it, staring at my hands folded in my lap. I stretched my feet till they tapped the bleacher below. "But I've heard Geraldo call them all freaks. I've heard others say it, too."

He laughed. "Geraldo! Who could be more of a freak than that guy? He's probably got ten children in every town we pass through."

His voice was so loud, I looked around the tent to see if anyone had heard. The Kriminov Twins were still practicing—Masha flipping from Sergei's shoulders to the floor. It was beautiful. There, a perfect moment, right in the middle of a long afternoon. Why wasn't I happier than I was, surrounded by such things?

"Ana told me that we don't mix with them, that her family never does," I said.

Suddenly I heard Ana's voice that first day: *Aren't you in the ten-in-one?*

No! I thought. *Clementine is the freak.* I thought of the wings stretching out of flesh and bone. The disgusting fusion of feather and bone and blood and flesh.

Mauro turned to me. "Are you okay?" he asked. "Why do you care what the Vadalas do? They think their Italian blood is more pure than our blood."

"I'm fine," I said, but could feel my face scrunching up and tears burning at my eyes.

"What is it?" he asked, taking my hands in his. "Why don't you talk to me?"

I just stared at the twins, at Masha practicing the stilts while Sergei watched. The words beat at me, but I could not say them. I looked up at his beautiful face, his black eyes.

"Why do you like me?" I blurted.

"What do you mean?" He was genuinely shocked. "Tessa, I love you. You know I love you."

"Don't you think I'm a freak?" I asked, without even thinking.

"Why would I love a woman I thought was a freak? What are you talking about? I don't even think that way in the first place."

I could feel my face flushing. "What about Clementine?" I whispered. "Isn't she one?"

Mauro's face eased. He laughed out loud and pulled me to him. "*Eres celosa!* Jealous!" He leaned back and looked at me. "Please do not be jealous of her," he said. "That was long ago and so unimportant. Not nearly so important as what we have. I am proud of you, Tessita, how beautiful you are, how talented. You are small, *sí.* Perfectly so, like a piece of embroidery. Clementine was not for me. If she had been, we would have married."

"Married?"

"But I didn't marry her. And not because of people like the Vadalas.

Because it wasn't right; she wasn't right for me." I looked up at him. His face shifted and got soft. "And besides, I want to marry you."

I was suddenly aware of the landscape outside, the lush green grass and the mountains hovering around us on all sides. I could feel the hazy summer air, the trees and grass. The sharp scent of the sawdust.

"What?" I whispered, foolishly.

Mauro cleared his throat. "I planned to do this later this week, Tessita, but now how can I wait?" He smiled. "You're lucky I don't trust anyone enough to keep this on the train." He pulled a twinkling diamond ring from his pocket and slipped it on my finger. "Will you marry me?" I saw that his hands were shaking.

"Yes!" I cried. "Yes!"

The Kriminov Twins stopped and looked up at us. The lion tamer looked up. Carlos, standing near the opening of the tent with the elephant girl, looked up. So did Ana and Bici the clown and a Polish contortionist with fake yellow hair, Petra.

The whole day turned dizzy and light. Mauro leapt up the bleachers and balanced himself on the outer edge. He shifted back and forth on the ledge and shouted down, for all the big top to hear: "TESSA RILEY IS GOING TO MARRY ME! WE ARE GOING TO BE MARRIED!"

Mauro rushed down and scooped me up in his arms, then flipped me up in the air. I had never seen him so silly. Within minutes word had gotten out, and Lollie was there beside me, roused from a lazy game of cards in the cookhouse, along with other friends.

That night we celebrated after the show, dancing around the fires outside the train car, opening bottles of champagne that Carlos had run into town to get. The corks popped off and the champagne shimmered down into our plastic glasses. Lollie raised her glass again and again to us, getting more misty each time. Had I been more grounded that night, I might have paid more attention when Geraldo didn't even show up, and I might have seen how sad Lollie was, underneath the surface of things.

The next morning it was in all the local papers, and there we were, in a photo someone had taken: Mauro and I, side by side, he towering over me as I sparkled up at the camera in my rhinestone leotard. *Circus Royalty to Wed,* a headline read. "Tiny Tessa, 18, famous for her one-arm swing-over, and Mauro Ramirez, 22, of the Ramirez Brothers tightrope act, announce engagement."

There we were. I thought for a moment of Mercy Library, all the newspapers and documents stored in the file cabinets downstairs, where I had first seen my name in print alongside my mother's, father's, brothers' and sister's. This photo seemed to blot out all of it. With a fluttering heart, I clipped out the article carefully and put it into a file alongside all the other articles from that first season, when, for me, the whole world was remade.

We were married the following winter in Mexico City. Returning to the villa was like coming home. I hugged Luis like a long-lost brother—my *real* brother, not the ones I'd been born with. I embraced Mrs. Ramirez as if she were my true mother. Paulo's Serena and baby, Pilar, had moved into the house earlier in the fall, and we all rushed to see the beautiful fat baby with tiny gold hoops dangling from her ears.

Mrs. Ramirez and Victoria oversaw the design and making of the intricate lace dress I wore at our wedding, and Mauro and I were married before a gold-covered altar with the Virgen de la Macarena in front. Carlos gave me away. Lollie and Serena and Mrs. Ramirez stood in a line next to Mauro as I walked up to him, a bouquet of white gardenias in my hand. The other brothers formed a line on the right.

As I walked toward Mauro, so handsome in his traditional black suit, I had to force myself to walk in long, graceful steps, to keep my veil and train in place and not yank off the lace and run, laughing, right into his arms.

I was happy, happier than I'd ever been. For the first time happiness was a condition of my world, not a moment that sparked and burned away. I loved being married to Mauro. During my second season, when the Velasquez Circus grew even more popular and well loved, he kept me centered. He formed a cocoon around me as reporters became more and more common on the lot and people began waiting in lines that wrapped three times around the tent to get in.

The years passed in a dizzying array of colors, a thousand colors flashing and sparkling along endless horizons. I practiced less and less and spent more time with my new husband, my family. I continued to work on the rope and hoop. I increased the number of swing-overs I could do at one time to nearly two hundred and began working more on the rope ladder and silks. As for the flying trapeze, I just let it go. I worked so well alone in the air, it didn't seem necessary to punish my body and heart anymore, to fling myself into empty space again and again and feel that cold fear erupt inside me. I was happy now; I didn't need to claw my way through whatever it was inside me that would not let me just *go*.

Paulo didn't mind by then either. He married Serena and brought her and Pilar on the road with us. Before long they had a second child, Eduardo, born my third winter in Mexico. Lollie doted on Pilar and Eduardo, who seemed to calm her anxious, starved heart, and Paulo and Serena seemed to be made for each other, always laughing as they wandered the lot with their toddling babies. Even José found happiness with

Ana's older sister Bettina Vadala, who confessed her attraction to him one night after too many glasses of homemade sangria by the fire.

So time passed, and though I still woke sometimes certain that I could smell Mary's scents of clove and cinnamon, calling me to the past and the future, I just let them sweep by.

✳

CHAPTER EIGHTEEN

One night during my fourth season with the circus, a knock came at my door as I prepared for an evening show. We were somewhere in the middle of the country, outside Kansas City—close enough to Oakley that I probably should have been a little nervous, but I had begun to feel immune to the outside world by then, I guess. If not for my name emblazoned on the door and the sheaf of articles that had been printed about me in newspapers and magazines, no one would have recognized me as the same Tessa Riley who had scrunched down into knots and crept through the fields of Riley Farm.

I opened the door and thought I was looking into a crazy funhouse mirror, the kind that could shrink you down to one foot or stretch you out to the size of a building, depending on your angle. There outside my door stood a girl with my face—the same rounded eyes and bow-shaped mouth, the same sloping nose—but about three times my size, as if I'd expanded overnight.

The girl looked at me with even more shock than I felt.

"Tessa?" she asked.

"Yes," I said, looking at her.

It hit me like a slap. It was a moment I'd dreaded ever since I'd first seen my image on the posters that were splashed through every town on the circus's route. She was different and yet the same as I re-membered.

"Geraldine?" I asked, my mouth hanging open.

And I had the sudden, sinking, grief-stricken sense that all of life had passed me by.

S he had come to make peace with me, she said. We sat in my dressing room, I on the chair by my vanity and she on the tiny sofa shoved against one wall. She had slimmed down over the years. I was surprised at the delicacy of her fingers, fine long fingers that cultivated orchids and other blooms in a flower shop in Kansas City, as she later told me.

I could not believe it. Geraldine grown, sitting in front of me, an al-most elegant woman with long-fingered hands that would never spoon sugar straight from the bag and into her mouth.

"You left Oakley?" I asked.

"Yes," she said, "as soon as I could. Not too long after you left, Tessa."

"I always thought you would be the same," I managed to get out, "that all of you would be the same."

"Things changed a lot after you went away," she said. "Dad never spoke another word to anyone, just sat on that stupid chair and rocked himself to death. Mom cried and howled all those last months, but once Dad died, she became a new person entirely. It was as if she'd been freed, and she started letting other farmers court her, and then Mr. Briggs from down the road moved in with us. He seemed okay, but that's around when I left."

She took a breath and stopped. Geraldine seemed nervous sitting there with me, as if she were afraid to sit in silence for one second. I did not know what to say to her. She was like a ghost out of some other life—a life that still had the power to devastate me and strike me down, no matter how far I traveled away from it.

"Oh, these are for you," she said quickly, handing me a small bouquet I had not noticed before then.

I looked down at the exquisite arrangement of lilacs and daffodils, then stood awkwardly to find a jar to put them in. I could not look at Geraldine's face as I brushed past the couch to the bathroom faucet.

When I stepped back into the room, Geraldine was staring at the cosmetics littering my vanity, the couple of sequined caps tossed to the side, the pot of glitter next to the smooth silver hairbrush with my name engraved on the handle.

Geraldine met my eyes then and smiled quickly before looking down. "She missed you, you know," she said then. "I mean, I know they weren't the greatest parents or anything, but Mom cried for days when you went away. She kept saying she'd failed you."

Slashes of pain went through me as I let her words sink in. "What about Dad?" I asked, after several moments.

"He didn't say anything," she said. "I mean, I don't know what he thought or felt. He was always going off by himself, you remember, and then at a certain point he stopped talking at all."

She looked at me.

"Why did you leave us?" she asked after a long pause, her face twisting slightly.

We sat in silence for several minutes then. I didn't know what to say, just stared at her tapered shoes. "Was it Dad?" she whispered.

I looked up at her, searching her face. "It was everything," I said finally. "I couldn't stay there."

"It's okay, Tessa," Geraldine said, and reached out for my hand. "I know you were sad at home. I knew things weren't right, somehow, for you. I always hoped you were okay after you left. I would try to imagine where you were."

I was surprised to see her crying, and even more surprised to feel the tears sliding down my own cheeks.

"Why are you here?" I asked.

"You're my only sister," she said. "I wondered if you thought about us, knew what happened to us the way we knew about you, all this time. I mean, we saw you in the papers. We saw pictures of you on the trapeze. We saw pictures of you when you were married."

My whole world seemed to shift over one notch more with each thing she said. "I never thought you could see me when I couldn't see you," I whispered. "It was always the opposite, when I was growing up."

"I felt that way, too," Geraldine said, "when we were growing up. I felt invisible, though I was hideous and gigantic, and I could never hold myself in the way I wanted to."

"Really?" I said.

She nodded, smiling at me.

"I'd see that woman Mary sometimes when Mom took me to town, and even though Mom yanked me away and got furious at me, I'd stare at Mary and imagine spending time with her like you did. I was always jealous of you back then. I was so lumbering and slow, and you could run for miles."

"You remember her?" I asked quietly. "Really?"

"Of course," she said. "I remember the first time I heard of her. Mom was yelling at Dad and saying he couldn't bring books into the house. She always thought they'd had an affair. God, she talked about it enough."

"Yeah," I said, remembering that long-ago day. "I remember."

"She got so mad sometimes thinking about you working there, but she wouldn't dare say anything. I mean, with the money, and Dad."

"Did he ever say anything?"

"No," she said. "He never did."

She looked to the ground for a second, and suddenly I just knew. "Geraldine," I asked slowly, "did Dad take you out in the fields, too?"

The room was silent for several long moments. Her shoulders crumpled, and she bent her head down.

"I never knew," I whispered. "I thought it was only me."

"I don't know what was wrong with him, Tessa," she said, looking up. "Why he was like that. Mom was always worried about Mary Finn and every other beautiful woman, but it was us. Just us."

"But why?" I asked, knowing, of course, that Geraldine didn't have the answers any more than I did. And yet it was the first time I was able to just ask that question, in all its purity: *Why?*

She shook her head. "Look at you now, though," she said, smiling shyly. "Going all over the place, a circus star! When I first saw you in the paper, I couldn't believe it. I wanted to jump up and down."

Her smile was genuine, spreading across her face. I smiled back at her. I couldn't place my feelings exactly, and didn't try. I thought how the world works in messy, imprecise ways, smashing itself together when you want to keep it apart, breaking into a thousand slivers when all you want is peace.

We stretched out on the bed and sat with our backs against the headboard. Geraldine told me of her life and job, the farm, and some neighbors I only vaguely remembered. She told me that Mercy Library had been turned into a supermarket that my brothers sold crops to, and all the books had been donated to a new school the town had built a couple years back.

The day slipped into dusk. At one point, late in the day, Mauro stopped into our car and almost jumped when he saw Geraldine. Then he looked at me, twisting his head back and forth in confusion.

"Mauro," I said, "this is my sister, Geraldine. Geraldine, meet my husband, Mauro."

I laughed out loud as her eyes grew wide and she looked him over slowly, from top to bottom. "Wow," she breathed, flushing all over.

Mauro was no less taken aback. *"Tu hermana?"* he asked, looking at me and shaking his head. I smiled and shrugged. "Well, then," he said, putting out his hand to her, "I guess that makes you my sister, too. Come, join us all for dinner. You have to tell us all of Tessa's secrets, since she has so many." He looked back at me and winked.

I couldn't believe how well we all got along that night. Carlos took one look at Geraldine and sat next to her until showtime, enthralling her with stories about Mexico and the Ramirez family's colorful history. Lollie looked from Geraldine to me and back again, smiling.

"You are both so beautiful," she kept saying. "Like two petals on the same rose."

I gave Geraldine a front-row seat for the show that night, and as I twirled inside the hoop and on the rope I felt her eyes watching me, seeing something that she thought might help her on her way. I didn't know what it was. I thought of my dream, years before, of my family sitting under me, watching me the way the rest of the crowd did.

After the show we drank sangria in front of a huge bonfire. My husband on one side of me and my sister on the other, Paulo and Serena's babies—three of them by then—running around screaming and naked, Carlos and José laughing and telling Geraldine stories about how scared I had been when I'd first come, how mean Lollie had been, while Lollie and Ana and the twins and everyone else just laughed and talked and drank.

There was so much more I wanted to say to Geraldine that day and couldn't. I could not tell her how much I had always longed to sit with her the way we were then, as friends, as sisters. I could not tell her how the mention of my father turned my blood to ice, or that just hearing Mary's name made her more real to me than she had been for years. My Mary and the one Geraldine spoke of were the same—not the woman on the flying trapeze, but the town librarian who drove men mad and set them to dreaming. I could not believe that the world I'd done everything to suppress was still out there, beating with life and love and heartbreak, like every other place.

Before she left Geraldine took me aside, by the fire, and just held on to me. We were both drunk and happy, standing in the hazy light.

"I'm sorry," she said. "For everything. I'm sorry I never came to you." "I'm sorry, too," I whispered.

G eraldine's visit awakened something new in me, something that nagged at me over the next few years and brought back memories I'd thought were gone forever, flashes of the cornfields behind our house, empty and bleak as a nightmare. My family took on a new shape in my mind—no longer frozen in Mary's world, they had lives that extended parallel to mine, with new loves and careers and regrets and sadnesses. All the souls from my past began inhabiting my life like ghosts. Sometimes my memories were so strong I would barely see Mauro in front of me, touching my face, taking my hands in his own.

Until then the circus had seemed like a separate, magical world existing outside time and space. It had its own force and energy, its own rules as it moved from one town to another. I had always felt a little like if I stepped away from the circus, time would restart: my father would reemerge from the fields, push me back down into the dirt, and block out the moon.

But Geraldine's visit set something in motion, set my heart to remembering. My perspective started to shift, bit by bit, and memories that surprised and shocked me began to occupy my mind, chipping away at the layers of myth and story the circus had given me.

I began recalling sights and smells and voices, began staring at Mary's picture and remembering what it had felt like to sit next to her on a wooden floor, watching the sun go down, dreading the walk home. I reached past the pain of family and leaving, back into my childhood, to death and the river and Mary's hair wrapped around her neck, the water droplets clinging to her skin. And the more I reached back, the more I came to the question that had hovered around the edges of my life for years: *Who was she? Where had she come from? Why did she die?* All the unanswered mysteries at the heart of my childhood. A woman had come into my life and handed the world to me, had *seen* the world in me, but I had been too young to see her back then, as she was.

If I had I seen her, I thought, I might have been able to save her.

PART THREE

*

A few years after Geraldine's visit, during the beginning of my seventh season with the Velasquez Circus, a breeze rose up in the south of Mexico and swept over the Mayan ruins and up the coastline, carrying the scents of clove and cinnamon into the southern states. Clothes hanging out on lines dried instantly. People stepped out of showers, reached for their towels, and found their whole bodies had gone dry. Women could no longer wear skirts in the street. The trees whipped about, tossing their heads, while flower petals spun off their stems and into the air. People began sprinkling hot chocolate with cinnamon and brewing vats of cider to satisfy the cravings the spiced air left them with. In the Velasquez Circus, we looked up and wondered at the flapping canvas, the Ferris wheel spinning too fast, the slight swaying of the train on the tracks. The scent wafted over our bodies and seeped into our skin. I was plagued by strange dreams every night, the kind that trickle into your waking life and unsettle you. We all grew restless, and took to wandering the lots and towns during the day instead of gathering in the cookhouse.

I was affected more than anyone, I think. A cough and a fever forced me to cancel performances for the first time ever and take to my bed. Mauro held me as I moaned and cried, as I writhed in my sleep and held up my arms to protect my face from lashing rain, from sweet smoke curling into my mouth and choking me.

Mauro shut all the windows and locked them, but still the breeze pushed its way into our car and under the blankets. Mauro packed me in as tightly as he could, but nothing helped. The breeze rubbed up on me like a cat. The spice scent crept into every pore on my skin, every strand of my hair.

I stayed in bed without moving. I could not even enter the ring, let alone curl my hands around the *corde lisse.* Lollie could not perform either, and Geraldo was forced to go out in the ring alone—though without her he just swung through the air uselessly, stretching out his arms to empty space. The audiences complained so much and grew so belligerent that Mr. Velasquez was forced to reduce ticket prices by as much as half.

There was nothing I could do. Mauro would sing and whisper to make me sleep, but I'd bolt awake from nightmares filled with dread and loss. I'd wake with my heart pounding in my chest, and the breeze would rustle through the sheets like an intruder. Mauro could not even touch me; he'd take my hands in his and then drop them as if they were two suns. He brought all my meals to me—plates of beans or shredded beef I left sitting on the table untouched—and he read me stories and poems. Carlos came by, too, to read, and his voice was so seductive and the stories told through it so riveting that I knew once and for all how he was able to capture all those women's hearts, in every town we passed through.

The fever lasted for three weeks, as long as the breeze whisked through the circus and back again, trailing the scents of spices and stirring up longings of every kind. Mauro took to the bed with me some nights, nuzzled his face into my neck, and spoke of Mexico. Clementine fell into bed and dreamt of water; Ana dreamt of perfect white horses galloping as fast as light.

José was one of the worst afflicted. Clara haunted his dreams mercilessly and followed him throughout the day. He swore she toppled all the glasses of water he set down in his train car or on the long tables in the cookhouse, messed up his hair just after he'd painstakingly smoothed the pomade through it, and danced and jumped on the wire just ahead of him, trying to make him lose his balance. His girlfriend Bettina said he had bags under his eyes an inch thick and could barely concentrate on what was in front of him, worsening to such a degree that the brothers were forced to cut him from the act, at least until things returned to normal. But as one day faded into the next, with the breeze showing no signs of calming, none of us knew when that might be.

As for me, the world outside our train car no longer seemed to exist. Mauro kept pressing wet cloths to my forehead and bringing me plates of food, but the fever did not let up. I felt like I was drowning, caught underwater where all I could see was Mary's face next to me, staring at me through a tangle of weeds. I tried to pull myself up toward Mauro's voice and hands, but for those three weeks I could go only where the fever took me—deep into the river, to where the thousand colors of the opal stone glittered from Mary's neck.

The day my fever finally broke, a stranger showed up at the Velasquez Circus. We had arrived at a new lot only hours before, and had begun the laborious task of setting up the entire circus and midway, starting with the big top itself. The lot was mostly empty of townies except for a few of the usual autograph-seekers. But when the man with the sleek cat's eyes set foot on the lot and started striding purposefully toward the tent, we all knew he was no normal kind of fan. He looked like someone out of a story, with his tall, lanky body and dark hair, his soft green eyes and cruel, curving mouth. He had a bit of gypsy in him, too; his long black coat scraped against his knees as he walked, and his boots were black and scuffed. A camera hung from his neck, a large duffel bag from his back. Drawn by a strange sort of feeling that lifted me from my bed and to my window, I threw open the curtains just in time to watch the stranger striding into the big top.

"What is it?" Mauro asked.

"I don't know," I said. "A stranger has come."

I realized then that my skin was drenched in sweat, no longer burning the way it had been for twenty-one days straight. Suddenly I could not stand the four walls of our train car; every fiber of my body was bursting to get outside—to the sun, the air, and the big top, where the stranger waited between the open flaps. I did not even know why I was so compelled; a sort of panic had come over me, filling me only with the desire to get to the stranger as quickly as I could. I raced to get my clothes on.

Mauro and I rushed out of our car to find Lollie standing outside, dressed in her best blue flowered dress with long, draping sleeves and a swishing skirt.

"Did you notice," she asked, "that the breeze has stopped?"

Inside the tent, the oppressive atmosphere outside gave way to an electric kind of excitement as circus folk of every stripe crowded around the stranger. The whole Vadala family was there, all the brothers, Geraldo, the twins, the new contortionist act from China, the clowns. I could hear his voice—a rasping, rich sound with an accent that spoke of verbs so complicated they would take years to learn. A terrible feeling of déjà vu came over me as we approached the middle of the tent, though we'd gone through these motions a thousand times before, a stranger showing up with a bit of news or a story to tell that'd make the children's mouths drop and set all our hearts to racing. We were all eager to hear of life in the cities and towns we passed through but never inhabited, and we treated these travelers and storytellers like royalty on the lot, lavishing them with front-row seats, hot meals, and a privileged spot by the bonfire, where we always gathered to listen.

This time something felt different. Perhaps it was the breeze he came in on or the two kiwi-colored eyes that hit me like pistols as I approached, but I knew that this stranger was not there to tell us of a scandal or affair. Something about his face stopped me cold.

"Here she is now," someone said then, pointing to me.

Before I had time to think, the stranger reached his enormous hand out to me and said, "My name is Costas."

I just blinked at him, a world taking shape in my mind.

"I have come from Turkey," he said. "I am looking for information about Marionetta the flyer." If Mauro hadn't been just behind me, his hand resting protectively on my back, I think I might have tipped over and fallen to the floor.

"It's okay," Mauro whispered, but he could not help me. I tried to stop my hands from shaking. A grief welled up in me, so strong I thought I might be dying. My loss overpowered me; the ache came from my blood and my bones.

It was the boy from Mary's story. It had to be.

I looked at his face, and everything Mary had said came rushing back to me. It was crazy, how it could all return in an instant, no matter how much time had gone by, no matter how far away I was from all of it. Within one moment everything that had happened between then and now had been stripped away, and I was still that girl lying on the floor of Mercy Library, dreaming of a boy with eyes like kiwis, hidden away from the beauty of the world the way I had been.

"Forgive me," he said. "I understand that you knew Marionetta. She was my mother's sister, my aunt. I am on my way to Rain Village."

I stared at him. It was as if Mary had stepped straight out of the past and found me in front of the courthouse once more. Even as we stood there I could see Costas walking with his father in the sun, see the flicker of fish out of the corner of my eye. I could hear Mary's voice in my ear, talking about her sisters, their stone house, and the forest surrounding it. I could see her behind her desk in Mercy Library, weaving a tale about a boy who grew up in the middle of nowhere.

I felt Lollie's hand clasp mine as she moved beside me. "Mary spoke of you," I said then, trying to keep my voice from trembling. "She told me a story about you, about a boy whose father raised him without love, but I never imagined you were someone real, someone I would meet one day."

"Who are you?" he breathed, looking into me. A strange, delighted smile spread slowly across his face then, and his eyes lit with recognition. "You are the girl from the library," he said, "aren't you?"

"Yes," I said.

Everyone was quiet, watching us. More and more people filled the tent. Once the news began spreading that a stranger had shown up with the name Marionetta on his lips, not one soul stayed out on the lot.

He stepped forward. The camera dangled from his neck. "I had hoped to find my mother's family," he said. "She was dead, and I started searching for her sisters. I have traveled so long, searching for my family. For any link. I traced Mary to Oakley, and I went there to find her. I heard she had died some years ago, and then I heard about you and how you'd joined the circus."

As he spoke, I thought he was the most beautiful person I'd ever seen, and then I realized: he looked just like Mary. I thought of him in Oakley, speaking Mary's name and then mine. Walking through the town square, under the oak tree, past the post office and stationer's. A longing moved through me, but I wasn't sure what it was he was stirring.

"I am searching, too," I said, and it was only in that moment that I realized it was true. "Everywhere."

"Yes," he said, looking at me. "Have you been to Rain Village?"

Silence drifted over the tent like a billowing sheet. I could hear Mauro breathing behind me then. Not one of us hadn't dreamt of the rain and the river, heard the slap of fish on boat decks or the rapping sounds of rain pounding into mud.

"No," I said, my heart pounding. "Do you know where it is?"

Even Lollie had admitted that she did not know whether Rain Village really existed, despite all she had heard of it from Mary and all she'd seen in visions, years before.

"Yes," he said—just like that, as if it were the easiest thing in the world. "My mother wrote of it before she died."

"We never knew where it was," Carlos said, stepping forward. "In all our travels, we've only heard rumors about it."

"Come," Mauro said then, an edge in his voice that only I recognized, "let's eat. Our guest here must be starving." I looked back at him in surprise, but he didn't meet my eye.

Costas looked at Mauro gratefully, and it was then that I noticed how dirty he was, how his hair was matted against his head and the skin on his hands dark with grime. Lollie stepped up to him. "Come with us," she said, smiling.

Costas turned to Lollie and took her arm, bowing graciously. I stood there barely able to move as I watched them walk away.

"What are you doing, Tessa?" Mauro asked sharply, turning to me. I looked up and saw the hurt on his face. He could see right through me, the way he always had. "Aren't you hungry? Let's go."

Mauro's steps were heavy and quick as we walked. I could feel the words bursting at his lips.

"This *gitano*, I don't trust him," he said, finally, in a low voice.

I didn't speak. My world collapsed and broke open at the same time. The life I had built—with Mauro, with the circus—seemed unreal suddenly, less real than the memory of the riverboat moving up and down the pink-fished river, the rain that never stopped falling over it. I stared at Costas's body ahead, watched the fluid way he moved, the way he stepped back and guided Lollie into the cookhouse.

When we walked inside, Costas looked up at me and smiled. His eyes were beautiful. Casually, as if it were part of his body, he lifted the camera, adjusted the lens, and snapped a picture of us walking in. Mauro didn't even notice. We sat across from Costas, and Carlos and Lollie brought back heaping plates of roasted pork and rice for all of us. I couldn't even look at my food.

"You're a photographer?" I asked, shyly. I could feel Mauro tense beside me.

"Yes," he said. "Back in Athens, I worked for a newspaper. But I take many kinds of pictures. People, landscapes."

"Do you have any here with you?"

He looked around self-consciously.

"Yes," said Carlos, setting down his fork. "Please show us."

Costas looked back at me, then lifted his bag to the bench beside him. He reached in and felt around, and brought out a small, thick folder.

"Here are some," he said. "I just carry small prints with me. I have rolls of film in my bag to develop when I get the chance." He smiled. My heart was pounding as he handed the packet to me. I opened it excitedly, pulled out a stack of photos.

I spread them out like a deck of cards on the table. The images were vibrant, bright: a beautiful Turkish woman with a starry scarf wrapped around her head, a lime-green parrot sitting on her shoulder; two young men smoking at a café, a sign behind them like a prophecy, written in thickly slanted letters; an old Hispanic man standing next to an elaborate wrought-iron cage filled with doves, his smile crinkling across his face; waters so blue and perfect the photos themselves seemed to be wet.

"These are wonderful," I breathed. But piercingly sad, too. I thought of the poems Mary had read to me, the thick novels that had left me gasping and in tears.

It seemed like everyone started talking at once. Costas was quiet, eating his pork and watching us.

After a few minutes he reached into his bag and set another packet in front of me. These were black-and-white, swirling photos filled with light and dark. I saw sun-bronzed fishermen hauling up nets filled with salmon, women and men dressed in flared skirts and pants whirling across an outdoor plaza, a group of dirty children standing in front of a squat building, men pushing carts of vegetables through crowded streets.

"All different places I've been to," he said, "in my travels. I haven't been home for three years."

Lollie leaned over me, picking up a photo of a man surrounded by hanging sausages. I studied the photos, enthralled. What kind of vision would you have to have, I thought, to see these things? I flipped one photo over and almost gasped.

"Oakley," I said, looking up at him. I turned to Mauro next to me, glanced back to find Lollie. "Oakley," I repeated. "The town square." In the photo I could see the hanging trees, the tavern in the background. The park benches.

Mauro picked up the photo and looked from me to Costas. "This is where you grew up?" he asked.

"I went there," Costas said. "Trying to find Mary."

"Yes," I said to Mauro, and then looked to Costas. I felt unmasked suddenly, after so many years, as if they could look into the photograph and hear the kids calling me freak, see my father hunkered over me. "I used to eat lunches with Mary in that park, every once in a while. I passed through it every day. I practiced hanging from the branches of that tree, the one on the right."

Mauro laughed, but as he studied the photo and Lollie leaned in to look over his shoulder, part of me wanted to yank it from his hands and rip it to pieces. Mauro was so *separate* from all of that, I thought; everything in the circus was. My head spun. Before I could really process what was happening, Costas sifted through the photos and pulled out a second one, pushed it toward me. "This is what used to be the library," he said.

I looked down, and the words "Grady's Grocery" stared out at me, printed on that same creaking sign out front that used to say "Mercy Library." The front door, the steps—all of it was the same as I remembered, except for the men and women walking out with brown paper bags full of food. I wondered what had happened to the thousands of books and papers Mary had kept track of so carefully. I thought of her room and her boxes downstairs, the leotards and the trapeze, all the trinkets scattered over her front desk, and I felt such a tremendous sense of loss that I almost couldn't stand it. She had deserved better, I thought.

"Yes," I said weakly. "The sign is changed, but other than that it's the same."

"How long did you work there?" he asked, as Mauro leaned down and picked up the photo. I looked away. I didn't want to study the photo. I could imagine my mother, maybe at that exact moment, walking out of the store with a bag full of beef for a stew or roast. I could see Mary returning to the library with her basket filled with papers and herbs, asking what had happened to her books, her overflowing file cabinets. My head was pounding. I felt as if my heart had just been ripped open. *It all still matters*, I thought. Underneath everything, there was always *this*.

"Four years," I said.

"I missed you both by a while." Costas smiled.

"Yes," I said, sitting back, letting my breath go from ragged to almost normal. "You did." Mauro handed the photos back to him, and Costas slid them into their packets and back into his bag. I watched, helplessly. He looked straight at me and I could feel Mauro's hand grip my knee, but I could not look away. His face so like Mary's but his own, too. The set of the jaw. The determined air underneath the gypsy clothes.

It was Lollie who broke the tension. "Where do you come from, Costas?"

Everyone waited expectantly for Costas to tell us about Rain Village and Mary and the rest of his life before, the way most travelers sat back and found relief in the telling of their tales.

"I come from Turkey," he said. "I'm going to Rain Village to find my family's past, my mother's past."

"Your own," I said.

He looked at me in a way that made me blush, and I looked away quickly, flustered.

"But please," he said, turning to Lollie, "tell me about Mary, when she was here. I want to hear everything about the circus," he said, glancing over at me, "and Oakley."

I looked down at my plate, determined to stop blushing. Lollie didn't seem to notice. Speaking in her animated way, she told the story of Mary coming to the circus, back when she had followed Juan Galindo like a dog after he'd come upon her in the barn, covered in ice. She moved her arms through the air and slapped her thigh for emphasis. It was a story we'd all heard a thousand times and could listen to one thousand times more.

"I wish I could have known her," Costas said afterward. "I wish I could have seen her perform."

I could almost feel the longings in the air: for Mary and for all the people and places that had dropped away. I held tightly to Mauro's hand.

Suddenly I was dying to speak. I had really only spoken of Mary to Lollie and Mauro, in private, but a new feeling passed through me that night. For the first time I wanted to announce my story, fill the air with the sound of my voice speaking Mary's name, and so I did: I told of the day in front of the courthouse and my first visit to Mercy Library. I told him how we had brewed tea and shelved books, and practiced the trapeze in the quiet afternoons. I spoke of the last day I saw her, how her body had floated in the river like a child's.

"Did she drown herself?" Costas asked then.

"Yes," I said. It was the first time I'd said it out loud.

At that point Mr. Velasquez entered the tent, looking wan and tired. He too had succumbed to the illness that had afflicted us, following us in on the breeze. We sat at attention as he surveyed the cookhouse.

"I hope you're all planning on performing tonight," he said abruptly. "Because we need the goddamn *dinero.*" With that, he turned on his heel and left.

We had been so swept up in stories that we hadn't seen how dark it was or heard the sounds of the Ferris wheel and the crowds that now filled the air.

"Let's go," Mauro said. He stood, dumped his half-eaten food into a trash can, and stalked off. I followed.

Outside, the midway was alive and bustling with movement and laughter. We could see it past the big top. I was surprised that any time had passed since I'd emerged from the train, my sickness. Other performers and concession workers and roustabouts raced around us, muttering about sinuses clearing and fevers suddenly breaking.

Mauro and I raced back to get ready, I at my vanity and he by the bed. He was quiet, angry, and I knew better than to say anything in the mood I was in. But as I slipped off my clothes and pulled on my new sequined leotard, I could think only of getting back out there to Costas, as if he were a mirage that could disappear at any moment.

That night I performed on the silks, wrapping and unwrapping my body in sheets while the band played wistful violins. I moved more beautifully that night than I ever had before. The air seemed to reach out and embrace me, pulling me through itself and sliding down my skin. When it came time for my swing-over routine, I went and went and reached two hundred and fifty, the audience still chanting out each turn.

I was too obvious, trying to impress him. *Look what I can do,* I might as well have shouted. *Look how beautiful I am, in the air.*

When I dropped to earth and bowed, my white-slippered feet digging into the sawdust, I looked straight into the front row and at his face. I reveled in the power my body gave me, in its effect on him. I smiled and bowed, then left the ring.

Later, when we all gathered in front of the fire, Costas strode right up to me and put out his hand. His face was shining with excitement, and he was looking at me with something like awe. "That was amazing," he said, taking my hand and shaking it, then bringing it up to his mouth for a kiss. "You were brilliant up there. So powerful."

I blushed and smiled, and a moment later Mauro was there beside me.

"My wife is the best in the world," he said, gripping my hand in his. I was annoyed, and then guilt washed over me. I loved Mauro; he was my husband. I tried to convince myself that it was the lure of Rain Village, of Mary and her secrets, that stirred me so strongly. Nothing else.

"Thank you," I said, to both of them.

Mauro didn't leave my side for the rest of the night.

Everyone crowded around Costas. The fire flickered on our skin. Mauro kept his palm pressed into the small of my back as we talked and laughed with the others. I tried not to look over at Costas; whenever I glanced up at him, it seemed our eyes met within seconds and I had to look away. Even if I wasn't looking at him, even if I was deep in conversation with Ana or someone else, I was aware of exactly where his body was, its relation to the fire, and to me.

But more than that, I had the strange feeling that Costas *knew* me. Knew the dark places that lay burrowed inside me, the absence and loss that were always there. I wanted so badly to ask him about Rain Village—how much he knew, where it was, how long it would take him to get there.

Later, when everyone began drifting off to bed, I heard Lollie offer Costas her empty compartment or Geraldo's car, which he almost never slept in.

"No, thank you," Costas said. "I prefer to set up my own tent. I've been sleeping in it for weeks now." I heard him laughing and thanking her, thanking everyone. I heard Lollie direct him to the sideshow camp where most of the other tents were set up.

"Let's go," Mauro whispered, and pressed my skin with his hand.

"Okay," I nodded. I looked up again at Costas. "See you tomorrow," I said. "I would like to hear more of your stories."

"Yes," he said, and smiled.

"Good night," Mauro said curtly, and we turned back to the train. I resented him so much at that moment it was like a tangible thing burning inside me. *Stop it,* I thought. I threw my arms around him and kissed him before we went to bed, trying to reassure him, trying to block Costas out of my mind.

"I love you," I whispered.

That night I could not sleep. Mauro pulled me into him and I lay with my head against his smooth chest, watching the moonlight that streamed in through the slats of the window shade, illuminating the room. His skin was warm under my cheek. I could hear him breathing, knew he was still awake, lying there watching the light like I was. Keeping my eyes closed and pretending to sleep, I rolled over onto my side and hunched up with my knees to my chest and my back to him. The minutes and hours passed.

Finally, late into the night, when I was sure Mauro was asleep and when I couldn't bear the silent car any longer, I slipped out of bed as quietly as possible, inching my way off the mattress and to the floor. I leaned over the bed and put my face close to Mauro's to make sure he wasn't awake. I pulled on a shirt and skirt, then ran out of the car and into the empty moonlit lot.

I was just taking a walk, I told myself. I stepped lightly over the candy wrappers, cups, and programs that littered the ground. The Ferris wheel loomed over the lot like a monster from the sea. I had forgotten how eerie the circus could be, how quiet and shimmering.

I crept over to the huddle of tents, past the big top and scattered throughout the midway. I recognized Costas's tent right away, the pale green canvas I'd seen him carrying earlier. It was apart from the other tents, closer to the edges of the midway. My heart started pounding so loudly it drowned out everything else. I had such a good life, performing with the Velasquez Circus, traveling all over, living with a man I was in love with and who loved me more than anything. It was crazy for me to think that I needed anything else.

But I found myself standing in front of his tent, crouching down to it. Tapping the canvas. Bending down and crawling into the tent when he lifted up the flap. Sitting with my legs crossed next to him. With the flap tied open, I could faintly see him in the moonlight spilling in.

"I was hoping you would find me," he said.

I looked at his gypsy face and green eyes. He sat facing me, and our knees touched. I felt as though I could tell him anything, and had to remind myself that he was a stranger. For several long moments we just looked at each other.

"You were really the boy in the story, weren't you?" I asked, finally.

He laughed. "It's amazing that you heard of me and my story. That Mary knew." His voice was soft, deep.

"Tell me about the place you grew up in," I said. "The way you were kept from the world. It's all true, isn't it?"

He smiled. He pushed back the hair that had fallen over his face. And then he told that ancient story, the one Mary had whispered in Mercy Library as the sun slanted through the windows. The hair stood up on the back of my neck and goose bumps rose on my skin as Costas spoke of the father who had kept him hidden away from everything, out in the middle of the country.

"For over seventeen years I lived in the center of Turkey with no one but my father for company," he said. "When I turned eighteen, he decided to introduce me to the world. We threw our clothes in a bag and walked out together, farther and farther, and everything changed as we walked. We came upon roads and wagon tracks; the trees changed color; and I began to see little houses and then a girl I might have dreamt of, if I'd known to dream of such things before."

"The girl with red toenails and black hair down to her knees?" I asked, unable to sit still.

"Yes," he said, laughing. "Yes. Poppy. I married her, and we have a son."

"Oh," I said, wincing a little. "It is a story Mary told many times. I would ask her to tell it to me when I was most sad, and imagined what it must have been like, seeing those girls with jewels in their hair. I always felt hidden away, like you were."

"It was wonderful," he said. "Everything opening up, like all the flowers blooming at once."

"And you have a son with Poppy?" I asked.

"Yes," he said. "A boy. Four years old. And you are married to the tightrope walker?"

"Yes," I said, blushing and looking down. "What happened then?"

"We moved to Greece," he said, "and broke my father's heart. We were happy for a few years, until I started thinking about the past. And started this journey. First to find Mary, and now the youngest sister, who is still there. In Rain Village."

I remembered them from Mary's stories—Katerina, the older sister who'd left when Mary was a child, and Isabel, the young one Mary had left behind.

"Isabel," I said. "The youngest."

"Yes," he said, looking straight into me. "I've left my wife and son to seek out my own past and history. My aunt, my family. To find what beats in my blood. Do you understand that?"

"Yes," I whispered.

I looked at him, unconsciously tracing Mary through his features and gestures. I watched his face as if it could explain to me why it was so important for us to find out who we are and where we come from. Why we think that history can fill the holes that nothing else can reach.

"I dream of it, you know," I said. "Rain Village. All the time."

"So come with me."

I felt his gaze in every part of my body. I felt as if I had found a crucial part of myself, like my whole life had led me to that moment.

"I don't know why it's so important," I said. "To go there."

"Is it?"

I looked at him. "Yes," I said, and then the feelings rushed over me, the thoughts crystallizing even as I said them. "Without her, I never knew anything good. She *gave* me my life. And I never even knew her, what made her so sad. What made her walk into the river. I hate that I don't know that. I have to know that. Is that crazy?" I almost couldn't look at him. It seemed insane that I could even think to tell him these things.

He leaned forward. "No," he said, gently. "It's your past. Who you are. I was happy, too, but never whole, never. There was always something missing."

"They don't understand," I said, swallowing back tears. "Not really. She changed my life. I mean, she gave me my life."

He stretched out his hand, placed it over mine. "Is that really true?" he asked. "Sometimes people just spark things in us that are already there, don't you think?"

"No," I said. And then, more emphatically, "No."

He watched me, waiting.

"She taught me how to read," I said. "How to *see* things. She taught all of us that. Everyone in Oakley took to books and reading, because of her. Except my family." I thought of Geraldine sneaking under my mattress to find my books. "She gave me words," I said, "and vision. She taught me how to see the world differently. Do you know what I mean?"

"Yes," he said.

"It's like when you walked into the world after all those years of being hidden away. That's how I imagined myself, as like you. Except with me it happened on the floor of that library. She'd tell me stories and read poems to me, and it was like the entire world just cracked open and was different. Because of her."

"It must have been very hard for you when she died," he said softly, leaning toward me.

"Yes," I said, conscious of his skin, his smell. He could touch places in me that Mauro couldn't, I realized. "It was."

"It must have been hard to see that she could not save herself, when she had done so much to save you."

"I never understood," I said. "She showed me that there was the circus, and then she wouldn't leave with me. I asked her, you know. To leave with me."

"What did she say?"

I felt I was half there with Costas, half back in Oakley with her. Sitting by the river eating strawberries, listening to her describe her fate. "She said she couldn't leave. That sometimes the world closed down until there was no room left. She wanted me to go without her."

"That is a terrible story."

"She was done with life. I didn't know that then. I don't understand it now."

"Have you never felt that way?" he asked.

I stared at him. "Have you?"

"Yes," he said. "Many times. I've always felt there was a hole at my center, that I had no place, no home."

"But you have a wife and a son."

"And you have a husband," he said. "And the circus. I have never seen anything so extraordinary as you in the air, Tessa. And yet here you are."

"But I have never felt like I was done with life," I said then, defensive suddenly, a new feeling moving through me, something strong and ferocious. "Even at the moment when I knew Mary was gone and I felt that I had nothing in the world."

Suddenly his palm was on my waist and his face moving toward me. His eyes fierce and blazing. I felt my whole body tense, my hands shaking.

"I should go back," I said, pulling away.

"I'm leaving the day after tomorrow."

I nodded, unable to look at him.

"I'm sorry," he said, reaching for me, and I ran out into the night, disheveled, my heart racing. I couldn't see straight. I ran past the big top, stopped in the menagerie, and leaned against the tiger's cage. Tears rolled down my face. The tiger crept over to the bars. I reached out and touched her fur.

It all hit me then: how I had never really known so many things about Mary, never known what had made her so broken or what had made her step into the river and drown herself that autumn day. How I hadn't known about the crazy ring that had gleamed from her neck, the one she'd told me about in her story of the peasant girl. How I had never even known what had led her to that library in Oakley to read thick books and turn her back on her own life. *I had visions of people following me, hunting me down,* she had said. She had given up on life, left me alone to face the future. I sobbed, and the tiger pressed her body against the cage, comforting me. I thought then that what Costas had said was true for me, too: something had been missing in my life, hovering around the edges and flashing in my periphery, a nagging sense of having left something half done. I needed to understand what had happened to her. I needed to understand it so badly that it seemed crazy I hadn't been to Rain Village already.

Sunlight crept over the lot. It was one of those moments in life that seemed to have always been there, when you know so strongly that something has to occur that it may as well have already happened.

When I got back to the car Mauro was sitting up on the bed waiting for me.

"Where were you?" he asked. His anger was a palpable presence in the room, making its own shadows against the wall.

"I took a walk," I said. My eyes filled with tears. I was grateful for the window shades blocking out the dim sunlight. "I couldn't sleep."

"You saw him."

"Yes," I said. "Just to talk. I needed to talk to him."

"I don't understand. Why?"

I stood there. "Because of *Mary*," I said, my voice breaking. "Don't you see? Because of everything that happened." I gestured helplessly.

"Tessita," he said, softening. "That was so long ago. Why do you keep it so close to your heart?" He came over to me, cupped my face in his palm. "You have to let go of it, all that *dolor*."

I leaned in, let him pull me to his chest. I wanted to believe that there was nothing beyond this, right here. That the pain inside me didn't matter.

"You don't understand," I said finally, pulling away and looking up at him. "This is my one chance. I can put everything right."

Even in the pale light I could see the stricken look on his face. "Your chance?" he repeated. "Chance for what?" He flung up his hands. "What can you set right?"

My face was raw with tears, my throat sore from crying. "I think I have to leave, Mauro," I said, before I even realized I would say it. My voice cracked as the words poured out. "I have to go to Rain Village. I have to see it, put all of this to rest."

He looked stunned. "What? You just mean a visit, both of us?" He stared at me and then looked, suddenly, as if I'd smacked him across the face. "With the *gitano*," he said.

"Not because of him." Even as I said it I was not sure what was true, and what wasn't. "It's something I feel in my bones, pulling me. I will come back. I will. I just need to *see*."

"What about the circus?" he asked, pacing the floor, red with anger. "All of this? You're just leaving to go to some imaginary place? This man comes and that's it, *adios*? How do you know he's not just telling stories?"

"I'm coming back," I said. "I just know I have to go there. It's like one of Lollie's visions. I just *know*."

"You just know that you have to go with *him*."

I didn't know if he was right. Suddenly I wasn't sure of anything. If the crazy fever still had me under its hold or if Mary had come straight from the past to yank me from my future.

He turned around and looked right into me. "Why do you want

to bring out all this pain, Tessita? We're so happy. Why can't you let it alone?"

My heart ached for him. "I just can't," I whispered. "It's always there. So many unanswered questions."

"What if the answers just make you more unhappy?"

"I'm sorry," I said.

"What if it doesn't change anything?" he asked, taking my hands in mine.

"Then I will come back," I said. "And we'll be happy again."

He got very quiet then, still. "And what if you don't?"

I looked up at him and felt like my heart was breaking. I started sobbing, big wracking sobs, and I doubled over, the pain was so intense. Mauro leaned in and gathered me up, wrapped me in his warm body.

I thought of our first date in Mexico City, of our wedding. He carried me over to the bed then and stayed pressed against me, shushing and lulling me to sleep. "I do not understand this, Tessita," he said. "Why you cannot leave the past behind you. Why you can't understand that this is your life now, that the past just brought you here."

When I woke up a few hours later, Mauro was gone. The room seemed eerily silent, the sun much too bright flowing in. It all came back to me. The night before. Costas, Mary. Rain Village. I turned on my side, and my head throbbed with pain. Slowly the sounds of the circus drifted in—the laughter and voices, the roars of the tigers, the tinkling music and popping of the sideshow games.

The door pushed open then, and I sat up, immediately self-conscious. Mauro walked in carrying a cup of coffee and bowl of fruit. I was so relieved I jumped out of bed and ran to him.

"Oh, Tessita," he said, setting the tray on the edge of the bed and pulling me into him. "No more tears." He sat down and I leaned into his side. "So what are you going to do?" he asked.

I clung to him, holding him as tightly as I could. "Please understand," I said, talking into his ear, his hair. "Please forgive me. I will come back to you."

His body was stiff, but he relaxed it then, held me tight in his arms and pressed his face to my neck. "Then go," he whispered. I could feel wetness on my neck. "The *gitano* is leaving tomorrow. You have much to do."

He pulled back, and I stared into his black eyes, the curving lashes. "Just come back to me," he said. "Don't lose your heart."

"Thank you," I said. My whole body was trembling.

"I will not stay and watch you go with him," he said, stroking my face and hair. "Do not ask it of me. I'm going to stay in town for a day while you pack up. If you change your mind and are still here, I will be the happiest man in the world."

"I will be faithful to you," I said. "I will come back."

He leaned down and kissed me, his lips as soft as pillows. "Good luck to you, *mi amor*," he said. I watched him stand up and turn to the door. So proud, a star of the circus. He slipped out into the day, leaving me alone.

I spent the next several hours wrapped in the sheets, crying, wishing I could stop time. Over and over I wondered if I could let Costas go and keep my life the way it had been before, but his presence and Mary's story had burrowed into me, illuminated every missing part. Everything had changed. It was early afternoon by the time I forced myself out of bed. Mauro was right: I had a lot to do.

After I dressed and bathed, I went to the tents to find Costas, trying to avoid the curious faces turning to me as I went by.

"I'm coming with you," I said, as soon as I came upon him. I saw the relief in his face, but before he could say anything, I turned away.

I spent the rest of the day doing chores. I gathered my things and set my wages and contract in order. After listening to him plead and bribe and shout for most of the afternoon, I worked out a settlement with Mr. Velasquez for all my future missed shows, and then I cleaned out the train car and packed one large duffel bag. I had accumulated a chunk of money over the years, and I gathered as much of it as I could and sewed it into my pockets. I knew I was taking far more than I would need for a short journey, but I didn't think about what that meant.

When I told Lollie I was leaving, she promised to keep my costumes safe, along with whatever else I could not carry with me.

"I knew this day was coming," she said. "Just be quick, *chica.* And come back. Don't mistake her past for your own future."

"Why, Tessa?" Paulo asked, when I told him. "Aren't you happy here?"

"Yes," I said, "I am. But I just know this is something I have to do." He shook his head and walked away.

That night, the night before Costas and I left together for Rain Village, I spread glitter over my cheeks for the last time, staring into the mirror at the woman I'd become. I had to reapply my eye makeup several times to fill in the paths of my tears. I stuck my feet in my sparkling slippers, draped a cloak over my rhinestone-covered leotard, and set out for the ring.

The circus makes everything beautiful, transforms any pain. As I twirled over the crowd, I just let the air hold me, make me into someone new. Even the tears that fell down my face sparkled like diamonds under the light.

Afterward we walked silently from the big top to the backyard. No one was smiling or laughing the way they usually did. Carlos, furious, wouldn't even look at me. The dark, silent mood seemed in direct contrast to the whirling lights and music and shouting coming from the midway and front lot. When I returned to the empty train car, I took off my costume with shaking hands and carefully folded it into my open bag. I reached into the pile of clothes and pulled out my pink lace skirt. Taking a breath, I split open the hem, let Mary's opal ring spill onto the table. The swirling colors lit up the room, and dazzled me. Suddenly I was so sad I could barely see straight. I slipped the opal onto my right ring finger and held up both of my hands to the light: everything I loved and wanted in the world seemed reduced to those two blinding spots on my hand. My wedding ring, and the ring Mary had fastened to a chain around her neck before she walked into the river.

CHAPTER TWENTY

Costas and I set out into the early morning. The ground seemed empty and stunned under the hot sun; my body felt thick above the concrete and sidewalks. We walked into town, and I felt unmoored, like I was exchanging one self for another. I imagined Mauro alone in a hotel room, preparing to head back to our empty train car.

"How do you feel?" Costas asked, turning to me.

His voice caught me off guard. I turned to him, surprised. I looked up at him, then flicked my eyes quickly away. "Terrible," I whispered. "Heartbroken."

"Are you sure you want to come?"

I nodded. "I need to do this," I said. There was no question: Rain Village might as well have been my destiny, my pull to it was so strong.

We bought our tickets and boarded a northwest-bound train an hour later. Over the course of the day we watched the land go from dry and dusty to green and lush. I had so many questions, but my head was muddled. I kept imagining Mauro getting ready for the evening show, moving across the wire as if he were walking on air. I couldn't pin down what I was feeling: heartbroken, yet detached somehow, as if the only thing real was the clanking and rumbling of the train beneath us. I closed my eyes, let the steady clang of the wheels soothe me to sleep.

The next morning Costas's face was the first thing I saw. It jolted me into the present. I turned to the window; flowers began coating the fields the train passed through, and a light breeze whipped through the train car, fluttering through my hair and clothing. We rode silently. It made no sense, but I *knew* him. Our longing and sadness formed a bridge between us. In my years with the circus I'd been surrounded by huge, heaping families sprawling across the lot, families who passed their gifts from one generation to the next. Costas knew what it was to feel adrift and alone in the world, no matter what places you found, from time to time, to rest in.

We stayed on the train for two days. We slept sitting up in our seats, our bags propped on the seat next to us. When I woke that second morning and saw his face right there next to mine, I thought for a fierce, crazy moment that I was back in Mercy Library, the sun slanting in through the windows as Mary and I sat by the front desk, stamping people's books and drinking herb tea. I felt a deep, sudden sense of being past pain. As I focused in on Costas's face, his beauty, his eyes, there was sadness and guilt and love and desire all at once. It was intoxicating, strange. The past raging back to life. *What am I doing?* I thought, again and again. But Rain Village lived inside me, moving me toward itself like some undertow pulling me out to sea.

I sat back and stared at the changing landscape, the giant trees and the distant sparkling snow, and thought how everything before this moment seemed like something I'd dreamt. I thought of Mary, how she had left the circus, too, for reasons I'd never understood. Did she feel this same way, anchorless and suspended? Did everyone feel it who left one place for another? I thought of the glitter-covered girl on the trapeze, dangling from a rope, spinning like a windmill in the air while the audience counted each turn and waited for her to fall. I thought of my father carving our hedges into the shapes of animals while Geraldine and I watched from the porch. I thought of being hunched over a sewing machine in Kansas City, and the only thing that seemed real was the glass pane in front of me, the faint smudge blocking my view of the passing towns. I pressed my hand against the glass and stared at the starfish-shaped imprint it left.

"What was she like?" Costas asked, late that night. I blinked my eyes open and turned to him, saw the pale green of his eyes in the dark. "You call her name in your sleep; did you know that?"

"No," I whispered. I wondered if I always had, if Mauro had simply never told me. Costas smiled encouragingly. "Describe her," he said.

I looked at him for a moment and then thought back on all those moments, every single moment I had spent with her. With Costas there next to me, I felt safe. I thought of her rasping voice, her laughter as she swung through the air above me or steadied me with her strong, ring-covered hands.

"She was the most beautiful woman I had ever seen," I said. "Around her everything was different. Everything."

He smiled and closed his eyes. I was grateful that I could talk to him about Mary without my heart splitting in two. With Costas my life seemed so rich, so bound up in myth. Mauro had Mexico and his raging history, this wonderful larger-than-life family he had taken me into. I had Mary and the river, her hair coiled wetly around her neck. Whispers and secrets, like Costas had.

"She came in and wrapped everything in mystery. It was like one of the piñatas the circus kids have on their birthdays. The way the world turns over, is almost too much to bear when all those toys and coins and candies come raining down."

"Yes," he said, looking at me. "I know what you mean."

I wanted to tell him everything. I wanted to spread myself bare, everything that was wounded and scarred and ugly. Things with Mauro were so pure and soft, soothing. Mauro healed and protected me, made me forget the past, sink into the present. I worried that I had failed Mauro, that I was failing him now. I thought of Mary then, and suddenly I felt in my blood how utterly I had failed her. I had shut myself away, let myself drift away from her until there was barely anything there. I hadn't even shared the swing-over trick with her. I had left her alone in that library, to her demons.

"Well," I said, breathing in. "When she died, I felt like everything she'd given me was gone. As if *she* had taken it all away from me. I never even thought about why she did it; I just knew that the one person I had, my one friend, had left me. And everything else back then, it was so miserable. All the time. Even talking about it now I just feel blackness."

"What was wrong?" he asked. "What was so bad?"

My father's face loomed down, the memory of his callused farmer's hands flipping me over, rubbing into me, opening me up. Me washing and washing and washing in the river water, when it was through. Closing down until I could barely see the world around me. I thought of Mary. Back then I'd been so dazzled by her; I always should have seen her better than I did.

"My father hurt me," I said. Tears broke over my face, and tore me up from the inside. "From when I was twelve till the time I left home."

I could feel the words hanging there before me, as if they could push every molecule of air out of the car. When a long moment of silence had passed, I looked up at him. I could almost imagine I was setting things right, saying now what should have been said before.

"Did she know?" he asked.

I was disoriented, could barely breathe. "Who?"

"Mary. Did she know?"

I was about to shake my head when I remembered her face. *You can always leave,* she had said, again and again. *There are always more selves inside you that just need to come out.* She must have known, I thought. She must have felt all that grief and shame; I must have worn it on me like a banner. I remembered running to her covered in bruises, the day she finally set up the trapeze for me and gave me my first lesson, though she hadn't wanted to. She hadn't ever wanted to face the past, I thought. She had always turned everything into stories.

"Her father, too," Costas said, interrupting my thoughts.

"What?"

"Her father. Katerina said that their father molested them, too. First her and then Mary. That is what my father told me. He said that Katerina was the woman of his dreams but that she was all twisted up and broken inside. Always running from Rain Village and longing for it at the same time, to set things right."

A strange sense of vertigo swept through me, and I clutched my head, squeezed my eyes shut. For a moment I felt like I was that girl again, sitting in front of the courthouse, wearing my father's hands like a brand on my skin. I was innocent then, but it must have been there the whole time. That mark.

Suddenly it was impossible to pretend the past was something separate from what I was. Costas brought something with him that cut through the power of the circus, made me suspicious of the way it transformed pain. Made me suspicious of the stories Mary told, of the lights and the spangles and the glitter, the Ferris wheel going round and round. Made me suspicious, I realized then, of Mauro, too.

I couldn't stop the guilt that came over me then, that horrible sense that I had failed Mauro, and Mary, and everyone. That I could have saved her.

As we made our way north, the trees expanded and grew so tall we could see only the trunks from the train, giant pillars whole families could fit into. I sat back and stared out at them, the snow you could see glittering in the distance. I remembered how giant everything had felt when I was growing up, how my parents and sister and brothers had seemed to tower over me, to fill up whole rooms. "Look," I said to Costas, pointing to the trees.

"It's like we've entered a fairytale," he said.

He leaned back and I smiled at him. "I wonder what Rain Village is like," I said. "She always made it sound so magical."

The sun caught his eyes and lit them bright green. Suddenly I wondered how different my life would be with someone like him. It seemed astonishing, sometimes, how much the world could change, depending on where you were and who the person was next to you. I imagined what my life would be like if I lived in Turkey and Greece, had hair thick with salt.

For a second I thought Costas would kiss me. His face was so close to mine. His eyes moved down my face, to my lips. The light shifted then, and I saw my face in the window behind him. His eyes went dark again, and I turned away, swallowing. Don't lose your head, I thought. It would be too easy to think I was someone else.

Hours passed in a strange sort of haze. Costas slept next to me. I looked back out at the landscape, watched it become green, luminous. My thoughts returned to Mary, to what I was trying to find. We were in her world now, I realized. After all this time. As the train crossed the countryside I could practically see the clear air turn to mist, the ground become soaked with water. When we started heading still farther west, the whole world lit like an emerald, and the trees seemed to tap the sky.

I wondered if this was what Mary had seen when she'd left Rain Village, tears streaming down her face and trailing out behind her: these trees, this falling rain, these little towns that seemed equal parts wood and mist.

"Why did your mother leave Rain Village?" I asked Costas in those endless hours as we sat side by side staring at the wet landscape. "Was it because of her father?"

"I only know what my father told me," he said. "I never knew her at all, you know. But she said her father beat her and hurt her and that no one said a word about it. And that one day she finally left. She wandered all over the world, he said, before she and my father fell in love."

"What happened to her?"

"One day right after I was born, she walked into the ocean and kept on walking."

"I'm sorry," I said, breathing in. "That's terrible. She drowned? Like Mary did? Like William, too?"

"I guess," he said. "William?"

"The one Mary was in love with. The reason she left."

He looked confused. "I don't know about William," he said. "What happened?"

"I just know that he drowned. That Mary was in love with him and he drowned, and she left soon after, went out into the world. I don't think she ever went back."

"It is a hard thing," he said, "to leave the place you come from."

I thought of Oakley, the tree in the town square, the hedges that lined our yard. For a second I wondered if he was making fun of me. I looked up quickly, but he seemed to be somewhere else completely.

"You must have a lot of guilt," he said. "To drown yourself after that. You know?"

"Yes," I said. "I guess so." I was embarrassed to have never thought of it and looked down, tapped my foot on the seat in front of me.

Of course Mary had felt guilty. Every time I thought of her, she seemed to take on a new shape, a new dimension. I wondered if it was ever really possible to know someone else.

Day moved into night, and rain pounded against the train-car windows, hammering and beating down, never letting up for a minute. By the time we arrived at the tip of the country, it seemed like we would never see the sun again. The rain pounded down and the sky was like a sheet of rock as we boarded a small bus that would take us to the riverboat, the one Mary had described, and at long last into Rain Village. Time shifted and took on a new form. I had no time to gather my thoughts, but the world was always like that: no matter how much you prepared for something, there was always that moment when you had to leap off the platform and fly toward the catcher's hands.

The bus was quick, and soon a strip of blue revealed itself. We pulled into a small dock. The sun poured onto the water like melted butter. The air seemed different there, somehow. Costas and I walked down to the water—quietly, as if we might wake something. We looked down and saw fish as big as watermelons. Trees circled the riverbank, and the leaves hung heavy with sunlight, casting a spell on the water.

She has been here, I thought. I could feel her presence. I imagined Mary leaving Rain Village so many years before, her tears falling in the water, the memory of William burned into her heart and breast. She would have walked from the riverboat to the dock and into the world for the first time. Right here. Soon Juan Galindo would find her, changing everything from that day forward.

I looked at Costas, my eyes filling with tears. "It feels like we're at the end of the world," I whispered. As if we were about to step off it. I thought of Mauro and the trapeze, of circus lights and glitter and the elephants' swaying trunks, the tigers' soft fur, the crazy banners and colors of the sideshow, the sawdust and cotton candy and miles of faces staring up at us with astonished, blissful expressions, and wondered once again what I was doing in this huge, lonesome expanse where time seemed to have stopped. The rain seeped through my shirt, ran down my skin.

"I know," he said, grabbing my hand. His touch comforted me. I hadn't realized how rigid and tense I was.

When a boat appeared down the narrow path of the river, it seemed like a mirage. It shimmered through the leaves and rose straight up into the sky.

We stood together and watched the boat approach. It pulled to a stop with a heavy, wheezing groan, sank from our weight when we stepped on the deck. The captain took our bags and fare quietly before heading back to the helm. The few other passengers didn't seem to pay us much mind.

I don't know what kind of journey it was, really, that brought Costas and me to Rain Village. It did not feel like we were traveling the way a boat travels through the water; rather, we seemed to move the way a dream passes from loss to memory. I was inside the vision I'd had, when I'd first seen her, and Mary's voice whispered in my ear. Was I a child again, listening to one of her stories? I sat on the deck of the riverboat, leaning my back against the railing, and the wood under my hands felt like the planks that made up the floor of Mercy Library.

The rain pattered against our skin, onto the deck and the water. The air was so delicate. Looking above me, I saw the rain lit up by the sun, and the leaves overhead were like petals, almost translucent with the sun coming down through them. I looked over at Costas, watched him change the film in his camera, lift the camera to his face. *He's documenting this,* I realized then. *He wants to get it all down.* I thought of Mary standing in Mercy Library, surrounded by files and books.

We moved slowly down the river, watching the plants and trees and water, and then, in the distance, we saw people waiting on the shoreline. A burst of color in the melancholy landscape.

"Rain Village," I whispered. I climbed up on the railing and held the top rail with my hands.

As we approached, I saw that the people were wearing shiny hats that kept the rain off their faces. I glanced at the other passengers, saw a woman with long hair so black it was like a pool of ink I'd dip a quill into, standing along the railing, waving. She glanced at me and smiled. I smiled back, then tilted my face up to let the mist of rain coat my face.

The boat bobbed on the water as we anchored at the bank, and the fish thumped against the sides of the boat. "Look at them," Costas whispered, pointing.

The captain helped me down from the boat; my hand reached for the railing and my skirt grazed the water as I slid onto the riverbank. I stepped forward and nearly fell. When I took my second step my foot felt more assured, the mud less slippery, the riverbank more steady. I could feel the place closing over me, could almost smell the spiced oranges, feel the brush of dark coils of hair on my skin.

Our feet sank into the ground. We walked up the riverbank and onto the earth above it. People milled around us and headed toward a path lined by trees. I saw the woman from the boat, watched as her galoshes navigated the muddy paths effortlessly, as if she were walking barefoot over cement. She ran to a tall man and hugged him. His hair was the color of peanut shells. When his eye caught mine, I turned away, embarrassed.

I recognized other people from the riverboat moving alongside us, caught snippets of conversations about their trips. Costas smiled down at me and I thought how right he looked, being there. His long coat, his thin gypsy body. His eyes were the colors of the leaves drifting all around, hanging from the trees like feathers.

We began walking with everyone else, down a path surrounded by trees. The world, the trees, everything around us was so lush. Vibrant.

Soon the path opened onto a street, and Costas and I stopped in our tracks to take it all in: the twisting street lined with stores, people everywhere, the treetops jutting over the buildings like knife tips. The soft, glowing colors, the pinks and yellows and greens like hard candy piled in a bowl. I looked into the distance and saw small houses, their tipped roofs pointing to the sky.

We moved into the street, stepped up on the twisting sidewalk. Every block or so there was an opening between shops, revealing a path to the forest.

"We're here," I breathed, suddenly seized with joy.

The thrill of being there—seeing it all right there, straight from her voice and into the world—overtook me, made me mad with pleasure. I couldn't drink it all in quickly enough. We passed a clothing store with bright jackets hanging in the window, a candy store lined with bins of licorice and chocolate. We passed a small grocery store crowded with people, several of whom met my eye as we went past and then quickly looked away. Many places sold fish, or rods and tackle, shimmery fish-shaped lures. One store only sold the rain hats I had seen people wearing. A tiny inn sat at the end of the street, like something from a fairytale.

It was all just as Mary had described. She'd told me about the street and the shops and the fishermen, the forest stretching behind everything. She must have been the same age as I was now, I thought, when she'd left. I imagined her standing here, the rain caressing her skin. How different it must have been for her to travel with the circus, I thought, and to fall in love with a dark-skinned man like Juan Galindo. How alive she must have felt.

We entered the inn, paid for two rooms for that night. The man at the front desk handed us our keys without a word. As I dropped my bag onto the bed, I found myself alone for the first time in days. I walked to the window and stared out at the rain-soaked ground, the sturdy people walking past, oblivious to the water running down their skin.

"Mary, are you here?" I whispered. "Is it okay that I've come?"

Costas appeared at the door a few minutes later. "I'm starving," he said, smiling. "Let's eat." We walked to a restaurant we'd passed before, and the smell of frying fish wafted past our faces. When we swung through the screen door a moment later, our hearts were light. A red-haired waitress handed us menus. We ordered fish and wine. Fish crackled on the stoves in the kitchen, and we could hear them even from our small table, which sat just under a window looking out onto rain and mud. The waitress brought our wine and we toasted each other, drank it down. Minutes later we were served two platters with thick pieces of fish flesh spread upon them; I took one bite and felt it melt on my tongue.

"This fish is nothing like what they used to pull from the water back home," Costas said, his face shining with pleasure. "It's as soft as custard."

"Yes," I said. My fork cut through the flesh and pulled it apart in smooth, long pieces. I looked up at him and thought how I could have kissed him, right then.

"I've traveled so long," he said, "to be here."

"How do you feel?" I asked.

He took a long swig of wine, then leaned in. "Like I can finally stop searching. Like this is where I was supposed to be all along."

Afterward we strolled through the streets, taking it all in. The trees, the mud, the rain that made everything seem hazy. I felt like the child who'd seen Mary walking toward her in front of the courthouse and the adult who'd lost her, at the same time.

"What do you know about your mother, anyway?" I asked, as we headed back down to the river, following a trail of people. "Do you know how she and your father met, anything like that?"

"I just know what my father told me," he said. "But I never knew if what my father told me was true."

"What?"

"He said that when he was young, he met a girl named Katerina and thought she was the most beautiful woman he'd ever seen. They were both working on the boats on the Aegean, I guess, in Turkey."

"What did she look like?" I immediately imagined Mary with Costas's eyes, his mischievous look.

"She had long brown hair she'd tie up with silver strings, lashes like Greta Garbo's, lips that looked like wet fruit. He always got teary describing her. When he met her, he said, she was only nineteen, living with this family who'd found her on the docks and taken her in. She'd steal past the mosquito netting and out the window every night to my father's little boat he kept docked at the harbor."

"How romantic," I said.

When we arrived at the water, there were a few small groups gathered around fires. The people glanced up as Costas and I stretched out along the bank.

"Yes, I guess they spent their nights drifting on my father's boat out into the sea," he said. "I know my father tried to impress Katerina with his bravado, diving into the water and coming up with a small octopus wrapped around his hand. The next night he'd serve it up to her, tentacles and all."

"What happened?"

"They finally ran away together, to Greece. The town was an hour from Greece by boat, so they just kept going one night, to an island called Kos, and they moved into a small house with a white tile floor. They spent their days planting flowers and hanging curtains and swimming in the ocean and eating vats of yogurt piled high with fruit. That's how he used to describe it to me."

"It must have been hard for him to talk about it to you after everything that happened," I said. I thought of the riverboat, imagined Katerina going halfway across the world just to fall in love with a man on the water.

"It was the best time of his life. He always talked about it. It's one of the reasons I realized I had to make this journey, so I wouldn't be filled with regret the way my father was. I felt like I would never be myself until I came here."

"When did things go bad with Katerina?"

"Well," he said, "the way my father tells it, she used to talk about this place, dream about it, mumble about it in her sleep. Always talked about coming back, and one day she just snapped and walked into the water."

I couldn't help but feel shivery, imagining it. "That's terrible," I said. I wondered if Mary had wanted to return here, too.

"Yeah," he said. "I get the feeling there is a lot of sadness here, because of the place. I don't know why I feel that way; right now I'm so at peace. Are you?"

I looked at him, not sure how to answer. "Yes," I said, finally. I *was* at peace, but I was everything else, too. Happy. Filled with remorse. Detached from everything, as if I were reading it all in a book.

We stared out into the water, the tangle of trees and foliage hanging over it, the people scattered across the bank. I could not get over the feeling that we were at the edge of the world, and that we could do anything. My heart reached for Mauro, but it almost didn't feel real, as if he were a character I was remembering from a story. It was a dangerous moment, a moment when a person could forget everything that had come before, and disappear. After a while the sound of the rain and the weight of memory took their toll. Barely able to keep our eyes open, we watched night descend over everything—slowly, like a parachute falling to the ground.

Costas turned to me. "It feels like you're home, doesn't it?" he asked suddenly, his face earnest and intent. "Does it feel that way for you?"

"Yes," I said, watching the water, trying to imagine the feel of the bar in my hands, the feel of the rope wrapped around my wrist. Everything from my former life seemed far away. "Yes, it feels like that," I said.

I looked out at the water again, saw a few fishermen drifting out in their boats. I didn't want to look at him, I realized.

The murmur of voices blended with the slapping of the water. The moon cast a silver glow over everything. I thought of the cornfield, the moon, all the ways the world can hide us, and suddenly the night and the rain seemed sinister in a way they hadn't before.

"What happened to her?" I whispered. "What happened here?"

"Tomorrow," Costas said, "we'll find out everything."

I nodded, trying to shake off the feeling that had come over me. That something was wrong. That we were disturbing the dead.

Back in my room, I moved into a deep, long sleep swirling with dreams so real I could feel the burn of my father's palm on my skin, see his face leaning down into mine, smell the dirt underneath my back, in the cornfields. I saw my mother's face right before mine, her skin creased and her eyes damp with tears. I saw Mary lean in so close that I could feel her hair brushing against my shoulders.

"What are you doing here?" she asked, as if all were right in the world, when suddenly the air turned black and water came gushing out of her melting face. "What are you doing here?" the voice repeated, no longer recognizable.

In my dreams, it felt like days passed. Days, weeks, years. I was in Mexico, and back in the cornfields, and in the herb garden behind the library. I saw Mauro looking at me from underneath his curved lashes, Luis at the table as Victoria smoothed pomade through his hair. The lemon-grease smell. That perfect confluence of lines and the beams overhead, my hands folding over the bar and coming to rest. The claw-shaped corn. *I am going to Rain Village to find what beats in my blood,* I thought. *To find out what happened to her, what I had failed to see.*

I started, blinked my eyes open, all the hairs on my neck prickling against my skin. I sat up straight, convinced I was being watched. But the room was dark, empty. The only sound was the constant, prattling hum of the rain on the window. Suddenly I felt like weeping. Like clawing off my own skin. I was not just burrowing into Mary's past, I thought. I walked to the window and stared out into the dark night. What if it is just grief, I thought, at the bottom of all of this?

✴

CHAPTER TWENTY-ONE

When I woke the next morning, I felt as alone as I'd felt years before, that night by the train tracks, waiting for the Velasquez Circus. The world was completely open now as it was then, yet all I wanted to do was sleep, to slip back into dreams and memory. The rain outside was soothing, soft; the bed was warm. I stretched out and turned to the window, where I could see just the tops of the stores and buildings, a bit of the treetops that shadowed all of them. What was Mauro doing right then? I wondered, and I tried to imagine the tents, the train cars, the wire stretching from one side of the big top to the other. I grasped at the images, but they seemed too far from me to reach.

The dread from the night before was gone, and the world seemed light and inhabitable again, but changed. There was a sadness in me that had always been there, I thought, that the circus had only concealed. I got out of bed, my head pounding from lack of sleep.

Outside, Rain Village was beautiful, like a painting. Pastel and shimmering.

My body felt dull, slow. My muscles ached for the bar, I realized, as if they could remember what my mind and heart couldn't. I must get back soon, I thought. A ferocious longing moved through me then, searing through the rain and mist and memory. But even if it was crazy to have come here, it was time to put my dreams to rest, I realized, and find out what had happened to Mary, after all this time.

I took a shower and threw on my clothes, ignoring my headache. A minute later I was banging on Costas's door. He appeared, his face sagging with sleep.

"What is it?" he asked. "Tessa, are you okay?" He reached down and touched my cheek with his fingertips.

"I'm fine," I said, stepping back. "I just want to get started. I need to know what happened here, why her presence is so strong, why it's all so sad. Do you want to come with me or not?"

"Yes, of course," he said. "But what's your rush? We're here now. We have all the time in the world."

I looked at him in surprise. "I don't have all the time in the world," I said. "I have a life to get back to. We need to find out what happened here, Costas. That's why we came. Why I came."

"Yes," he said, dreamily, watching me, and it occurred to me then that he planned to stay in Rain Village, that he would never return to his wife and son.

"This isn't home," I said, carefully. Lollie's words echoed in me: *Don't mistake her past for your own future.*

He nodded but didn't seem to be listening. His eyes bored into me, made me feel strange and exposed. "Just give me a few minutes to get ready."

I went to wait for him in the lobby. I was so anxious to get started I could barely stand still, and kept shifting from one foot to the other, clenching my fists and teeth. The wall was covered in old photographs. I walked up, studying them, all the sepia-toned faces staring back at me. One photo caught my eye: a young girl holding a dog, a black ribbon hanging down her hair, which was swept to the side. There was a haunting, lost quality to the image that was unsettling.

"Good morning," I heard.

I turned to the man behind the desk. I hadn't seen him when I'd walked in. I noticed a book lying on the desk beside him. Shakespeare. "Good morning," I said.

"Light rain today," he said, gesturing to the window. I looked out and was struck by the gentle sunlight, the rain like mist.

"It's lovely," I said, then pointed to the photo. "Who is this girl?"

"Her name was Lena."

"Was?"

"She died a few years after that was taken. A fire. That must have been forty years ago."

"How terrible." I stared at the girl's face, thought what an odd thing, to have been captured during this one moment in her life, sitting with a dog on her lap and a bow in her hair. I thought of Mary in the brochures, forever caught in that moment of flight. "Do you know of a girl named Isabel Finn, by chance? She had two sisters, Mary and Katerina."

"Sure," he said. "Isabel lives in a house in the woods. We don't see her around much in town, but she's out there."

"Do you know how we can find her?"

He looked at me curiously. "Now, what could you two want with Isabel?"

"Oh," I said. "My friend who came here with me. She's his aunt. He's come here to find her. And I knew her sister Mary, a long time ago."

"You knew Mary?" he asked. I noticed then that his whole face shifted, grew light. "Mary Finn?"

"Yes," I said. "She was the librarian in my town, when I was growing up. A little town in Kansas."

"Kansas," he repeated slowly. "Is that right?"

"You knew her?" I looked at him more carefully, realized he was probably her age. The age she'd be now.

"We lived not too far from the Finns when I was a boy," he said. "I had the biggest crush on Mary for years and years."

"You did?" I asked. I felt a strange uneasiness move through me, a sense of no longer knowing where I was. I tried to shake it off.

"Do you find that hard to believe?" he asked, laughing. "We all had crushes on her, but she only had eyes for William Jameson. We were all sorry when she disappeared." He looked at me, studying me. "Most of us just thought she up and died after William did. You say you knew her?"

"Yes," I said, hesitating. "She joined the circus after she left here. Became a trapeze star. She traveled all over the world."

"Isn't that something?" he said. He shook his head. "I bet she was a sight."

"Yes," I said. "No one ever forgot her."

"Well," he said, nodding, "we've never seen another like her."

"What about Isabel?" I asked. "Isn't she like her?"

"Isabel," he said, drawing out the word. "No, she's not really like Mary. Never was. She's a bit more ... quiet, I guess."

"Where did you say I could find her?"

He smiled, hesitated. "She lives in the forest," he said. "Close to the river. If you follow the river west enough, you'll come to a little cross. Where they found William. The Finns lived just north of it."

I shivered slightly and nodded. The spot of that ancient tragedy. Just then the door opened and Costas walked in, freshly showered and holding his camera. His hair was still wet, combed back from his face.

"Ready to eat?"

"Okay," I said, looking up at him. It struck me, how handsome he was. "Our host was just telling me how to find the Finn house."

"Great," he said. He nodded at the man, then put out his arm to me.

Outside, the rain seemed to lick and fizzle at our faces. I caught it on my tongue.

"It's gorgeous here, isn't it? I feel so relaxed," Costas said.

"Yes," I said, staring out at the hazy street, the fishermen tromping across the muddy road, to the river. Leaves seemed to be dangling over everything, and the trees hovered on top of us, the thick darkness of the forest. "It's all leaves and water and mud."

"Where I was raised, it was just flat and hot. Like nothing. It was like being in the middle of blank space. Here I feel embraced by something."

He was practically glowing, I saw. The rain running down his face didn't seem to bother him, while I found myself with my palm at my forehead, wincing. The line of shops stretched out in front of us, like a railway track, blurring in the distance. He raised his camera, capturing all of it.

Costas laughed as we arrived at the restaurant. I almost slid on the step, and he steadied me. The rain lashed over the wooden planks as we stepped inside. "Doesn't it explain so much, just being here?"

We sat down at a table. His eyes were cat's eyes. "You're so much like her," I whispered.

He reached over and put his hands on mine. I jumped slightly, then settled into his touch. So much was going through me, and it was hard to understand: how much was him, how much was her, how much was just what was inside me

We were quiet, taking each other in. The waitress brought us coffee, and I released his hands, took a long sip. The anxiety moving through me didn't fade. I stared out the window, at the muddy street outside. I focused on a familiar-looking woman and for a moment my heart leapt, until I realized it was the black-haired woman from the riverboat. I looked around the restaurant at all the men and women eating and talking. Everyone's eyes seemed to be bright blue or green, the colors of the river and the leaves.

"You knew her, Tessa," Costas said then. "I never knew my mother or anyone related to her. I would give anything for just a few minutes with her. It was just my father and me, always, in the middle of nowhere."

Something changed in the way he looked at me. I could feel myself blushing and glanced down, embarrassed. "I'm just afraid that you want too much," he said.

The waitress set our eggs in front of us, and I looked up, met her eye. She smiled vaguely. I looked over at Costas and then back up at her. She was so pale, with long, black hair. She looked like Mary, and like Costas. You could tell they all came from the same part of the world. I had a strange, sudden sense of being all alone.

"Excuse me," I said. "I'm wondering if you remember a girl named Mary Finn."

"I don't think so," she said, squinting at me.

I nodded, tried not to show my disappointment. Costas began eating his eggs.

"She lived here a long time ago. Maybe you're too young."

"Actually, that name does sound familiar," she said, wrinkling her forehead. "Finn. I know that name." She held the name out on her tongue, then shook her head. "There was this girl I vaguely remember, a sad, thin girl who lived in the woods. I don't remember anything else about her really. I think she disappeared or something."

"Do you know anything about a boy named William who drowned in the river?"

"No," she said, shaking her head. "That's all I know. I'm not even sure if I'm remembering right." She smiled the same vague way she had before and left us to our breakfast.

Outside, the mud collected at our feet like coffee grounds. We followed the river down the line of stores. Most of the stores were raised off the ground, with wooden steps leading up to them and awnings keeping the steps dry. I was quiet as Costas took photo after photo.

"They were both just girls, so many years ago," I said. "Maybe we do want too much from this, from coming here. But someone must remember."

"It's this place, part of why my mother left, I think. The rain wipes everything out," he said, and I realized that something more was bothering him, something bigger than what was happening right now. "Who we live next to, who dies, what they meant. No one should vanish without a trace."

I laughed at that, brushing past leaves dangling in front of me. Trees hung all about us. "Oh, I bet you could walk through Oakley today and it would be like I was never there. That's what it was like when I *was* there."

Costas stopped, turned to me.

"What do you mean? In Oakley everyone remembered you."

"They did?"

"Yes," he said, giving me a funny look. "Did you think people would forget someone like you?"

"I don't know," I said, shrugging and suddenly feeling self-conscious. I thought of the kids who'd pointed and laughed at me in the town square. I thought of Geraldine, how astonished I'd been to learn that they had seen me in the papers when I thought I'd been able to vanish into thin air.

"People talked about you at the library, how sweet you were, and smart. How you could look at someone and know what kind of book they needed to forget all their troubles."

"Really?"

He laughed at my surprise. "Of course."

I was silent for a moment, thinking about what he had said. It didn't make sense to me, but then I remembered that what Geraldine had said hadn't made sense either. That she had envied my lightness, my book learning, my friendship with Mary. It was frustrating, knowing we could be so wrong in the way we saw the world.

We had almost reached the end of the street, where a large white building marked the beginning of the woods, which spread out in front of us. Just leaves and wet, wet earth, running up against the river. I almost imagined I could hear the movement of the water, shifting and becoming more intense, ominous. These were her woods, her river. I squinted, thought of Mary barefoot, wading into the river, carrying a basket full of herbs.

"Look," Costas said, pointing.

His voice startled me. I looked back to what he was showing me. It took a second to make out the black letters stamped over the door of the white building. *Library*. I almost gasped out loud.

"I need to go inside here," I said, my voice trembling.

"Okay, let's go," he said, taking my hand. "Are you okay, Tessa?"

"I'm fine," I said. "But please let me go in alone."

Costas looked at me and nodded. "Should I come back for you in an hour? I'll just keep talking to people around here."

I nodded, grateful.

With quick, nervous steps, I walked up to the front door and pushed my way in. It felt exactly like being a child again, back in Mercy Library. For several long seconds I just stood there, taking it in. Feeling the past and present run up against each other.

I could feel it in my skin and bones, Mary's presence, more vividly than I'd felt it on the street or the riverboat or by the river. I hadn't been in a library in years, I realized. The musty smell of old books, the shelves rising toward the ceiling, the piles of books on the front desk.

I walked down an aisle of books, fingering the spines, peering through the space in the shelves, and I almost expected to see Mary sitting there with Mrs. Adams, the other woman's palms in her hands. I wondered why I had never thought to visit libraries in the towns we'd passed through with the circus.

It was coming back to me slowly, the numbers we had arranged the books by, the way we had kept an order to the library even as the library itself was pure chaos, and I made my way to where I knew the poetry would be shelved. I turned down the aisle, felt a calmness fall over me as I saw volume after volume line the shelves, as I'd known they would. The book was right where I knew it would be. I hadn't even known I was looking for it until I saw its old cracked leather binding, the gilded pages. I turned the pages, and for a moment I was sure she was right next to me, her black hair curling down and tapping my shoulder.

I felt suspended. Thinking of Mary as a girl, bent over this book, and remembering the two of us in Mercy Library, the words of the poem making everything in the world drop away.

She was like me, I thought, and it was less a thought than a feeling of recognition I had never had before. And then: *Why didn't I tell her about my father?* That day, by the river eating strawberries. I had come so close. I winced, thinking of it, the two of us sitting by the water, occupying different worlds utterly.

"May I help you?"

I looked up, startled, slamming the book shut as if it contained something forbidden. I had almost forgotten where I was.

"I am just reading a bit," I said, looking up at the old woman standing over me. I was struck by her pale pale skin and light-blue eyes, the white wispy hair pulled back from her face.

She looked down at the book in my hands. "You like poetry," she said. A strange expression came over her face, and she knelt down beside me. Her body was surprisingly graceful and agile. "Tennyson," she said, her voice growing soft.

"Did you ever know a girl named Mary Finn?" I asked. "She was from here and became a librarian in the town where I grew up."

"Why, yes." She looked at me carefully, surprised. "Where are you from?"

"Kansas," I said.

"Ah." She stared at me for a moment, then smiled and shook her head. "So she ended up in Kansas, did she? And she's a librarian?"

"She was, yes. A great one."

She kneeled down next to me. "I shouldn't be so surprised. She spent a lot of time here. I'd be ready to close up, thinking the library was empty, and then I'd find her off in some corner buried in a book. She would just be lost in it. I'm glad to hear that she went and made a life for herself."

"Oh, she did," I said. "She was in the circus, too. She became a trapeze star."

"The circus," she repeated. Her face became girlish, soft. I couldn't help but smile.

"Yes," I said. "She was called Marionetta. She wore red sequins and people lined up outside her door to give her flowers."

She nodded, her face wondering. Her eyes moved over my fingers, my hands. I clasped them together. "You are a bit like her," she said. "How she was. Do you know that?"

"Me?"

"Your expressions and gestures," she said. She fingered my long skirt, the little ribbons hanging off it. "Your clothes."

"Thank you," I said, feeling myself blush. "She was like the perfect woman to me, a movie star. I always wanted to be like her."

"Well, some people just blaze through the world," she said. "Mary was always like that. I just can't get over it, though, hearing about her now. We always wondered what happened to her."

"After the accident, you mean?"

"Yes," she said. "After William died. Her lover. No one ever really knew what happened, whether it was an accident or not, what she did after. Did she tell you about it?"

I shook my head. "She said that he drowned, and that she left shortly after. I know it broke her heart. I was hoping to find out more by coming here."

"Ah," she said. "I'm not sure you'll find what you want here, then. When it happened, this place was crazy. There were all kinds of rumors about what had happened. Some people swore Mary came running out of the woods with a bloody rock in her hand, screaming about murder. Some said William had betrayed her, had another lover. Others said that she just went mad one day for no reason at all. Most believed it was just a tragic accident—they were arguing and he fell, they stayed under too long, he got a leg cramp. We all know the river has a strange way of taking its own. And then there was a whole slew of people who swore that Mary and William were attacked by some crazy man passing through. People claimed all kinds of sightings. Our doors were bolted shut for months after. I know I had a nightmare or two myself."

I listened to her, my heart heavy, dull. *I will never know what happened.* The thought moved through me with a sickening clarity. "I wish I'd asked her more about it, when I had the chance," I said.

She was silent for a moment. Her hands were like bird's wings on her knees. So delicate and thinly boned. "So she passed, then?"

"Yes."

She nodded. "Some people said she ran away, but I think most of us thought she'd died back then. That she wouldn't have been able to go on with William gone. He was her whole future, people said. Of course, plenty of people just thought she couldn't live with what she'd done." She looked at me and smiled sadly. "There have been so many versions of the story over the years. You'd hardly even recognize her if you heard one of them now."

"Well, thank you for talking to me about it," I said.

"No, thank you," she said. "I was always real fond of that girl. Always felt a bit bad for her, growing up the way she did, in that house. The way she always needed to escape into these books. I'm glad to hear she had a good life for herself after she left here." She stood then, smiled down at me. Her pale eyes and skin seemed translucent.

"What do you mean, that house?" I asked.

"It just seemed bleak there. Grim. Nobody cared much for her father, I know that. She sure didn't want to be at home. I would tease her that she read too much, that her mind was getting so crammed with words there would be no room left. She'd say that was impossible, that there was so much room in her she'd have to read every book, go to every city, meet every single person to fill it."

"Do you know Isabel?" I asked. My mind leapt and grasped. If anyone could tell me what had happened that day, I thought, it would have to be Isabel.

"Her sister?" She squinted. "I guess. She must still be around. I don't really know." She paused, looked down at me. "Mary was always partial to that book. I don't know that anyone else in this town has ever even read it."

I smiled, clutching the book in my palms, and watched her thin, elegant body walk away. I leaned back against the shelves. Pulled the book to my chest. I might never know what had happened to Mary, I thought. What she'd witnessed that afternoon on the river. What she had done. The thing that had made her leave me.

Closing my eyes, I imagined myself back on the floor of the library, sixteen years old, with no idea what the world had in store for me. Me with the smell of my father on my skin, the familiar ache in the center of my body, thinking only of the rope and the swing-over and the trapeze. And she, the whole time, putting one foot in front of the other, moving out of my life forever, walking toward the river and her fate. Taking all the answers, all her mystery, with her. Over and over I imagined myself standing up and running to the back door, past the herb garden with its buried silver key, into the grass beyond that led to the river. Coming upon her as she dipped her foot into the water, felt the cold of the river soak into her shoes.

"Tessa?"

I looked up, startled. I had almost forgotten where I was.

Costas stood over me, looking confused.

"I waited and waited for you," he said, leaning in. "Have you been crying?"

"No," I said, standing up and shoving a book back into the shelf. "Let's go to the river. Let's find Isabel."

"Are you okay?"

"Yes," I said. "I'm fine. What about you?" I looked up at him then and saw that he looked more than fine. His face was open, alive. There was an energy to him that hadn't been there before.

"I am great," he said. "I was just waiting outside, talking to people. You know, the river, it's so beautiful. I feel as though I could stay here forever. We could stay here forever. It's where we belong. Don't you feel it, too?"

I stared at him, not sure how to answer. I gently touched his arm. "Let's go find Isabel now," I said. "You need to meet your family before you start thinking too much."

He placed his palm under my chin, stared at me intently. I felt a shiver run through me. I was so full of emotions, desires, I overflowed with them. I felt almost as if I had seen Mary, and now I wanted the world to be as stark and raw and real as possible. I wanted to touch Costas's skin, I realized. Feel him over me and inside me. I moved my face against his palm.

Then I caught myself. A pang of guilt passed through me, and I came to my senses. "Let's go," I repeated, lifting his hand away.

Outside, the rain was hammering down. It was afternoon already, I realized with surprise. The whole world seemed washed through with gray and silver, and the woods stretched out in front of us in a tangled mass. Costas walked easily through the thick mud while I kept sinking into it, pulling out my feet with loud sucking noises, feeling the mud fling up and slap against my leg. As we moved into the woods, the whole world seemed to change. The leaves simmered against the dusky afternoon. Flowers sprouted from the ground, spreading out like jumbles of curls.

I pushed my way past a tree branch hanging in our path. The river rushed to our left, the rain pummeling it and making it wild. "The librarian knew Mary when Mary was young," I said.

He nodded.

The leaves overhead were like a canopy; when they opened up we could see the sky and the splinters of rain. When they closed again the world became dark and hushed, the earth solid beneath us. I prayed Isabel would be home, that we could find her. Just a little bit more, I thought. Right into Mary's heart, into that memory, us at the riverbank. I wanted to burst it open. How many times had I dreamt of it? Going back in time to tell Mary that I understood her, that I loved her, that I knew what had happened to her and that bad things were happening to me, too. This is exactly who I am, I would have said.

I pushed through the trees, started running through the mud. I looked back, saw Costas smile and start running behind me. I laughed. My body felt good. I let my arms swing out wildly, my legs push and push. My muscles burned and then loosened, spun out. My lungs strong, my muscles warm and relaxed. When I saw the cross by the river-bank, surrounded by flowers, I stopped short. Costas nearly ran into me.

"What is it?" he asked, breathing hard, bending over.

I pointed. "The cross. Where it happened."

I walked up to it, trembling. The river rushed past, just inches from where I stood. I knelt down. The cross stuck out of dry ground at the base of a tree.

I turned to face the river, the rain falling over it so lightly now that it barely broke the surface. I could almost see her there, with him. She seemed to emerge from the forest with her black hair flying around her face and hanging past her shoulders, her feet bare, her hands full of herbs and plants.

I reached down, ran my palms over the mud, the stems of the lilies. "She changed everything, you know? She made everything different."

"I wish I could have known her."

I thought of Luis, falling falling to the ground.

"It always seems so strange to me," I said, "how one moment can change everything."

It had happened right here. Why hadn't I listened to her? The river looked so beautiful, tranquil now. The rain just skimmed the surface of it. I closed my eyes, breathing in.

✳

CHAPTER TWENTY-TWO

It did not take long to find the Finn house. We turned from the river and walked through the wood, and when it appeared to us it was as if I had visited it one hundred times before. Mary had described it to me so vividly. The stone, the front porch, the twisting path leading to the front door. I glanced at Costas, wanting to make sure I wasn't just imagining it.

"Is this where they were raised?" he asked, breathing in. For the first time he seemed nervous, unsure. "My mother's home?"

"Yes," I said. I touched his arm.

We stepped out of the wood and onto the brick path. The house seemed like something out of a fairytale with its sloped roof, black shutters, and bright red door. I could see Mary slamming out of it, running into the wood, her hair flying everywhere. I looked up at the second-story windows and wondered which had been hers. I knew she had sneaked out into the night, climbing out that window and down the rain gutter to meet her lover at the river. I thought of myself running from Riley Farm to Mercy Library, remembered the exhilaration I had felt, that feeling of being unleashed on the world.

We walked up the front steps and knocked. We waited, looking at each other nervously. There was no answer. After a minute I knocked again.

"It looks like someone is home," Costas said, peering into the small window I was too short to reach. "This isn't how I pictured it."

"What do you see?"

Just then the door wheezed open, and a beautiful woman appeared in front of us. Her hair was long and pale, and she had black-lined eyes the same blue as Mary's, but shaped like large almonds. She was older than I would have thought. I had always pictured her as a little girl, I realized.

"Yes?" she asked. Her eyes fixed on Costas. "Do I know you?"

I frantically tried to remember everything Mary had said about her.

"I am Costas. I am your nephew. Katerina was my mother," he said. "I've come back here to find you."

Her face had a stunned expression. "You look more like Mary," she said, finally. Something broke on her face when she said Mary's name, I noticed, and then slipped past. "Where are you from? What happened to Katerina?"

"She ended up in Turkey and Greece," he said, "with my father. I never knew her. She died soon after I was born."

"Ah," she said. Her eyes didn't move from his face. "Katerina and Mary looked alike. Mary is my other sister, you know. I took after our mother more, I guess."

She was silent then, taking him in, looking right through me where I stood in front of him in the doorway.

"You are very beautiful," she told him, finally, "the way she was."

I looked up at him, twisting my head behind me, and was surprised to see the expression on his face. He was staring right back at her, fascinated. Something was happening between them, I thought, and suddenly I felt queasy.

"My name is Tessa," I said, holding out my hand to her. "I knew Mary when I was a girl. She lived in my town in Kansas."

When she looked to me her eyes were so blue they didn't seem real. "You knew her?"

I was about to respond when she seemed to catch herself suddenly and stepped back. "I'm sorry," she said. "Please come in and sit down."

We followed her through the hallway and into the living room. She was stunning, wearing a bright silk dress even though she was alone, her body slim and slight, but she seemed much less vibrant than Mary. *It's this place,* I thought. A large fireplace cast a glow over the room. The house smelled of smoke and wood. Outside, the rain pummeled down.

"Please sit," she said, gesturing to one of the old-fashioned couches. I smiled politely at her, but she just looked back at me. The couch was like a slab of stone.

"Mary was a librarian in my town, when I was young," I said, as she sat across from us. Her chair fanned out behind her like a peacock's wings.

"A librarian," she repeated, as if she were feeling out the word. "She always loved books so much."

"Yes," I said. "She taught me to read, and to love words and stories."

"Oh," she said, looking at me as if Mary had come to life again for her, just for that second. "How is she? Is she alive?"

"She died," I said, "some time ago."

Isabel took in the information, her face blank. She leaned back into the chair. I was surprised at how uncomfortable I felt with her, and with being in the house in general.

"I tried to find her, you know," she said, after a minute. Her voice was much lower now, sad. "I wrote letters to her, but I never knew where to send them."

I looked over at Costas, who was staring at her, rapt. He must see himself in her, I thought. His whole past and future. It seemed crazy, suddenly, that he and I had taken the same journey at all.

"Mary told me all about this place, all about growing up here."

"Then you don't know anything." She looked right at me, and I was surprised by the harshness of her look. Then her face softened. "Would you like some coffee?" she asked. "I think I have some biscuits, too, if you'd like."

"We'd love some," Costas said, before I could answer. I could have slapped him. "Let me help you." He jumped up chivalrously and helped her to her feet. She led him out of the room, smiling back at him.

I shook my head and looked around. The fireplace crackled, spit. A large family portrait hung above it, I saw then. A mother and father sitting on two formal chairs, with the three daughters standing at the mother's side. My heart twisted up inside me at the vision of Mary as a child, the same age I'd been when I'd first met her. She was at the side of the painting, resting her hand lightly upon her mother's shoulder. Much older, Katerina stood behind her. The two looked almost identical except that Katerina's hair was stick-straight and Mary's tumbled down her breast in a mass of dark curls. Isabel stood to Mary's right and looked only slightly younger. She and the mother had the same pale hair, finer features. You could see that Katerina and her father carried the same haughty expression.

I wondered what was in the rest of the house. What Mary's room had been like. I thought of Riley Farm with its acres of cornfields and grass. The way the cornhusks flared up and curled over themselves like claws. That was all part of me, I thought, the way all of this had stayed inside Mary.

Isabel and Costas came back into the room, laughing together as he balanced three steaming cups in his hands and set them on the coffee table, pushing one toward me. He looked up and winked at me. She seemed much more at ease, which made her even more beautiful in her pale, slender way. I could only imagine how he'd charmed her with a phrase or story, his kiwi eyes.

He was about to sit when he noticed the portrait. "My God," he said, walking up to it. Isabel glanced at me and then went to stand beside him.

"I don't know why I keep that up," she said, "when they are all gone. Yet I feel as though something terrible will happen if I take it down, even after all these years. I haven't touched anything, really."

"I understand," Costas said. "I take photographs. I won't ever destroy a photograph of someone."

I stared at them, how beautiful the two looked together. I almost felt the way I had the first time I'd seen Mary walking toward me. Awestruck. Isabel's pale, moonlit hair hanging down her back, her hips curving under her gauzy dress. Costas's dark hair folding over his black collar. He was having as much of an effect on her as she was having on him, I saw, and she kept looking up at him, her face warm and open. I felt smaller than I had in years. It was strange how it could still come up on me, that feeling of being a freak. I sank back into the couch.

Costas asked Isabel about her father and mother, about what his mother, Katerina, had been like when she was young. I tried to focus, but it was all so much. My mind went back and back to those moments on the river, with Mary and William together by the water, what might have happened just before it had taken him from her. I tried to remember everything she'd ever said about it, but all I could think of was her face that day she'd told me she couldn't leave Oakley. *I am marked by fate,* she had said, *for what I have done.*

"What did you do?" I whispered. It all came down to that, I realized. I was so close to her, it. I didn't need to know anything more.

Outside, the rain was coming down in sheets now, smearing the windows. I could see the forest through a strange watery haze. What would it have been like for her, growing up in this house, sneaking out at night to meet someone like William? I felt a shadow come over me and almost jumped, but it was only the light shifting. Costas and Isabel were deep in conversation.

I stood up. "Do you mind if I look around?" I asked, interrupting them.

Isabel turned to me. She seemed taken aback.

"If you don't mind," I added quickly. "It's just that Mary described this house to me so many times."

She relaxed. I realized she was a woman always slightly on edge with people, whereas Mary had been so sure of herself all the time. "Of course," she said. "Go ahead. Look in her room if you'd like. It's at the end of the hall. We never touched it, you know. We always thought she might come back. At least, my parents did. But I always knew she was gone for good."

I stood and watched her for a second. I wanted to ask more, but she had already turned back to Costas. I watched her lean her body into his. I couldn't deny the stab of jealousy moving through me and berated myself for it. *This is not about him,* I thought. I slipped up the winding staircase, ignoring the dust that rose up around me as I moved over the carpet, trying not to feel self-conscious. They weren't paying any attention to me, anyway.

As I moved through the upper hallway, which was covered in flowered wallpaper and cloudy mirrors that hung in a row, I looked into each room: the ornate canopies, shelves lined with dolls, the busy wallpaper. Dust seemed to coat everything. There was something not quite right about any of it, about Isabel living in a house that felt crumbling, barren, frozen in time. I passed what had to have been Katerina's room, the parents' room. At the end of the hallway, I recognized Mary's room right away. The piles of books, everywhere. The ornate red quilt covering the bed. I felt my whole body clench.

I stepped into the room tentatively, as if I expected her to pop out at me, a specter telling me to stop disturbing the dead. But it was empty. It *felt* empty, like a room in a museum. I spent several long minutes touching every object, trying to imagine what each thing might have meant to her. I picked up a small jewelry box with a ballerina on top, opened it and saw a girl's silver bracelet, a little bird pin with carved feathers, a gold ring. Was there something of her left in any of this? I thought of my old room in Oakley for the first time in years. Geraldine snoring on the other side of the room, the window that looked out over the fields. There was nothing of me in that room, I thought. I had only passed through it, as if I hadn't been there at all.

I could hear the rain funneling through the gutter, making a hollow whooshing noise. I walked to the window and tried to lift it. It took a moment to get it to budge. I closed my eyes, imagining her before her life was marked by tragedy and regret, when everything was open to her. The window slid open, flinging dust everywhere, and the scent of rain burst into the room. Or had she just been anxious, I wondered, waiting for her one chance to escape, find something new?

The room felt hushed, strange. Rain slammed onto my hands, which rested on the windowsill. I closed my eyes, trying to will myself back home to that day by the river, her voice in my ear and the grass blades rubbing against my back. Twisting her curls around my fingers as she spoke. I wished more than anything that I could go back in time. *What were you trying to tell me?* I would ask. *What was happening to you?* I could remember the way the weeping willows looked hanging over the river, the way the grass had that warm summer smell to it.

You cannot escape your fate, Tessa, or where you come from, she had said.

My mind strained against it. Maybe there is no secret, I thought then. Nothing to find. Maybe her lover died and she could not find happiness in the world after. Couldn't it be as simple as that? Whatever happened, could it really matter now?

My head hurt. Mary, and then my father, and then Mauro—it was all crowding my vision, swooping through me like the wind that had brought Costas to the circus and led me here. The pain of loss and memory passed into my gut. I thought of my father and a rage came up from deep inside me. *You took me away from her,* I thought.

I threw her jewelry angrily back into the box. How could the memory be so fresh after so many years? No matter how far I went, how much I succeeded, it was always *this.* This anger, this loss. Everything circled back to it.

I felt I had grasped nothing, trying to piece together who Mary was, why she had drowned herself in the river, why she had picked me out of the crowd and seen something in me that no one had seen before.

I walked to her bed, bent down, and rested my head on the quilt. I breathed in, imagined the imprint of her body on the fabric. How could I get any closer to her than this? No matter what I found in Rain Village, it couldn't change the fact that she had left me, that I could never get back to her, never love or know her more perfectly than I had. It could never change what my father had done to me. It could never change that there had been a sadness in her I couldn't understand.

I might never learn the truth, I realized. But even if I could whirl back in time and stand right there next to her as she confronted her fate, standing by the river on that long-ago day, it wouldn't change who Mary was. What she had meant to me. What I had lost when she left.

When I finally dragged myself back downstairs, it felt as though hours had passed. I thought how hard it would be to get back to the hotel, through the tangled wood. The stairway was so dark I had to feel my way down the banister, into the dim light of the living room.

Costas and Isabel sat side by side on the couch, barely looking up when I entered the room. She was telling him stories, I realized, about his mother, about his grandparents, and as I walked toward them he looked up at me.

"Tessa," he said, "are you okay?"

Isabel stopped midsentence and followed his gaze. "You miss her," she said simply, her expression suddenly serious.

"Yes," I said. I was crying. I brought my hands to my chest and realized the whole front of my shirt was wet with tears.

"I still miss her, too," she said.

I wiped my face, sat in the chair she had occupied before. I looked at Isabel. Her hair glimmering in the dim light. Her blue eyes focused on mine, sparkling out at me. This must be hard on her, I thought. Learning so much in one day, having the whole world come hurtling through the front door after all the care she'd taken to keep it out. I looked at Costas. It seemed clear then that this was what he had come here for. To be with her, to help her. I wanted to remind him of his wife and son, to tell him not to forget them, but it hit me, right then, that he had left them long before now.

My heart ached. I thought of Mauro, missed him so much it was actually as if a part of me had been cut out.

I turned to Isabel. "Do you know what happened that day?" I asked, finally. "What happened between Mary and William on the river?"

Her face changed. I was surprised at the sadness there. It was clear that she carried grief within her, and now it was all right at the surface. In this old house, surrounded by dust and bones, the rawness of it was almost absurd.

I leaned forward. Met Costas's eyes and then looked back at her. It didn't matter to him in the same way, I thought. Knowing what had happened.

"Well," she said. She opened her mouth to speak but then closed it, bringing her hand to her face. After a moment she tried again. "I haven't spoken about Mary in years. All I remember is how wild she was that night. Wild with despair. I remember her and my father yelling. Him calling her names, her screaming back at him. I remember lying under the covers in my room with my hands over my ears, willing it to stop. And then she was just gone. I felt like it was my fault, as if I'd willed her away. The house was always quiet, every day after."

"I am sorry," I said. "She spoke of you, you know. How much she missed you."

"She did?"

"Yes."

Her face lit then, and I told her everything I could remember Mary saying about her. How smart Isabel had been. How terrible it had been to leave her behind, how Mary hadn't had a choice.

The way she had left me, I thought.

"Thank you," Isabel whispered, close to tears. I felt thankful then that I could give this to her.

"Did William give Mary a ring?" I asked, suddenly inspired. I didn't need to be there anymore, I realized. In Rain Village.

"Yes," Isabel said. "An opal ring. He said it would bind her to him forever."

"The peasant girl," I said.

'Yes," she said. "That old story the old folks tell. Mary always liked those stories; she was always repeating them to anyone who would listen."

I smiled at her, genuinely then. "I'm going back to the village," I said. "It's getting late."

I looked at Costas, but knew he didn't want to leave. I had no idea what would happen to him. All I knew was that the Velasquez Circus was in the last weeks of the season and would be in the South by now, in Mississippi or Florida or some other state with trees that dripped and dangled over swamps. It seemed strange to think about the planned-to-the-minute schedule of the circus train and caravan, when in Rain Village it felt like time had no meaning at all. But the circus was the world I knew. My world.

"I'll stay just a little longer," Costas said, smiling at me softly, wistfully. "Can I meet you back at the hotel? Will you be all right?"

"Yes, I'll be fine," I told him. I would miss Costas; he was something like a brother or a best friend.

On my way back down to the river, the rain had let up and the moonlight guided me. Something had shifted, and the evening was so bright I had to squint when the trees parted and the light shone directly in. I leaned against a tree and took Mary's ring from my pocket, holding it in my open palm. I had considered, briefly, giving the ring to Isabel, but I thought the last thing she needed was to be bound to the past more than she was already. We had enough burdens, I thought, all of us. I couldn't save Mary, I couldn't change a damn thing, but I could do one thing more.

The ring sparkled and exhaled in the moonlight. I followed the soft path Mary must have walked down hundreds of times before. The ground was wet at my feet, covered in leaves.

When I reached the river, I knelt on the muddy bank and stared into the water. The moon had clouded over, making it difficult to see.

A terrible, piercing longing moved through me. An ache so powerful I could only clench my teeth and wait for it to pass. I bent toward the river, and it was just at that moment that the moon shifted, lighting the surface of the water so that it looked like glass.

I leaned forward, my heart in my mouth.

It was her, unmistakably, on the surface of the river. Mary Finn, just as I remembered her. Her cat's eyes staring out at me, her long black hair so wild it was like a field of weeds, her silver hoop earrings dropping to her shoulders. Her brown, freckled skin. Her lips the color of coral.

I felt a radiance inside me. A sense of pure light. "Mary," I said, reaching out to the water.

She smiled at me with her crooked teeth, her full lips curving into a bow. "Did you know that stars die, Tessa?" she asked.

"Yes," I whispered. I reached down to touch her face. I expected to feel her skin, which had always been soft and warm, like bread just out of the oven, and was shocked when my fingers dipped into the water. Her image scattered over the surface, then disappeared.

I stared into the water, barely able to breathe. As the surface stilled again, I sighed with relief, seeing the contours of her face and shoulders and hair returning. Her long coiling hair. Her blue eyes. Her strong shoulders that could hurl themselves over and under the bar, that could propel her body through air, slice right through it.

It took me a second to realize it was not Mary in the water, swaying slightly across the surface, looking out at me, but my own face coming into relief. My own long hair, my own wide blue eyes staring out at me. I looked up frantically, up and down the stretch of the riverbank, but I was all alone, just as I had been before. The only sound was the faint lapping of water, the dull wind fluttering over it.

I looked back at my reflection. What I saw surprised me. There was no shock or disappointment or heartsickness breaking over my face. Instead I looked luminous, even beautiful. Like a streak of light on the water. I thought, suddenly, about my thirteenth birthday. How I had stared into the mirror, my face covered with glitter and Mary standing behind me, and realized, for the first time, that I was almost pretty. Not like Mary but not so unlike her, either. *People try to shut out beauty wherever they can in this world,* she had said, *but it's a mistake.*

The moon shifted again, and I watched my image cloud over. I sat back. Stared at the leaves whirling on the surface, the puffs of mud that seemed to churn up from the bottom of the water.

I sat for what seemed like hours, running my fingers through pebbles and grass. I stared into the river and saw myself swinging over and over the rope, creating circles in the air, twirling and stretching into one gleaming white line. I saw my body arcing through the canvas tent, my starfish hands reaching for the bar. Suddenly I was so homesick for the circus, for Mauro, that I couldn't see straight. *That*, I thought, was all mine. The circus, my husband, my family. Flight. That feeling of being unbound, of cutting right through the air. Mary might have given it to me, set me on this path, but it was mine after all.

I stood up and wiped gravel from my hands and clothes. The river seemed to rush in my ears, the smell of flowers and spices swirling around me. In one movement I dropped the ring into the water and watched it disappear. Then I turned back to the woods and began walking.

It was only in Rain Village that I realized my life had a shape to it, one that went beyond the outlines of Mercy Library, beyond Mary Finn and Rain Village, past the imprints my father's hands had left on my skin.

What was all mine, I thought, was sitting with Mauro under the lemon trees, watching Lollie spread glitter across her skin, listening to José's bitter denunciations of love and all its follies—those moments were as much a part of me and my story as Mary was and always had been, from the day she'd befriended me outside the courthouse in the center of the town square.

I understood, finally, why Mary had worked so hard to keep the names and numbers straight in Oakley, why she had to take life and pin it down in the lists and charts she kept filed away in bursting cabinets. But I wondered what truth Mary had thought she was recording in all those charts and lists and clippings. Did she record the way a girl's heart can gape open like a wound when her father comes in from the fields? Or the way the tears streamed down her own face as she fled Rain Village and everything she knew, the blood of her lover on her hands? My name was in those files she kept—*Tessa Riley*—right next to my father's name, my mother's name, and the names of my brothers and sister. But nothing about that name suggested the way my heart broke when Mary Finn died in the river, leaving me alone to my fate.

The train ride home seemed to last for months. I couldn't stand being away from Mauro another minute. Anxiety gripped me, yet all I could do was sit, staring at the wedding ring gleaming from my finger. Waiting. Praying that he would still want me, that all of them would take me back. I was suspended between lives, as if I had just leapt off the trapeze and toward the catcher's open hands.

A C K N O W L E D G E M E N T S ✳

I would like to express my love, gratitude, and eternal devotion to:

Greg Michalson, for guiding me through this process with such grace, intelligence, and generosity, and everyone at Unbridled, especially Fred Ramey, Caitlin Hamilton, and Cary Johnson. Elaine Markson, for believing in me for so long, through so many drafts, and her assistant Gary Johnson, for answering 5000000 emails without calling me a stalker. Paul West, in whose classroom I began this book over a decade ago, for opening up all possibilities of language and imagination to me, and for being an inspiration, then and now. Jennifer Belle, for helping me so thoughtfully with these pages, and for being so supportive in every way, at every point. My parents, Jean and Al Turgeon, and beautiful sister, Catherine Turgeon, for all their love and support, copyediting prowess, and general familial awesomeness. And for forcing all their friends to read this.

Massie Harris, who inspired Mary Finn in all her splendor, for being ferocious, devoted, and brilliant, and for writing teenage diary entries predicting this event. Eric Schnall, for all the Doma sessions and incredibly sensitive, thoughtful, spot-on *commentos*, which helped me see everything more clearly. Tink Cummins and Anton Strout, the Dorks of the Round Table, for all the support, feedback, advice, strategizing, and cheese-filled dinners—for everything, that is, except the name Dorks of the Round Table. Joi Brozek, for all the writing inspiration as well as general fearlessness, brilliance, and glamour. Brenna Tinkel, for reading draft after draft in two seconds flat and giving much sparkling and brainy advice. Peter Schneeman, for setting me on the right path many, many moons ago.

And: Alfred Triolo, for those Italian stories; Richard Morris, for early support; Jonathon Conant, for trapeze stories; Sangeeta Mehta, for so much help and advice; Christine Duplessis, for going to bat; Rachel Safko, for fighting; Dr. Bernard Bail, for endless patience; and J.D. Howell, for talking to me about Washington. And to my gorgeous friends who saw so many drafts over the years, and even read them—Chelsea Ray, Heather Freeman, Barb Burris, Mark Berman, Rob Horning, James Masland, Erika Merklin, Pete Heitmann, Jacob Littleton, Tony Begnal, Robert Wolf, and everyone else—thank you.